THE BLACKNESS

Joseph Hyman

Aventine Press

The cover photo image is provided by
G. De Marchi (STScI and Univ. of Florence, Italy) and
F. Paresce (STScI)/NASA, ESA

Published by Aventine Press
750 State St. # 319
San Diego CA, 92101

ISBN: 1-59330-547-8

Library of Congress Control Number: 2008931397
Library of Congress Cataloging-in-Publication Data
The Blackness

1

General Dudorov Blunders

Mexico City, circa. 2050

No one saw it happen. More exactly, those who saw it disappeared in a matter of seconds. There was a flash, a great roaring sound. The Eurasian Embassy, where the explosion took place, vanished. The buildings close to it vanished. For a quarter of a mile on each side the buildings were torn apart, blasted apart, collapsed, came down on the people inside them. Beyond that quarter mile radius there was more damage, more fire.

It was impossible even to guess how many died. The street had been crowded. The Embassy itself was swarming with the usual staff and visitors, engaged in its great work of expanding the power and prestige of the Union of Eurasian Republics. The buildings around it were alive with the daily busyness that makes up the life of world cities.

The official count of the dead was something over 200,000, including an estimate of the numbers of whom no trace could be found. The injured were three times that number and of these many died. The rescue operations were made difficult by the fact that the ruins were radioactive. The bomb or whatever it was had been thermonuclear.

Within minutes after the explosion there was the usual call: the Sons and Daughters of Moctezuma took credit. They were said to be the militant faction of the Aztec Society, dedicated to a restoration of the old time religion and language. The day of the blast was the anniversary of the battle for the city in 1521, in which Cortes, probably without knowing it at the time, achieved the conquest of Mexico.

Actually the Sons and Daughters of Moctezuma also took credit for a minor explosion in the Embassy of the United States. It was a small, apparently conventional bomb. Only 11 people were killed and 40 some injured. Both explosions came at the exact same minute.

The echo of the explosions was heard far from Mexico City. Within minutes there were reactions in Moscow and Washington. The world waited, anxious, concerned, at least the world that was involved with or aware of grand politics. Those who did not were merely population statistics, and could be disregarded as meaningless people. In Moscow the news came as a shock. V. I. Cheka, Chairman of the Eurasian Union, had been expecting a call from the Embassy, waiting with his closest colleague, J. V. Ulianov, head of all the Security Agencies.

"It's about time," Cheka said.

Ulianov looked at his watch. "About time," he agreed.

"Our Dudorov," he added, "is always reliable."

Cheka nodded his head in agreement. "Our Dudorov is always reliable. I expect very good results from his Mexican visit. Very interesting results. I think the key will turn in the lock."

Ulianov lit his pipe, nodded and smiled. It was not a heartwarming smile. "Vladimir Ilyich," he said, "I salute you for having created such a beautiful plan. A real work of genius. A masterpiece of political art."

Cheka lifted his hand deprecatingly. "You overdo it," he said. "Not a bad plan. In time we shall see how it works."

"No, no," Ulianov insisted, "Vladimir Ilyich you are always too modest. The details, only you could have thought out the details. To have an explosion in our own Embassy at the same time is nothing but genius. No one but you could have added that touch."

Cheka sighed. "That will have its advantages," he conceded. "But I regret some of the consequences. There are those who think otherwise but we are human beings, Josef Vissarianovich. Our feelings are humane. Lives will be lost. Our people will be injured and suffer."

"In a good cause," Ulianov said. "In a great cause. For the advancement of all mankind. What can be nobler?"

"Nothing," Cheka agreed. "Nothing at all. So we have the plan and we should have the call from Dudorov in another minute. You said he was to call at three minutes past three."

Ulianov shrugged his shoulders. "You know the communications people," he said philosophically.

They both looked at the screen. There was still no Dudorov.

"Let us ask our communications people if there is anything wrong with the message center in Mexico City," Cheka proposed.

Ulianov touched a button. "We are waiting for a call from Mexico City," he said. "Have you any word from the Embassy?"

"The message center went dead four minutes ago," said a voice. "We were talking to them till then." There was a noise that could be described as offstage. "Excellency," said the voice, "there is word from Mexico City but not from the Embassy." The voice was very unhappy. "Excellency, I suggest that you look at the general broadcast. I regret. I regret," said the voice.

"What?" said Cheka more or less to himself.

Ulianov turned on the general broadcast. Someone was talking in Spanish. It meant nothing to him. But Cheka understood Spanish. Cheka knew everything. Cheka listened carefully. His knowledge of Spanish may not have been what Ulianov supposed but he got the idea. It was no wonder that there was no call from Dudorov. He listened for five minutes, eight minutes. Ulianov suffered in ignorance. He too would take Spanish lessons. Prospectively they had, would have a great many orders to give in that language.

Another few minutes and Cheka turned off the broadcast. There would be reports from experts and more experts, analyses, recommendations from Institutes, investigations and investigations of the investigations, learning piled upon learning, deep thinking. He inwardly groaned.

It was a waste of everyone's time but society was basically organized for the orderly wasting of time. Without the reports and the Institute studies, the writing, the copying, the circulating, the reading, reviewing, the committee meetings to consider and make recommendations, the intellectual types would have nothing to do but get into trouble. He would face the routine, listen, preside. But he had only two or three questions which could be answered quickly. As always he saw only the opportunity in every disaster.

Ulianov when he thought it discreet to speak up asked the obvious question. "What has happened, Vladimir Ilyich? Tell me. What happened? What happened?"

Cheka looked at him and grunted. "A change of plans. Something new."

"What, Vladimir Ilyich?"

"A horrifying disaster in Mexico City."

"Oh," said Ulianov.

"But," Cheka went on, "a surprise. It was our Embassy. Nothing is left of it. Not a trace, not a grain of it. Everything, everyone, gone. There was a minor affair at the American Embassy. A handful of casualties. Around us the damage is endless. Your Sons and Daughters have taken the credit. I am not blaming anyone. But, Joseph Vissarionovich, how do you explain it?"

Ulianov was stunned. He felt cold, very cold. How could he explain it? Dudorov was reliable. His major generals were always reliable. Cheka looked at him. "So. Again, how do you explain it? I can imagine this. I can imagine that. There are ways to account for everything in this life. Tell me, what do you think?"

Ulianov felt even colder.

"Perhaps," Cheka suggested, "we underestimated. No, say I underestimated the North Americans. Could they have had what we had?"

Ulianov finally spoke. This was a question he was sure he could answer. "No, my people said no."

"They were positive?"

"Positive. They have ways of knowing. Proved over the years."

Cheka was thoughtful. Even if the North Americans had the means, they would never have used them. He had seen their President Blossom, for Blossom a great event, for him nothing important. He, Cheka, was 70. He had seen many men in the course of a lifetime. As Chairman for 20 years, he had seen and judged, and, for that matter, devoured more heads of state that he could remember. He could judge men. Blossom was a fellow well named. Very tender.

Before he was Chairman, Cheka had headed the Security organs. He had made a specialty of the Americans, studied their system. As a young man he had been posted to Washington, then to New York. It was a good, a sound education. He was no fool. The one thing he knew was that no one could know anything, really know. The people who called themselves scientists were so many children, deceiving themselves. He encouraged them in their Institutes. Half, partial knowledge was useful. You could at least kill people, destroy whole cities with it.

His partial knowledge of the Americans, of what they called their institutions, which meant their habitual ways of doing things, also had its uses. For practical purposes, which were the only ones he was concerned with, he would assume that what had happened in Mexico City was not the North Americans' doing. He looked at Ulianov. "So then what happened?" he asked. "Could Dudorov have made a mistake?"

Ulianov answered the question. He had been considering it while Cheka was thinking whatever he thought. He was inclined to be positive but he checked himself. He knew something of Cheka's way of looking at things and he accepted it. There was wisdom in not being sure. Also he could expect to be Cheka's successor so long as Cheka approved of him, left him in place.

The succession was from the Security Forces to Chairman. So long as Cheka thought him sound, thought him worthy, he would continue as heir and in time would inherit. And to fall might be to go under the ice and never come up. To fall was in fact to go under the ice. They had all seen it happen and they had averted their eyes as familiar names disappeared.

His answer was careful. "Vladimir Ilyich," he said, "you have seen Dudorov."

Cheka nodded. He had seen Dudorov. A good major general. And so was his father. And his grandfather before him. The Dudorovs were in a way hereditary high officers in the Security organs. They went back to Dzerzhinsky, back to the beginning, able men, knowing what was required and doing it, earning their positions and holding them. Four generations, trained engineers to begin with, ambitious but not too ambitious, men who valued their families. They could do with more Dudorovs, but Dudorov could make a mistake.

"Constantin Constantinovich," Cheka said, "yes, I have seen him. Of course I have seen him. He came into the service under me. His father worked with me as a colleague. I learned much from his grandfather when I was a beginner. That goes back 50 years."

"Could he have made a mistake?"

"A deliberate mistake? An accidental mistake? Which do you propose?" Cheka asked.

Ulianov said nothing. He understood that Cheka would ask this question and answer it. Some of Cheka's questions required replies. Others did not. At the highest level they knew this, were trained to distinguish questions that called for speech from those best met by silence.

"Accident?" Cheka said. "Joseph Vissarionovich, you showed me the packages. One, very small, one larger, not large but larger. One was wrapped in red -- the small one. You see, I remember it. The other was green. Could Dudorov have been what they call color blind? Even so there was the difference in the size of the packages. The point of the size was important, decisive. It was something we talked about. The point of the device was its size. Its effectiveness was its size. It was a midget. A dwarf. Easy to place, to conceal. You told me and agreed they were right. Your engineers were proud of themselves. They had worked at an impossible task and what they produced was a miracle. We saw the uses. The other device was routine. Constantin Constantinovich was intelligent, a man with technical training."

"Then there were the other plans, his other assignments," Ulianov ventured.

"Exactly," said Cheka. "The other plans. The other assignments. The whole exercise. He was to have had five, shall we say, of these cartridges?"

Ulianov nodded.

"Five altogether. So he had to know what we know. I rule out an accidental mistake."

"And deliberate?" Cheka went on.

The very thought made Ulianov cold again, freezing cold. Dudorov was his man. He had chosen him for the mission with Cheka's approval but the rule below was that the agent's failure was the principal's failure. The agent's transgressions were paid for by his superior. At the top it was different. The result could be "yes" or "no." The top was a different world. He had had Cheka's approval. But that was not binding on Cheka when Cheka came to make his decision.

A thought occurred to Cheka. "Also," he said, "I rule out an engineer's failure. The cartridges, the device, could not have gone off by itself. We might have considered it possible, but we had the little affair at the American Embassy. Dudorov was on schedule. There was nothing off schedule. So again, was it deliberate?"

"How, how could it have been, Vladimir Ilyich. We were agreeing that Dudorov was always reliable."

"In the past," Cheka said. "In the past. People change. Stresses. Strains. The human heart is a mystery. My mother was wise. I learned that from her. It was one of her sayings. I would ask you if Constantin Constantinovich sought the comfort of death if it is a comfort. But we are not sure that he died in the blast. He could be anywhere. And the other cartridges. That gives us a technical problem. Was the blast one cartridge or was it five? We will send people there. They should be able to tell us tomorrow. Would Dudorov have had any reason to destroy our Embassy, his Embassy since he was or is one of us?"

Ulianov had a suggestion. "Troyenko," he said. "He had no love for Troyenko. The Ambassador, so he told me, had been rude."

"Troyenko," Cheka said, "is a boor. I have no love for him. Had no love for him, I should say, now that he is so many atoms. He was not a likeable man but he had his uses. But even not liking him, would I have destroyed the Embassy and everyone in it?"

Ulianov shook his head. The answer was obvious.

"So we agree," Cheka went on. "Not an accident. Not what they call a technical failure which means only that we trust the engineers within engineers' limits. We are not even humanly certain about whether Dudorov lives or is gone. You are discreet, Joseph Vissarionovich. You will ask. Were there family troubles? Were there other troubles, personal trouble, illness that we did not know about? Defection," he said, "that too is an illness, the result of an illness. Were there any signs? You must be very discreet. It is not something to suggest."

The possibility was too much to contemplate, too disturbing. Ulianov did not want even to think about it. A major general in his Security Forces, a senior major general, an honored family, a man who knew the plans, who knew the exercise step by step. Then, worst of all, there were the four miniatures, the cartridges as Cheka had called them. Ulianov pulled himself together, as the phrase goes. He had instructions. He knew how to get information without causing alarm.

"Vladimir Ilyich," he said, getting up, "you have given me things to do. I will do them. First I will get our best men to Mexico City to examine, report, tell us about what they can deduce from the ruins."

"You go," Cheka said, "attend to these things. Later we will talk more. I see opportunities, I told you that. There are opportunities in every misfortune, even disaster. We will talk later. We will make the right moves."

Ulianov left. He was troubled, but he felt better, less cold.

2

Cheka's "Frighten to Death" Scheme Fails

The United States of America was founded by men of small means and narrow education. For generations such men dominated its affairs and managed its government. They were largely of British stock, Protestant in religion, and they were a meager soil out of which institutions could grow.

The Founders and their descendants had no understanding of the broader purpose of government. The Congress in which the legislative power was placed was an almost primitive body until the beginning of the 20th century. It met for short intervals, living for the most part in boarding houses and poverty-stricken hotels.

There were no offices for its members and no paid staff to advise them. More important, the stipend was too small to attract to the public service men with vision and force. The members were in the main simple lawyers and merchants, out of small towns, with small, modest origins. They regarded their constituencies as men of the same breed and stamp as themselves.

It was not until the population was enriched by immigrants from Eastern and Southern Europe, from the Caribbean Islands, from Asia, that the Congress, and the whole government, grew and unfolded and bloomed. The judges were transformed from men devoted to property interests to men of compassion.

The executive branch was made over. Presidents like William McKinley had such successors as Woodrow Wilson, Buchanan Flowerbush, Harry Midgett, the great Omar Jenkins. The African population was drawn into political life and flourished. Capitol Hill -- not much of a hill -- which had been barren for over a century, was covered with monuments, magnificent buildings teeming with true representatives of a now diverse, vital people.

Revenues which had been niggardly and dispensed in a beggarly style, swelled to a flood. The flood was diverted in generous channels. The whole motive of politics changed and the aim of those who engaged in it was the doing of justice, the righting of wrongs. Men who were not moved with this purpose were no longer elected to office. Those who had been victims had voices to speak and act for them. In the third century after the American revolution men began to see its promise fulfilled.

It was only to be expected that the first official reaction to the blast in Mexico City would come in the House -- the House of Representatives, which was beginning to see itself as the prime political agency. The members were engaged in the usual business, curing the public ills by the appropriation of money. An aide hurried in and spoke for a moment to one of the principal members, the member from the 9th Illinois, the conscience of the Chicago Mexican barrios as they spoke of it, the leader of the Hispanic Caucus, Jesus Maria Castillo y Aragon y Hohenstaufen.

Castillo, as he called himself, was the embodiment of the new leadership of the country. Small, dark, slight, of Guatemalan-Mayan descent as he described himself, he had the advantage of a very large personal fortune. His father had been what was called an "illegal" in his generation, a man of great competence and a large factor in the importation of cocaine by way of Colombia where he had family connections. Castillo spoke of his father with pride. He always referred to him as the Patriarch.

"The Patriarch," Castillo would say, "was a resolute man, a man with pride and with hope. He risked everything for his family. And," he would add, "he made his way and his fortune in the free market. No monopoly, nothing. He saw the need and he met it. I try to honor him each day by the little good that I do."

Castillo, of course, had his detractors. They pointed out that the market in which the elder Castillo carried on his really large operations was not an ideally free market. There had been arrangements, even violent arrangements, to control competitors. There were old newspaper files, they said, recording unsolved disappearances, unidentified bodies, unsolved execution-style killings, to use the newspaper phrase of the day. Some detractors went so far as to question the desirability of the use of cocaine, or even the quality of the product the elder Castillo supplied.

Almost all pointed out that Castillo had bought his position of leadership, first buying his Chicago district from those who managed such things in Chicago and then buying the Hispanic Caucus with gifts and loans on easy terms to its members. But, as Castillo said, the fortunate of the world must always expect to be envied and slandered. Even his detractors would have conceded that fortune had favored him.

The declared premier objective of the Hispanic Caucus was the repeal or, more exactly, the abrogation of the Treaty of Guadalupe Hidalgo. Everyone knew that the immortal Emancipator in his one term in the House had condemned the Mexican War. As spiritual descendants of the Emancipator they proposed to undo it. Castillo on this afternoon listened to the report from his aide. He nodded. He heard opportunity knock. He rose and asked to be heard.

"It is my sorrow," he began, "to bring tragic news to this House. There has been a prodigious explosion in Mexico City. The Eurasian Embassy has been completely destroyed. The entire area in which it stood has been shattered. The carnage is frightful. No one can say at this moment how many thousands of good and innocent lives have been lost. We cannot judge who is guilty of this vast crime. I pray to Almighty God that this blood is not on our hands, that this is not our doing. Our shame is enough as it is. We must restore what our forefathers stole and make reparations for that."

"I call on this House," he concluded, "to appoint a select committee to investigate the tragedy that I have reported. I ask further that we adjourn for the day in memory of the innocent dead, our Eurasian brothers and our Mexican brothers and sisters," he added. It was nothing notable, but enough for the present.

The House adjourned on a standing vote of those present after voting that the Speaker should name the select committee to investigate and report to the House as to the blame for the disaster in Mexico City.

There were questions here and there before the afternoon ended. Why had Castillo said nothing about the explosion at the American Embassy? Why had he said nothing about the Sons and Daughters of Moctezuma?

Castillo's comment would have been, if he had been asked, that his aide, a trusted aide, had said nothing about the Sons and Daughters and that the affair at the American Embassy was trifling, at the most a matter of a few lives, a few injuries. And, he might have added, criminals were known to cover their tracks, red herrings and so on. After all, the select committee would get at the truth and he had no doubt of what the truth would be as reported from the committee.

As the journalists always liked to put it, at the other end of Pennsylvania Avenue the President, Walter Blossom, was discussing the Mexican problem with the Secretary of State. Castillo had been maneuvering for something to be called the Commission for the Abrogation of the Treaty of Guadalupe Hidalgo. So far it was nothing but talk, thanks to the more respectable Populars in the House. But their authority was not what it had been. The Hispanic Caucus and the African Caucus, the Asian Caucus and the Appalachian Caucus, the Gay Caucus, and the Structurally Unemployed Caucus taken together combined into a great many votes. And they had kind looks and sympathy from the standard liberal Populars.

The major stars in the media sky argued about it. Either the institutions of the Republic were falling apart and chaos was threatening; or, as most saw it, the institutions were taking on a new shape, were making new growth. There were only good and great expectations and cause for rejoicing. To his surprise, as a truly liberal Popular, Blossom had less confidence in a happy ending than he liked to admit.

Walter Blossom knew from his course in American History in high school that Abraham Lincoln had disapproved of the Mexican War. Like all good Americans he revered Abraham Lincoln. He wished he could have Abraham Lincoln to guide him. In fact he sometimes sat in the Lincoln Room at night hoping that he might get a message.

Not that he believed in messages from the Beyond. He was an educated man who knew the difference between what was real and unreal. He was a rational graduate of his State University, a sociology major, an honors graduate of its law school. He was the son of a rational cashier in a bank and a rational teacher of Home Economics. He had had a rational wife. Nevertheless, he sat on many nights in the Lincoln Room and hoped for the best.

He kept asking inwardly what his most loved and profound predecessor would have done about the fruit gathered at the end of the Mexican War, now, at this point. Lincoln was shrewd, a smart trial lawyer before becoming a saint. Texas, strictly speaking, was not part of the loot as Castillo called it, of the Mexican War. But if we were righting old wrongs, it would have to go back to Nevada, California, New Mexico, Arizona, much of Colorado and, maybe, Utah.

He was not certain about the geography. There were people in those states, some people, who would not want to be Mexican citizens. They would want to leave. Where could they go? What would happen to their property rights? Then there were the public improvements, the dams and public works, paid for out of the taxes levied not in those states alone but from the people at large.

The Mexican states, as the Hispanic Caucus referred to them, were reliable Popular states, liberal Popular states. Their loss might cause serious damage to the existing political patterns. Lincoln was a politician and would have seen that. Choices were always difficult problems, complex. Until he had the message, he could only do his best to fend off the Commission.

But he could see the merit in Castillo's objective. The greatest of human desires was the desire for peace, for an end to bitterness and demands from those who were wronged or thought they were wronged. By restoring to Mexico what had been taken unjustly, peace would be advanced a step at least. There would then be, the objectors said, more demands. The Indians had a standing claim to the whole continent, including Castillo's Mexican states.

There were arguments, of course, about the Louisiana Purchase, the two Floridas. Some descendants of the slaves brought from Africa demanded that the old Cotton States be given to them by way of reparation for their ancestors' labor. The claims all overlapped. Nevertheless, all

15

had some justice. Lincoln had achieved immortality by preserving the Union and Walter Blossom also saw that as his duty. He was saying as much to his Secretary of State and she had agreed when he heard about what had happened to Mexico City.

The word came from the Vice President who had been listening to the news broadcasts for want of anything more interesting to do. He had become Vice President for much the same reason. Besides, it was not a bad gamble, something he knew as the son-in-law of Omar Jenkins who had become President long ago when Jack Suitor disappeared on a space tour in one of the earlier rockets.

"Walter," the Vice President said. -- he and the President were "Walter" and "Charles" to each other. "Forgive me, Marietta," he added, nodding to the Secretary of State. "Something you ought to know." He hoped that the news was, as the reporters said, an exclusive. He told them what he had learned and was gratified that they had not already heard it. "Porfirio Aleman is speaking in a half hour or so," he concluded.

Blossom groaned. Eurasia was a perennial problem. Mexico, which had been a problem for the ancestors, was beginning to be a problem again. But Eurasia was the large cloud that hung over everything. There had to be a way to dispel it so that the sky would be clear again. Some presidents loved foreign affairs. There was Woodrow Wilson. Buchanan Flowerbush shone at them and naturally knew that he did. Conceivably the world was more difficult now as a result of some of the Flowerbush triumphs.

When Blossom took office he was resolved to dispose of all the issues between the United States and the Eurasian Republics. Essentially it had to be a matter of trust and confidence and good will. He was a good man; Cheka had to be a good man. They would only want the same thing. Cheka was older and he would treat Cheka with deference. They would meet and each would see the other as human. If he trusted Cheka, Cheka would have no choice but to trust him.

The thing to do was to reassure Cheka that the United States was not hostile, that the Eurasian Union had no reason for fear and suspicion. He and Cheka could deal with each other as friends. If concessions were needed to prove his good faith, he would do what was needed. He had persuaded Cheka to meet him in Geneva and had been impressed. Cheka understood that they were both men of good will and had held nothing back.

The Eurasian peoples had their tragic history. Their Union was a shelter for the hundreds of millions with long, tragic memories and a need for assurance, constant assurance that no one could harm them. Cheka explained it all carefully. He had to reckon with fear, constant fear. Then he had to deal with his colleagues, with Semyon Semyonovich Grabkin, Double Marshal of the Eurasian Union, always demanding what he called a margin of safety. They had parted with toasts to friendship and Blossom felt that friendship would flower. He came away certain of two things, Cheka wanted what he, Blossom, wanted, peace, and Cheka was sincere, a man to be trusted.

Blossom's whole aim was to turn his hands to domestic affairs. He could act there with confidence. It was a matter of money in the right place and everyone would be happy. If he enjoyed Cheka's confidence there would be even more money available to insure universal contentment at home. This development in Mexico City -- everything had to be thought of as a development -- would have upset Cheka and threatened the friendship. Blossom's vision of the Americans happy at home, men, women and children, or better, women, children and men, was in danger. He wondered what proof he could give Cheka to restore the human tie they had both felt at Geneva.

"This," he finally said, "could be the worst day of my life. A bomb in our Embassy. The Eurasian Embassy gone. The whole area leveled. Who could have done it? Who could have done it?" As a boy, as a young man back in Wiscota, nothing had prepared him for this kind of evil. "Who could have done it?" he asked again. "Who could have done it?" No one, no one dared to strike at the Eurasian Union. There were always terror and bombings, but nothing ever touched the buildings or people of the Eurasian Union. They were safe, unlike those of the United States whose people served abroad at the risk of their lives.

"I think," the Secretary of State suggested, "we had better get hold of the old man."

Blossom touched the button. In a matter of seconds the old man appeared on the screen, Michael Carmody, the perpetual Director of the Intelligence Group. He had been there for 40 years. Apart from those who saw him as the guardian of the Republic, everyone feared him. The Intelligence Group was able to gather domestic intelligence and with intelligence gathered abroad this in some way made Michael Carmody omniscience incarnate. Liberal Popular opinion was that it was best not to offend him. One or two presidents had suggested that he retire and enjoy his leisure. He assured them he preferred to be busy, to perform the work to which he was accustomed. There was no point in arguing. The members of the Congress, for their own reasons, would not consider the name of a successor.

"Yes, Mr. President," the old man said. He was a formal old man. He kept moving his fingers. His one admission of age was his arthritis.

"Mr. Carmody," Blossom said, "Mexico City."

"Yes."

"Do you know more than we know?"

"I don't know exactly what it is that you know," said the old man.

"Only what has been announced from Mexico City -- what the Vice President has heard and told me. Could you add anything?"

The old man nodded.

"Then?" Blossom asked.

"I had better come over," the old man said.

"You can tell us now. The line is secure."

The old man shook his head. "Mr. President, with all deference, no line is secure."

"But this one, from my office to yours?"

The old man shook his head again. "No line is secure," he said firmly. "I will come over at once."

While they waited for the old man, they saw and heard the President of Mexico, Porfirio Aleman Villa, Porfirio the Inscrutable, the number one oligarch, numero uno, covering his awareness that the foundations were being eaten away by being inscrutable. This time he was shaken. He knew enough about the Aztec Society. He knew enough about the Sons and Daughters. So far as he could, he had known Troyenko and the goings on in his Embassy and its staff of over 2,000.

Every day a score or more members arrived and departed. A large, expensive staff had to be paid. Money flowed in and out of bank accounts but who could say where it went or how it was used? Moreover there could be payments offshore and who could tell anything about them. He, himself, was an authority on money offshore. Exchange controls were a farce in a country with so many borders, so many coasts. The Eurasian Embassy was a hive, ceaselessly busy. After dark its lights burned, a reminder that the Eurasian Republics were present and present and present.

Now there was only an enormous crater where the Embassy had stood no more than an hour ago. He knew the grand rule of cui bono. If anyone benefitted, it was, maybe, he, Porfirio Aleman Villa. He had resisted but he had finally made the command appearance in Moscow. So he had seen Cheka and Moscow. He was in no position to cross the Eurasians. They would make demands. The thing for him was to be more impassive than ever, the Mexican sphinx. So he spoke.

He was shocked, horrified. He mourned for everyone, the Eurasians, his beloved friend the Ambassador, his own uncounted sisters and brothers. But he thought it best to say nothing about the minor accident at the North American Embassy. Every effort would be made to find and punish, to determine and place the guilt where it belonged. Never blinking an eye, expressionless, he played his part, an Indian of the Indians.

By the time the old man arrived the Mexican broadcast was over. Blossom had done the messages of condolence, to Cheka, to Aleman Villa. He motioned the old man to a chair.

"You heard Aleman Villa?" Blossom asked. The old man nodded.

"And your reaction?"

"Frightened," the old man said after a pause. "An unhappy Indian."

Blossom expressed surprise. "We were impressed," he said, "by his control, by how quiet he was."

"Too quiet," the old man said. "Too much control. But we can talk about Aleman later."

"Yes," Blossom agreed, "you know why I want to talk to you, why we want to talk to you." He looked at the Vice President and the Secretary of State.

"Perhaps you had better be more exact," the old man said, "so that I don't take up too much of your time."

Blossom felt uncomfortable, intimidated, much as he had been by his own father almost up to the end. The generations ahead always had an advantage however much you sought to deny it. When they began to break, the advantage moved; but the old man gave no real sign of breaking. He did not have to say that he had known Aleman Villa for years, had sat drinking with him. And the old man had done his share of the drinking.

"This is disagreeable," Blossom said with an effort. "But you know that the Intelligence Group has its critics."

The old man was calm. "How could I not?"

Blossom made a still greater effort. "There will be, let me be blunt, suspicions, those who will wonder, wonder now, if the Intelligence Group, your Intelligence Group, was responsible for the destruction of the Eurasian Embassy.

The old man moved his fingers. "I won't ask if anyone here has such thoughts," he said. "Such an act is forbidden by law and my strongest critics have never proved I was lawless. But more to the point, the United States has nothing that could have been used to do what was done today in Mexico City. To go back to Aleman for a moment, that is why he was frightened today."

"Do you know who had the means?" Blossom asked.

"We all know," the old man said, "you, all of us. Cheka. Ulianov. The Union of Eurasian Republics."

"And you mean to tell us that they destroyed their own Embassy? No, that's going too far. You can't expect us to believe that." The old man was breaking. This was the first sign, the foolishness that goes with living too long.

"Take my word for it, they did it," the old man said. "I was brought up a good Catholic," he went on. "I believe that the Lord knows everything, understands everything. No one else does." Suddenly he looked younger, ten years younger, 20 years younger. "Still, let me tell you a few things, but only if none of you will repeat them, only on that condition, except to Miss Clymer."

"Mr. Carmody," Blossom said, "you really are asking too much. How can you?"

The old man interrupted. "Lives are involved. Other men's lives. Sources of information on which the safety of the United States could depend. Your own safety."

Blossom was sure the old man was what his children would have called gaga, senile. However painful it would be, the time had come to replace him. But for the present the thing to do was to humor him.

"I will answer for all of us," Blossom said.

The old man, as always, was sitting very erect in his chair. "A month ago," he began, "a man whom I have known half a lifetime and have always had reason, good reason, to trust told me he had learned from his people that one of Ulianov's technical institutes had created a device such as was used today in Mexico City, a miniature, a truly miniature thermonuclear bomb. It was, he told me, beyond his engineers and his mathematicians but they knew that the physics and the mathematics were possible. I did not need to tell him that we had worked in the same direction and gave up because our technicians declared it was an impossible project. He knew that. In fact I had told him."

Blossom would have rebuked the old man for the disclosure but the old man gave him no time.

"My friend told me that Cheka had approved what my friend called Ulianov's schedule. First they meant to wipe out one of our Embassies. Next they would turn to New York. Then Chicago or perhaps a city on the west coast. Washington was the last target -- the place where we sit, the Capitol. On the same day. The device he said was so small that in a sense there was no guarding against it, that the only protection was to learn the identity of the agent or agents involved with the schedule and follow him."

"I can't believe it," Blossom said, half to himself.

"The agent arrived in Mexico two days ago, but I learned it only after he had got to their Embassy."

"I don't believe any of this," Blossom said. "But, all right, do you know his name?"

"Only the name that he has given us," the old man said slowly. "He has come to our people. He claims to be seeking protection."

3

Cheka Looks for New Way to World Dominion Short of War

There were always opportunities as Cheka saw it. The trick was to distinguish the true from the false, the safe from the dangerous. There were times, of course, when he wondered about the very concept itself. An opportunity was an occasion for advancing, for obtaining an objective, for moving toward the ultimate goal. The Romans had triumphal processions to mark each step on their way. They exhibited prisoners then strangled them when the ceremony was over. Their goal was never quite clear. Apparently it was to swallow everything in their reach. Then Augustus, and after him Hadrian, had set some kind of limit. They could swallow only so much. Perhaps setting the limit contained the seed of their ruin. Or perhaps setting the limit had insured their survival for the two or three centuries before their collapse. It was a question that he often thought about.

He had proposed it as a subject for the Institute for the Study of Past Human Societies but Director Smerdyakov had evaded and dodged. The question was dangerous unless the Institute knew the answer that would satisfy the highest authority. And Cheka had not given any instruction as to the answer.

The presumption was that the Eurasian Union would expand endlessly, not perhaps endlessly because the Earth was only so large. But the Union would, could expand to that limit. The Romans in their best days had, when you thought about them, small resources. Their legions had to walk wherever they went. Their weapons were trifling. They had to cut and jab and kill in a primitive way, not much better than so many savages. Such machines as they had for killing were nothing. It was retail killing at best so their conquests were overwhelming to them, but modest on any present day scale. Cheka thought at times about the blood, the grunting and sweating as the Romans extended their power. It had been the same with the Persians, the Assyrians, all the old imperial peoples. They had probably caused terror wherever they went, everyone paralyzed by their noise and numbers, everyone conscious of the inevitable slaughter they faced.

The biggest slaughterhouses had been managed by Genghis, Lord of All Men. He and his sons and grandsons had reached out further than anyone who preceded them but what they had grasped broke into pieces. The marvel was that starting from Moscow it had all been put together again. The process, sometimes interrupted, but then resuming as in 2020, had gone on for centuries. The Eurasian Union since the Merger embraced everything the Mongols had touched or seen and a little beyond. Could it go further? Could it contain the whole planet?

The instruments for conquest were ready at hand. There was no need for chop, chop and men with strong arms and stomachs. Thanks to the technicians in their white smocks there could be storms of fire out of the sky, claps of shattering thunder that no one would hear. Those who were marked for destruction would be ashes before the sound of thunder could reach them. Fear of the fire and the thunder alone would suffice. No one would resist, or almost no one. The few who did could be tracked down, caught and disposed of in the old way alone in their prisons. The Eurasian Union would take over what now lay outside it, intact and undamaged. It was all very simple. He had spoken of the key fitting the lock. Fear was the key to the lock. Fear would open the door.

Long ago he had talked of these things with the present Dudorov's father, perhaps the most intelligent man he had known, perhaps a too intelligent man. They had talked not long after Cheka had become Chairman -- the title was General Manager then. Semyon Semyonovich Grabkin, Marshal of the Eurasian Union -- his Double Marshalship was still in the future, was eager to take all Western Europe, to extend the Union to the Atlantic. He promised success and Cheka was tempted. The elder Dudorov-- grandson of the first Dudorov -- was close to him then and he asked his opinion. In those days talking to Dudorov was like talking to himself, easy, free.

"Vladimir Ilyich," Dudorov had said, "it may not be so clear as our Semyon supposes. Let me think about it overnight, maybe write something down. I know your rule is never to write but writing can clarify thinking."

Cheka remembered laughing at Dudorov's reference to his rule. Dudorov was correct. Paper was dangerous. Words once written could be used as a witness. It was not always wise even to talk. Nevertheless, Dudorov went away and came back the next day with his comment, addressed to no one, unsigned, typescript, anonymous. Cheka still had it, a voice, a sensible voice. Dudorov's anonymous paper lay on his table. He regretted Dudorov's death not long after that particular passage, accidental, a lost plane. He had wondered at times if Grabkin knew much about it. In a way it was Dudorov who had kept Grabkin from marching and Dudorov was known to have more influence than went with his rank.

He read the paper again: It would be in my opinion ill advised to adopt the proposal of the military to overrun Western Europe at the time proposed or any other time. If the operation were successful, as I assume it would be, the result would be ruinous. I am also assuming that the United States would not intervene to any serious extent and that the result would be achieved without the risk of using nuclear weapons. Nevertheless my expectation is that we would be victorious in the military sense and would die of acute indigestion, having swallowed 50 million Germans, 50 million Frenchmen, 50 million Italians, 40 million Iberians, 15 million Belgians and Hollanders, plus 20 million Danes, Norwegians and Swedes. If we were to swallow the British Islands as well, we would have another 50 million people of a kind to make our indigestion even more painful.

There are not in Western Europe large groups that would serve us as we were served throughout our 20th century ups and downs by local East Germans, Poles, Hungarians, Czechs, Rumanians and Bulgars. We would meet almost nothing but hostility from the Westerners. Our own people could probably police them but they would be, as I see it, unequal to the stresses and strains within a short time. Our troops taken as a whole would be corrupted by what they would see in Western Europe. And we do not have enough reliable cadres to control both them and the 200 to 250 million Western European peoples we would have brought into our system.

He and Dudorov had on occasion talked about the theology of the System. The icons, as Dudorov called them, Marx, Engels, the holy writings of Lenin, the sacred word, Communism, by which they were all supposed to be living, the mystical brotherhood of the Party -- or its innermost membership, the combination Dudorov defined as the System.

"Our Church," Dudorov once proposed, "is not what it was. Is that so?"

They agreed that their Church was not what it had been. Even when revived by Cheka, its True Believers were few. There were more what Cheka thought of as Formal Believers. Dudorov had suggested that Grabkin was a prime example of a formal believer; Semyon Semyonovich was the son of a loyal and loving soldier of the revolution whose happiest memories had been of raping German women in Berlin as a boy lieutenant. Dudorov regarded Globus as a specimen of the rare True Believers. Globus had been a deputy in the Ministry of Foreign Affairs when Cheka became Chairman. Now he was the Minister, a concession Cheka had made to the Party. Party elements had to be pacified.

Globus, Dudorov claimed, was potentially the outstanding theoretician of his generation, literal minded and narrow minded, stupid, explaining everything to himself and to anyone who would listen by quotations from Marx, Engels and Lenin -- or even Stalin, depending on Stalin's standing at any particular moment. Osip Gabrilovitch Globus was moved by his duty to forward the work begun by the grandfathers and carry it to its logical end.

Cheka looked at the clock. It was almost time for the meeting. Globus and Grabkin had asked to see him to discuss the action that must be taken as a result of the horrifying destruction of the Eurasian Embassy in Mexico City. Grabkin saw the affair as involving the honor of the Eurasian Republics. To Globus it involved duty, devotion to the principles of the World Revolution. Ulianov, of course, would be there. And the ghost of Dudorov and the mystery of Dudorov's son. Ulianov arrived a minute early through the door from Cheka's private apartment. The Double Marshal of the Eurasian Union and Globus arrived after the clock sounded the hour. They had waited in Cheka's anteroom for a few minutes out of respect for his primacy.

"Well, here we are," Cheka said, with everyone seated. "You speak first, Semyon Semyonovitch, as, shall we say, senior officer present."

Grabkin demurred. "Only in years, Vladimir Ilyich, only in years." He was a large, bulky man in the style of earlier commanders of the Eurasian armies, with the heavy moustaches that were also part of the style. His medals recorded 40 years of the latest restoration of the Republics, every move, every morsel devoured, every new expansion of power. No one had ever had such a collection. But no one before him had ever been Double Marshal.

Cheka lifted his hand. "Semyon," he said, "you begin. Tell us. What do you think? You asked for a meeting."

Grabkin lit his pipe. "You understand my concern," he began. "An old soldier, but not too old to serve our great Union. This deadly blow. The rule of my lifetime is that we meet blows with blows. You attack when attacked. This is an insult. We do not accept insults."

"And more specifically, Semyon Semyonovitch?"

"As Minister of Defense and Double Marshal I can tell you that we can strike anyone who strikes us. We can go to the Channel -- but you know that. We have talked about that before." Grabkin still regretted, would always regret, that he had not been allowed to go to the Channel at the second time around. What a time they would have had in Paris, in Brussels, in Amsterdam. What plunder and other enjoyments. "And as for crossing the Channel, that would not be a problem." He had worked out the solution a half dozen times and was confident of it. "And if you say the word we can strike anywhere. Through the air, under the sea. Tell me to go to Mexico City. We will go to Mexico City by the thousands, by the tens of thousands. Compared with us, there is no one. We can deal with any rabble that might try to oppose us. Look at me, Vladimir Ilyich, I am an old man. But I have good years before me. It would be the crown of my life to punish these Indians who thought they were safe from us.

"So," Cheka asked, "you think what you call the Indians destroyed our Embassy?"

27

Grabkin puffed on his pipe. "But who else is in Mexico City?"

Globus slowly shook his head. Poor Grabkin, a good soldier, but soldiers only saw the surface of things. "Forgive me, Semyon Semyonovich," he said, "if I disagree. This is only another outrage of the great imperialists. Your Indians may have known about it, or maybe not. Only the great imperialists would have done this. I know them. I see them and deal with them. They may try to conceal it but they are choking with envy and hatred. Their sun is setting. They see our sun rise. The rubbish heap of history waits for them." The last was a phrase that Globus loved. It was the ultimate summing up of mankind's experience. History would settle everything in the right way. History maintained a large rubbish heap.

"You have proof?" Cheka asked.

"I know it in my heart of hearts," Globus said. "In my bones. Logic is logic. But you, Josef Vissarionovich, you are our eyes and our ears. You know I am right."

"I know what I know," Ulianov said. "You must not ask me more."

"Of course," Globus said, "you need say no more. Knowledge is always a burden. And I have no wish to carry your burden. Your silence tells me enough. We have all sacrificed our lives to the mission, to free the oppressed, to liberate those who suffer wherever they are. We are all moved by the same purpose."

Cheka looked at Globus, well fed, dressed by what could be described as the best imperialist tailors, the nephew of an uncle who had been Minister of Foreign Affairs in his time. It would be interesting to know what sacrifices Globus thought he had made. As Foreign Minister, Globus, like his uncle before him, had felt called upon to maintain the honor of the Eurasian Union by living in a suitable manner, which meant with an elaborate residence, elaborate dinners, crystal chandeliers, a retinue in attendance. But no doubt Globus could present a list of his sacrifices if asked: the modest life which he would have preferred, a life of study and thought, a life given to the Party alone and the reward for such dedication. The Foreign Ministry had its advantages, but with his talents Globus might have been expected to get where he, Cheka, sat, Chairman and to have been a Grand Theoretician, his books consulted and quoted, a latter day Plato, Mohammed and Moses, a sage of sages, a lawgiver and ultimate guide.

"We cannot recall our ambassador from Mexico City," Globus went on. "Poor Troyenko. But we can make demands for reparation. So much for Mexico. But we can and, I urge, must act against the great imperialist power, the central imperialist power."

Grabkin nodded agreement. Globus and he saw eye to eye. He was sure of it.

Globus corrected him. "Not that I urge going as fast as Semyon Semyonovich. We will recall Scriabin from Washington and leave only a skeleton staff. We will demand that they acknowledge their guilt and make restitution."

"Restitution?" asked Cheka.

"Not," Globus conceded, "that they can bring back Troyenko and all those others who have been killed. But payments can be made to their stricken families. Payments can be made to us – our obligations to their banks can be erased. Delivery of goods can be made in amounts that we set."

"An idea," Cheka said. "And if they refuse?"

Globus was sure they would not. They were guilty. The whole world knew they were guilty. He would go first to the World League and it would declare that guilt, solemnly, finally. There would be no choice for the great imperialists.

"But if they refuse?" Cheka insisted. Not that he thought Globus was wrong. The United States was not what it had been. Blossom was weak; a well-meaning man, a man who wanted and needed approval, his, Cheka's, universal approval. And the politics of the United States invited being stirred up with a stick. He could take care of his own too ambitious. In the United States ambitious men did as they pleased, pursued their own interests. It would be easy to bring on a storm. He and his predecessors had done it before and always with profit.

"You may be right," Osip Gabrilovich," he said after a moment. "But assume the improbable, if they refuse?"

"It would be out of my hands. I am only the Foreign Minister of the Union. It would be a matter for you and Semyon Semyonovich."

"We have our plans," Grabkin said.

Cheka knew they had plans. Soldiers, if that was what they were, always had plans. They spent their lives making plans and it apparently never occurred to them that their plans might not work, in fact seldom worked, that life was full of surprises, sometimes unpleasant surprises. People made unexpected responses. Even machines did not behave as they were intended to. Moreover, once the soldiers' plans were taken out of the files and acted on, it was difficult to draw back, maybe impossible. Grabkin could go through the air or under the sea, but there was always the question of what would happen when he arrived. The plans called for no more than x resistance but it would always be x 1/2 or 2x or even 5x. People had peculiar reactions. The Americans were an odd mix and could be maneuvered in any direction. But no one could be certain of what they would do if they were driven into a corner, forced into a corner.

"Your plans are very sound plans, Semyon Semyonovich," Cheka said. "Still invasions are risky. The Swedes, the French, the Germans learned that from us."

"There are other means, Vladimir Ilyich," Grabkin said.

Cheka knew the other means too. The fire and the thunder out of the sky. The fruit of the Tree of Knowledge, gathered over generations by the various Institutes, all competing for the honor of having gathered the deadliest harvest. There were assurances that the Eurasian Republics would strike without being struck. Their enemies would be destroyed in a matter of minutes without retribution. Yet on the other side they had the same promises. The computers on both sides gave the same messages: you may proceed without risk.

By definition computers made no mistakes. Nevertheless, one set of computers had to be wrong. More to the point who could be sure what would happen when the buttons were pushed. The marvelous toys had never been used, by their nature could not have been played with, put to the practical test. Mice could have eaten the wires that governed them, parts could have corroded. Maybe half would respond, maybe all, maybe none. In theory they were watched over like so many children with nursemaids, attended to daily. But if the nursemaids were drunk, or lazy or stupid who could be sure about the state of the children? Cheka knew enough to be wary, always assuming the toys had been properly designed and correctly built to begin with.

"Yes," Cheka said, "we have other means."

"The birds," Grabkin said. "We could let the birds fly." he had faith in the white smocks and their learning. It was all past his understanding and therefore all the more credible. So far as he was concerned they were a set of magicians. He looked at them as his grandfathers had looked at the priests. The white smocks had access to a mysterious power.

"Not," Grabkin added, "that I would like to make use of the birds. There will be no pleasure in acquiring nothing but ruins." They would gain something. The last enemy would be literally wiped off the Earth but it would be sad to be made to forfeit all of the last enemy's wealth. New York -- he had been there, Washington -- he had been there. Splendid cities. To take them would be better, more satisfying to him, than taking Berlin to his father long ago.

Globus agreed. Their aim, after all, was to liberate, to lift up the lowly. He would regret having to slaughter the oppressed with the oppressors. He knew that making an omelet entailed breaking eggs and that the makers of the Revolution had broken eggs by the dozens. Nevertheless, if it could be avoided, it would be better to have the liberated North Americans work and produce. Their farm lands were good; their peasant population alone would be a great gain.

"Enough," Cheka finally said, "I have listened and I know what you think. We will proceed. Osip Gabrilovich, you will recall Scriabin to consult for a few days. We will use the World League as usual. You will draft notes for me -- to Porfirio Aleman and President Blossom. We will go over them. And you, Semyon Semyonovich, will announce that the armies of the Republics stand ready to do whatever their duty requires. I have a few questions to ask, Joseph Vissarianovich."

When Grabkin and Globus had left, Cheka turned to Ulianov. What had he learned?

"The area in Mexico City is radioactive of course, as we expected. Our people have measured it. The indication is that only a single cartridge, as you call it, was used. Our inference must be that Dudorov was not in the Embassy or that he had left the other four shall we say in a hiding place?" The worst was to come.

"And you think?"

"I have a postscript, Vladimir Ilyich, which I now add. We have information, roundabout, from their Secretary of State. Dudorov has gone to them for protection. More exactly, he has gone to the old man." It was not good news.

"And you believe it?"

Ulianov shrugged. "It could be a story made up for our benefit. But how would the old man have known just the right name? How would he have come up with the name Dudorov?"

"We both know the old man," Cheka said. "He hears things. He may only want to alarm us. But if he has Dudorov and the four cartridges we have things to think about. We may have a wreck on our hands. We will accept that we do have a wreck. The problem is to salvage whatever we can."

"We have done it before," Ulianov said, not at all happy. The temperature was dropping again.

"We might begin," Cheka said, "by getting up the usual demonstrations. You must be able to find some Sons and Daughters in the debris. An interesting place," he added reflectively, "thirty million people living on top of each other. A human volcano. Perhaps the time has come for an eruption."

Ulianov nodded. He hoped that enough of his contacts -- the technical term -- had survived. Surely all of them had not been in the Embassy. He nodded again.

"And," Cheka suggested, "there should be sympathy and mourners north of the border. Nieces, daughters, cousins, the usual family ties, sons, nephews. You will know what to do."

4

Dudorov Too Big a Fish?

Walter Blossom's election as President was in a way accidental. To begin with he was a man. During the new millenium the Populars had become basically the women's party and had for more than a generation named only women as its candidates for Chief Magistrate. The Popular ticket was, as it was described, balanced by having a man as Vice President. And Walter Blossom had been agreed on for that post. The difficulty was that the Populars were divided between the liberals who supported Marietta Snow and the conservatives who had united behind the candidacy of Louisa Clymer.

The nomination and election of Miss Snow had been expected and universally approved by what considered itself the Fourth Estate of the nation. This was the whole body of observers and reporters and interpreters of what Blossom, for example, referred to as developments. Some of them wrote for the press in the old-fashioned way, others, maybe more, were faces and voices, explaining the meaning of each day's events, foreseeing consequences, reading the future. There was a whole galaxy, stars of great and small magnitude. The brightest were so many friends and familiars whose presence was looked to and welcomed five days a week, six days a week. They had immense followings. And they were paid in proportion. Their standing, or rating as it was called, was in a sense a function of the amounts they were paid. To receive 20 million dollars a year was to be assured of a vast audience. Money, after all, was the final proof of achievement and commanded respect even from those who pretended to make their own judgments. The common and the sound view was that the advertisers who provided the funds were prudent and knew the value of the insights and opinions they, in effect, paid for. No one had been paid as much as Marietta and no one had received as much admiration.

Marietta had not only brought the news three times a week to almost everyone in the country for 25 years, but she wrote a piece that was printed once a month in the New York Gazette, entitled "If I Were President." In these monthly pieces she criticized and corrected, explained and demonstrated what had been done and what should have been done by whoever was President. Quite reasonably she found no President perfect. From time to time she gave them the marks she felt they deserved. A "B" from Marietta was an event. Most Presidents had to make out with "C's."

The last Unpopular President had only "F's" during his eight years in office. In a way the surprising thing was that Marietta had not become President earlier. The support was there but for years she had misgivings about involving herself with the business of politics and the men and women engaged in it. As she said, it was her function to think. She had no desire to mediate between the factions and the ambitions of their promoters and leaders. Some thought this position inconsistent with Marietta's "If I Were President" pieces, but her reply was that she considered the Presidency should be concerned with the making of policy rather than what she called housekeeping duties. In fairness it should be said that Marietta had proposed constitutional reforms that would create four Vice Presidents for operations, leaving the President free to devote herself to the larger issues and problems. In spite of her known reluctance to move to the White House there had been an irresistible Snow for President movement and Marietta had, as the phrase goes, bowed to it.

The opposition had come from the more conservative Populars who supported Louisa Clymer. She had been a leading member of the New York bar before becoming President of the Fiscus Eternity Trust Company and then President of Technamics Corp. The Snow and Clymer groups were equally strong and each canceled the other. Neither could get a majority. After seven ballots the Convention agreed, not very willingly, to accept a man as its candidate for the first time since 2020. Blossom was liberal, but less so than Marietta. He could expect the votes of most men, who were a minority but still very numerous. The Clymer group came around grudgingly. Louisa's pride was in what she referred to as her realism. She looked on Marietta as not only soft -- to use her word -- but a fraud; no more than an actress. Blossom she thought of as a weak sister. If she herself could not be President, she would make Blossom President. And she did. Nothing pleased her so much as the spectacle of Marietta weeping when the eighth ballot was over.

Blossom did his best in the aftermath. He offered Louisa the Department of State. She declined. Her preference, she said, was the Department of Defense and the Treasury, both of them. There was no precedent for the arrangement but Blossom accepted it. Then he had a question: would Louisa object if, as a matter of politics, he invited Miss Snow to take the Department of State."

"Good Christ, no," was the answer. Louisa's style was to be blunt and a little profane. She considered it useful in dealing with men. She was a woman -- which was no more than an accident and one she could not have prevented. Being ladylike was a matter of choice. "Only," she added, "don't expect any sisterly feeling. I despise her. She probably loathes me. Probably thinks I am jealous of her role as everyone's teacher. And bear in mind that my two departments are not bound by any opinion of your Secretary of State. I do my own thinking. You understand, Walter?"

Blossom understood. He persuaded Marietta to come into his cabinet as Secretary of State. She had been for years really more interested in foreign than domestic affairs though, as she observed, she was equally well informed about both. She was to have a free hand -- almost a free hand in dealing with the interests of the country abroad.

"Miss Clymer," Blossom explained, "is coming in as Secretary of both Defense and the Treasury. It was," he went on, "a matter of politics, something dictated by the need to hold the Popular Party on its true course. Miss Clymer," he continued, "will have a voice in foreign affairs to the extent that they involve her, shall we say, interests."

Marietta listened and judged. The Secretary of State had the most dignified part in the play. She sat on the President's right, had precedence at all gatherings. She would listen to Miss Clymer as she would to anyone else. In effect, as she saw it, she was consenting to allow Miss Clymer to sit in the Cabinet and to speak at its meetings. She was being, she felt, more than gracious.

"Mr. President," she assured Blossom, "I understand the situation perfectly well. I am giving up my career for the present in the hope that it will help you and the people at large. I think of us both as devoted to relieving world tensions." World tensions were bad and could be relieved. Relieving world tensions would benefit the whole race of mankind, or better, all humankind. She saw herself as a kind of Co-President.

For Marietta the Geneva meeting caused a mild crisis. As Secretary of State she had recommended a meeting with Cheka. But Cheka as a head of state could meet only with Blossom. As a foreigner, of course, he could not understand the existence of an informal Co-President. Marietta could meet with Globus but only Blossom could informally confer with the Chairman. So Marietta made the acquaintance of Globus and concluded he was an intellectual but not one that she liked, too stiff and too narrow. As for Marietta and Cheka, they met. Cheka watched her. Marietta watched him. He was, she decided, a man of great charm and, correctly, brighter than Globus. She regretted, naturally, that the Eurasian Republics were not under the management of a woman. She accepted, however, Blossom's estimate of Cheka as a man of good will and she agreed that he was sincere, very sincere. Cheka understood his own women: a woman as Secretary of State, all American women, struck him as odd. This woman presumably was important, that is, officially certified as a person of consequence. He was inclined to regard her as a female version of President Blossom. As for Louisa, he met her too and was a little disturbed.

Louisa had insisted on being one of the group that went to Geneva. Marietta had objected. It was a meeting devoted to foreign affairs, to our relations with the Eurasian Republics.

"Look, Walter," Louisa had finally said at the Cabinet meeting. "Cheka and the rest of his crowd affect what we do at Defense and the Treasury. I want to see them and make my own estimate of them. When I was in practice, at the Bank, at Technamics, I made a point of seeing the people who created the problems. I've seen pictures of Cheka and everyone else. The pictures may not do them justice. I intend to see the whole lot for myself."

At Geneva Louisa's formal partner was Grabkin. She pleased him by getting him to tell her about the overwhelming power of the Eurasian Republics. When he announced -- this was after a great deal of drinking -- that the United States of America was no longer much of a force in the world, she led him on to explain why he thought what he did. For whatever good it may have been, she learned more from Grabkin than he learned from her. At least she discovered that the Double Marshal, and presumably the single marshals as well, thought Mexico was important. The Double Marshal's report was that the American Secretary of Defense was a well-behaved woman who listened and said very little and could be ignored.

Cheka's reaction was different. When he talked with Louisa he was reminded of one of his strong-minded aunts, who also listened and said very little. She seemed to know something about the Eurasian Union's credit arrangements, about its investments and about some attempts to get information from Technamics through the back door. His impression was that she might be difficult like his aunts, more difficult than women should be.

Remembering what the Double Marshal had said about Mexico, Louisa was curious about the explosion in Mexico City. Her people reported at once that the debris was radioactive. Her people had theories but no explanations. They had no device and knew of no device that could account for the blast, at least nothing on the list that was known to them. She had, of course, not been at the White House when the old man was there but she knew he had been there. On the following morning she went to call on the old man herself.

"Didn't the President tell you what I reported?" the old man asked after Louisa explained why she had called on him.

"No," she said, "Mr. Carmody. All I was told was that you had disclaimed responsibility."

The old man half laughed. "You know," he said, "I don't think they believed me. But the President and the Secretary of State have more confidence in Cheka than they have in me."

"I don't."

"That's a kind thing to say," the old man went on. "Did they tell you that an agent who claims to have set off the blast had come to us for protection?"

Louisa shook her head.

"Odd," said the old man after a moment. "Odd, very odd. Perhaps I ought not to have mentioned it."

"Well, you have," Louisa said. There was nothing surprising about their having held back information. People were always doing that to each other. Blossom should have known better. After all she had for all practical purposes put him where he was. But she knew how people behaved. She had used and discarded people herself as she moved up in the world. Brilliant careers, like money, as someone had said, were not made in the light.

"I haven't seen him," the old man said. "But he will be here tomorrow. The affair is puzzling."

"You say the man claims to have set off the blast?" Louisa asked.

"Maybe not that. To have made the arrangements -- both Embassies. It makes no sense. Less sense than usual. If he's telling the truth we have caught a large fish, maybe too large a fish."

"How too large a fish?"

"I told the President," the old man said, "so I might as well tell you that friends let me know several weeks ago that the Eurasians had something special and to make a long story shorter were likely to destroy our Embassy in Mexico City. They planned something on the same scale for New York and another city or two with a grand finale in Washington."

"Friends? Not your people. Friends?"

"I have friends. We have friends. Not very many. We trade information and these friends have good information. I listen to them when they speak. They told me this. They told me that. Then they told me the man in charge had gone to, was about to arrive in Mexico City. My people missed him. Then you know what happened. And then he came to us, giving a name that means something."

"I won't ask the name."

"You needn't," the old man said. "Not a name that you know. No former client. No one with an account at your bank. Not one of your business acquaintances. But an acquaintance of mine to the extent that I know the name."

"But the fish," Louisa said. She wanted to know why the fish might be too large.

"That," the old man said, "is a question that involves the larger issues, the fundamentals. How you see our relationship with the Eurasian Republics. To me, we have been in a long mostly stalemated quiet war that they began long ago. None of your important people agree with me. The Presidents -- including your President -- are always about to get the lion to lie down with the lamb. Your Secretaries of State are always about to negotiate what are referred to as the outstanding differences. But the war always goes on. You talked to the Double Marshal, the monument with the medals?"

"Yes," Louisa said.

"He's my age," the old man said, "maybe a year or two older. He hangs on. He wants to go to the Channel. He wants to go further. The Merger was good for his health; made him feel 20 years younger. Cheka keeps him in line. Cheka's no fool. He plays his own hand. Then he plays ours."

Louisa listened. The old man was crazy. Everyone knew it and everyone said so but it was an interesting craziness.

"Cheka knows that a noisy war, the kind Grabkin thinks of, would be a disaster, could be a disaster. Risk. Too much broken. The weapons too large, out of scale," the old man went on. "Out of proportion. The engineers and their customers lost touch with reality a long time ago. The whole business has been out of control, senseless, a waste of money and time. It's been a process of buying elephant guns for hunters looking for rabbits. The planet isn't big enough for the weapons, too small, maybe too fragile. You ought to know more about this than I do. Space stations. Space weapons. If all of it worked -- and nobody knows that it would -- we would have the end of the world. Cheka sees it and I give him credit for that."

"You know that?" Louisa asked. And she was not so sure the old man was crazy. There was a point in what he said about rabbits and elephant guns.

"Dear lady, like most things in this life, a matter of inference but only in part. He and I had a conversation in private once, a long time ago."

"I never knew that," Louisa said, really surprised. It was difficult to imagine how or where Cheka and Michael Carmody could have got together and talked.

"It was just after he had become what they called General Manager. I heard he was coming here, informally, to see how everything looked. I had never seen him in all the years he was what people call my opposite number but I knew him from photographs. There was a party in their Embassy here, presumably for his informal benefit. I went. I spotted him as one of the waiters. A peculiar lot, the Eurasians. More imagination than we have perhaps. You can't imagine one of our Presidents getting him or herself up as a waiter. Anyhow, I saw him, asked if there were a quiet corner where I could sit down and have a drink, alone, by myself. He suggested the Ambassador's special retreat, led me there, locked the door and we talked."

It was quite a story as the old man told it and if you believed it. They had sat and talked for an hour. They had exchanged compliments. Each knew what the other was up to -- within limits. Each knew the other was formidable. Cheka was candid. The United States was on the defensive. The Eurasian Union attacked, expanded where it could safely. Cheka underlined safely. The armed forces and the arms -- even then -- were nonsensical. The objective was not to take over ruins but to have the gates opened, to take intact the whole prize. The trick was to get the gates opened.

"It will take time," Cheka had admitted, "but the one thing we all have in abundance is time. How old is the universe?" Cheka had asked. "How long will it last? Whatever answer you get, from the Bible believers, from the science believers, it is always the same. We have plenty of time ahead of us. Our advantage is time.

"I have walked around, looked around," Cheka had added. "You build, tear down, rebuild. You are always changing. Your people are wound up too tight. Everything is running too fast. Everything vibrates. It's like a machine out of order. No one wants things to be stable. They want nothing but change. As we build up the pressure, you will disintegrate. You will have movements and movements. Resistance takes patience and you have an impatient people. The gates will be opened."

"Dear lady," the old man said, "Cheka has been very patient. He did the Merger, which all our wise people said was impossible. The pressure has never relaxed. I have never seen glaciers but I have read about glaciers. They creep. The Eurasian Union creeps like a glacier. It may seem to move only two inches a year but it moves. And Cheka was right about us. We don't have the temperament or character that resists. We expect quick, easy solutions. Painless salvation. It's been a long time since I talked with Cheka and the pressure is high. Very high. But," he concluded, "I shouldn't have talked so much. You didn't come to hear me dredge up my recollections of a conversation a long time ago or my opinions about the state of the world."

Louisa reflected. For more than 20 years she had made constructive use of her time. She had risen and risen. Her career was a model. Compared with her the old man was poor. She had more and better honorary degrees. She outranked the old man at parties, though he never went to them. In those same years the old man was stalled, not a new idea in his head. He had sat with his eyes fixed on Cheka, fixed on a conversation that may or may not have occurred. However she had been to Geneva. She had talked to the old Double Marshal. She had had a look at Cheka. They were not the kind of people she was accustomed to.

The old man was the victim of what people called monomania. Conceivably Cheka was too. Their craziness in a way reduced, could reduce, her career to nothing more than frivolity. From the Bank she knew that Cheka was engaged in peculiar and immense transactions. At the Bank she had approved vast loans to the Republics herself. No one really knew where the credits were used. There were stories that the Eurasian Republics had large, maybe controlling holdings in the great American companies -- even, some people said, in the Bank. There was Omnium Corp. -- a giant investor, in and out of the market. And again there were those who claimed that Omnium acted for Cheka. She asked the old man what he knew and got the expectable, uncomfortable answer.

"Cheka understands the way we do things," the old man said. "We live to lend money so, of course, he borrows. The Republics borrowed so much long ago that all your people can do is to give them more credit. Cheka buys with our money, buys where he thinks it may be useful to have a position. It doesn't cost anything. It's a kind of present. Some holdings provide him with income. If he sells them, they give him profits or at least money to use in another direction. The essential thing is that these dealings create the right kind of atmosphere, the right point of view. As a matter of business the people who count realize that it would be unwise to be unfriendly to the Eurasian Republics. It's a matter of common sense. You don't rock the boat. You must have learned that as a practical woman."

Louisa nodded. She was a practical woman. And what the old man was saying recalled conversations in board rooms, conversations at dinners.

"So," the old man concluded, "if my visitor tells us that he had instructions to level Manhattan and blow up the Capitol, the sensible thing for the practical people will be to call him a fraud. And if he isn't a fraud, the thing to do will be to ignore him. Unless, of course, Cheka pushes too hard."

"I'll be back," Louisa said, "after you talk to your fish."

The old man told her she would be welcome.

5

Hispanic Caucus: "Give Back Mexican States"

"I'm a beer salesman," Harry Fresser said. "I sell whatever it is that keeps my brothers and sisters from stinking. I sell anything and my concern is only with money. Which is why Planet has swallowed all but the competition my brother Eliot allowed to survive. But, by God, I think you went too far in that special broadcast of yours."

Miss New looked hurt. She was the number one news star now that Marietta had gone out of business and had allowed herself to become Secretary of State. Her contract gave her complete control over what the lawyers called the content of her broadcast.

"Oh, I know that," Fresser told her. "I also know all about the sacred nature of the First Amendment. I speak only as one of the audience. Explosions in Mexico City. Blowing up a Eurasian embassy. Neither one makes me ashamed to be an American."

"I'm sorry, Harry," Miss New said. "What I mean is that I'm sorry to know that you feel as you do. I've had thousands of calls and telegrams and they all approve. No one, absolutely no one shares your point of view."

Fresser knew the ultimate truth; the audience ruled. He and the late Eliot had believed in the audience as their forebears had believed in the Lord God Jehovah and their rewards were considerable. They had been the well-known billionaire brothers. Now Harry had the whole lot. Planet, the investments, all the billions were his. Eliot looked down from Heaven.

"I'm always careful," Miss New declared.

"I never questioned that, Dorothy," Harry Fresser conceded.

"But," Miss New added, "I'm also sincere, Harry. You know I'm sincere."

Harry agreed. There was no reason to argue about Dorothy's being sincere. Her sincerity had made her Marietta's one serious rival. She spoke from the heart. She said what she felt. It was not her thinking but her feeling that made Miss New what she was: America's conscience.

"I am not a polls addict, Harry, unlike some people we know." She had Marietta in mind. Marietta was known to have had her own organization -- that was her word -- for the purpose of keeping her close to the public, asking questions, sampling public opinion, getting up the usual percentages.

"Like Blossom and friends," Harry suggested. The politicians generally had no faith in astrologers but they counted on regular surveys of the political market. A product was a product and its appeal had to be tested before you invested. Ideas, programs, policies were all of them products.

"I regard Walter Blossom as a sincere person," Miss New said rather primly. "I wasn't thinking of him."

"My apologies to Walter Blossom," Fresser said. "But I still think you went too far in the broadcast. I'll be damned if I feel ashamed to be an American." He was relieved as a practical matter that not many listeners or viewers or whatever they were had shared his reaction. Business was business. Nevertheless, he wondered why he was unique. Why should he be ashamed?

"It's quite simple," Miss New explained. "I don't mean to offend but it is mostly a matter of age. I am my age. You're a long generation older." Dorothy was in her late 30's -- pushing 40 harder than she liked to remember. Harry Fresser was further around the track by a good 30 years. "There are many people your age," Miss New conceded, "and some of them tend to think as you do. Younger people are, to be plain about it, more open."

"More compassionate?" Harry suggested. It was a word he disliked.

"Exactly so," Miss New said. "We're concerned about other people, their hopes and their needs."

"So I'm a mean, selfish old man? You can say it, Dorothy. You won't be the first one to say it."

Miss New smiled. She really liked Harry Fresser. Not many men faced the truth about themselves as he did. In spite of the billions he was really quite human. To be selfish was human. She might be selfish at times though she left the selfish details to her agent and lawyers. Harry could face the truth about himself but he did not, maybe could not face the world as it was.

"No," she insisted, "I won't say that you're what you said you were. Your problem is that you won't admit that the world is different now, that there have been basic changes. You grew up in a different time. Your premises are no longer valid."

"Such as," Harry asked.

"There's the Eurasian thing, for example. You grew up in an atmosphere of dislike and fear of the Eurasian Republics. You haven't got over it. You haven't -- I dislike to say it -- been able to outgrow your prejudice."

"Tell me more," Harry said. No doubt she was right in a way. There were things he would never learn and also some he would never forget.

"You don't appreciate how strongly people feel about the Mexican issue -- about doing something to return what was stolen. It's much worse now after what we've done. Killing all those innocent people."

"How do you know that we did it?" Harry asked.

"Everyone knows we did it," Miss New said. "1 spoke to Harrison. He told me that Cheka is about to reveal the evidence they have." Harrison was Harrison Swing, the Planet correspondent in Moscow. "Harrison says the evidence is overwhelming. They know it there. He said feeling is running very high, that they're very disturbed, but that Cheka is trying to keep it under control."

"Harrison is our correspondent," Harry said, "and he makes a nice appearance." Swing was always described as distinguished. He had a fine head of gray hair and a dignified manner. "But," he added, "Harrison was never the brightest fellow I knew. He believes whatever he's told."

Miss New wanted to know if that were so why Harry sent him to Moscow, kept him in Moscow.

"That's easy," Harry explained. "He's the only kind of fellow they'll take. They kept expelling all the fellows we had there before we sent Harrison."

"That may be so," Miss New conceded. "But the evidence is so clear. The whole thing was so obvious."

"Obvious?"

"And clumsy," Miss New said. "That small explosion in our own Embassy to cover our tracks."

"Small?" Harry asked. "A dozen people were killed."

"That only shows that we are both stupid and ruthless. The whole affair is disgusting. We kill our own people to conceal our guilt for the thousands of lives that we took. You've got to admit that what we did was vicious, horrible."

"I don't admit it," Harry said. "But tell me, Dorothy, since you're so certain, who could have planned it? Who could have been so -- to use your word -- ruthless? You tell me Blossom is sincere. Blossom?"

"No," Miss New conceded. "I don't think Walter could have known about it. He would have forbidden it."

"Marietta?"

Miss New's face tightened a little. She did not like Marietta. And she did not like the idea that Marietta had the power, the authority to give orders, such far-reaching orders. She shook her head. It could not have been Marietta.

"No, Harry" she said. "Not Marietta. It would have been, it was our Mr. Carmody. No one else would have dared or would have had the means. It's shameful but no one can control him. He's been involved in every evil in the world for as long as I can remember."

"You confuse him with the Devil," Harry observed.

"He is no one to joke about, Harry," Miss New said. "He is a danger to all of us. Forever stirring up trouble."

"Speaking of people stirring up trouble, your friend Castillo was doing his best today."

Miss New was displeased. "Mr. Castillo is my friend, Harry. And Mr. Castillo was only doing what his conscience required."

"Whatever prompted him, he didn't get very far."

Miss New was disappointed but not surprised by Harry's reaction. She had regretted the scene in the House. The Speaker was too old. He should have retired or been displaced years ago.

The proceedings in the House, as they were still called, were broadcast each day. The Speaker had not approved of the idea but oddly enough he had been the chief beneficiary. The audience had kept growing. They watched the proceedings because they admired the Speaker. Harry Fresser had said that he wished he could hire him, that he was the only rival of his own stars, that the Speaker had style and presence. He looked like what he was -- a man with both authority and experience. He was considerate and courteous but his will was his will.

Manners -- the Speaker was Francis Manners -- had lived in Pennsylvania, in their county, since before the Revolution. A Francis Manners had sat in the Continental Congress, had served in the Pennsylvania Line and then sat in the First and Second Congresses. Other Manners had sat in the House, doctors and lawyers, never rich, never poor, reasonably well-to-do competent men serving as officers in the various wars, well thought of and trusted. The Speaker's career had been a surprise to him. He took it as being in part a legacy from his forebears. He had felt at home in the House because of them. He judged that he had been accepted and respected because his family had been part of the House for generations. Accordingly he set store by the past and its arrangements. The talk about Guadalupe Hidalgo offended him. No one could dismantle the Union as though it were a kind of machine. That had been settled, probably in Pennsylvania, at Gettysburg. If the States of the Union could not break away by themselves, it was impossible that they could be, so to speak, given away, could be surrendered to Mexico or to any other foreign power.

The day after the destruction of the Eurasian Embassy Castillo had asked to be recognized. His purpose, when asked, was to seek unanimous consent to consider a resolution for the appointment of the Commission to consider abrogation of the Treaty of Guadalupe Hidalgo and retrocession of the Mexican States.

"So long as I am in the chair, or present and a member of the House," the Speaker had said, "there can be no unanimous consent to consider such a resolution. And I add there are no Mexican States as the gentleman from Illinois refers to them. There are only States of this Union. I will now hear a motion for adjournment." And the gavel came down.

Castillo grinned. The Speaker had shown his hand. The Speaker was blocking the road but there were ways to remove an obstruction. Nevertheless it was not his most agreeable day. As Harry Fresser had noted, he, Castillo, had not got very far.

"I'm interviewing Castillo tonight, Harry," Miss New announced.

Harry grunted. He did not approve.

"I think he's entitled to say what the Speaker prevented his saying today on the floor. It's a matter of fairness. Some one must teach the Speaker that he can't stop people from expressing opinions."

"Tell me, Dorothy," Harry asked, "are these fellows kidding us? Is Castillo kidding us? Do they really want to undo everything that has been done for the last 200 years or more? It doesn't make any sense. What do they get out of it?" He was puzzled.

"You don't understand them, Harry?"

"No. It's an honest question," Harry insisted. "What are they up to? Who benefits? I don't get it, to quote Brother Eliot." Eliot either got or did not get whatever it was.

"It's a matter of justice to Mr. Castillo, to him and his group. They are Spanish. They are men with pride. They want to right a wrong done to their ancestors. The Spaniards are a proud people."

Harry objected. "I'm about as Spanish as Castillo," he said. "Or the rest of what they call the Hispanic Caucus. You know that, Dorothy. They're a collection of Indios."

"Indians, Harry, are a proud people, too."

"Well," Harry said, "what about us? Or aren't we entitled to be a proud people? Why can't we hold what we have. You don't doubt we can hold it."

"Yes, I do," Miss New said. "We have world opinion against us. There is no greater force, Harry."

Harry thought that was nonsense. He wanted to know what was going to happen to the people in the old Mexican territories. "They're twenty per cent of the population of the United States," he pointed out. "What do you expect them to do?"

"They can stay where they are," Miss New said. "Castillo has already said that."

"He's also said that all the property there should go to the Republic of Mexico as what he called delayed reparations. After all, Dorothy, your family lives in California. What are they going to do?"

Miss New had given that thought. She would provide for them. Fortunately they had no reason to worry. She could provide for them. Other people would, could do as much.

Harry was not convinced. There were 60 million, maybe 65 million people involved.

"Don't forget," Miss New reminded him, "half of them are Mexicans."

"A happy thought," Harry said. "To quote Eliot again, your friend Castillo is playing with fire." Eliot thought there were dangers in playing with fire. "You're playing with fire yourself, Dorothy."

"I told you," Miss New insisted, "that everyone shared my point of view. The Americans are better, more moral, than you suppose, Harry."

After Dorothy's interview of Castillo that evening, even she thought she might be playing with fire. Castillo had made the best of his opportunity. He was, he had said, convinced that the time had come for self help, a principle enshrined in the law. What he had to say was, he explained, really addressed to the Mexican people. If the Congress would not act, if justice was to be obstructed, there was no choice. Those who had been wronged should seek redress in their own way.

The people of Mexico, the poor people, should simply roll over the border. A mighty flood was what he envisioned. They should come by the millions. No one could stop them. The old Mexican states were there, ready and ripe to be taken. Rich land. Rich fields. Handsome cities and towns. There were houses for those who were homeless. Magnificent roads, magnificent bridges and dams. This was all part of their long withheld inheritance. And all right-thinking Americans would welcome their coming. The national conscience once cleared, the United States would live in eternal friendship with the Mexican brothers and sisters, or preferably sisters and brothers.

Miss New was moved by the eloquence but, as it went on and on, a little uneasy. As for Harry, he was appalled. Castillo was in effect giving away twenty per cent of the market. Even worse he was involving Planet in what looked like a plain case of arson. The audience in California, Texas, Arizona, New Mexico, wherever Castillo was asking for trouble, would, and as he could see, not without reason, regard Planet as an accessory to Castillo in starting the fire.

6

Cheka Demands Return of "Dudorov Assassin" and State Property

Cheka was celebrated for being quick witted, a most adjustable man. Those who dealt with him were always being astonished by his talent for recouping what seemed to be certain losses. The Merger was perhaps his best known recovery. The situation was hopeless and Cheka came out of it with the Merger. The Eurasian Union was, or seemed to be, stalled, to be on dead center, when he became number one. He had started it moving again. He had thought out new combinations, slipped around obstacles, found openings which no one had seen.

The destruction of the Embassy in Mexico City and the Dudorov business had only intrigued him. Another man in his place would have contented himself with blaming and punishing underlings. Cheka's reaction was to explore the ruins and put them to use. The Embassy was gone and with it the objectives that Troyenko had been told to achieve. He could get along without Troyenko and whoever else had been in the Embassy. Troyenko was an ill-tempered man whose principal claim had been that he had married Globus' daughter. The destruction of the Embassy only opened new and more interesting vistas.

If Dudorov had turned himself in to the Americans, he knew the answer. Sitting alone thinking it all out by himself, he could see the moves clearly. The American Institute had rooms full of experts. But they were too full of facts. They lived by computers. They were data retrievers and like retriever dogs had no idea of what a living bird was about. He knew the Americans. He had a feel for the Americans. He had been there and worked there and moved about there, understood the American currents and tides. When he was satisfied with his plans he sent for Ulianov.

Poor Ulianov. He was heir apparent but heirs apparent had vanished in the past, with only families and close friends left to mourn for them. And the happy prospects that had disappeared with them. The Embassy in Mexico City had been reduced to molecules or atoms or electrons or mesons or gluons or something. The Mexican Program had gone up with the Embassy. Dudorov, from whom better was expected, had taken sanctuary with the always sinister Carmody.

It had been years since the Security Services had to account for such a disaster. And he, Ulianov, was the one to be brought to account. Cheka was merciful compared with some of those who had preceded him. Unlike the revered Stalin he did not favor closing accounts with a bullet fired into the back of the head. He did not favor working and beating and starving the transgressor to death, an anonymous number, in the course of reeducation.

But Cheka could be severe. He, Ulianov, could complete his career as a teacher in the third grade in a provincial elementary school, instructing Bashkirs or Yakuts in arithmetic or the geography of the Eurasian Republics. And a man, any man, would feel concerned for his family. Ulianova, of course, would divorce him. She was a sensible woman.

The prospects of his children would be blighted unless they disowned him. They were intelligent and they would disown him. But even so they would all lose by his disgrace. He was despondent when he obeyed the summons from Cheka. The only thing to do was to brace himself for the blow. At least Cheka was not a cat and mouse man. Cheka would come to the point and he, Ulianov, would not beg, would not get down on his knees. The Ulianovs had pride. He would listen, accept his fate, and take the punishment Cheka decreed.

To Ulianov's surprise Cheka was in a good mood. Cheka was buoyant. There was no frown, no air of being withdrawn.

"Sit down, Josef Vissarionovich," Cheka said. "Why are you standing?"

Ulianov sat down. He wondered if he were wrong about Cheka. Cheka had never been a cat and mouse man.

Cheka looked at the ceiling. Then he looked at Ulianov. Suddenly it occurred to him that Ulianov might be uneasy, that he expected reproaches, that he thought that he, Cheka, blamed him for having created the problems for which there were such brilliant solutions. Ulianov was clever enough but too serious, maybe not enough bounce. The real gift was to bounce. Not to worry, but to think, use imagination and bounce. He must get Ulianov bouncing again.

"You're so solemn, Josef Vissarianovich," Cheka said. "Take it easy, as the Americans say." Cheka liked to use American phrases. They were a demoralized, even a degenerate people but their language had spirit. Ulianov took heart. Cheka had surprised him before. It was best to be careful but it was possible that Cheka would surprise him again.

"Our problems," Cheka went on, "I have been sitting here with our problems. Now I have suggestions. The smaller problem is Dudorov, but Dudorov could upset everything else. Our sources tell us that he is safe with an old friend, Mr. Carmody, but fortunately, most fortunately our sources are wrong. We know better. Dudorov is dead."

"Dead?" Ulianov asked.

Cheka nodded. "Dead. Very dead. We have discovered the body. Dead at the hands of parties so far unknown, though we shall soon know them. The man with our Mr. Carmody may well be the murderer. Without question the man with Mr. Carmody is, shall we say, an impostor, a man who may have stolen Dudorov's papers and other state property that were in the late Dudorov's custody."

Ulianov listened, admired. No one was the equal of Cheka. "But the body, the identification. How do we do it?"

"In the usual way," Cheka explained. "Dudorov left a widow. There is always the family. Dudorova will view the remains. How can she fail to recognize Dudorov after being his wife for 20 odd years? You will have the press there. We will have a few questions and answers. You must be sure that Mr. Swing attends but that should be easy. Everything will be recorded by cameras so that Mr. Swing can make his report."

"And Dudorova? Will we have to prompt Dudorova?"

"She is a woman of good sense. But my advice is to spare her the strain of what I have in mind. She is also a sensitive woman. She will make an appearance by proxy. There are armies of actresses. The

Eurasian theater is world famous and you will have someone who is enough like Dudorova to be her own sister."

I hear and I obey, Ulianov said to himself. He nodded. He had his instructions.

"We will naturally want the impostor returned to us. I will leave it to you to find a name for him, a suitable missing citizen of the Republics. The suspect murderer when returned will be tried in accordance with law, given all his rights. The Americans will want that assurance and we will be happy to give it. You will get the most distinguished lawyer to act and speak in our name in the American court. There, as you know, everything is done in the courts. When the court has ordered the impostor returned, the most delicate conscience will have no cause for concern. The Ministry of Justice will look to you for guidance in this important and delicate matter. Dumkov, after all, is your subordinate in all State Security business. So much for Dudorov. You agree?"

"Vladimir Ilyich," Ulianov said with sincerity, "when you speak, I agree. You see everything clearly. All of us hear and admire, and I more than any."

Cheka half smiled. Ulianov overdid the flattery but he had done the same thing in his time. It was a kind of court ceremonial, a kind of church ceremonial. Ulianov had probably come expecting a kick and a curse. Instead he had something like a pat on the head. He had his new orders which amounted to forgiveness and a new lease on life -- again an American phrase. Whoever was General Manager, whoever was Chairman -- whatever the title, held thunderbolts in his hand, held the keys, as the Roman Catholics put it, the ultimate power to loose or to bind.

"So much for Dudorov," Cheka said. "As for Mexico, we will proceed as we said when Grabkin and Globus were here. What we want is confusion and noise. And you, Joseph Vissarionovich, have done very well."

"Done very well?"

"Your little man, Castillo," Cheka suggested. "You are resourceful. Miss New."

Ulianov reflected. It was best to be cautious and make a disclaimer. If he took credit for Castillo today, he might have to take the blame for Castillo tomorrow. Castillo was certainly not a reliable man.

"Vladimir Ilyich," Ulianov said, "I must be honest, Miss New, Castillo, I am not responsible for them. They act and speak for themselves. They are not on our rolls. Miss New makes public opinion in her own way though perhaps she is inspired by people we know, but indirectly. Always by indirection. And Castillo has his own aims. They are obscure. They may coincide with ours. But we do nothing for him except as we do with Miss New. From time to time we inspire through friends, young friends. We have made indirect contributions to Castillo's causes and projects, subsidized his progress but he would not know it."

"Would prefer not to know it, perhaps?"

"You are right, always right," Ulianov corrected himself. Cheka as always was right. No man could be sure of the extent of another man's knowledge.

"Turns a blind eye," Cheka suggested, another American phrase. "I approve. I applaud." The best servants were those who did not know they were servants. They were all the more zealous, all the more useful. To feel independent made a man bolder. His motives were pure. No one could attack them. They were his own. A man taking orders was always unsure of himself, on the defensive, however unconsciously. But maybe not always. A Castillo might ignore what he knew for his own reasons. Rascals were rascals whatever language they spoke. And the Americans had more than their share. Perhaps it was the climate, the air, the water that produced men like Castillo. He, Cheka, had known and watched the Americans for half a century and marveled that the fools and rascals flourished there as they did. Perhaps it was a greater marvel that the Americans had survived even as well as they had. Certainly their future was doubtful.

"I approve and applaud," Cheka repeated. "Everything is proceeding but you have not told me about the Sons and Daughters, the Aztec Society."

"We lost some but there are always more to recruit. Fortune was with us. Medusa Mendes was in California at the time of the accident.

She knows what is required and, as she says, never fails. A remarkable woman."

"So far, so good," Cheka said. "For the moment we must make sure that Dudorov does not spoil our plans. We will need the most distinguished voice to speak for us."

"Dodge?" Ulianov proposed.

"No one," Cheka said, "is more respected and deservedly so. "

7

Dudorov Tells How Cheka Plotted Terror

It had been an unhappy choice for Dudorov but he could see no alternative. The Embassy was gone, the Embassy quarter was shattered. The damage was like nothing that he had imagined. There had been a mistake but the destruction would have been the same in a sense even without the mistake, the same number of deaths, the same number of victims broken and torn. He could guess what had happened. Troyenko had destroyed himself and everyone with him.

But that was nothing to explain to Ulianov. There had been orders and he, Dudorov, had not followed the orders. Moreover he had other orders which he would not obey. He had faced what men had once called a moral crisis, but moral choices and moral crises had been obsolete, old-fashioned figures of speech, out of date for 50 years at the least. In the real world, the world in which he had grown up, there were those who gave and those who took orders. Some, like himself, did both. The orders given and the orders obeyed fitted together, combined into a kind of perfection. Otherwise there was confusion, chaos, anarchy in which the universe would come to an end, his universe, every man's universe. To disobey was to ask for punishment, appropriate punishment.

What he proposed to do was the ultimate crime, to reject the order and avoid the punishment -- if that were possible. He would turn to the Enemy, to Carmody who would receive and despise him. But he would be free from the orders that troubled him. He knew where to go and he went there, saying he was Constantin Dudorov and that he must see Mr. Carmody, must see him at once.

There was no need to ask the computers to identify Dudorov. The old man knew the name. Dudorov I was a hero of the Revolution, zealous, devoted. His good fortune was to rise high but not too high. He had his honors but he survived the worst of the storms, a Major General of the Security organs. He married late and his name and his honors were a legacy to Dudorov II, with the warning to avoid the dangers at the top of the mountain. The old man had known Constantin Dudorov II as someone close to Cheka, maybe too close. Now he was about to talk to the third generation. He looked at the pictures -- I, II and III. There was a family resemblance -- lean men, intellectual types if types existed or a man's appearance gave any clue to his character.

A voice announced that Johnson was waiting. Johnson was delivering Dudorov from Mexico City. Johnson came in. The introductions were made. The old man would talk to Dudorov alone for the present.

"Here I am," the old man said when Johnson had left. "You wanted to see me. You see me. You have things to tell me. You'll find that I'm a good listener."

Dudorov told his story. He had his orders from Ulianov. The first order was to destroy the American Embassy in Mexico City. Cheka had decided there would be a minor, a routine explosion in the Eurasian Embassy at the same time -- or so Ulianov had said. He was to tell Troyenko and arrange that the explosion in his Embassy be in an area where there would be only moderate casualties. An agent in the Embassy, Karpovich by name, was to take and place the bomb in the American Embassy where he had friends. He was to take his instructions from Dudorov but Troyenko objected.

"It was a personal thing," Dudorov said. "Something that went back a long way. Something that had to do with a woman. A rebuff for which he thought I was to blame. Actually it was my wife. He wanted to marry her but she preferred me. So he married Globus' daughter and made his career -- for which he should have been grateful. But to go back. He refused to allow me to see Karpovich. He, Troyenko, was in charge of the Embassy. Mexico was his province. Only he had authority over people assigned there. It was all very rough. The time had been fixed. The device was already armed. "I could not appeal to Ulianov. There were no secure channels. The plan, the project was not to be the subject of messages."

The old man understood. "So what happened?" he asked.

"I gave Troyenko the two devices," Dudorov told him. "It was wrong. I violated my orders. And then Troyenko began to ask questions. Both devices were small but the one for the American Embassy was so small he was suspicious. Had I made a mistake? Could I be trying to harm him by placing the larger device in his Embassy. He claimed I was his enemy, had made reports to Ulianov that were intended to harm him. Globus had told him."

"I get the picture."

"There were words and more words," Dudorov said. "Troyenko was a disagreeable man, a most disagreeable and a dangerous man. Globus was his wife's father and Globus is Globus. Finally I left. What I did was irregular. I should have insisted on seeing Karpovich and following orders. In such a situation after all I outranked Troyenko. It was a security matter and as a Major General of the Security Forces I had authority over an Ambassador, any Ambassador. It was my saying so that made Troyenko lose all control of himself. I finally told him that I would hold him responsible in place of Karpovich for seeing that Ulianov's orders were followed and left, went to one of our houses and an hour later heard the explosion."

"I can guess the house," the old man said. "And what did you do then?"

"Started back toward the center of the city -- Learned what had happened -- that it was our Embassy that was gone. Saw the outer edge of the damage. Went inside -- what do you say? -- the perimeter. Saw some of the victims." Dudorov grimaced. "It is very easy to talk about war and killing," Dudorov said, half to himself. "I remember being told that the great Napoleon enjoyed riding over the battlefield and surveying the wreckage, the battlefield sights. An odd taste. I think even he would have averted his eyes from the sights that I saw.

"It was a slaughterhouse of a kind that no 18th century mind could have pictured. I have a strong stomach. I vomited. It was too much. It was not only seeing. There were the screams. There was the smell. I could not tell this to Ulianov. I could not tell this to Cheka. I had had enough, more than enough. I thought of you, Mr. Carmody, I am a man who needs help."

"Help? What kind of help?" the old man asked. He was willing to believe that Dudorov was Dudorov. But was he a talented actor? And what part was he playing? Was this one more script that Cheka had written, and one in which Michael Carmody was to have a role of some kind?

"Look," Dudorov said, "in this business we are all mind readers. You think I may be one more wooden horse, that Cheka is playing a trick, that Cheka has sent me here as part of a scheme." He reached in his pocket, took out a small case and put it on Carmody's desk. "Empty the case and tell me what you see, Mr. Carmody. No harm will come to you."

"We will both hope not," the old man said. He opened the case, took out its contents. There were four cylinders, no bigger than cigarettes. He lined them out on his desk. "I see them. Now tell me, General, what do I see?"

"I had five when I arrived in Mexico City," Dudorov told him. "The fifth caused the blast that killed how many people? One hundred thousand? Two hundred thousand? No one knows. No one will know. They are still counting bodies, pieces of bodies. Two hundred and fifty thousand? Who can ever count those who disappeared in the fire and smoke?"

The old man looked at Dudorov, looked at his desk. So this was what his friends had told him about. They learned about everything. He could never guess what their sources were but what they had told him and what Dudorov told him fitted together so far. "One of these, one of these by itself?"

"Another triumph of the human mind," Dudorov said. "The tree of knowledge, you remember the story. These are some of the fruits, prize apples fresh from the tree. Now, Mr. Carmody, let me tell you how these four are to be used -- were to be used. You have them now. I have nothing further to do with them. But I was to use one in New York."

"Where?" the old man asked.

"I was to use my judgment as to the place. Downtown, midtown. At noon -- to do the maximum damage. We wanted chaos in the streets."

"What would it do to buildings, big buildings, strong buildings?"

"The makers were hopeful, more than hopeful, confident. And you know what it did in Mexico City. Their expectations were justified."

The old man was thoughtful. His friends had known the plan for New York. "That would leave three."

"Then another city -- Chicago perhaps. Los Angeles maybe. Again it was a matter of judgment. You understand. They trusted my judgment. I am part of the nobility as a Dudorov."

Nobility. The old man was interested by Dudorov's use of the word.

"That was what my father called it," Dudorov told him. "A reflective, intelligent man, my father. His death was the greatest loss in my life. A great teacher, but gone before the course was completed. I often recall conversations that I had with him and think about the meaning of what he said to me."

"I saw your father once or twice," the old man recalled. "Attractive. He was coming and going here. I knew him by reputation and made a point of having a look at him. We were told he was close to Cheka."

"Too close."

"With prospects, great prospects," the old man went on.

"Too great," Dudorov said. "Without such a possible future, he might have lived longer.

"We understood each other," the old man assured him. "We heard the story, the rumor, the accident, Grabkin. It was a very tense time. But about the nobility?"

"My father used to say that we were rid of the old grand dukes, the old princes and counts, and had invented new ones. A new emperor, but the old empire and everything that an empire needs. He used to laugh and point out that there were half a dozen families that claimed to have a grandfather who had the glory of giving the coup de grace to the Romanovs in the cellar at Sverdlovsk. That, you see, made them members of the nobility. It entitled them to honors, a place of distinction."

An interesting way to look at it, the old man thought to himself.

"Medium nobles," Dudorov went on, "but good enough, very good for opening doors, for getting a start in the world, the right world. Your intellectuals, journalists and so on, they don't understand us at all. Things are open but they generally go by inheritance. Globus had an uncle. Troyenko had a father-in-law. Grabkin also had an uncle and Grabkin has sons. Ulianov had claims as a cousin."

"And Cheka?"

"Cheka is the exception. According to my father Cheka never talked about family. There was something hidden. My father's guess was that the name was invented, taken to cover over old nobility. But that was only a guess."

"Not the kind of name I would have chosen," the old man observed. "But an able man, Cheka. And what were you to do with the last of these objects?" So far Dudorov had confirmed the information passed on by the friends.

"Here. Washington." Dudorov looked at the old man. "The White House. The Capitol. The same day."

"It sounds wasteful," the old man commented. It also sounded like Cheka.

"Symbolic," Dudorov said. "On this one I had no discretion. Take the radius of the blast in Mexico City. Here we get the shrines, the White House, the Washington Monument, the Lincoln Memorial. We also get a good many Departments. And with the Capitol we get your Supreme Court, the Libraries, the House and Senate, the members, the staffs. You see the point."

"Maybe I do," the old man conceded. "But then maybe I don't. Who planned this? If you know. You had your orders from Ulianov?"

"From him," Dudorov said. "But the plan had to be Cheka's, was Cheka's. Ulianov told me as much. This was my reward. They were giving me the best assignment of all. It would make me famous forever. I was to end the stalemate, win the game, trump all the cards, sweep the board. Put it anyway that you want. That was the program. That was the prize."

The old man picked up one of the cylinders and held it in his hand. Cheka had talked of opening the gate and it was with this that he intended to do it. A patient, astute fellow, Cheka. There would be five blows -- or really four. The Embassy would disappear in Mexico City with all the attendant shocks and alarms and uproar. There would be a tremendous crash in New York itself, then in whatever city Dudorov chose. Everyone would cry out for protection. They would all feel naked, exposed.

Then the final smash in Washington City, <u>umbilicus mundi</u>, at least the center of part of the Earth. There would be no point in protests and notes. They would have been sent already, perhaps, though Blossom would have wanted proof, the press would have demanded proof that the Eurasian Union was indeed responsible. He, himself, would have known, but no one would have listened to him. He and his friends were suspect as declared enemies of the new order. They would have been suspect themselves. He might have picked up Dudorov's trail. Could he have picked up Dudorov's trail? Dudorov doubted it.

"I don't think you would have found me," Dudorov said. "I would have come in with all the right papers. You have and we have libraries of whatever is needed. I could have had my American passport, returning from business abroad. No one would stop me. The Americans are forever moving around, business or pleasure. They move by the thousands, the tens of thousands each day. I look like everyone else and I can always change my appearance a little. I would have been in New York, but how would you find me? I would have gone to Los Angeles, say, but many people go to Los Angeles. Washington is a center for business, a place to visit. There is nothing remarkable about a man who chooses to go there. Those," he pointed to the cylinders, "would have been in my pocket in a cigarette package, perhaps. And at the end I would have been off to London, always the normal, commonplace traveler. In between, we have our houses."

The old man said nothing. There was no reason to tell Dudorov that he had slipped by in Mexico City though they had watched for him, knew he was arriving there. Dudorov had probably told him the truth but with Cheka you could never be sure. As for the cylinders, they were something for his agents to look at, his experts or those of his friends. And he would give them to no one else. He weighed them in his hand.

Dudorov watched him. "Cheka waited for those for years," he said. "He sees himself as a peacemaker and those were to bring peace by ending the struggle with you. There would be one empire, a single authority his and his successors."

"Peacemaker and war maker. War maker and peacemaker. The same thing, given Cheka's point of view," the old man suggested.

"Right," Dudorov said. "My father knew Cheka well. What I know of him, I know in part through my father. For him everything is conflict with the United States of America. But he never wanted war as Grabkin and the lesser Grabkins understand it. He has paid them, given them honors, supplied them with weapons but he has never had any use for them or their plans. He has had his own ideas and his own ways. Those things in your hand were to break any will to resist." He paused and thought for a moment. "The only thing that went wrong was that he chose the wrong agent."

The old man nodded. "I won't ask why you were the wrong agent."

"I don't know, myself," Dudorov told him. "I couldn't have predicted my own behavior. I really can't say why I'm here. Too many orders. Too much obedience. Maybe too little faith in Cheka's idea of peace. Perhaps too little belief in the perfection of a world subject to a simple unchallenged will. So here I am, needing help."

The old man put the cylinders back on his desk. "I'll be honest," he said. "I never trust anyone. A very bad habit. You will understand, though, that I look on Cheka as a dangerous fellow and you come from Cheka. But you can count on me to give you cover so far as I can. If what you've told me is true Cheka is going to do everything possible to get you back -- and to get these." He looked at his desk.

"I'm a heavy burden," Dudorov said.

8

Moscow Funeral for Dudorov
"Murdered by U. S. Agent"

Cheka regarded the Dudorov murder broadcast as a credit to Ulianov. The world press was there in full force. Dudorova was led in to view the remains. She identified the body as that of her husband, burst into tears, was prostrated, had a fit of hysterics, fainted, was led away sobbing. There were then pictures of Dudorov's great grandfather, grandfather and father, Dudorov as a boy, as a young man, as a new major general, at the time of his death. Ulianov, who was present, announced the posthumous promotion of Major General Dudorov to full General and the award of the rarely given decoration of Very Special Hero of the Eurasian Union.

Harrison Swing who was dean of the press corps described the occasion that evening as the most solemn and moving that he had witnessed in all his career. He promised his audience a broadcast of the state funeral that had been ordered for Dudorov and an interview with Dudorova as soon as she recovered from the first shock of Dudorov's death.

Dudorov watched the proceedings in Mr. Carmody's office. The old man congratulated him on his promotion and on his award and wanted to know how many full generals there were in the Security Service.

"One at a time," Dudorov said. "Ulianov. Cheka was the general before him."

"Did you recognize the photographs of yourself?" the old man asked.

Dudorov shook his head. "No one I know. They could have been anyone. Probably done for the broadcast."

"A good touch," the old man commented. "You understand where they're heading."

Dudorov understood.

"And the widow?"

"Again no one I recognized. The right age. The right size." Evidently they did not trust his wife. He was pleased but still he regretted. What would happen to Dudorova would depend wholly on Cheka. At least Cheka was not a reincarnation of the immortal Stalin who, as Cheka said, could always rise above human feeling.

"And the corpse?"

"Who can say," Dudorov answered. "There are always bodies available. Moscow is a very large city." In spite of himself he was depressed. He was officially dead, with more honors than he could have expected. As he had said to Mr. Carmody, he knew where they were heading.

On the following day the official Eurasian news agency announced that it had been confirmed that the killer of General Constantin Dudorov was an agent of the American Intelligence Group. He had escaped from the Eurasian Union with state property of the greatest value. The name of the agent, a native of Moscow, was Yuri Bolkonsky. The official understanding was that he had arrived in the United States and was under the protection of his employers. The Eurasian Union would take whatever steps were needed to see that the brutal killer of General Dudorov was brought to trial in Moscow, the site of the murder. The Eurasian Union would also ask for and would recover the property Bolkonsky had stolen and which had, so to speak, inspired the killing. The Eurasian Union would, if necessary, proceed in the American courts in which it had confidence. Counsel was being engaged -- eminent counsel, the best.

The eminent counsel, the best, was Boregard Dodge, Mr. Justice Dodge in his time. He had been appointed to the Supreme Court by the last Unpopular President and confirmed over great opposition. No child of parents who had named him Boregard -- whatever the spelling -- could be a reliable Justice. He had sat on the Court for years, most often dissenting. After 20 years he resigned.

"Too many women," was his explanation. "And I was the last white man on the Court. There was my brother Lumumba and my brother Hu Hih and my six sisters. I was handicapped too by being a lawyer. I thought we were a court. They thought we were a combined center for social studies and legislature. The Bible case finished me."

The Bible case was Outrage v. The United States of America. Outrage was the chairman of the Society for Mutual Equality. The Society's view was that tax exemptions for churches using the Bible violated the First Amendment, the establishment clause, and also the Equal Rights Amendment forbidding discrimination on sexual grounds. Both attacks were equally pertinent and persuasive; but the Court based its decision largely on the later Amendment.

Genesis was the heart of the problem. Genesis said in so many words that God had created Adam first, that Eve was an afterthought, had been Adam's rib. The inner meaning was that women were secondary, inferior. Moreover, Genesis with its account of Sodom and Gomorrah, reflected a judgment in favor of one sexual preference over the whole variety of such choices. The case was of the greatest moral importance.

The Chief Justice insisted on having a unanimous Court and in the end made a concession to the stubborn quality of her brother Dodge. The Court would allow the exemption, after expressing its doubts about Adam and Eve and the rib, if the Bible were reviewed and, as it wrote, "brought into harmony with the views herein expressed." The Court appointed a master, more exactly a mistress, "to review and correct the offending passages in Genesis and else where in the now received text." Outrage was not wholly satisfied but the revised text was some consolation

"At that point," as Dodge once explained it, "I got the Hell out. Enough was enough. Also I was poor as what used to be called a church mouse. It was time to make money. I had a choice between a half dozen places where they had a 1000 or 2000 lawyers. They were even willing to print up new letter heads, change their names. Instead I set up by myself, got a couple of customers, hired some help, got some more customers." The customers paid what Dodge asked and got the service they wanted. In point of fact they were surprised. They thought they were buying a name and discovered they had considerably more. Boregard Dodge was good in the office, good in trials, good on appeals. The charges were high but that gave the customers confidence. They wanted the best and Dodge's fees were the best in the business. If there was such a thing as a legal celebrity, it was Boregard Dodge.

Among Dodge's best customers, Omnium Corp. perhaps stood the highest. Its interests were on the grand side, its problems expensive. He was not surprised when Omnium's chairman, George Sidon, called and made an appointment. George, as Dodge had described him, was one smart Lebanese. Omnium had a mainly Lebanese staff, always a little mysterious, and George was always wrapped in what Dodge thought of as his Near Eastern veil.

"Mr. Justice," Sidon began when he and Dodge had concluded their usual compliments, "I have been asked to approach you on an interesting and delicate subject." For Sidon that was the usual opening. He operated in an interesting and delicate world.

"I listen," Dodge said.

"You know about the tragedy in Mexico City. Of course, everyone does. And the Dudorov business. Or should I explain it? You are a busy man, a scholar. Perhaps you do not watch the news broadcasts."

"Thank God, not all of them," Dodge told him. "But enough to know something about what you call the Dudorov business."

Sidon smiled at Boregard's joke. The Justice was a joker. It was one of the odder American traits. "You know that the killer is in the custody of a Mr. Carmody?"

"That's what I hear. That's what I read." Mr. Carmody was old Mike to him. They were about of an age. He did not think of himself as old Boregard Dodge but Mike was old Mike.

"I will explain my being here by saying that one of my stockholders has asked me to recommend counsel to act for the Eurasian Republics in extraditing the person in Mr. Carmody's custody," Sidon went on. "Unofficially, I emphasize unofficially, it is a matter of the highest importance that the request for extradition be honored, the very highest importance."

"So."

"So inevitably I offered your name as that of the most desirable possible counsel. My mission is to ask if you will accept a retainer. The financial terms will be whatever you like. I am here unofficially, socially. A gentleman from the Embassy will call on you and make the formal request and arrange the retainer if you are available."

So far as Dodge was concerned, business was business. The Eurasians were a roundabout crowd, anything to avoid being direct. There were stories that the Republics were the controlling stockholders of Omnium and Sidon's visit seemed to confirm it. Why Sidon first and then a gentleman from the Embassy? And what gentleman from the Embassy? "Extradition is a little off my usual road," he said after a moment. "But I'll talk to the Ambassador and only to the Ambassador as someone I know. I'm too old to enjoy talking to strangers." He might have added that he talked only to men with authority.

The conversation with Scriabin took place the same day and went off very well. Scriabin, in Boregard Dodge's phrase, was an old settler. He had been around for a generation or more. He gave his assurance that Dodge would be paid whatever he wanted. The essential thing was to recover the killer of Dudorov and the state property. Moscow would produce any proof that was needed, any proof, any witnesses. Justice Dodge had only to list what he wanted and Moscow would be sure to provide it. Had he seen the proofs? He had not but he had confidence in what he had been told by the ministries concerned with the responsibility for bringing Dudorov's killer to justice. Cheka was not named but Dodge understood that Cheka felt Dudorov's death very deeply, and was determined that the killer be punished. As for the state property, it was of a unique kind and its recovery was a matter of honor to the Republics.

When Scriabin had left, Dodge reflected on the two conversations, Sidon, Scriabin. Clearly the affair was important and he had been hired to insure the desired result. It was high politics disguised as a lawsuit. He had no doubt that Moscow would provide whatever proof he required. The sensible thing would be not to ask too many questions. If Moscow said the fugitive was Yuri Bolkonsky that would be his proven identity. Fingerprints were infallible and there would be fingerprints.

Scriabin had confirmed that the fugitive claimed to be Dudorov and that, apart from the fingerprints, there would be more fingerprints and photographs and witnesses to refute such a claim. Nevertheless, he wondered what the Administration would do. Old Mike Carmody was protecting the fugitive. Would Blossom support him? But why was old Mike protecting the fugitive? And would he give up if instructed? There was obvious room for maneuver. He would have the papers prepared. Before they were filed he would do some exploring.

That evening, without calling ahead he went to visit old Mike at home. It was a small house to which Carmody had moved after the death of his wife. He shared the house with a daughter, his only child. The daughter answered the bell. Then the old man came to the door.

"Well," the old man said, "this is a surprise. Not many people take the trouble to call on me. Come in, Mr. Justice. Join me in my one evening drink."

"One?" Dodge asked.

"One," the old man repeated. "Things aren't what they used to be. One is all I'm allowed."

Dodge condoled with him, got his drink, settled down. There was the obvious question: why he was there.

"You read my mind. As I told you, not many people call on me."

"Dare to call on you," Dodge amended. "But I have a good reason. This Dudorov business."

The old man looked at him. "Let me read your mind, Mr. Justice."

"Come, come," Dodge said, "you've known me as Boregard for half a lifetime."

The old man made a gesture. "All right, Boregard. You've been approached to act for the Eurasian Republics. Or, perhaps, you've been more than approached. Perhaps you have been retained. You've spoken to Sidon. Maybe to the Ambassador."

Dodge nodded. "You're just as sharp as ever," he commented.

"I would have to be pretty dull not to know that much," the old man observed. "Sidon is a regular messenger boy. But you represent Omnium so you must know all about that. Anyhow Sidon is a minor angel. He announces the archangel's coming. Scriabin is the local archangel."

Dodge nodded again. The old man had a nice way of putting things. "Bolkonsky, would Bolkonsky go home without going to court, waive extradition?" he asked.

"The name is Dudorov," the old man pointed out. "I don't know why he came to us but I have no question about his identity. He doesn't want to go back. And I wouldn't let him go back if he wanted to."

"Does the Administration take the same view?"

"We haven't discussed it, Boregard. But I doubt it. You know the kind of people we have."

"Look," Dodge said, "I've signed on. I'm committed to putting Bolkonsky, give him any name that you want, on the rocket for Moscow. The necessary proofs will all be produced. The man you have is Bolkonsky. The court will find he's Bolkonsky. There isn't a thing in the world you can do."

The old man shook his head. "For one thing I could convince you that you're being used. Oh, I know you've got a strong stomach. And I know the duty lawyers have to their clients in return for their money. But you don't need the money."

"I've got expensive children and grandchildren."

The usual plea," the old man observed. "Have you any idea what this is about? You haven't asked about the state property which you are supposed to recover. I assume your retainer covers that too. Do you know what it is?"

"They didn't tell me. Not in so many words. But Scriabin made it clear that they want it."

"Scriabin doesn't know what it is. He is only the chief local messenger. He isn't important enough to know everything. Let me tell you what you're playing with. How big is your thumb? Or your little finger?"

"Normal," said Dodge.

"You know about the blast in Mexico City. Everyone does. And the returns are just beginning to come in, so to speak. You're a rich man. You probably dabble in real estate futures. Omnium is short on California real estate futures. And Texas futures. And in all the so-called Mexican states. Maybe you are too, Boregard."

Dodge smiled. Old Mike was smart. "For the present I am," he conceded. "But what has that to do with the state property?"

"The blast in Mexico City was set off by something about the size of one of your fingers. There were five of these fingers. Dudorov brought four along and I have them. Do you follow me?"

Dodge shook his head. It was not easy to know what to think about Michael Carmody. He had known him for years. Old age affected some people, made them lose touch with reality. Fortunately he, himself, had been spared. He was, as he liked to say, still in full panoply and harness, unimpaired, only older and smarter, richer by so much experience. But old Mike was probably living in some kind of fantasy. He shook his head for a second time.

"You drop one of those fingers in a trash bin on a street in Manhattan, walk away. At the time set, a large part of Manhattan is gone. You can do the same thing wherever you choose. Dudorov had orders to place the first one in our Mexico City Embassy. What happened isn't as clear as it might be. Something to do with Troyenko, if the name means anything to you."

"I recall Troyenko," Dodge said. "I did some business in Mexico City and I had occasion to see him."

"Dudorov was to go on to New York and do a rerun of Mexico City. The last target was Washington, downtown, the Hill. It was Cheka's way of bringing peace on Earth, perfect peace. This state property that you want to recover was supposed to convince us that we had better see things Cheka's way, had better give up. There would be a few hundred thousand casualties. Everyone else would be, as the children used to say, frightened to death. Do you follow me now?"

"And you believe this? This is what the man you call Dudorov told you?" Dodge wanted to know.

"You mean, am I losing my grip?" the old man asked. "My weapons experts wouldn't believe it at first. A matter of pride. Cheka's people couldn't do what they couldn't do. They're beginning to be a little more modest. Eurasian mathematics and engineering are better than they had supposed. You go think about it. Get your damned order. It's a long time since I had any respect for judges or lawyers, junior or senior. When the time comes I intend to do whatever I think has to be done."

"You are pretty persuasive, Mike," Dodge said after a moment. "Maybe some day you'll let me see Dudorov. All lawyers are whores -- not that the word means anything now. But I still have some scruples. Or maybe just pride. I'll think about what you've told me this evening."

9

US Cabinet Meets on Cheka Demands: Let Court Decide?

Cheka had been pleased with the notes as he had rewritten them. The drafts from Globus had been too stiff, too wooden, the usual rhetoric. Globus was hopelessly married to all the old formulae. As the official notes went out they were universally praised by the world press, expressing more sorrow than anger, conciliatory but firm, reasonable was the word.

The note to Porfirio Aleman was one of condolence for the precious lives that had been lost. It dismissed as impossible that the Mexican people could have had any part in the destruction of the Embassy of the Eurasian Republics. That, the note stated, was the work of an agent or agents of the United States of America. The wanton destruction of Mexican lives was regrettably part of a pattern going back to the seizure of Texas, continuing through the Mexican War, to long exploitation of Mexican mines, to border war at the time of the Mexican Revolution, a sacred event. The Eurasian Republics were aware that the Republic of Mexico sought the abrogation of the Treaty of Guadalupe Hidalgo, the return of the Mexican states and an indemnity. The Republics sympathized with and supported their sister republic. The Republics considered the matter one to be resolved by the World League as the ultimate agency of world justice.

The note to Walter Blossom expressed sympathy with him as a man of good will and with the people of the United States who were indeed a great and good people. Blossom and the Americans generally were no doubt shocked by the actions of lawless elements who had acted in desperation to estrange the peace-loving people of the Eurasian Republics from their American sisters and brothers. The Republics asked only that the United States of America acknowledge that their agents -- agents out of control -- had been responsible for the blast in Mexico City, bring them to justice and compensate the Republics by payment of a sum to be determined by the World League. The Republics also attached a copy of the note to President Aleman and expressed the opinion that the United States could have no objection to the proposal to refer the claims of the Republic of Mexico to the same unprejudiced body.

Finally the Republics called for aid in the return of one Yuri Bolkonsky who had brutally murdered the late General Constantin Dudorov and sought refuge in the United States, together with certain state property of considerable value. The Republics hoped for an early and favorable reply to their note.

There was also a private note to Blossom signed by Cheka, writing as he said not as a head of state to another head of state but as one human being to another, recalling the feeling for each other that had come into being at Geneva and expressing the belief that nothing could destroy that feeling. Cheka had thought at length about a suitable ending. He was pleased with his choice of words. The note concluded with "Most sincerely your brother in peace -- V. I. Cheka"

When the notes arrived Blossom read and reread them. The official note was far kinder than he had expected. His good will was assumed and the good will of the American people. He was deeply moved by the personal note. He called a meeting of the inner, the senior cabinet to decide what should be done, the two ladies and the Attorney General, Lester Luanda. There he handed out copies of the personal note.

It was not a harmonious meeting. Blossom began by saying that he thought the personal note from Cheka was, as he said, heartening and indeed moving. Marietta agreed. She thought it was a beautiful note, one of the most beautiful in all her experience. Luanda agreed; beautiful was the word he would have chosen. Louisa dissented. So far as she was concerned the personal and the official notes had to be taken together. Looked at that way the personal note, in her opinion, was nothing but cynical. The most sincere brother in peace language disgusted her.

After an uncomfortable silence, Blossom suggested they consider what reply should be sent to the longer, official note. What was their reaction? Marietta, as Secretary of State, made the first comment.

"I regard it as very fair, very temperate in view of the facts," she began. She had thought about the note, sketched out a reply and intended to deal with the issues at length but Louisa interrupted before she could go on.

"In view of the facts?" Louisa asked. "And what are the facts?" Louisa's question and manner could be described as unfriendly.

"I had thought," Marietta said, "that we all knew the facts, had all agreed on the facts." She looked at Blossom but Blossom offered no help. "Do you want me to tell you the facts?"

"That would help," Louisa suggested.

"The facts, the main fact is that we destroyed the Eurasian Embassy in Mexico City with a great, a terrible loss of life and are now responsible as a government to the Eurasian Republics and the Mexican people. In comparison the Dudorov thing is minor but we are equally responsible there."

"That isn't the way I've heard it," Louisa said.

Marietta bridled. "From whom?"

"From Mr. Carmody," Louisa said. "He repeated what he had told you and Walter, the whole story, about the explosion, Dudorov, the so-called stolen state property."

"And did he approach you?" Marietta demanded.

"No. I went to see him. I knew he had talked to you on the day of the explosion and I wanted to know what he had said. Neither you nor Walter -- nor the Vice President for that matter -- had passed on anything to me.

Marietta had every right to be indignant. These were matters of foreign relations, international affairs. She had the monopoly and she said so.

Blossom intervened. It was necessary to keep peace in the family. There were decisions to make. The public was anxious. The media restive. There were beginning to be demonstrations. Castillo was stirring the pot. The whole world was waiting. "All right, all right," he said. "Marietta, you're the Secretary of State. We all acknowledge it. But

Louisa is concerned. This is a cabinet matter. I have to prepare a reply to Cheka and I want everyone's views. You spoke to Mr. Carmody, Louisa. You say you believe him. Tell us why."

"Because my people told me the destruction was done by a thermonuclear weapon and Defense still has the monopoly there. Nothing is missing from our inventories. I've had them checked and rechecked. Logic is logic. We couldn't have had anything to do with what happened. That's to begin with. My people also told me today that they're forced to accept the Carmody story about the state property. They were skeptical. They didn't want to believe it. Now they've talked with the Intelligence weapons experts, seen the data, seen the items. They don't want to but they're changing their minds."

"The old man," Marietta said, "is clever, too clever for his own good. He knew how to cover his trail. No one has dared to control him for years. I thought and I still think that he set off the explosion to prevent our coming to a decent settlement with the Republics. Cheka sees it that way, which I think very generous. Harrison Swing says Moscow has proofs and that they have let him see enough to convince him."

"Great God," Louisa explained, "you're not telling us to rely on Harrison Swing."

"I know Harrison," Marietta said coldly. "I have always found him well informed and reliable. He has a very special position in Moscow. He's thought of there as friendly, fair minded. They open themselves to Harrison. It would be against their own interest to mislead a man with his standing as our unofficial ambassador."

It was painful for Blossom to have such disagreement. He had Cheka's notes and he had to reply. Louisa was telling him to reject them and he had obligations to her. His lawful Secretary of State was proposing that he accept Cheka's premises, probably accept Cheka's terms. He said so -- but without mentioning his obligations. Perhaps there was an alternative course.

The Attorney General had a suggestion about the Mexican states. It would be embarrassing to go before the World League. There would be, perhaps an element of coercion in doing that, at least the appearance.

He had done some research, discussed it with his ablest assistants. They agreed there could be a more graceful approach. The United States had as their boast that they were governed by law. The issue could be and should be resolved in the usual way and by the highest tribunal.

Blossom felt a little relieved. There had been voices objecting to his choice of Les but he was proving that he was equal to the office he held. "Les, please be specific," he asked.

"Of course, Mr. President," Les said. He felt himself more of a great officer of the government if he addressed Blossom formally. "I go back to the Constitution. We always go back to the Constitution. That is our foundation, our bedrock. So. Article III, Section 2, the first paragraph." It was like quoting the Bible, something his father as a minister had been accustomed to do. "You understand, Mr. President -- as a lawyer." All lawyers knew the Constitution by heart.

Blossom nodded, but not at all sure of himself. "Go on," he said. After all the Secretary of State was a layman, more exactly a lay person. Lay woman was out of the question.

"The Ambassador of the Republic of Mexico files a petition in the Supreme Court which has original jurisdiction over his suit, asking the court to set aside, to rescind, as we say, the Treaty of Guadalupe Hidalgo on the usual grounds. The treaty I see as a contract. Equity can set aside any contract brought about by coercion. The origins of the treaty are well known. I see no difficulty." Les was proud of himself.

Having heard Les, Blossom could only admire. It was perfectly simple. But would the Court do it?

"I would expect a unanimous Court," Les assured him.

"It's a very good Court. It prides itself on being the national conscience."

Marietta agreed that the Court was the national conscience. Women, most women, were sensitive to the distinction between right and wrong. There were exceptions. But the Chief Justice and her six sisters were models of what women should be. And the Attorney General's proposal should be attractive to Cheka. She expected him to be graceful about it. Though she did not say so she was astonished that Les was such a sound constitutional lawyer. She knew he had a fine practice, a really fine practice managing the affairs of the big earning African artists and athletes. The story was that Les took only clients with incomes of two or three million dollars a year and was a genius at taxes. He had what were spoken of as the finest offshore connections -- tax free connections.

The sour note came from Louisa. "It's an idiot Court," she began, "but even they are likely to see that they have no jurisdiction over such a petition."

"But I wouldn't oppose the petition," Les assured her.

Louisa looked at Blossom. "You've got to appear and oppose," she said. "In case you don't remember, Walter, the Constitution guarantees the states republican government."

"Oh, that's all right," Les assured her again. "I've thought of that naturally. But if the treaty is set aside the relief goes back to 1846, the states as we know them were never properly states of the Union. They have no claim under Article IV. Moreover," he went on, quite satisfied with himself, "the petitioner, through the Ambassador, is a republic, the Republic of Mexico. The areas would still enjoy republican government."

"Good God," Louisa said when he was finished. "More nonsense." She turned to Blossom again. "Of course you've got to oppose such a maneuver. The governors of the states concerned will come in, if you don't. You're all talking nonsense."

Walter was a little upset. The brilliance of Les' proposal was a little less bright. Louisa had after all been a great success as a lawyer. She had had the certified best conventional clients. If you reckoned prestige by clients, she outranked Lester Luanda.

Louisa wanted to say that Walter and Marietta and Les were even bigger fools than she had supposed. So she said it.

There was a minute of silence, broken by Marietta. "You can always resign," she commented.

"But I'm not going to," was the reply.

Marietta turned to Blossom. "But if the President asks for your resignation."

Walter said nothing.

"He's not going to," Louisa said slowly. "He knows and you all know that I'm responsible for him. I made him President and I'm going to see that he doesn't make a fool of himself."

There was another minute of silence.

In such circumstances Marietta and Les could have said that they were resigning but they did not want to resign. In the broadest sense they had a duty to Walter, to their supporters, to themselves for that matter to stay where they were. Actually their duty was to the country which was facing a crisis in which they were needed. Even in the most bitter personal conflicts, the voice of duty was strongest.

"Let's just agree to leave Les' proposal on the table," Blossom finally said. "We can all think about it. And I know, Louisa, that there is still sentiment for preserving the Union." The essence of statesmanship was to conciliate, to reconcile warring elements. "Let's go on to the Dudorov matter."

On this Marietta could only say that if they were not accepting Cheka's major proposal, they had to accept the minor one. "It's only one man," she pointed out. "And Cheka has really been gracious. The note doesn't say that Bolkonsky is our agent. We can be friendly and cooperate without any embarrassment. Not, of course, that Bolkonsky wasn't acting on Carmody's orders."

Les started to say "Amen" but he corrected himself. He was accustomed to saying Amen -- like his father. "I join," he said, "with the Secretary of State."

"And you, Louisa?" Blossom asked.

"I've already told you my position," she said. "I believe Mr. Carmody. We can't turn back the Yuri Bolkonsky they ask for when the man we have is Dudorov. Again, logic is logic. Dudorov is alive. Obviously there's no one to extradite or turn over as Dudorov's murderer."

"Perhaps," Blossom said. "Perhaps. But it's a matter of fact, an issue of fact. It's something to leave to the courts. Cheka understands that. I understand the Republics have retained Justice Dodge."

Marietta had a suggestion: not that she knew, not that she was a lawyer. "But wouldn't it be more dignified if we did what Les spoke about, give the Dudorov thing to the Supreme Court to decide?"

It was his idea but as Attorney General Les still liked the thought of having the Supreme Court rule on all the big issues with the Republics. Doing it that way would be dignified. But the Secretary of State had made a good suggestion -- the Administration would take a neutral position. Dudorov could, of course, have a lawyer.

"What," Louisa asked, "if Mr. Carmody wants to appear and oppose extradition?"

"Les just said we'd be neutral," Marietta observed. "Officially all we do is observe. If Mr. Carmody tries to confuse things, Walter can stop him. Lester can stop him. As Attorney General only he can speak for the government."

Blossom nodded. He hoped it was simple.

But it was not that simple to Louisa. If Dudorov was Dudorov, they were morally obligated to say so and oppose the Republics.

"No," Marietta insisted, "our real obligation is to the people of this country, to the whole human race, to achieve permanent peace." It was a very powerful argument.

Enough was enough. Blossom wanted to think about what he had heard. Blessed are the peacemakers -- he had heard that somewhere. If Cheka consented -- and in general Cheka was, he, Blossom, felt, more than willing -- he could be a real peacemaker. He thanked everyone. They had all been very helpful.

On her evening broadcast Miss New had important news. President Blossom would ask Chairman Cheka to join in submitting the issues raised by his notes for consideration and solution by the Supreme Court in accordance with law. He had also asked for the resignation of Louisa Clymer and Director Carmody, effective as of noon on the next day.

Finally Miss New had spoken to the Chief Justice and been told by her that while she could not comment on a matter that might come before her she could say in all honesty in all its long history the Supreme Court had found the Constitution equal to the needs of the people. Miss New had hoped to interview the Secretary of Defense and Director Carmody before her evening broadcast for confirmation. But she had been unable to reach them. She had not had time to talk to President Blossom but her information came from her usual, unimpeachable sources. It was a big broadcast.

10

TV Report of Old Man, Louisa Firings Retracted

Within a few minutes after the broadcast Cheka was wakened to receive an urgent call from the Minister of Foreign Affairs who had in turn been wakened by an alert Deputy. Globus was calling to inform him and warn him against the latest imperialist scheme, a scheme that was meant to outwit him. Not, of course, that Globus could say that or really suggest it. By definition no one could outwit the Chairman of the Union of Eurasian Republics. It was one more plot by the desperate Westerners doomed to the ashbin -- or was it the rubbish heap -- of history. Cheka heard him and thanked him.

After the call was over Cheka thought about the Americans. He had lived among them but how could he explain their peculiar ways to an ignoramus like Globus, a man who believed everything was explained by two or three not very well-written books, books written by men who by the circumstances of their own lives knew very little about even the world of their own time.

The Americans were well known to be a thoroughly secular people, free from the restraint of religions, emancipated from priests, a model collection of atheists. And yet they had their pieties. Among them was that towards what they called Law and Judges and Courts.

They revered judges, who were lawyers of uneven quality, and generally retired minor political types or at least parasites on the political body. They wore black costumes and sat on chairs on platforms in the public rooms where they performed. The amount of respect given to judges seemed to be in proportion to the elaborateness of the rooms in which the performance took place. The higher the ceiling, the more extensive and expensive the paneling, the greater the veneration accorded them.

Their Supreme Court was supreme probably because its building contained the most marble and its stage set had higher ceilings and more marble pillars than those of any competitors. Perhaps it was for that reason that no one could or would question anything that it said. If it said night was day, it was day. There was no limit to its absurdities but there was equally no limit to its authority.

As his own American expert, Cheka kept an eye on the Supreme Court of the Americans. Seven women, and what women they were. Two men, a Chinese and an African. Cheka had nothing but faith in them. For generations the supreme black robes had been at work dismantling the old institutions of the Americans. He was confident they would dismantle the Union itself if given a chance.

And as a humane man -- which was how he saw himself, as someone who had kept the Double Marshal and the single marshals under control, he preferred to have the Americans commit suicide rather than administer the coup de grace on his own. If Blossom wanted his consent to commit suicide, he would give it. He fell asleep framing an appropriate note in reply to the note he could count on from Blossom.

Even before Cheka had fallen asleep, Harry Fresser had his own call from Louisa. He had turned to her to represent him in various hours of need when she had been a leader of the grand corporate bar. He had heard Miss New. Louisa was being forced to resign. Perhaps she was calling to remind him that she might be, would be in practice again. He would be cordial, though he had found Louisa perhaps a little imperious, and inclined to be highhanded with clients. He liked Louisa but no nonsense women were disconcerting, especially when he was paying their imperious fees. In due time he would indicate as much to Louisa. But she was not looking for business.

"Harry," she told him, "I've got you out of trouble, serious trouble before. You can find someone to protect you and explain for you this time. You're in real trouble now. The worst trouble you've ever had. And I'm an expert on this particular subject."

Harry knew Louisa was right. She was an expert. But what was the trouble?

"You're a rich, rich man, Harry, and like all rich men you're always looking for quick easy ways to make money. Am I right that you're very short on real estate futures in what we're supposed to call the Mexican states?"

"Very short," Harry said.

"You're a big operator, Harry," Louisa went on. "Big operators often have little operators around them. Is that true of you?"

"Such as?" Harry asked.

"Would your Miss New, for example, be short on these real estate futures?"

"She may have said something to me, asked my advice. Lots of people ask me for advice. But you shouldn't ask me questions like that. These are personal things."

"You heard Miss New this evening, Harry," Louisa continued. "That broadcast is going to have quite an effect on real estate futures tomorrow. It should be a happy day for the shorts."

Louisa was right. It would be a good day for those with foresight and confidence in their judgments. "You're probably right about that," he conceded. It would be only polite if he expressed his sympathy with Louisa so he added that he had been genuinely sorry to learn of the latest developments.

"You don't have to feel sorry for me," Louisa assured him. "I'm feeling sorry for you."

"Why?" Harry asked. Louisa was never easy to read but this time she was being illegible, if that was the word.

"Some people are going to suspect that Miss New's big story was intended to break the real estate future   s market wide open so Harry Fresser could make his usual killing -- with a modest helping for Miss New herself. But unfortunately, Harry, the story was your Miss New's invention. And beyond the small issue of your and Miss New's speculations, you have created a nasty situation for the entire damned country."

Harry was silent. He could see the complaints being filed. He could total the damages asked. He could see himself answering questions and not just in courtrooms. There would be an official investigation. He had more than Planet but it was Planet that made him a power. If Dorothy had gone off the track Planet could be badly hurt. However Dorothy was experienced, not the best, but an experienced performer. He felt better. It had to be Louisa who was reacting to being made to resign. Even a woman like Louisa would under pressure break down and behave the way women did, the usual female hysteric. The proper thing for him to do was to make an effort to calm and comfort her. Actually he was fond of Louisa. In her large way she was a beautiful woman.

"No," she insisted after he made a graceful beginning, "you're the object of sympathy. Get it straight. I haven't been asked to resign. Mr. Carmody hasn't been asked to resign. We are not asking any court to give away seven states of the Union. Your President is almost angry at what you have done to him. Luckily Walter doesn't have quite enough energy to get really angry at anyone."

"But you did consider it. You did have a meeting," Harry said. "There had to be some grounds for Dorothy's broadcast."

"You can guess what happened. Anybody can guess it. Your former number one star and your number two star, Marietta and Dorothy, talk. You know, Harry, girls always talk. Maybe Marietta was trying to force Walter's hand. Maybe Dorothy got too excited to listen. Maybe she jumped, as we say, to conclusions. Maybe this. Maybe that. And incidentally Miss New did not try to call me. You know important people all have telephone logs. She didn't try to call old Mr. Carmody. Of course she says the story was too big for her to confirm it at the White House."

There was no point in arguing -- unless Louisa had gone over the edge, was out of her mind. For better or worse Harry's experience with the victims of advanced nervous breakdowns was limited. Louisa seemed under control. No screaming, no sobbing, nothing out of the way. Probably the best thing to do was to give up. Harry surrendered.

"All right, Louisa," he said, "I know you can't be my lawyer, but tell me, what do I do? You tell me the move."

Louisa was amused. Harry Fresser with his billions, one of the great of the Earth, greeted and bowed to and reverenced as the embodiment of human felicity did not know what to do. His instincts were sound for reaching and grabbing and piling up money. He was as a simple child at this moment, waiting to be led by the hand. He found himself in a corner and he was not accustomed to corners. He needed a guide.

"You get hold of Miss New," Louisa explained, "wherever she is. You get her back on the air. She makes what we call a retraction. She takes back her story. She was misled. She is sorry. She corrects what she said. And she does it on your prime time. Tonight. You don't waste any time, Harry."

"But what if I can't find her," Harry objected. "Dorothy isn't the most accessible person. She has her private life. What if I'm unable to reach her?"

Louisa laughed. "You make a nice appearance," she told him. "You can go on yourself. It would make an even better impression. You apologize. You make the retraction."

That was out of the question. There was something referred to as stage fright. He could not, as Louisa said, "go on the air."

"Then get someone out of your stable. You have a room full of pleasant faces with agreeable voices that you pay to speak the lines you give them. What you run is a kind of model agency, Harry. Order up one of your models."

Harry still had objections. "That's easy to say," he pointed out. "Harder to do. Suppose I find Dorothy and she sticks to her story. Suppose she refuses to do what you say. She has a contract. She has rights under her contract. Independence."

Louisa was firm. "Then fire her or whatever you call it. Let her sue and be damned to her."

"But to go back," Harry said. "If I can't find her, she would be furious if I take back her story without giving her a chance to defend it, to prove it. After all, let's be fair, her reputation's at stake."

"To Hell with Miss New's reputation," Louisa commented. "Planet has crossed wires that carry a very high voltage. Apparently, Harry, you aren't bright enough to understand the extent of the damage that Miss New's broadcast can do. Let me tell you some of the probable damage."

Harry listened and suffered. Planet was supposed to be a money-making not a serious enterprise. He was always uncomfortable when he was reminded that what it did could have serious consequences. It was designed for vacant people with vacant minds, to help them kill time. In the modern world the great blessing was supposed to be leisure, which translated as boredom. The more advanced the society the more leisure everyone had and the more acute the attacks of ennui.

Tuberculosis was the scourge of the early industrial age. Currently the population was ravaged by galloping boredom. The well-to-do sought refuge in travel. Some consumed oceans of beer. Some committed murder to get the money to maintain the traffic in drugs.

Planet offered the cheapest relief, day and night, noise and pictures, intended to help the weary endure from hour to hour and to have no effect on anything.

As Louisa talked, he could see what had happened. Being a practical man he ignored subjects like the conflict with the Eurasian Republics. It was real to the extent that it made it easy to play games with real estate futures. But Louisa was telling him it was a dangerous conflict. Wheels were turning. There was a kind of giant machine of world power and Dorothy had jumped into the machinery, taking Planet along, maybe even all of his beautiful fortune. In spite of himself Louisa had scared him.

"You win," he said. "I'll do what you tell me." He even thanked Louisa for calling him.

Harry Fresser was right. It was not easy to get hold of Dorothy and no pleasure to talk to her when he did. Her story was correct in every detail. Whatever Louisa said was a lie. Louisa was trying to save herself. It was as simple as that. She, herself, had not called the White House. She had confidence, absolute confidence in her source. Who was her source?

That was something she would never disclose, could not disclose. The First Amendment protected all sources. The existence of the country, of a free people depended on a free press. Even if the story had been premature, events would show she was right. So she was saying the story had been premature?

"That was not my understanding, but anything is possible," Dorothy conceded that much.

This was taking too long. Harry had an idea that a change of tactics was called for; perhaps an imaginary call direct from the White House would help. He excused himself for a moment. He had a call on his number two line. Dorothy was, please, to hold on. After five minutes he was back to report that Miss New's broadcast had seriously embarrassed the White House. It depended on Mr. Fresser for the appropriate, immediate remedy.

Having heard Harry, Dorothy was too upset to make another appearance. It would kill her to make a retraction. Nothing like this had ever happened to her before. The humiliation would be too much. Harry was human. He could get someone else. He understood. He would get Howard Pleasants. But he wanted Dorothy to remember that they and Planet might not be out of the woods. There could be repercussions.

To make it more dramatic Harry had Howard Pleasants break into the primest of prime times, regretting the error in Miss New's nightly news story. She had been led to believe that certain decisions had been made by the President. They had not been made. No resignations had been called for. No decision had been made to ask the Supreme Court to deal with the issues presented by the notes from the Eurasian Republics. Planet deeply regretted. Planet had pride in the truth of its broadcasts. Everyone could always be sure that Planet would never mislead them. However Pleasants personally wished everyone a good, pleasant night.

When the Pleasants performance was over, Harry Fresser felt better. However he hoped that Dorothy would not ask any questions at the White House about who had called him direct. Anyhow, Louisa's call was enough. The voice was Louisa's voice but the hands were the hands of Blossom.

In fact the Pleasants retraction was a great relief to Walter. He made it a point to listen to the Planet evening news broadcast. He felt it gave him perspective. Moreover he was, as he would have said, a fan of Miss New. She was blonde and he thought she was pretty. Secretly he wished she were in the Cabinet rather than Louisa, who was good looking but large, and Marietta who was too thin and intense. After what he thought of as a hard day he had turned on -- as the phrase went -- Miss New.

He had sat there, quiet, relaxing. And suddenly he had begun to focus on the big story. He might have wished it were true but it wasn't. He would never have the nerve to fire old Michael Carmody any more than he could have fired his father. He could never have the nerve to fire Louisa -- or the ingratitude. He knew that Louisa had made him President when the liberal Populars had him down for Vice President.

It was a main principle of the liberal Populars that only women were fit to hold what they always spoke of as the Chief Magistrate's office; and for better or worse he was the wrong gender. Moreover Louisa's style of thinking was helpful, less principled than the liberal Popular line to which he tried to be loyal but touched by practical concerns that would not have occurred to him.

For example, Louisa had pointed out that the governors of the Mexican states might not be silent if he took Les Luanda's advice. Apparently Les, himself, had not thought of that possibility. Marietta would have ignored it; but Louisa had been right to remind him that there could be opposition to the Mexican claim. He had to assume that the opposition would disappear if the Supreme Court set the treaty aside but it was a factor, like a datum that was fed into a computer.

Before he could decide what to do, Louisa had called. He was inwardly sorry to spoil Dorothy New's story and day but he had to tell Louisa the truth. For Louisa that was enough. She knew what to do. And she reported later that Harry Fresser had his instructions. It had been a full and difficult day. He had the retraction but he still had his problems. As the commentators all said, the Presidency was a burden.

11

Cheka and Court Join in Welcome to Court Jurisdiction

Cheka was not upset when he heard that the account of the American President's decisions had, in effect, been denied. That gave him the initiative. It was his move and he thought the result might be a checkmate. He would send Blossom a note.

An hour later Cheka was satisfied with his handiwork:

My Dear President Blossom:

There was an indication in your press yesterday that you would invite the Eurasian Republics to submit to your Supreme Court the issue covered by my notes with reference to the larger issues between your government and the Republic of Mexico and those relating to the destruction of our Embassy in Mexico City, including the recovering of our state property and the return of General Dudorov's murderer. That procedure impressed me as superior to any other that might be available and, indeed, preferable to that which I had suggested.

I share with all mankind the greatest respect for the legal institutions of the American people which have been perfected over the more than two centuries of their existence. Your Supreme Court is in every way the embodiment of human law in its highest and profoundest development. With all deference to the Supreme Court of the Union of Eurasian Republics, your Supreme Court and its members must be accepted as preeminent among all existing fountains of justice.

Having said so much I propose that we submit the various matters and issues referred to above to your Supreme Court for its consideration and judgment. The Eurasian Republics will, of course, ask to be represented by counsel and they will be bound by any judgment like all other parties.

I write this with confidence that such a solution will be in the best interests of both our great peoples and will contribute to the cause of world peace and brotherhood.

As before, I am your most sincere brother in peace,

V. I. Cheka

It was, perhaps, a little flowery, a little, perhaps, overdone; but flattery was flattery. The American judges would love it. The Americans generally would take it as a compliment to themselves. Conceivably a few cranks would find fault. Even some might be wary. Nevertheless, he had the satisfaction of precedent; the Trojan horse was successful. He sent for Ulianov to make the arrangements.

Ulianov was pleased to find Cheka in such a good humor. He read slowly and carefully; he looked at Vladimir Ilyich. The Americans would never accept the jurisdiction of the Eurasian Supreme Court. Cheka was asking the Americans to be their own Judges. It was an obvious point but he felt obliged to say so. He was sure Vladimir Ilyich expected such an objection.

Cheka laughed. Ulianov, none of them, understood the Americans. "I am not a reckless man, Josef Vissarionovich," he said. "No one is more careful. When I see opportunity, I also see danger. I look at both sides. Here we are safe. You have the files on the Chief Justice and the rest of them. They are very fine moral people. They will, as the Americans say, bend over backward. More important they are lovers of peace. Even more important they are thirsty for glory. They act now on a national stage and dispose of national issues. But that is only one continent. Here they will be on the world stage and there will be world issues before them. Add it together and you will get the result. This is their chance for approval and praise from the whole human race. Only their decision for us will assure that. We have the key in our hands."

"And then what, Vladimir Ilyich?"

Cheka was amused. Ulianov was the child. He was the father. Ulianov was asking to be told what the promised land would be like. For the Americans there was one last vestige of their vanished religion. Towards the end of the calendar year they went out and spent money freely, buying things to give to each other. They exchanged gifts on one day of the year, as costly as they could afford, maybe more than they could afford. Ulianov, the whole crowd, they were all imagining the triumph of the Republics as a never ending American Christmas. There would be presents, big presents. Cheka recalled a story about Marshal Blucher taken up to a height so that he could have a full view of London. He saw it; he marveled. What a lot of plunder, he said.

That was how Ulianov and the lesser Ulianovs saw the American prospect. There might be disappointments. The Supreme Court would rule. Being righteous and generous at no expense to themselves, its members would probably decree that all the property, real and personal, accumulated in the territory being given back to the Republic of Mexico, should go with the territory. Fifty or sixty million people would be penniless. They would, probably almost all of them flee. Probably even the Mexicans in the treaty states would move with the rest.

There would be chaos, disorder as the millions crossed the new border. The United States would fall apart under the strain. Riots, a kind of civil war, would almost certainly follow. He was a realist. He had no desire or intention to get caught in such a convulsion. Later, when the convulsion was over, the Republics could intervene but by that time there would be a poor kind of Christmas, something like Grabkin's Berlin, politically speaking a prize. Only politically speaking a prize. The major objective was power; the Christmas presents, the plunder were minor.

After Cheka had explained it all, more or less, Ulianov was visibly saddened. "Maybe," he said, "the Dudorov plan was better. Maybe that key was better." Properly managed, terror produced a good crop.

"Unfortunately," Cheka pointed out, "we no longer have a Constantin Constantinovich. Mr. Carmody has him and with him, no doubt, the cartridges. And what our people invented, his people will duplicate. We counted on the shock of surprise. There will be no surprise. And they might match blow for blow. For example, Leningrad for New York. President Blossom is an idealist, but not Mr. Carmody. The idea was sound but ideas are only sound in their time. The Mongol horsemen with their Chinese engineers could conquer their world. Horsemen are not what they were. You must always think of time, Josef Vissarionovich."

For Cheka, however, there would be rewards even before the Americans had brought the roof down on themselves. It was too early to discuss them even with his likely successor. Cheka had them clearly in mind and they pleased him. For generations, the Republics had been fed on by parasites, petty sultans and sheikhs, heads of states that existed by courtesy of the competing bounty of the Republics and the Americans.

The bounty being money and arms for their often ragged praetorians. Cheka would invite them to a grand celebration of the triumph over the imperialist monster. They would be met by squads of soldiers. Instead of the customary luxurious motor cars, they would be transported from the airport in trucks, not to the Marx Palace Hotel, but to barracks. Again in trucks, they would be delivered to the usual banqueting room, but the food would be black bread and cabbage. Then he would speak to them.

Cheka could see them all in his mind's eye. Some of them liked flowing robes. Some distinguished themselves with elaborate turbans. A large number chose to present themselves in uniforms, soldiers whose conquests had been telephone exchanges, radio stations, local power plants, soldiers who had fired mostly at victims tied to a stake. They considered themselves tough fellows, swaggered around, wearing berets, owning automatic weapons that insured respect for themselves and used up cartridges by the shipload. Some liked gold braid. Those who considered themselves more up to date dressed themselves simply as sergeants or privates on the theory that such simplicity had a menacing quality.

The trucks and the barracks, the black bread and the cabbage would have set the tone for the evening. His honored guests would have begun to grasp that they had no bodyguards, no praetorians with them; that they were in a place where their will meant nothing, defenseless, exposed.

He would begin by saying that the sun had gone down. The North Americans were no longer competing and the Eurasian Republics no longer had use for them. He would tell them that what they called credits were no longer available. There would be no more grain, no more lard, no flour, no machines, no engineers, worst of all no more weapons or spare parts for weapons.

They could hereafter use knives or stick each other with spears, brain each other with clubs. The Eurasian Republics were done with them. Those who wished to go home could go home, if they could manage it. Those who would feel safer not going home would be given appropriate jobs. They could enroll themselves in schools and learn trades. The choice was theirs and they would have the same rights as all citizens of the Eurasian Republics. He would have saved the Republics a vast yearly expense. And then he could close down 50 Institutes and put their employees to more useful work, even if they were only reassigned to mop floors.

But it was all to be a surprise and it was better to surprise the whole world, Ulianov included. Also the chickens were yet to be hatched. Ulianov could help in the hatching.

"The note," Cheka said, "will go out today. This evening we will have the world press assembled to hear it read. The effect will be very good. You will have copies on hand. You might even let Mr. Swing have a copy early enough for use on his regular broadcast. I am having Globus and Grabkin in to tell them the course we are following. They will protest. They always want to take what they call a strong line, not being able to think of anything except threats. You will have another world broadcast. And be sure the widow attends."

That evening the Moscow correspondents gathered and heard the historic news. The Eurasian Republics were submitting their claims rising from the destruction of their Embassy in Mexico City, including the recovery of the person of Yuri Bolkonsky, to the Supreme Court of the United States. And presumably, subject to the agreement of President Porfirio Aleman Villa, the Court would be asked to rule on the binding effect of the Treaty of Guadalupe Hidalgo.

The universal reaction was one of approval united with astonishment. Nothing could be more fair. Nothing could prove more fully the good will of the Eurasian Republics and their devotion to the cause of world peace. Harrison Swing had tears in his eyes when he concluded his broadcast. This was a new era. The Republics had shown their faith in the impartiality and honor of the greatest institution of the American people.

At the Supreme Court itself the excitement was greater than any time in its history. Its reputation had grown over the past generation as it went from reform to reform. Now it had received the ultimate accolade, the confidence of the Eurasian Republics. From the Chief Justice, herself, to the least of its 9,000 employees, the Supreme Court as a body was thrilled.

The Court, as its members liked to recall, had humble beginnings. At the outset there was little to do. In the Old Stone Age of the Court members resigned to go home to their states. It met in the Capitol cellar, or something very much like a cellar. In what could be described as its New Stone Age the Court began to assert authority and moved up a flight, on a level with the Senate and House.

At the start of its Modern Age the Court moved into what was now called the Old Building from which it began to issue orders to its inferiors, the states, the Congress, the Executive branch. Its full Modern Age began with the appointment of the first Madam Chief Justice, Wanita Pfuhl of Ohio.

She came to the Court after three terms as governor and with the standing of one of the most powerful of the new Popular leaders. As she said later, her eye had never been on the White House. From girlhood on she had looked to the Chief Justiceship as the place from which to apply her ideas and ideals. Presidents came and went; the Chief Justice had tenure for life and no need to bargain or trade in fixing the course for the country. She arrived at the Court fully prepared. She had a program.

The weakness of the Court to her mind -- and she had a clear mind -- was its dependence on the accident of the cases brought to it. It was a poor basis for moving the country on the path it should take. The staff of the Court, moreover, was too small for the responsibilities that it bore.

Her first major improvement was to set up a large research staff to study and assess the social and economic needs of the nation.

Twice yearly it published its list of issues to which the Court should address its attention. There was a simple rating of issues and needs, from highest priority to lowest priority. There were high priority and low priority and medium priority ratings. The Court invited litigation focused on matters high on the scale. And since everything could take the form of a lawsuit, litigants and lawyers assured the Court an efficient agenda.

The first goal was to abolish old wrongs and old wrongs having been analyzed and listed, were brought before it and dealt with. The second goal was positive, to achieve an equal and perfect society. A larger research effort was needed and the Court's staff of sociologists and economists multiplied. As order after order went down Chief Justice Pfuhl found herself -- and her Associate Justices joined her -- dissatisfied with the manner and speed with which they were enforced.

The answer was to create the Court's own Bureau of Enforcement. By the end of her tenure, Congress, perhaps grudgingly, appropriated the money to build the new Court Center, the Pfuhl Memorial as it was commonly called, nearly equal in size to all the buildings occupied by the House and Senate combined and a monument to Wanita.

Her successor, as she had long hoped, was her niece, the present Chief Justice, a child of her own sister, Bonita Jackson. In her ten years on the bench, the niece had been loyal to the principles and memory of her aunt. The resources of the Court expanded. Its computer was acknowledged to be the most fully informed computer in the whole world. Its sociological and economic experts were the most learned members of their professions. And its Enforcement Masters were famous for being tireless at their work.

The first comment of the Chief Justice when she was told of the Cheka note was beautifully human. She was reported as saying that she wished her aunt had lived to see the Court so respected, enjoying the confidence not only of all American citizens but that of the Eurasian people as well. She said much the same thing at her daily press conference.

12

Congress Leaders Move to Block Court Action, Preserve Union

The sociologists all found that it was a homogeneous country. Everyone talked alike, dressed alike, cooked alike, thought alike. But Bright Dismukes, as he said, was so old that he had the last Southern accent. He was also old enough to have sat in the Senate for 44 years and to have become its oldest member. He was distinctly a conservative Popular but the young liberal Populars treated him with respect. They were wise. Actually a couple of liberal Populars had campaigned against him in a primary several years earlier and had lived to regret it.

As Chairman of the Committee on Appropriations, Bright Dismukes could be obliging to friends and difficult with people who crossed him. He could, as he put it, turn off the water. The two liberal Populars who thought he was old enough to be beaten had thereafter lived in a desert. Their states suffered with them until they retired the offenders on the understanding that the water would be diverted back once the offenders were gone.

There was a theory that Bright Dismukes was so old that he had no idea of what was going on in the world. Another theory was that he was so old that he no longer cared what happened outside his Committee. Neither was right. When he heard about Cheka's latest letter to Blossom and that the Chief Justice was taking it as a personal tribute he was alarmed. Deciding that the time had come to do something, he arranged to have breakfast with Francis Manners, the Speaker.

"I don't like the situation," Dismukes said after he and the Speaker had compared information and what each thought was likely to happen.

The Speaker nodded agreement. They both saw the same prospect. The Court would take jurisdiction. The Chief Justice would write another

101

landmark opinion with the help of the family computer. She would dress it up like a Christmas tree, with all kinds of precedents. But basically, as always, she would act on the principles of natural and historical justice. Everyone knew the incantations and formulae. Then there would be a solemn decree sweeping away the wrongs of the past. The Court's duty would be painful but clear, the more painful, the clearer.

"We'd better stop this thing now, before it goes any further," Dismukes said after a moment.

The Speaker agreed. What did Bright have to suggest?

"We could talk to Blossom. When we were young, the thing we did was to go to the White House. Thinking back, Omar Jenkins, Harry Midgett, Burt Rohrback didn't amount to much as great statesmen but they had some authority. Blossom is nothing."

They talked about Blossom. Cheka had asked his consent to the proposal he made in his letter. But there was no chance that he would withhold it. The swarm that made its living making what it called public opinion, male and female, high priced to low priced, were all for the Cheka proposal. They had already begun to crank the polling machine. The public was eighty-three percent in favor of peace and quiet which meant it was eighty-three percent for anything Cheka proposed. Another poll showed that ninety-one percent of the people were in favor of enjoying life, and ninety-four percent believed that this was the only life they had had or were going to have. Adding it all together the polling public were all in favor of taking Cheka's magnanimous offer.

"But who," Bright Dismukes asked, "is this wonderful public? You and I have 150 years between us. I've never known anyone who was asked his opinion. How about you?"

The Speaker had never known anyone questioned by anyone in the business of polling. "All the same, Blossom will be persuaded. He told me after he had been to Geneva or Zurich or wherever it was that he saw himself and Cheka as a couple of Princes of Peace."

"There's no point in our wasting our time or Blossom's," Dismukes went on. "Madam and company want to perform. With or without Blossom's consent they're going to say they have jurisdiction -- even if Blossom rejects the proposal."

The Speaker agreed. "So we're going to have to do this on our own."

"And we're going to have to act quickly. You remember the old movies, Francis. We have to head Madam off at the pass."

The speaker took a paper from his pocket, unfolded it and handed it to Dismukes who read it and nodded.

What the paper said was that no court of the United States has or shall have authority to declare invalid or to set aside any treaty of the United States entered into by them with the concurrence of the Senate as provided in Section 2 of Article II. It was an amendment to the Constitution.

"I would like to go further but this will do for the present. I have the votes for it in the House. You have the votes, We put it in and pass it today."

They considered and counted and recounted the votes. Beginning with the Guadalupe Hidalgo states the votes were certain. There was Texas, not one of the Treaty states but the Texans were subject to the same claim. There were the states that bordered on the Treaty states and would be uneasy at any change in the existing arrangements. The Treaty state delegations were large. Everyone had a friend.

"How long is it going to take for ratification?" Dismukes asked.

"I spoke last night," the Speaker told him, "to the governors of Texas and California. They called me back later. They said they can count on 44 legislatures, including their own, to act within a week or ten days. They had done some soundings -- no particular language. An amendment to protect their states and their people, to prevent the country from being broken apart. Everybody is willing to act to prevent it."

"Except the President and the Chief Justice," Dismukes corrected him.

"And some other people whose motives we won't discuss now."

"So far, so good," Dismukes said. "But I think we might make another move. I would like to let some gas out of the Court, deflate it. We've made a great mistake in letting it swell up as it has."

"I follow," the Speaker agreed.

"It's bad for people to have too much money," Dismukes observed. "We've all seen it with people we know. Money corrupts. Too much money corrupts absolutely. You know the old tag. What if we reduce the Court's allowance, put it on a strict diet, even reduce it to starvation rations? They tell me it has some eight thousand or nine thousand employees. What if it had, maybe a hundred. The old Court wasn't so bad -- nine members, a law clerk apiece, a library. Why can't we go back to that?"

"You have no objection from me," the Speaker said.

"We do your amendment when we meet today. Then we amend the Court's appropriation. You and I will agree on a number. Madam has friends but not enough to create any problem."

They agreed on a number. They had met for breakfast at six. They had plenty of time to prepare for the morning.

It was a vile, a foul, dirty day's work; the press, the media expressed nothing but outrage. Marvin Mazo, the chief of the Washington Bureau of the New York Gazette, called it a senile and cowardly attack on the fortress of the American conscience. The Chief Justice agreed and complimented him on his choice of words.

"I liked what you said, Marvin," she told him. "Senile and cowardly." They were in bed together. Marvin had been her Aunt's good friend. Now he was her special friend. It was both a sentimental and a practical friendship. Marvin spoke with the highest authority by virtue of being the Washington voice of the New York Gazette, which was useful even to Nita, as she liked to be called. And Marvin got special insights into the workings of the great institution of the Court, past, present, even prospective. Marvin even advised and offered suggestions.

If Nita sometimes thought Marvin was a little old for her, she really liked Marvin and he was a suitably dignified match for that matter. She could have married Marvin -- he was a widower -- without being ashamed of him. Still the arrangement was satisfactory as it was and she was faithful to her aunt's advice, that marriage was a trap for women and was designed by men to prevent women from realizing themselves.

As Chief Justice, Nita, of course, had realized herself career wise, as she thought of it; but looking at herself in the mirror she had to concede that she was very attractive. She might want to pair off with a younger version of Marvin. She definitely preferred the intellectual type.

"It was a bad day, Nita," Marvin said sympathetically.

"I'm not going to worry about it now," Nita assured him.

She had been working on her opinion in the Eurasian-Mexican cases when she heard of the senile and cowardly attack in the Congress. Working on opinions early was something she had learned about from her aunt. Cases could be seen and understood more clearly before they were confused by records and arguments. The essential thing always was principle and principle was not subject to change. It was Marvin who had broken the news to her. He had come straight from the Capitol.

He had begun by saying that he was unhappy to have to bring her bad news. Both the House and Senate had got out of control. One of his young men got wind of it and had called to tell him to come up to the Capitol at once. When he arrived he went to the House side. The Speaker was on the floor, going from one of the older members to another.

Marvin had got hold of Castillo to find out what was going on. Castillo told him the Speaker had an amendment to the constitution ready to introduce. He, Castillo, had not seen it yet but he was, of course, going to oppose it. Anything that the Speaker proposed was bound to be vicious. And he had reason to think that this was the Speaker at his worst. Actually when the amendment was introduced and Castillo got up to oppose someone had spoken to him and he sat down again. The vote was a formality, Marvin had said. It was a put-up job, to be vulgar about it.

Then, Marvin reported, when he went over to the Senate he found that the Senate had approved the same amendment and old Bright Dismukes had a bill amending the Supreme Court's appropriation. The performance, Marvin had told her, was incredible. He had seen nothing like it for years. No one opposed. A half dozen members were absent. Three were present and abstained from voting. When the Senate's bill was walked over, the House passed it, with Castillo and a few others opposing.

Nita heard it all. She was a heroine meeting adversity, Cleopatra hearing that Caesar was about to appear, Maria Theresa after losing some battle. However, her situation was better than theirs. Law ruled everything and she was the law. Marvin's report had upset her at first. After all she was human. She had feelings. All women had feelings and what the congress had done was insulting. The thing to do was not to feel so much but to think. She had her own weapons.

It was after she told Marv she was not going to worry about the events of the day that the solution came to her. Perhaps it was a message from the spirit of her aunt; or it might have been nothing but her own inspiration. Marv was a man of the broadest experience. He had a marvelous mind. He was there. She tried the solution on him.

"Marv," she said, "I've got the high cards."

"You've got what, Nita?" he asked.

"The high cards," she repeated. "You know like in games. And I've got the high cards. There's nothing to worry about."

"Tell me. Explain, I listen."

"Injunctions, Marv. I, we, the Court deal with all this with injunctions."

"Keep on talking, Nita." Marv knew about injunctions. Injunctions were great. But what kind of injunctions?

"Look at me, Marv," Nita commanded. "Look at me and what do you see?"

It was an interesting question. What did he see? A small, confident woman as the Lord made her. He answered by saying he saw the sun and the moon and the stars, his Queen of the May.

"The correct answer," she told him, "is that you see the judicial power of the United States in its full glory. You know all about the separation of powers. What you are looking at is the prime, number one power."

Marvin Mazo looked and admired. Rightly or wrongly she was sure of herself. He admired resilience.

"You see," she went on, "a woman who can hold everyone in contempt, the Speaker, old Senator Dismukes, anybody you name. I've got it clearly in mind now. I know just what I'm going to do. "

It was simple. The House and Senate had wasted their time. The proposed amendment was nothing. The Court would issue injunctions. The governors would be enjoined from calling special sessions to ratify the amendment. Injunctions would go out to the members of the legislatures in session forbidding them to approve the amendment. Moreover anyone who defied the injunctions would be in contempt of the Court. The penalties would be heavy, fines and imprisonment until purged of contempt, large fines, very large fines.

The appropriation problem had an equally simple solution. The Court would send a draft to the Treasury for the money it needed, cast in the form of a mandatory injunction. It would simply be an order to pay and failure by the Treasury would be an act of contempt. The order would be directed to the Secretary; the Secretary would be personally liable.

It sounded too easy to Marvin. But he was not the Chief Justice. Contempt. Imprisonment. Fines. The procedure sounded irregular. At least he knew of no precedent.

Nita understood. Men were more timid than women. "The great thing I learned from Wanita," she said, "was that the Court should always be bold. Suppose Columbus had been afraid to steer a new course? The Court is like Columbus. It explores. It keeps the Constitution vital, equal to the needs of each crisis." She was echoing Wanita's wisdom.

Wanita had told her that she herself had had two truly great predecessors: John Marshall, Earl Warren. A pair of busted politicians Wanita had called them but men who could still hear opportunity knock. They knew that you created power by using it, really by no more than asserting it. Marshall said the Court was Supreme which made it Supreme. Warren said he was the moral arbiter of the ages and could prove it from sociology studies which made him a one-man church militant. All they were doing, Wanita concluded, was working off the frustrations of political failure. And they had got away with it.

All of which was why she had always had her eye on being Chief Justice. Once there she would be in charge of everything and that was what she had been. She managed the Court and no one could question what the Court did. Any Chief Justice worth her salt could, as Wanita summed up, do as she damned pleased.

Marv heard it all and had to agree. Everybody jumped when the Court told them to jump. They jumped, in fact, when any court said to. It was an essential part of the American character. Stone masons were paid so much an hour to carve on public buildings that the United States was a government of laws, not of men and supposedly people believed it.

An occasional heretic suggested that it might be useful to inquire as to the source of the laws, not the laws as enacted but as read and applied. But a heresy, by definition, does not have general acceptance. Marv had applauded almost every judicial performance.

At least all the big decisions were headed in what he thought of as the moral direction. Some of Wanita's medicine had been swallowed grudgingly. Some of Nita's doses were equally bitter. The elected law makers were increasingly jealous of what could be called the appointed law makers, hence the Speaker's and Bright Dismuke's successes that day.

"Nita," Marv asked her, "let's call what happened today a rebellion. Do you think you can put it down with these injunctions of yours?"

Nita was sure that she could.

"And Nita, will the rest of the Court see it your way?"

Nita assured him. "We're always a unanimous Court," she pointed out. "Once I make the decision, the sisters and brothers sign whatever I tell them."

13

Chief Justice Nita Warned: Congress Will Impeach You

It was very helpful to have a computer which knew both the names and addresses of the governors and all the members of the state legislatures. By mid-morning the Chief Justice had every thing ready to go out to the United States marshals in the various districts. At that point she called her sisters and brothers together.

The sisters and brothers heard and approved – one thousand per cent. They had been shocked by what the Congress had done. In the rhetoric of the Court, the action of the Congress had had a chilling effect. They had never thought that it would turn on them and bite them. Was it a serious bite? Could the bite even be fatal?

For years the Congress had been an obedient dog, not exactly a pet but a dog to put up with. They were all happy to hear that there was a remedy, that for all practical purposes there was really no bite.

The senior member of the Court, Ms. Justice Drain, spoke for all of them when she declared after Nita was finished that only Nita could have analyzed the situation so quickly and neatly. They had all been applying their minds to what looked like a serious crisis, a serious constitutional crisis. The crisis disappeared as Nita explained it. An inherent power of the Court was to pass out injunctions. The proposed injunctions disposed of the issues. The dog would wag its tail and be a good dog.

"Another thing," the Chief Justice said, having thanked them for their confidence and for being a unanimous Court, "you all know of Mr. Cheka's letter and I'm sure you all take pride in it."

They all knew about the letter. They all took pride in it.

"I've been told," she went on, "that the Republic of Mexico is willing to submit the validity of the Treaty to this Court for its decision." Miss

New had called her to tell her she had glad tidings from Mexico City: Porfirio Aleman had appointed counsel to act for him, had completely committed himself. "I would like to announce that we are in agreement that the Court should hear the claims of the Republic of Mexico and the Eurasian Republics when they are presented."

They were all in agreement. They were a court. The purpose of courts was to do justice. The claims were for justice. It was as clear and as simple as their injunctions. Moreover, as Ms. Justice Drain pointed out, they would be ploughing new ground. They would have a change from their usual diet. They would be dealing with the broadest of issues and, acting wisely, they would be "bringers" of peace.

"Quite so," Nita assured her. The prospect was sobering but she knew it exhilarated them.

The Chief Justice's press conference that day was beautiful. Dorothy New used that word in describing it. The Chief Justice, Dorothy said, had never looked more serene. She had never had more important announcements to make. She had been, the word was, majestic in disposing of the foolish and hasty -- this was Dorothy's language -- attack on the Court by the Congress. She had been doubly majestic in stating that the Court would accept the responsibility of ruling on the too long festering issue of the Treaty of Guadalupe Hidalgo and both the Eurasian and Mexican claims rising out of the terrorist destruction of the Eurasian Embassy in Mexico City.

There had been no questions when the Chief Justice completed her statement. No questions were needed. Everyone knew, Dorothy said in completing her broadcast, that the country was in strong and good hands.

Nita listened to Miss New's broadcast with Marv and was moved by it. Offhand she could not remember having been called majestic before. She wondered if Marv thought her majestic. He called her Queenie at times but that was a little familiar. "I knew Dorothy liked me," she commented to Marv, "but I never thought she .... " She left the sentence unfinished.

"Dorothy New is Dorothy New," was all that Marv said. He had a poor opinion of Dorothy. A second string Marietta and the first string was not very much. It was best not to say so. Nita would have told him that men were always jealous of women, envious. He was an old style print journalist as the phrase went. The Dorothys were paid five times what he had from the Gazette. Eliot Fresser had aired him -- as Eliot phrased it -- a few times and decided that he was wanting in radiance, again Eliot's word. Eliot was sorry but radiance was the quality that you had to have on the air. Dorothy shone. Marietta shone. The Marvin Mazos were dull.

The truth was, according to Eliot, that women made up the meaningful, the really significant audience. And women essentially did not trust men and their point of view. Men were cynical. Also men were not much to look at, even those who tried to make the best of themselves. Women wanted the woman's view of what went on in the world because women knew what was important, had more feeling, knew how to dress, in short women were radiant. Nita was looking at him. He told her that Dorothy had done no more than give her her due. But he had his doubts. Louisa had talked to him.

Blossom had also looked at the broadcast of the Chief Justice's press conference. They were held every day and he did not, as he said, view all of them. He had, however, been alerted, put on notice, that this was likely to be a special one. The action of the Congress on the previous day had been disconcerting. He had even felt almost offended.

What the Congress had done was unusual. It could even be described as momentous and he felt that he should have been told of it beforehand, maybe even consulted. Not that he had much to do with the Congress or had much acquaintance with the old timers like the Speaker and Senator Dismukes. They seemed to him more or less obsolete types, the last known examples of a vanishing species. He knew they had some nominal standing but he had not thought of them as capable of the kind of thing they had done.

Blossom had a feeling at times that the Court tended to crowd but he accepted the fact that it had the last word on everything. Like God, it was the Court that disposed. By the old standards the Court might be regarded as perhaps overblown but its development, as everybody agreed, had been no more than natural. The late Wanita had no more than speeded the process.

For the Congress to strike at the Court was futile, no more than a sign of bad temper, not to speak of bad judgment. It had put him in the embarrassing position of having to take a position, to approve by signing, to disapprove by a veto. Inaction would be or could be seen as tantamount to a veto. The announcement of the impending injunctions had been a relief. To that extent he had liked the press conference. However, the announcement that the Court would act on the Treaty and the other matters struck him as tactless.

The Cheka letter had been addressed to him. The consent asked for was his. The Chief Justice and the Court were in effect taking over his mail and dictating his answer. He liked the Chief Justice personally. Nevertheless, he wished he could object. There was after all something to the separation of powers, or had been. It was all very complex and Louisa complicated it further.

The reporters, ever eager, had sought her out to get her reaction to the Court's mandatory injunction. Without consulting Blossom or the rest of the Cabinet she had told them she regarded the injunction as nothing more than a joke. "Farce, pure farce," was the way she had put it. Would she comply? The answer was no. But contempt, would she put herself in contempt of the Court?

"You people," she had told them, "are a few days early. If there is no veto, or if there is a veto and the veto is overridden, if the action of the Congress stands, of course I'll comply with it. And if the Court is not sensible enough to dissolve its injunction, then I will be in contempt."

"But if the injunction stands?" someone asked.

"Then, I'll be in contempt." She would say no more than that. She was, she said, the victim of her upbringing. She had been brought up to be polite about judges and courts.

Having dismissed the reporters, Louisa had called Marvin Mazo and asked him to come to the Treasury.

"Marv" she had said, "I want to talk to you in your role as friend of the Court, as <u>amicus curiae</u>."

"All right," Marv conceded, "I'm a friend of the Court."

"A word of caution. Your friends, your friend is asking for trouble. The Court has the last word but only up to a point. The Senate has the last last word when it sits as a court after the House votes to impeach."

"Are you being serious, Louisa?" Marv asked.

Louisa nodded. Of course she was serious.

"Have you spoken to anyone? Has anyone spoken to you? Do you know that anyone is really thinking these thoughts?"

"If they aren't," Louisa said, "they will be, even," she added, "if I have to remind them of what the Founders provided -- with their usual foresight. After what the Congress has done already, you don't doubt that it will go this last step. Or do you?"

Marv wasn't sure. There had been trials of strength before with the Court and nothing had happened. The Court always prevailed. Why would it be different this time?"

"Nita," said Louisa, "if I may refer to her as Nita, isn't leaving anybody much room. She's about to push us all out of bed, though maybe I ought not to put it that way. We've got no place to go. If she can tell me to pay whatever she says for the Court, she can appropriate money for everything else."

"I can see that," Marv had to admit.

"But it goes beyond that," Louisa went on. "She's evidently determined to set aside poor old Guadalupe Hidalgo. She is going to settle scores with President Polk. She is going to say goodbye to what we're told are the Mexican states and their people. Apparently the Court is going to conduct the foreign policy of the country in the guise of hearing a lawsuit."

"So," Marv asked, "what do you want me to do?"

"You can tell Nita for me that I say to lay off, to back away with as much grace as she can but to back away before she brings down the roof."

Marv wanted to know if Louisa spoke for Blossom, the Cabinet, anyone but herself.

"In the circumstances, Marv," Louisa said, "it's enough that I speak for myself. You know Blossom. Score zero for Blossom. Score zero for the rest of the crowd. But for these purposes you had better not ignore Francis Manners or Senator Dismukes. They see things the way I do and so will most people if this thing goes any further."

Marv looked at Louisa. "You're a formidable woman, Louisa." he said. Without question she was a large, good looking formidable woman.

"Will you break the news to the Chief Justice that this time she can't have her own way, that the old scarecrow no longer works?"

"Within my limits, I'm an honest man, Louisa," Marv told her. "And to be honest, I don't have the nerve. If she asks for advice then I can suggest what you've pointed out but I can't walk in and tell her that Louisa Clymer says to back down. You know about pride."

"A well known cardinal sin -- to which we're all subject."

"The Chief Justice of the United States has her share and more. It goes with the office," Marv added.

Louisa knew about women and men, men and women, liaisons, love, relationships, whatever they were called at any particular time. Nita loved Marv. Marv loved Nita. Or something. Marv couldn't tell the Chief Justice that she was an idiot. That the Secretary of the Treasury had told her to back off. That would cause trouble. The Chief Justice might infer that Marv liked the Secretary of the Treasury more than he should, that his affections were being transferred. A lover's quarrel might be the result, a misunderstanding, an emotional crisis. Only God knew what a Chief Justice might do in such an emotional crisis. Dido upon the wild sea strand was all she could think of offhand.

"Let me," Louisa said, "make a suggestion. Do this as one of your patented pieces, background, an informed source, six informed sources. You sew it together. You're looking at all the hints and veiled thoughts and this is a possible future development, the ultimate crisis, the result of a breakdown in communications between the three great branches of our great federal system."

"I'm the messenger boy?" Marv asked.

"A post of honor, the messenger chosen on high. Through you and you only divinity speaks to divinity, your special divinity. I'll guarantee your being Journalist of the Year, a footnote, even a reference in the text of all histories of our lives and times." Louisa looked at him. "I know you're a true liberal Popular, Marv," she added. "Faithful to the principles and nonsense of your lost youth. But this will be doing a favor to the liberal Populars. You'll be the lighthouse that kept them from breaking up on the rocks. You'll be doing Nita a service in saving her from herself. And I'll regard it as a favor to me."

Marv reflected. Louisa was right. This was where the old print journalism rose and flew far above the Dorothy News of the world. He would have a long piece, carefully written, quietly written, words quietly spoken at the highest levels, heavy with meaning. In another time, it occurred to him, he could have talked to Abe Lincoln, maybe to Jefferson Davis, to Robert E. Lee, put it all together, prevented the whole Civil War. No campaigns, no battle at Gettysburg, no Gettysburg speech, no Lincoln Memorial, everything would have been different. He regretted that the opportunity could not have come to him. He had been generations too late. He realized that Louisa was waiting for him to say something.

"You persuade me, Louisa," he said. "I won't talk to the Chief Justice directly but you can all read the Gazette in the morning." Louisa, he thought, is a real mover and shaker. She also had very fine eyes.

14

Leading Eurasian Assassin Drowned

Cheka was troubled for the first time when he read the Mazo story in the Gazette. Things had been more or less going according to plan. The action of the Congress he had regarded as no more than a last dying spasm, a last twitch as the spirit departed. The Supreme Court ladies had made their response. They were Supreme. They had, moreover, sent their own answer to his letter to Blossom. Of course, they had jurisdiction. Of course, they would exercise their authority, in their robes and their high marble hall.

But Mazo -- he knew all about Mazo -- was saying that he had heard voices, whispering objections and hinting at means to enforce those objections. Mazo was close to the Chief Justice, very close according to the Security files. Was Mazo speaking for her? Was she going to fail to perform her part in the play? That was impossible.

The Security files gave him perfect confidence in her character, a strong-minded woman accustomed to having her way, always having her way, a real old style Tsarina. In fact the Americans, by accident or design, had nothing but old style Tsarinas. The men were evidently so many Paul's or Nicholas II's, fellows to be removed or ignored.

That being so, whose were the whispers? Not Blossom's. He had seen Blossom, another weak Tsar. The old men in the Congress. They were too old, but he made a note to reread their files. The Secretary of State, the lady news star? Her heart was in the right place. He had seen her with Blossom. He knew the ins and outs of Popular politics and where the Blossom nomination had come from. The voices may have been, probably were, the voice of the woman named Clymer. He had seen her too, an attractive woman but not sympathetic to the usual universal ideals.

There was an old question: What would happen if an irresistible force was met by an immovable object? The Chief Justice was the irresistible force. If the Clymer woman were an immovable object, what then? He had sent word to Ulianov for the file on Louisa Clymer. It would be helpful to know as much about her as possible.

Ulianov himself brought in the file. Cheka motioned to him to sit down. He looked at the file.

"American women," Cheka said finally. "American women." Ulianov said nothing. What could he say? "This woman may be a problem," Cheka went on. "You remember her, Josef Vissarionovich?" Ulianov remembered her. Security people were trained to observe and to have total recall. It was an essential part of being a Security type, the essential trait of those who rose to the top. You remembered everything in detail, eyes, voice, bearing, the least mannerism. You saw someone once and never forgot a detail. You would recognize the person in question forever, even in any disguise, even after a lifetime. The Security mind took a photograph, filed it away, could retrieve it at will.

The Clymer woman was small, a small dark woman, almost a dwarf. "How could I forget her?" he said. Small women, all very small people, were troublesome. It was what was called compensation. They made up for being diminutive by asserting themselves. He had a friend or two who was difficult for that reason.

"The Clymer woman may be a problem," Cheka repeated.

Ulianov understood. He had removed problem people before. He indicated as much.

"I know, I know," Cheka said. There had been accidents to a head of state here, a head of state there. Air transportation was out of its infancy but still subject to accident in spite of every precaution. The appearance of good health was deceptive. The healthy were suddenly stricken, quickly wasted away. But they had been heads of minor states, satellite states. There was a risk even in dealing with them, but not much of a risk. Even there you moved with great care, made sure the successor would feel only gratitude, that the mourning would be, if sincere, mainly formal. With the Clymer woman, the considerations might be more serious. The Dudorov affair had to be thought of. No sensible man would trifle with old Michael Carmody, whatever his age. He explained all this to Ulianov.

"Even the sainted Stalin," Cheka pointed out by way of conclusion, "observed certain limits. He killed freely and widely but only those who could not strike back in either this life or, as they say, from the grave. He even let Hitler alone."

Ulianov nodded. They had talked about that before, many times. They had searched through old papers, all sorts of papers, for years. "He, Hitler, was a special case, Vladimir Ilyich. You think so. I think so."

Cheka conceded the point. When it would have been easy to dispose of Hitler, Stalin had disapproved the suggestion. Did Stalin act out of prudence, out of concern for retaliation or was there another and different reason? He and Ulianov had concluded that Hitler had been Stalin's invention, his agent, to smash the states in the West and the German Reich in the process. Then Hitler or the Germans generally had gone out of control, maybe only the Germans. Maybe Hitler had been a loyal agent. There were records and traces that suggested as much.

What had happened to Hitler was murky, even his death as reported. Hitler had doubles and doubles. After generations no one could be sure of anything that happened or was supposed to have happened. But in any event the Clymer woman was no agent of theirs. She was no head of state.

"It would be easy," Ulianov suggested. "Something for Speck."

Speck was a specialist with very special experience. They kept Speck as a kind of insurance when nothing else worked.

"It might be easy," Cheka said. "But maybe not so easy as you think, Josef Vissarionovich. For the present you had better not even speak to him. Not a suggestion that you may have an assignment. You understand?" Ulianov, of course, understood. Cheka would think. Cheka would decide. All the same the idea was his. Using Speck had been the answer to some difficult questions before. Cheka loathed Speck, or said that he did. But Cheka was practical. A last thought from Cheka. "The crowds," he said. Ulianov hoped the crowds were satisfactory.

"Very good. Not too big, not too small. They're building up as they should. But, Josef Vissarionoch," he noted, "the mix is too young. There should be more older people. Not old but mature, perhaps better dressed. The impression is better, more serious."

Ulianov said he would speak to Medusa Mendez.

The old Lafayette Duvall house and estate could no longer be seen from the road running by it. There was a high brick wall and it was the only visible wall. Inside it were, in a manner of speaking, invisible walls, barriers, alarm systems. The Lafayette Duvall estate was a very safe place, beautifully maintained, beautifully watched over. It was hard to get in; in some circumstances it was equally hard to get out. A very high class prison, a very fancy hotel. It depended on the guest's point of view. Old Mr. Carmody had himself driven there to call on General Dudorov.

They talked about Boregard Dodge who had interviewed Dudorov. Mr. Carmody asked how it had gone.

"How can I say?" Dudorov answered. "A very distinguished man," Dudorov knew a distinguished man when he saw one. He had been brought up in the world of men of distinction, marked by their position and the deference they were accustomed to. That was, to play on words, the way you distinguished them. "He has the highest regard for you."

The old man moved his hands. It was a bad day for arthritis. "Everyone does," he observed. "Did he believe you?"

"Because of his high regard for you," Dudorov said, "he is inclined to take me on faith. He has, he says, the usual overwhelming evidence that I am dead and buried with a full set of honors. Not the best but better than I could have expected."

"Did he say what he was going to do?" the old man asked.

"He was to talk to you. He told me there were complications. Something to do with the court to which he belonged. It was confusing.

"You have company," the old man assured him. "Everybody is confused." He took an envelope from his pocket and gave it to Dudorov. "Look at those pictures, General, and tell me if you know the face.

"Dudorov took the envelope, took out some photographs. He knew the face.

"The name?" the old man asked.

"He had, what do you say, lots of names. Maybe Speck was the real one. I know him as Speck."

The old man nodded. He knew him as Speck, knew of him as Speck. "A dangerous man?"

Speck was employed, Dudorov told him, to be a dangerous man, a highly paid -- as Security people were paid -- agent; very much of a specialist. Speck, he added, was proud of his specialty.

"Number one on your list of assassins?"

"Speck thinks so. I think he was right."

"Close to Cheka?"

Dudorov shook his head. "Cheka," he said, "was afraid of him. He used him but so far as I know, never saw him. They told me, somebody told me, Ulianov maybe, that Cheka would never let Speck come near him."

The old man thought he perhaps understood why. Cheka thought of Speck as bad luck.

Dudorov again shook his head. "It went beyond that. Perhaps you know about Speck. Or maybe, perhaps, I should tell you."

"You tell me," the old man said, moving his fingers.

"Speck," Dudorov went on, "began as a medical student. A medical background. Someone, I never knew who, brought him into the Security Service. A real find as it happened. The talent was there, the talent for what proved to be Speck's special career. He never liked using a gun. Speck was a knifer, a strangler, very good breaking necks."

"A strong man," the old man observed.

"A strong man, a very strong man. He was also a poisoner. He read books, old books, knew the old recipes and made up his own. Speck was supposed to favor the slow acting poisons, poisons that could make their way through a man's skin. That was the talk and Speck encouraged it. You know, the man of mystery type."

The old man nodded. He knew the type.

"Speck really was out of an old-fashioned novel. Did you ever read Balzac?"

The old man nodded again. He had done lots of reading in a long life. Balzac had been on the list.

"Speck saw himself, sees himself, as one of the people, men or women, out of Balzac's underworld. He could give an assignment, that was his way of speaking, a terrible disease, something forgotten by everyone else, but still available for the men who knew how to find it and use it. Or this was his claim -- not a claim, something he hinted."

"Mugoko," the old man said. An African ruler who died in a way that horrified everyone. Then there was the grand something or other in Teheran who died in a sudden and mysterious plague along with half of everyone else. The head of state in Bangladesh had overnight become the victim of a form of what was thought to be leprosy, a galloping leprosy. The whatever, he was in one of the Koreas, had wasted away in a week.

"You understand why Cheka wouldn't let Speck get near him." Dudorov said after a moment. "The President of Finland falling downstairs alone in his house, falling downstairs and breaking his neck was human. The others were different."

"Would I be right, General," the old man said, "if I said that no one should take chances with Speck?"

Dudorov nodded. No man in his right mind would take chances with Speck.

"I ask," the old man explained, "because I hear that Speck might get an assignment in Washington."

"Not you," Dudorov said. "Certainly not you. Cheka would never allow it.'

The old man said nothing.

"Speck's assignments have always been chosen with prudence. No head of state who could strike back or could strike back through his friends."

The old man noted that he was no head of state.

"You're close enough to it for Cheka to treat you like one. He is careful not to disturb you. Routine things, yes. But nothing to cause, how do you put it, personal feelings."

"All right," the old man agreed. I'm not the assignment. Another person. Someone important and maybe important to you."

"If I have an interest or if I don't have an interest," Dudorov said, "you had better act. I know enough about Speck. Maybe I can be helpful." He had never told anyone, but he thought Speck had poisoned a woman of whom he, Dudorov, had been especially fond.

Speck prided himself on being a strong swimmer. He liked to go down to his own beach near Yalta and swim out for a mile or so. Then he would lie back and float. He would make plans if he had an assignment, or, if not, he would sometimes talk to himself or simply shout whatever obscenity came to his lips. He was, he was aware, complex, very special.

Sometimes he thought of his professional career. He was sure he was envied. He had done things that other men were unable to do. He had very good decorations. He had his own house by the sea, a very good second class apartment in Moscow. It was true that he had no family but a man really needed no family. It was also true that in spite of the decorations he had never been given the rank he deserved.

He should have been more than a major in the Security services. After all that he had accomplished. Moreover his kind of career had to be more or less hidden. He would have liked more recognition. He was not morbid but he wondered at times if he would have a suitable obit.

His decorations had come to him with the instruction that they were not to be worn. He was not to attract any notice. He was not to indicate to anyone how he had earned his various ribbons and orders. Nevertheless he had his own satisfactions. He knew his own skills. He could count over his triumphs. The highest circles were in debt to him for his exemplary zeal.

On this particular day he had followed his usual routine. He sensed that he would soon have another assignment and they were all full of interest and challenge. His were always the best. He had swum out, was floating, was thinking his thoughts when he heard the sound of a motor. Boats were not forbidden but they were unusual. Only real dignitaries had the use of a motor boat.

When the boat came near he could see that there were three men in it. The boat circled him slowly.

"We've been looking for you," one of the men called to him. One of the men shut off the motor. Speck was puzzled. There had to be a mistake. He had never seen any of these men before. "You must be wrong," Speck said.

"You're Speck?" the first man asked.

"Yes," Speck said.

"So I'm right," the first man said good humoredly. "We thought you'd be around here."

Speck was more puzzled. How would absolute strangers know he would be floating a mile or more from his beach. It was his habit; but no one knew what he did with his time. He took care that no one should know.

"Do you mind if I join you?" the first man asked. He was very polite. If Speck wanted the sea to himself, the man would not make use of it.

"I can't stop you," Speck said. He was, perhaps, a little annoyed. He preferred being alone. That was clear. If he had wanted company, he would have gone to where there were lots of people around, or at least a few people. The question was stupid. He had by his actions indicated his preference; and, of course, he was in no position to stop anyone from getting out of a boat and into the water.

The first man shrugged his shoulders and spoke to his friends. Then he plunged overboard and came up within a few yards of Speck. He swam a stroke or two and dived, disappeared.

At the same moment Speck rolled over. The only thing for him to do was to start back to shore. He glanced at the boat, at the men in the boat, took a deep breath, or almost took a deep breath. Suddenly he felt himself dragged down below the surface. He struggled. As he came up he saw a second man in the water, beside him. The second man caught hold of Speck's hair and forced his head below the surface again. Speck tried to break free from the second man's grip but he felt the first man's hands close on his throat. Speck was not only a strong swimmer but he was strong. He kicked out. He thrashed. He tried to strike one of the men, to disable him. He could manage dealing with one. Together they were going to drown him.

In the last minute of his life Speck cursed himself for a fool. He had thought back through each assignment when it was finished. The kill -- he thought of them as kills -- had always been careless, left him an opening. Some he had seen die and always with a foolish look of surprise. They had thought they were alone; or they had thought he was harmless.

Now he was the one who had blundered. He had liked his solitary swimmings, the floating under the sky. He had enemies, would have made enemies. But he never left a trail to be followed. Moreover the Security Force protected its own.

Then a terrible thought -- could these men be Security Force? Had the highest circles decided that he was dispensable, something to throw aside, to destroy? There were things that he knew that could be dangerous to those who had made use of his talents. Who else could have sent these hunters to find and to leave him, a drowned man, a corpse, maybe found, maybe not? Speck, Speck missing, the men who had sent the hunters would know. He made a last, now hopeless, effort. It was no good.

The two men left Speck's body bobbing a little as the wind rose. The sky was beginning to cloud. The men climbed into the boat. The boat started up, moved away in the direction from which it had come.

"I never did anything like that before," the first man said to his companions.

The second man grunted. It was a first time for both of them. The planning was perfect. They had to admire their planners. And they knew about Speck from their planners. God would forgive their dealing with Speck.

15

TV Back-up to Court Decision Canceled

"My contract," Dorothy New reminded him. "My contract. I'm not just a face and a voice. My contract makes me a producer. I conceive, I make the program. I get one super special a year and this is my super special. I get three hours. Prime time. Everywhere. The full audience."

Harry Fresser was sick of the contract. "I know your damned contract," he said.

Dorothy pointed out that no one made him sign it. He wanted to sign it. He knew her value, had all sorts of studies, needed her when Marietta became Secretary of State. All she had asked for was in effect a copy of the contract Marietta had had, except that Harry paid her less money. She reminded Harry of that. For her the program, the scope, the freedom to present ideas was primary. Money was second. Marietta charged 20 million dollars a year. She was contented with ten.

"You know the program is big, " she insisted. "This is the biggest thing that has happened in anyone's life time. I'm going to call it Confrontation and everyone will know what it is. Aleman Villa confronting the U.S., calling his people at Chapultepec to go to the land of milk and honey. The Supreme Court confronting the Congress. Essentially, and I hope you take this in the right spirit, Harry, the women who know the difference between right and wrong confronting the old men who don't."

Harry thanked her for the compliment. "Maybe I don't know that difference, Dorothy, but I still know arithmetic. I know how to add. Do you realize how much money you're spending?"

Miss New said nothing.

"I've got five million feet of film. I have 60 hours of pictures of federal marshals passing out papers to members of state legislatures. And do you know anything about state legislatures? A collection of Popular barbers and real estate agents. Members of the ladies' auxiliary who go to bed with everyone at the Legion Post. Who wants to see them?"

"This is history," Dorothy said. "You are recording history. No one has ever done it before. The complete record. As the audience sees what I've got for them, they will see things as they are, the truth, the whole truth."

"The Popular barbers and the Popular lady auxiliaries versus your holy nine on the Court?"

"Yes, Harry, as simple as that."

"And where did you get those shots of the Speaker and old Senator Dismukes, looking like a couple of corpses?"

"My crews did the best that they could," Miss New assured him. "As a matter of fact I kept only the most favorable footage."

"The same, no doubt," Harry said, "was true of the governors."

"I know you're being sarcastic," Miss New said. Harry had a sharp tongue but she was patient. "But I did for them what I did for your friend the Speaker and Senator Dismukes."

"How come," Harry asked, "you have nothing on your friend Louisa Clymer and the service on her?"

"My friend Miss Clymer -- as you call her, refused to cooperate."

The Marshal of the Supreme Court, Olga Feemster, had gone in person to serve the order requiring Louisa to deposit a billion dollars or so to the account of the Court. A camera crew had gone with her. The Secretary of the Treasury would see the Marshal but be damned to the camera crew. The Marshal had urged that the camera crew be regarded as an indispensable part of the ceremony but Louisa brushed aside the suggestion. She accepted the paper, thanked Marshal Feemster for coming in person and said she would consult counsel, Treasury Counsel, the Attorney General, somebody or other.

"You understand," Olga Feemster had pointed out, "that the Chief Justice expects me to wait for a draft."

"I don't think she would want you to be absent from your office that long," Louisa had told her.

It was embarrassing but the Marshal had left Nita's chambers with the instruction not to come back until she had the money. The Court, the Chief Justice had underlined, did not have enough on hand for its next payroll. There was enough for the Justices, enough for the Clerk and the Marshal, enough for only a handful. But there were no funds for the thousands who made the Court a great social instrument.

For example, the Enforcement Bureau which was attached to the Marshal's office had nothing available in its account. It would be a terrible loss, if not fatal, to lose any of its highly trained personnel. Miss Feemster did not think it prudent to disclose everything to Louisa, but she hinted, she lifted the curtain a little. The words were all wasted. Like the camera crew, the Marshal went away empty-handed.

The Chief Justice and Miss New did not like such treatment. Miss New would have some shots of Miss Clymer, photographs from an unfavorable angle and in a not very flattering light. And she would report that there were those who regarded the Secretary as engaged in a scheme to sabotage the law of the land. For her part the Chief Justice ordered research on suitable penalties for Louisa's contempt.

"You know Harry, Dorothy said, "I'm not sure that three hours will be enough for what I think ought to be done." Contracts were contracts. She was due only three hours. Nevertheless Harry should see that this was his opportunity, not simply hers. He could make himself famous forever as the man who by his vision settled once and for all the struggle between the Judiciary and the two minor branches.

Harry listened.

They would begin in Mexico City, the Eurasian Embassy in all its magnificence, the earnest, serious Troyenko, the world class diplomat, the earnest, serious staff. There would be shots of the adjoining streets -- Mexico City, the best of Mexico City, with its pulsing, vital crowds. Then the ruins. The giant crater where the Embassy had been. The shattered dead. Empty rubble. The fires. The injured. Then the President of the Republic, dark, sober, somber, mourning the victims but always with dignity. There would be the gathering crowds, women weeping, the men quiet and, like Porfirio Aleman Villa, always with dignity, silent. Perhaps a shot of Aleman at Chapultepec, the massive crowd response.

They would cut then to Moscow, the towers of the Kremlin, more mourners, Globus the bereaved father-in-law. Cheka was difficult. There were no, almost no pictures of Cheka. A peculiar man who forbade the taking of photographs. None at all since he became Manager or whatever he was. Few, very few earlier. A quiet man always, modest, reclusive, quietly working for peace. Dorothy would search the library again, the libraries. Someone would, probably Harrison Swing, come in to read Cheka's letters, to talk about the murder of Dudorov and the concern at his death among a people for whom life was sacred.

"Then, of course, we would come home. First, Washington, Walter Blossom, the White House, the Secretary of State, expressing horror at the destruction in Mexico City, Miss New, herself, would come in to tell about the speculation on the cause of the blast." There would be a shot of the Intelligence Group complex, photographs of its head.

"You can't do that," Harry Fresser announced.

"Censorship," Miss New began.

"Censorship, my foot," Harry said. "You aren't going to get me in a libel suit."

"Oh, Harry," Dorothy said, "old Mr. Carmody isn't going to sue you for libel. Anyhow, you know the Supreme Court would protect you. I can say simply that there were people who said, that the Eurasians suspected. That would be good journalism. They explain that in all of the schools. You ask the lawyers."

"No." Harry was firm.

Miss New was hurt. However, she would use the same footage - - nothing was wasted when she came to the Dudorov sequence. The mysterious stranger, the killer, sheltered by the old man.

"Go on," Harry said.

"The Court," Miss New went on. "We do the Court. We would go to the First Chamber, upstairs to the old Senate Chamber, to the old new building, to the new new one. There would be a still -- they had no moving pictures of Chief Justice John Marshall, films of Earl Warren walking and talking, on the bench, in his Chambers. Then Chief Justice Pfuhl, the first Madam Chief Justice. A voice would read some of the noblest language of her great opinions as background."

"All right," Harry said. Enough was enough. "Let's get on to the niece."

Dorothy sighed. Nita had been very gracious. We saw her in her chambers, with the 1200 volumes of Supreme Court Reports on the shelves around her. Then Nita at home, tending her flowers, gracious and human.

"How about Marvin Mazo. Do we get him too or some other current companion?"

"You're being vulgar," Miss New said.

"I'm not objecting," Harry insisted. "I thought we were doing the human bit. Better a man than a woman."

Miss New said nothing. There was no point in commenting. It was like the ladies auxiliaries going to bed with the boys down at the lodge. Harry had no sense of how people lived, of how free their lives were. Harry was out of date, on the shelf. Things would be better when he retired or died. Everyone died. Oddly enough for a moment the thought was dismaying.

She had said that Nita was gracious. Actually they had a quiet, warm interview, a woman of great intellect and compassion. Then the Cheka letter press conference, the queenly Chief Justice.

"At that point, Harry," Miss New explained, "we go back to Mexico. Crowds in the streets."

Harry broke in. He hoped they weren't paying for the crowds. A big crowd was expensive. The crowds were free, Dorothy told him; all the crowds, domestic and foreign, and they were good, forceful and boiling. Lots of signs, lots of noise.

Dorothy went on. "We come to grips with the Treaty. Stills -- President Polk, Zachary Taylor, General Scott, Santa Anna. A map of things as they were -- Mexico as New Spain."

Harry grunted.

They would show the new Texas, the states in the southwest, California, the fine houses, the stores, the grand buildings of Houston and Dallas, San Francisco, Los Angeles, the fertile fields, the dams, the highways, the immense wealth that was stolen.

"Oh come," Harry objected, "none of that existed at the time of the Mexican War. It was a waste land, nothing at all."

"It was all there in embryo, waiting there in the future." She had charts -- the research people had made her beautiful charts. The charts showed the gold taken out of California, the oil. They showed the copper stolen in Arizona, the oil stolen in Texas. The old values, the real values. All this was capital that had been taken from Mexico. They were very clear and convincing, the charts.

"You know, Dorothy," Harry told her, "you have to know better than that."

Miss New sighed again. The Harry Fressers were hopeless, blind, rigid, fixed in their limited ways of seeing the past, present and future. "We'll go on," she said. "We are nearing the climax. Now we get to the confrontation."

"It's about time, Harry commented.

Miss New ignored the remark. Here the issue was joined. Here was the point of conflict. The Chief Justice and the Court knew what was at stake: justice to Mexico, an end to the shame of Guadalupe Hidalgo.

Even more the Chief Justice responded to man's desire for peace, for beating swords into ploughshares, for recognizing that all men are brothers, all women sisters, everybody brothers and sisters.

The confrontation was with those who preferred injustice, who wanted war and destruction. Another view of the ruins in Mexico City, another view of the injured would make it all vivid. They would show those who desired injustice and death: the Congress in session, members scratching their ears, picking their noses, the Speaker, Senator Dismukes, noting their ages, born long ago, brought up in darkness, the Congress acting with its abortive amendment, its attempt to destroy the Court. The Chief Justice had had the cameras in while she signed her orders. Dorothy had the signing.

"I know all about that. And I've seen the service bit. I've already complained about all the expense. Then what do you have?"

Miss New had the ratifications -- 49 states. Massachusetts had been the only state with the decency to reject the amendment.

"I hope," Harry observed, "you aren't going to give them 49 ratifications."

Miss New was reasonable. A couple would do. As for the Treasury's defiant behavior, they had interviews with the Court's staff, loyal, committed to performing their duty.

"Trusting to get their back pay," Harry said. "They could be wrong. Go back and see them in a couple of months."

"Be serious, Harry. We have to do this in the next week or the week after. What we want is impact, to .... "

"To what?" Harry asked.

"To mold them. To guide them. The audience. To make sure that they see things as they are."

"What do you want to happen, Dorothy?"

"What I expect to happen," Dorothy said. "The Treaty annulled. The killer of Dudorov sent back to his punishment. The property of the Republics restored. Reparations, just reparations for the horror in Mexico City. All the tensions relieved. Then peace."

"All passion spent, Dorothy?"

Miss New looked surprised. Harry was quoting something from somebody. She was sure she had heard it before.

Harry was pleased. "You won't believe it," he said, "but I went to school. In fact Eliot and I both went to school, and read books. I even remember some of them, even reread them. I don't suppose you ever read old books."

There were too many new books, too many new insights, Dorothy said. To keep up with the new books was enough for her generation.

"No old poetry Dorothy?"

"We, the people my age, live in the present." They certainly had no time to waste. They had the present and, of course, the future to think about and to shape.

"Going back," Harry said, "I suppose the Queen Bee told you the future she planned? They tell me she likes to write opinions early rather than later."

"I know – in confidence, of course – a draft opinion but she did not show it to me and I did not ask to see it."

"But you talked freely? An open, warm conversation?" Harry suggested.

Miss New told him he was being offensive.

"Madam is keen to have your big special before she gets down to business?"

"That is my impression, Harry," Miss New conceded.

"And you regard it as a great compliment, Dorothy."

"Yes, I do, Harry," Dorothy admitted. "And I was moved when the Chief Justice told me that she counted on me to prepare the ground; to be the teacher, to get everyone ready."

"A kind of Dorothy the Baptist."

Miss New looked disapproving. Harry was being profane.

"What it comes down to," Harry said, "is that your friend wants to borrow my ladder. She needs a ladder. I have a ladder. She assumes she can use it. She thinks you have the key to the shed where I keep it." Harry was angry, visibly angry. "I've told you I'm a beer salesman, that I sell any trash for so much a minute. But Dorothy, there are limits even for me. I'm not going to advertise the goods your friend wants to sell. You can go back and tell her. No more free time for her. And no paid time, for that matter. I own Planet. You don't. She doesn't. No Confrontation Special, Dorothy. In fact, no broadcasts at all.

"My contract," Dorothy began.

16

Cheka Sends Agent to Spur
"Chaos by Court Order"

"The Americans," Cheka said, "are like a dog chasing his tail. They are going in circles."

"In circles?" Ulianov asked. He had been following all the reports, all the stories. He could make nothing out of them. He was mystified. Cheka, of course, could explain it all to him.

"In circles," Cheka repeated. "As I say, like a dog, like a dog chasing his tail." This was one of the American phrases he liked. "You understand, Josef Vissarionovich, all the Americans tell each other that they are governed by laws -- not governed by men."

"But that makes no sense," Ulianov objected. "How can they say that?"

"They say it and they believe it. They all believe it. They carve it on buildings."

"That must be," Ulianov said, "very expensive."

"Right," Cheka agreed, "you are right. The carving is very expensive."

"And they believe it because it is expensive?" Ulianov asked.

"No, no," Cheka explained, "they carve it because they believe it."

"But they make laws all the time," Ulianov pointed out. "I have seen whole rows of books. Their Congress is always making new laws."

"You are right again," Cheka agreed. "They make laws all the time."

Ulianov remembered something of what his grandmother had told him. "It is like the virgin birth, Vladimir Ilyich?"

Cheka nodded. He was pleased. Ulianov was very intelligent to make such a connection. "Exactly," he said. "A matter of faith." Ultimately and basically everything was a matter of faith. The questions had to stop at some point even for the Eurasians but there was no need to discuss that with Josef Vissarionovich.

"And," Cheka reminded, "you have seen rooms full of the opinions the American judges write for their lawyers to study."

Ulianov had seen such rooms. But did anyone read them?

"By day and by night," Cheka assured him. "For the Americans, what the judges say is the law. They have the last word."

Ulianov had been told that. He supposed it was so. But how could it be so? A judge was a minor official, even highly placed judges. A judge knew his place, consulted his betters and decided accordingly. To pay much attention to judges was foolishness.

"The judges," Cheka explained, "the American judges decide what a law means after it is enacted."

Ulianov thought that was nonsense. "If there is any question about what a law means, Vladimir Ilyich, the sensible thing would be to ask the people who wrote it. They would know more than anyone else about what they intended and did." When he issued an order it was for him to decide how to apply it.

Cheka nodded again. Ulianov was right. What the Americans did was foolish but they took pride in their folly. It had been the cornerstone of their system. They were stuck with it, as they said. "So you see," he went on, "they are chasing their tail. Their Congress acts. The judges ignore it. They send out what they call injunctions. They are orders that everyone must obey. Their highest court wishes to give away a third of their people and break up the Union. Their Congress opposes but in the end they will have to accept this law that they worship."

"But," Ulianov objected, "they have their Mr. President Blossom. What does he say?"

Cheka opened his hands. "You saw their Mr. President Blossom," he pointed out.

Ulianov agreed. He had seen their Mr. President Blossom.

"A good man. A sincere man. What do good and sincere men do in a storm?"

"Not much, Vladimir Ilyich."

"Exactly," Cheka said. "I don't worry about Mr. Blossom, not for five minutes." That was one more American way of expressing himself.

"So you think everything will go well, will go as we want?"

Cheka nodded. It was so far, so good. The problem was to create disorder and then to increase it, to split and to fragment. The European states had had their chance to protect themselves from the rising American power but they were timid or, maybe worse, blind.

The Civil War, the War Between the States, whatever you called it, had been a lost opportunity. He would have known how to use it: help to one side, then help to the other, money here, money there, arms to the needy, more battles, longer campaigns. In the end there would have been exhaustion, a lasting division, perpetual enmity.

And the Americans would never have become the heirs of Europe, the colony intervening in the affairs of its elders and exercising the authority of numbers and wealth. But history was little more than a list of such blunders. So far as he could make out the troubles that came to a climax in Lincoln's election had been homegrown, spontaneous, unmanaged. He had sensed the present troubles years before, sensed their promise, helped them develop, indirectly, quietly.

All that was needed had been supplied: funds for good causes had been forthcoming, grants from respectable sources to insure that studies were made, books published, publications supported. It was a matter of insuring what the Americans valued and called a free intellectual climate. The money had been cost-free so to speak, part of the profits of Omnium. George Sidon was a celebrated financial figure and equally famous for his giving to cultural causes.

Confusion was ripening now into conflict. So far, so good. They had reached the critical point and they must make the best of it. Schmiedegen had been sent to Mexico as Troyenko's replacement, a much better man, and he was getting results. He had dictated the Chapultepec land of milk and honey speech and he knew how to make use of it.

They had sent Zenner to Washington to make certain that the lovable and familiar Scriabin understood his orders and made no mistakes. Zenner knew Medusa Mendes' assignment and would see that she carried it out. It was better to keep Scriabin in his usual role, the genial host, the senior diplomat present, living proof that citizens of the Eurasian Republics were sociable and a threat to nobody.

"I haven't heard from Schmiedegen today," Cheka said.

"He called me," Ulianov explained. "He did not want to bother you. Everything is in order. The mass is in movement, he says. He will need more food, more tents, more supplies and they are available. He estimates there will be at least ten million Mexicans to supply at the border by the end of the week."

"A respectable number."

"With more moving behind them. The Chapultepec speech was very effective, Vladimir Ilyich." The speech had been Cheka's idea. Ulianov's first principle was to give credit where credit was due.

Cheka nodded. Protocol required that Number 2 always compliment Number 1 on whatever Number 1 did. He had observed the rule in his time but he thought Ulianov overdid it. "And do our observations confirm? Our satellite pictures?"

Ulianov shrugged his shoulders. "Ants," he said, "long files of ants. Armies of ants."

"Schmiedegen has Aleman Villa on his way to the border? There must be more speeches, two, maybe three. He must encourage his people."

Ulianov nodded this time. The arrangements were made. Schmiedegen followed orders, unlike Troyenko who always was difficult. But Schmiedegen did not have Globus for a father-in-law.

"And the Alamo thing?"

"Schmiedegen says Medusa Mendes has scheduled it and has everyone ready."

Cheka was pleased. "A good report, Josef Vissarionovich. I like the way Schmiedegen attends to his business. And the Alamo will be useful. Medusa Mendes is a capable woman. When a project appeals to her no one is better and the Alamo thing will appeal to her -- as a beginning.

"She looks forward to San Diego, according to Schmiedegen," Ulianov observed.

There was no need for Cheka to comment. Like everyone with real talents, Medusa Mendes enjoyed exercising her talents. He was giving her a chance to use all her skills. When he was much younger he felt that his seniors did not recognize what women could do. In his 20 years as Chairman he had made a point of encouraging their taking a full part in the management of the Eurasian Republics.

Men were seldom as zealous. Women were unequaled at getting information from the reluctant. As prosecutors women were best. Women were faithful to the rules as laid down. Women could be counted on to reeducate those who needed reeducation. Women -- unlike even a Dudorov -- never faltered. Women had a strength of character that was unique -- but needed direction. Zeal always needed direction. And Medusa Mendes was a paragon among women to judge from her record.

Ulianov asked if Cheka were satisfied with Zenner's performance. His own feeling was that Zenner was good, very good. Again Zenner had been Cheka's choice.

Cheka was satisfied. Zenner was the right man at the right place at the right time. Cheka had listed the moves. Zenner was making the moves. Zenner had the right color, a leading intellectual figure, a writer well known as a poet, celebrated equally as a writer of novels, world class -- as the Americans said -- as a journalist. Versatile was the word.

There was speculation in some quarters as to who might have written the poems and novels but the books had Zenner's name on the flyleaf and they were officially Zenner's. As a journalist, Zenner talked to the great, explicated the past, looked into the future. Zenner was always photographed in his personal library, surrounded by books, in the 14 languages in which he was fluent, highly educated at six universities, a recipient of honorary degrees, Eurasian and otherwise.

Zenner was not only distinguished but he looked the part, a classic man of distinction, notable, too, for his somewhat old-fashioned beautiful manners. Cheka was proud of him, having invented him in a way. Only he and Zenner knew Zenner's real name or his history. Only he and Zenner knew the extent of Zenner's talents and Zenner's accomplishments and his usefulness. He expected good results from Zenner's assignment for the day -- an interview with the Chief Justice. Women responded to Zenner. They talked to him freely.

As Cheka expected, the interview -- which took place a few hours later -- was all that anyone could have wanted. Zenner had spoken to his dear colleague, Marvin Mazo. He had come to the United States to observe, to learn about the constitutional stresses and strains which seemed to be reaching some kind of climax. Watching and learning, he hoped he would be able to explain this distinctly American development to his own people, to interpret and educate.

After all, above everything, he and Mazo were both students and teachers. Mazo, he knew, was acquainted with the Chief Justice. She, he was certain, was busy, overwhelmingly busy. But if he could see her, however briefly, he would be grateful, eternally grateful. Mazo made the arrangement. The Chief Justice was, indeed, overwhelmed by her duties, but she would receive him in her chambers for a few minutes, a very few minutes.

Like everyone else the Chief Justice knew all about Zenner. In a way it was odd that he had not arranged an interview with her before and she would ask for an explanation. She would take and hold the initiative. She got herself up as though she were about to sit for a portrait. She intended to look her best when Zenner arrived. Marv was to bring Zenner to his appointment, make the introduction, and leave. She would begin the interview by asking her question: why had Zenner neglected her?

If Nita looked her best, Zenner matched her. He was in his best form. He thanked Marv as his dear colleague for his courtesy. He thanked the Chief Justice for allowing him five minutes of her valuable time. Marv left. Nita began with her question.

"You must forgive me," Zenner said, "if I postpone for a moment my answer. I was not prepared for what I see now. They had told me that you were a grand official, the grand official of the Americans. They had told me you were a great lawyer, a profound political thinker, a powerful political force. But they had not told me you were such a beautiful woman." He looked, shook his head. "If I were a painter I would ask only to paint you as you are now."

Nita knew her limitations but then she did not look at herself objectively or with the eyes of a poet and novelist. Zenner perhaps saw her as she really was, as even Marv could not see her. She was pleased, touched. Dorothy New had described her as majestic but she was too small for majesty. To be beautiful was better, much better. She blushed. She repeated her question.

"My answer," Zenner said, "is that I am not in your country often. And I thought of you as august, as someone remote, someone not to approach. I am only a journalist, but a man, a sensitive man. I could have asked to see you but I was hesitant. I feared a refusal. I did not dare to ask."

Nita heard and was flattered and once again touched. It was an explanation from a man who understood her position in the world and deeply respected her. "But now," she said, "you are seeing me now. You have, to use your words, now dared to ask."

Zenner bowed his head. She was right. He would explain. She had borne the burdens and responsibility of her own country for years. Now she carried those of the world, of all of its people. It was imperative that he should see her and inform his own people of the nature of the woman to whom they looked for liberation from the fears that troubled them.

"Dear and beautiful lady," Zenner explained, "you are now a world figure. Now you are the only truly world figure; the one person in the world to whom we all turn our eyes, on whose judgment and strength depend all our lives." Zenner's English was perfect but for artistic purposes he thought it advisable on occasion to scramble his syntax. "And," he went on, "I had no choice. I imposed on Mr. Marvin Mazo's good will and so I am here."

Nita listened. She knew she was important. It was impossible, as Chief Justice, to be unimportant. Certainly she was a national figure, probably a world figure. But it had not occurred to her that she was the central figure in the whole world.

"From North Pole to South Pole, from East Pole to West Pole, all mankind, all womankind, all humankind center on you."

They talked. Zenner made it clear that he understood the proprieties. No one should talk to a judge about a case pending before her. He even used the phrase sub judice. Latin was one of his languages. But this was not a commonplace case between a few parties. In the truest sense everyone was a party.

Over the years a special relationship had grown up between Mexico and the Eurasian Republics. Scientists had established that the Mexican people at the time of the Conquest were Asiatic in origin. Now the blood of the old Mexican people was once again paramount. So the Mexicans were, as Zenner put it, part of the family.

The Eurasian Republics were older sisters of the Republic of Mexico, with a strong interest in its well-being, a great concern about any injustice done to it. A wrong done to the Republic of Mexico was a wrong done to the Eurasian Republics. They were committed to wiping out the injury done long ago by the Mexican War. They preferred, longed for a peaceful solution. Otherwise. But they hoped there would be no question if otherwise.

And the old wound had been reopened by the recent tragedy in Mexico City. Moreover the Eurasian Republics were directly involved. Their Embassy had been destroyed. All the evidence proved that the explosive device had been set off in the Embassy.

All the evidence proved that the scheme was Mr. Carmody's scheme. Nevertheless, the Eurasian Republics did not blame the Americans as a people. They too were Mr. Carmody's victims. And it was Mr. Carmody who had brought about General Dudorov's death. Dudorov, a rising leader and heroic servant of the Republics had been brutally murdered so that Mr. Carmody could steal the state property of incalculable value in his possession.

Zenner read widely. He read even the Bible -- an interesting work. In biblical language we were walking through the valley of the shadow of death. And it was the Chief Justice to whom we looked. We could say that we feared no evil so long as she was resolute in her devotion to law and to justice. She alone could avert the storm that had gathered.

Nita listened. She was not easily moved, she prided herself on not being easily moved. Nevertheless, what Zenner said brought tears to her eyes. She saw that she was -- fate being fate -- inexorably everyone's mother, the universal protector.

"Perhaps," Zenner said after a pause, "I have said too much, imposed on your time."

"No," Nita assured him, "you have been a great help to me. You have given me a clearer understanding of what I must do."

Zenner pointed out what was obvious. The Chief Justice would be subjected to terrible pressure. The Americans were by nature a generous people but there were powerful and selfish elements too. These elements might go to any lengths to preserve their power and wealth. For them the greater world had no meaning. For them the world was only their own narrow interests. To do what had to be done, she, the Chief Justice, must stand like the very Rock of Gibraltar. Could she be the Rock of Gibraltar?

Nita nodded.

"I have no fear of your Mr. President Blossom," Zenner said. "No fear of your Madam Secretary of State. They are good. But Speaker Manners, Senator Dismukes, they are touched by the blindness and envy of age. They could do harm. Mr. Carmody is a danger, reckless with age. The Secretary Clymer is a threat to the future. But I do not have to name names or to warn you."

"No," Nita told him, "you do not need to name names but those are the right ones."

"And the people behind them."

Nita agreed. And the people behind them, whoever was meant.

"You will need to be bold, to strike at them before they strike at you. Your Justice Holmes, you remember, advised always to strike at the jugular." Zenner was pleased with the reference to her Justice Holmes.

Nita agreed again. Justice Holmes had been a wise man, rich in experience. Had Mr. Zenner any idea of what these dangerous elements planned. Had he any suggestions?

"You know what they have done," Zenner said. "Their amending the Constitution, their impeachment procedure. Your own moves have blocked them. What you have is a stalemate but that is because you are forbearing. You must throw thunderbolts. You will know what they are. And you must hurl them before. I hesitate. These are desperate elements. Before, I was going to say, before they turn violent."

"Violent?" The thought was disturbing. People acted by and through and on paper. Words were actions; action was words. But there was the tragic fact of Dudorov's murder. The explosion in Mexico City had not been a paper explosion. Old Mr. Carmody was a violent man. What could the Chief Justice of the United States do if threatened with violence. The office was sacred and had been in all of its history. There was no precedent to which she could turn. No. Violence was out of the question.

Zenner shook his head. Tragically, most tragically he could not agree. Of course the office was sacred. The Pope at Rome had been sacred but that, as she would recall, had not saved Pope Boniface from violence at Anagni. Even in modern times a Pope had been attacked, shot in the Square at St. Peter's. It was unfortunate, but it was true.

Nita was not very clear about Pope Boniface and Anagni. She had heard about the other affair. What then should she do? What could she do?

"You have two things," Zenner said, "your thunderbolts and the love of the people. Above all the love and faith of the people. If you speak out, if you let them know you are threatened you can count on them to rise in their wrath. Then no one can withstand you."

Nita heard, understood. Her next press conference would be one to remember.

"Mr. Zenner," she said, "all I can tell you is that I am grateful to you for your having come to see me at last."

Zenner was honored. He could ask nothing better of life than to serve such a wise and good and beautiful woman. He would tell the Eurasian people that she was obedient to the rule of justice under the law and that the world was safe in her hands. He made his apologies. He had expected five minutes. He had taken two hours.

Nita forgave him. They had been hours that she would always remember with pleasure.

17

Nita Enjoins Congress Action to Curb Court

An hour later at her daily press conference, the Chief Justice began by saying that she had a very important statement to make but that she would first deal with the Court's daily routine. There was talk, loose talk she hoped, of possible impeachment proceedings. The Court was enjoining, had enjoined, such irresponsible action. The injunctions were being served and the Court hoped for, expected, compliance.

The alternative to obedience could only be anarchy, the destruction of the American government. She had confidence that the leadership in the Congress would see that they were on a dangerous course and would withdraw. Had she discussed anything with the President? She had, very briefly, by telephone. He, with the Attorney General, understood her position. The Attorney General accepted the fact that the Court was the ultimate judge of its powers and that its position was sound.

Would the Court bring contempt proceedings against the members of the legislatures who had ignored the Court's earlier injunctions and ratified what she called the abortive Treaty Amendment? The answer was, no. The Court preferred to ignore their conduct and would satisfy itself by treating their votes as a nullity. Would the Court proceed against the members of the Congress if they disregarded today's injunctions? Again, the Court did not wish to engage in unnecessary conflict with anyone.

Did she mean that the Court would not act against anyone who failed to obey the Court's injunctions? The Court was conciliatory. It was not vengeful. It wished to avoid any lasting breach with the other branches of the government. The Court would, however, use its powers against anyone who was in contempt of a mandatory injunction. Did she mean the Court would take steps to enforce obedience from the Treasury?

"The answer," Nita said, "and I speak with regret, the answer is that the Court has summoned the Secretary to appear before the Court tomorrow at noon to show cause why she should not be committed to prison until she obeys the Court's order. The Court will also encourage obedience by imposing a fine of a substantial amount a day, a personal fine, not to be repaid from government funds. The Secretary is, as we all know, a wealthy woman in her own right."

Someone asked if the Court regarded the amended Appropriation Act as a nullity too? The answer was "yes." The existence of the Court was provided for in the Constitution itself and that provision implied that the Congress would make available such amounts as the Court required to perform its functions. Any other view, as she had already made clear, could lead only to anarchy and a breakdown of the government.

"Those matters," Nita said, "I regard as routine. They are part of the Court's usual business. I mean to talk about something quite different."

"I have been told," she went on, "by what you would regard as an impeccable source that there are elements in this country who contemplate the use of violence to prevent this Court from doing its duty in matters now before it. Any threat to this Court -- and to any of our courts -- is a threat to the people at large. This Court, together with all of our courts is the guardian of the Constitution. We are the priests who guard the ark of the covenant. We have heard and balanced the conflicting rights of all the minorities which make up the country. Any threat to us is a threat to the order that we have created. Speaking now for this Court I am calling on the people to give us protection, active protection as volunteer guards, defending the judicial process against its enemies, open and secret."

There was silence. Reporters enjoyed excitement. It was like a sauce that made food palatable that was otherwise dull. Excitement was what got people through from one day to the next. Without tension and noise and uproar reporters would have nothing to do for a living. Without them, people would expire from boredom. The ideal arrangement was to have a daily disaster, a giant fire, a volcanic eruption, but not close to home.

The press, the media, whatever you called it, had enjoyed the dance: the Congress, the Treaty Amendment, the appropriations affair, the

Chief Justice and her injunctions. Their hearts were all with Nita and her collection of judges. After all, for years they had tended and watered the judicial power and rejoiced as it sprouted and grew.

The judges could be counted on to bring about change, quickly, abruptly. Elected officials delayed, took soundings, were concerned about votes. Judges had tenure for life and could do what they wanted. But for the Chief Justice to talk about threats of violence and to call on the people to rise might be an invitation to have a fire, a large fire, in your own house. It was Dorothy, Miss New, who asked the first question.

The impeccable source? Would the Chief Justice care to disclose the impeccable source? The answer, smiling, was that the Court recognized the sanctity of sources under the First Amendment. Surely the First Amendment applied to the Court. When the Chief Justice spoke of violence, was she thinking of direct, physical violence? The answer, regretful, was "yes."

Did the Chief Justice think in terms of some organized guard force? The Chief Justice did. How large? How small? That, the Chief Justice said, would be for the people themselves to determine, would depend on their response to her call for protection. The Court hoped its call would be treated as a call to the performance of a basic civic duty owed by the people at large. That was all she could say.

Generally there was a scramble as everyone left. This time the ending was different. The new injunctions were news but no great sensation. But threats to use violence? And a call for a kind of judicial militia? There was talk back and forth. There were guesses as to the impeccable source. Was there a plot? Who would engage in conspiracy? There were guesses as to what the people would do. What people? How many people? Where and how would they act? On one thing everybody agreed: they had a story.

Even before the press conference ended Olga Feemster, the Court's Marshal, had presented herself at the Treasury. She had a summons for the Secretary. But the Secretary was across the river. For the present she was Secretary of Defense. The upshot was that the Marshal crossed the river, where Louisa made her wait for an hour. Louisa was busy. She was making arrangements to protect the Mexican border of the United States from invasion, however informal, and to maintain domestic order as well. Walter had not agreed to such action but she would see him at the end of the day.

"I have a summons for you," Olga said when she was finally admitted. She felt offended at having been kept waiting. It was an affront to the dignity of the Court. "You know what is in it, of course."

Louisa did not know and said so.

"You didn't see the press conference?" Olga asked.

It was hard to believe that there were people who did not watch Nita's press conference; especially someone who had defied the Chief Justice.

"You'd better give me the summons," Louisa observed. Olga gave her the paper. She read it.

"My instruction is to take you in custody and present you to the Court tomorrow at noon," Olga said.

Louisa looked at Olga. She studied her. "You don't really expect me to let you, as you say, take me in custody?" she asked after a minute.

Olga had her instructions. The Court was going to find Louisa in contempt tomorrow at noon. Louisa was going from the Court to a suitable jail. She was going to pay a large fine, a very large fine. The Chief Justice had explained it all to her. Eventually Louisa would purge herself of contempt -- that was the formula -- and the money would flow again. The sooner, the better. However for the present it would be better for Louisa to resist payment and for the Court to make an example of Louisa. But quite certainly Louisa was not supposed to resist being taken in custody. The law was the law. Everyone was presumed to respect it.

"Of course," Olga said, "I expect you to go with me."

Louisa looked at her again. A stupid woman she thought to herself, very stupid. "I'm very sorry," she said after a moment, "to send you away disappointed but this is a busy day. There are things to do here. There are things to attend to at the Treasury. Tomorrow will be a full day as well. You may tell the Chief Justice that I will not be there at noon. You may tell her also that I find her behavior annoying. It discredits the Court. And now, if you please, I will get on with my work."

Olga had a pair of handcuffs in her purse. Should she use them or not? She took them out, fastened one to her wrist, and held out the other to Louisa. There was no need to say anything. Her meaning was clear. She was inviting Louisa to go with her, quietly. In the alternative, she would walk Louisa out like any other prisoner in the custody of a court.

Louisa touched a button on her desk. A Marine Guard appeared. "Please," Louisa said, "escort this lady to the door where she has a driver waiting for her."

Olga looked at the young man. The young man looked at her.

Louisa touched the button again. A second young man came into the room. She turned to Olga. "The two young men," she told her "will see that you find your way out."

Olga sat and considered. She could make a scene, so to speak. It would be in the news broadcast for the day. She could make history of a kind. However there was the dignity of the Court to remember. If there were a struggle she would not look at her best if there were a photographer at the door and the Marshal of the Court was a high-ranking member of the Court hierarchy. Slowly and with dignity she removed the handcuffs and put them back in her handbag. She got up, walked to the door, turned back to Louisa. "I remind you," she said, "that the Chief Justice will expect you tomorrow at noon." The young men followed her out of the door.

Later in the day Louisa told Blossom about the incident with Miss Feemster. Blossom found it disturbing. He was neutral in thought and deed in any conflict between the Court and the Congress. He had told the press so. But Louisa was defying the Court. Moreover she was not only refusing to obey the Court, she was obeying the Congress. The proper thing was to go to the Court and explain her dilemma.

"Not a chance in the world," Louisa told him. "Madam knows all about my dilemma. She's told everyone she is sending me to the lockup and levying what she calls a personal fine. You can't allow her to do that. You're President, Walter. You're the Executive Branch. If Madam can get away with this nonsense, you become nothing but a ceremonial presence."

Blossom could see that Louisa was right. But he had talked to Luanda. Les had said that he had studied and thought. All his research led to a simple conclusion: the President swore to uphold the law and the law was fixed by the judges. As Les saw it, someone had to have the last word.

"Look, Walter," Louisa said after having had this recital, "you'd better get yourself another Attorney General. There must be a vacancy somewhere. Make Lester a judge. First Circuit, Second Circuit, any Circuit you have. You must have something respectable enough to satisfy Les. But get rid of him, Walter, and get someone else. If the worst comes to the worst, I can take over the Department of Justice on an emergency basis."

Walter appreciated Louisa's advice. He was grateful to her for her offer. "But," he explained, "if I drop Les I'm in trouble with the African Caucus. I promised them Justice. Les was their choice. You ought to know, Louisa, a deal is a deal."

Louisa knew all about deals but there were more important things to consider than contempt proceedings and Lester Luanda's legal opinions. She had come to talk to Walter about the Mexican border. They had made plans. They would act and early on the following day. Naturally, they needed Walter's approval.

"But I can't give it," Blossom said when she was done. "You know I can't give it, Louisa. How would it look to the Hispanic Caucus? It would be racist. It would be an insult to Mexico.

An insult to Aleman Villa. An insult to Castillo. How could I look Castillo in the eye if I do what you ask?"

Louisa's comment was that she doubted that anyone had looked Castillo in the eye since he was four years old, maybe three. "He's too shifty for anyone to look in the eye. And Aleman Villa," she asked, "what has he done for you lately? He made the great Chapultepec Park speech and you can guess on whose instruction he made it. He started this avalanche for his benefit. Not for yours, Walter. He won't be surprised if you try to stop it. If his feelings are hurt, so much the worse for Aleman Villa. And," she concluded, "as for the Hispanic Caucus, did it ever occur to you that there might be an American caucus?"

"A what caucus, Louisa?"

"An American caucus, a United States caucus, people who think of themselves as citizens of one country rather than members of some special group."

Blossom knew what she meant. But such people were a special group too, another minority. You could call them Anglos, or North Europeans, or maybe they included all Europeans. However you looked at them, they were separate from everyone else and they had their own peculiar point of view. They did look on themselves as what Louisa said, as Americans. They probably looked on the United States as a unity, as a country, their country but that was simply their way of seeing things.

They felt superior to everyone else. After all he was one of them. It was a prejudice from which he had freed himself. He had known it in his own family. Blossoms had been around for almost 400 years. They felt they had created the country. But he had educated himself to the broader view as a liberal Popular. The Blossoms had been the majority and they had become one more minority group, existing at the sufferance of all the other minorities.

Louisa was a bright woman. Women were a special group to themselves and bright women, like Louisa, were a separate group in that group.

For nearly a hundred years the intellectual leadership, the press, the elected officials, the judges had moved, slowly at first, then decisively, to create the fine balance of all the conflicting interests that had made possible the miracle of the survival of the United States. It was mainly the intellectuals, the free press and the judges, maybe mostly the judges who had worked the miracle. They had recognized and respected every line of cleavage, every weak point and acted to satisfy every demand from whatever quarter it came.

Thanks to the foresight of the Founders and the wisdom of the judges, the Constitution had covered every contingency, would cover every contingency. It was his duty to honor the achievements of the past, to be flexible, to avoid any action that would offend any element by whose consent the United States had survived.

"That's a beautiful speech, Walter," Louisa said when he was done. "Castillo would love it. The judges would love it. I can hear them now, all clapping their hands and saying amen. But it doesn't move me. Survival? You're ignoring one fact. You stay on this track and the United States won't survive. Your friend the Chief Justice is about to finish it off, she and your friend Castillo and your friend Aleman Villa and maybe Cheka, another dear friend. Your judges are about to give away seven states with everyone and everything in them. And after that you're going to have a state of affairs that will make the Civil War look like a dream of order and brotherly feeling."

"I wouldn't say this myself," Blossom explained. "I discussed the situation with Marietta this morning. I told her your view of it. She says, and I'm only repeating her words. I wouldn't use such language myself."

"And she said?"

"She says you're a hysterical woman."

Louisa looked at him and laughed. "Poor Walter," she said, "you're not allowed to call a woman hysterical. Women can say what they choose. I will tell you a secret, something you should have been told by your grandmothers. God may not be a woman. Do you understand? God may not be a woman."

Walter looked alarmed in spite of himself. Perhaps Louisa was losing her mind.

Louisa saw the look of alarm and laughed a second time. "This is heresy, Walter, but women are really no better than men. Not wiser. Equally foolish. Just as mean. Just as destructive. Women, Walter, are not even angels. Do you follow me?"

"Follow you?"

"What I'm telling you, Walter," Louisa said, "is that because some women want to take all of us over Niagara Falls in a barrel, I feel no obligation to join them. In short, I'm not going to let you commit suicide. The Chief Justice wants to abrogate the Treaty of Guadalupe Hidalgo. I'm going to abrogate her suicide pact. You can sign the order or not. The United States will defend its border with its armed forces beginning tonight."

18

Cheka Hears Voice: Mene   Mene   Tekel

The United States and the Eurasian Republics were equally dedicated to the advancement of science. Enormous sums were made available each year to what were spoken of as their scientific communities. Savants of all kinds were brigaded together to work on promising projects. The ever present objective was to arrive at the ultimate secret by which one could destroy the other with perfect impunity.

Unfortunately this perfection had never been attained but the seekers never despaired. The search and research went on. The best minds were engaged. Human knowledge was extended year after year. The species went on from triumph to triumph. But the absolute prize was elusive. The most profound mathematical minds were used and burned out. The secrets of the microcosm and the macrocosm were revealed and discarded.

If it was reasonably certain that the experts could destroy the universe, neither side could gain an advantage from the final catastrophe. Nevertheless, the explorations went on in space and, more lately, under the earth. Daily reports were made to the Eurasian Security Services. The American Intelligence Group also had its daily summaries.

Cheka distributed honors and laurels, but he had misgivings about the whole business. There was a Scientific Adviser -- the current one Grand Academician I. M. Brilliant by name. Cheka saw him, listened to him, made his own judgments, gave orders. Certain apples from the Tree of Knowledge provoked him to action. A few laurelist academicians found themselves detailed to lower school teaching at Tobolsk or Irkutsk or villages on Sahkalin Island. One or two or three had died on the operating table but those were rare cases.

Cheka knew that knowledge was power and he could see some practical use for something like the devices that had been entrusted to Dudorov but the really ambitious programs made him uneasy.

Brilliant was keen on what he referred to as tectonic destabilization. The continents were floating on plates. The plates moved, a very slow movement. The trick would be to jar the plate, speed it up, make the continent of North America move at, say, 100 miles an hour, down into and under the sea. If that was too much to hope for, the weather could be destabilized so that North America would be turned into desert, or glaciers formed to make it another Antarctica. Cheka listened to Brilliant. Cheka had questions.

If the North American plate moved at the rate of 100 miles an hour, if North America slipped into and under the ocean, what would be the effect on Eurasia? Brilliant conceded that they needed the answer. When they had it, he would report. And the glaciation, what would that do to Eurasia? Again Brilliant conceded that they needed the answer, etc. There was also thought being given, Brilliant said, to earthquakes, major seismic disturbances, to controlled volcanic eruptions, how to start, how to stop. He anticipated the question: they would bear in mind the need to determine what the consequences might be for the Republics.

"And these are all serious projects?" Cheka inquired.

"But, of course, Vladimir Ilyich, Brilliant assured him. "The problem is simple." He quoted Archimedes, who would move the world if he found a place for a lever. "We only need a place for our lever. The power is nothing. We are men, modern men. We have available infinite power from any source that we choose."

Cheka looked more than a little uncertain.

Brilliant explained. "The North Americans are looking in the same direction we are. You understand, Vladimir Ilyich, the scientific instinct moves all of us toward the same ends."

Cheka as always understood.

"Human nature, Vladimir Ilyich. You know human nature."

Cheka understood human nature. It was his secret misfortune that he also deplored it. An effect of age which Brilliant was too young to know.

This is, Cheka thought, still the only planet we have. No one had had any luck with colonies set out in space. They had been the great program in his younger days. There would be agglomerations in space, more and more, larger and larger. Everyone would be happy in space. Or we could settle the moon or the planets, our planets, or somebody's planets.

Earth was crowded, too crowded. The colonies would be like Carthage to Tyre or Magna Graecia to Greece. Earth was small and crawling with its inhabitants, parts of it worse than the others. The colonies would be an escape. People talked about space as their forebears had talked about the Americas, a place to go, a new home.

Unhappily the agglomerations were a fiasco. No one was satisfied. The colonists were dissatisfied. The atmosphere – in the general sense -- was all wrong. Worse, and this was a mystery, first one, then another, agglomeration came apart, disappeared. There was no signal, no warning, no communication at all. The history of the planet colonies was the same. And the American colonies ran the same course: disappointment and then disappearance.

Brilliant and the lesser Brilliants knew the story which was why they had, so to speak, begun to come back to Earth while puzzling over the failure of the colonial ventures. Brilliant thought he knew what concerned Cheka. Cheka was a realist.

"These are not fantasies, Vladimir Ilyich," he said reassuringly. "The earth like all of us has its faults." Brilliant was not without humor. "The San Andreas fault, for example. We could do things with the San Andreas fault. Properly managed we could slide at least much of California under the water. Maybe much of Oregon and Washington State. My people think that would be safe." They had calculated the dimensions of the tidal wave on their computers, that and the probable earthquake. There would be a bonus -- much of Hawaii, the settled parts, washed away by a flood. He gave Cheka the picture.

"And if the computers are wrong, Isidor Maximovich?"

"My best minds deal with the computers, Vladimir Ilyich. My very best minds." Brilliant explained. It went without saying that the best minds would never make a mistake and that the computers were responsible, reliable entities. By definition, the computers' response was infallible.

"Isidor Maximovich," Cheka said, "you, not you as a person but you as a body gave us the computers' conclusion on the colonies. Was it right? Was it wrong? You know what became of the colonies."

The answer was easy. "Those," Brilliant explained, "were older computers."

"And newer is better?"

"For our computers, our methods. Not for everything, Vladimir Ilyich."

"You have asked these newer and better computers about colonies, about living in space?"

That was an embarrassing question. Brilliant's people had not asked them that question. But there was no reason to ask it. They had newer ideas, newer problems to deal with.

"Of course," Cheka said. "Nevertheless, it would be something to ask them. A practical test."

Brilliant agreed. "I regard that as an order," he said.

"You understand what concerns me," Cheka went on. "This destabilization you talk of. We have only one house to live in. We don't want to destroy the house. A splendid idea. Your North American plate spins faster and faster and nothing is left. A lost Atlantis. We all know the myth. If a myth. We are not damaged. No one is damaged except our North American friends. A feat. A marvelous feat. No loss to our side. But, Isidor Maximovich, the North American lands produce wheat, produce food which is useful. There are more and more mouths to be fed."

Brilliant nodded. That was a fact to consider. He had hinted to the Double Marshal that perhaps Science could solve the American problem by drowning the continent. It was indiscreet on his part. As Scientific Adviser his ideas were for the Chairman alone to consider. But he and the Double Marshal had been seated together at a dinner.

The Double Marshal had asked if there was anything new. Anything really new. He had been surprised by the Double Marshal's reactions, disapproval more than approval. Enemies were to be vanquished but you wanted the taste of the pleasures of conquest. Also you wanted the fruits of the conquest. He hoped the Double Marshal -- he was happily somewhat forgetful -- would say nothing to Cheka.

"Your people," Cheka said, "your people were to give us the kind of climate we need. Less cold. Better rain. An improved growing season. Everyone knows what your science has done. Less disease. Longer lives. A new army of people each year. We need the climate improved. Or will we have to rely on epidemics and famines?"

It was a delicate subject. The really good minds concerned themselves with schemes like the tectonic plate project. Only the second rate, inferior minds were available for programs for improving the weather. It was, Brilliant supposed, human nature again, difficult to explain. The imagination responded best to the challenge of devising means of destruction. To ask his prime physicists to think about improving the climate was to invite them to boredom. He had tried. He had seen their response, understood their response. He felt as they did. No excitement, no interest. He had given up on his number one minds. The number twos and threes were doing their best.

"My people are trying," he said. A little progress perhaps. Nothing really encouraging. Cheka's bluntness, epidemics and famines, or was it humor? Cheka's sometimes odd humor was maybe close to the truth. Perhaps it was advisable to move the conversation in another direction. Cheka had some old-fashioned interests, surprisingly old-fashioned for a man of his character. He generally asked after one of the older programs, the search for what was called extraterrestrial intelligence; what was known as the messages or voices program to the best minds, who all thought of it as a joke. He explained to Cheka they were still looking, still listening.

"And?" Cheka asked.

"The more equipment we have, the better equipment we have, the more noise we find. The whole universe is noise, in a way nothing but noise."

"Voices?"

"You could describe them as voices, Vladimir Ilyich, babbling, discordant, nothing with meaning as we recognize meaning."

"The voice of a crowd?" Cheka suggested. The total sound had no meaning but if you could sort out the sounds, distinguish the voices, then you discovered intelligence, human intelligence. You had, of course, to know the language that the crowd spoke and to understand the language as well. Did Brilliant agree?

Brilliant agreed. Cheka always surprised him with his thoughts and reflections. Cheka would have been a useful member of his, Brilliant's, staff. Not a trained mind but an interesting mind.

"There is nothing that you can distinguish, no dominant sounds, nothing repeated?" Cheka asked after a moment.

Something occurred to Brilliant, something that the messages and voices types had reported and kept reporting. They were not first caliber people, not thinkers, not solvers of riddles, nothing but people who listened, recorded, did exercises comparing the sounds that they heard with any and every language known since the beginning of time. They had heard something, heard it over and over, for a day, then another day, more days, loud, diminishing, then louder. They had described it to him as assertive. The sound had continued, was continuing.

He had not listened himself -- Scientific Advisers had no time to waste on the less significant projects -- but he had given them a quarter of an hour to play some recordings. The sound was certainly distinct, a powerful sound, perhaps what Cheka called dominant, certainly repeated. He told Cheka about it.

"You say it was distinct? And what was the sound?"

"Sounds, Vladimir Ilyich, two different sounds, maybe three. My people can make no sense of them."

"You recall them" Cheka asked.

Brilliant assured him that he remembered them. But sound was not his special field, not even one of his fields. He could not give a really technical account of what he had heard. There was a special vocabulary for each set of specialists which was, of course, what made them specialists.

"Yes, yes," Cheka said. He liked learned men within limits, but their refinements and qualifications could be annoying. "So far as you can, shall we say, reproduce them. What were the sounds?"

"Roughly, apologetically," Brilliant said, "doing the best that I can, coming as close as I can to it phonetically, it was something like many many tackle. It means nothing to anyone."

Cheka said nothing for a minute. So many many tackle meant nothing.

"Or," Brilliant added, "it could have been minny minny tickle, Vladimir Ilyich. I do not have what they call perfect pitch."

"But the sound was strong? A mechanical sound? A sound like a voice?"

Brilliant thought. It was hard to be certain of the difference between what Cheka spoke of as a mechanical sound and a voice. It was a distinction that would only occur to a layman. To the scientifically trained a sound was a sound. To hear a voice without an accompanying body could be a sign of dementia. There were patients in hospitals who were treated for just such a disorder. And to hear a voice in space was an even worse symptom. But it did sound like a voice, if you could think like a layman. He told Cheka, yes, maybe, a voice.

"Authoritative?" was Cheka's next question.

Brilliant again had to think. The voice -- if a voice -- was strong. It had the ring of, maybe, Cheka's voice when he gave one of his orders or the Double Marshal's when he expressed an opinion about how to make war.

"Vladimir Ilyich," he said, " you are asking for a subjective opinion but if you insist I would say yes, a tone of authority."

"And the source? Can you fix a source for a voice in space, Isidor Maximovich?"

Brilliant considered. That would not be a problem for the messages and voices types. His best minds could perhaps deal with it if they were directed to find the source of a sound, an anonymous sound, not a voice, voice being a word to suggest a person. Yes, they could determine the source if they were managed in the right way.

"You will manage them in the right way, Isidor Maximovich. I have confidence in you. And you will say nothing about this until we know more."

When Brilliant left, Cheka thought about what Brilliant had told him. There were obvious questions and Ulianov could get him the answers. There were always useful connections with the American scientific performers. He wondered what Mr. Carmody knew about the voice -- or whatever it was. In the meantime he would listen to the voice -- not a recording -- himself.

19

Secretary of State Marietta Protests Louisa Move to Defend Border

It was a normal evening for Harry Fresser until he was told that Secretary Snow was coming to see him. He had listened to Dorothy's broadcast with the double big news of the day. The news was, Harry thought, like a suit with two pairs of pants, maybe more than you wanted or needed. The Chief Justice was recruiting what sounded like a private army to Harry. And the United States Army, or some of it, was being sent to close the Mexican border and was to maintain order generally where it was threatened. Dorothy had welcomed the first development, as she spoke of it, and had been outraged by the immorality of the other. Before she was through, there was some confusion in what Dorothy said.

As Dorothy stated it, the Chief Justice needed protection, the Court needed protection, the processes of justice needed protection. There were plots -- she, herself, had heard of unsettling discussions among enemies of the Chief Justice. The plots had to be dealt with.

The Chief Justice had appealed, and rightly, to the public at large for whom she was shepherd and watch person. Properly speaking, she might have asked for protection by the armed forces of the Republic. But, the Chief Justice, like everyone, understood that the Army, with a capital A, was not so much a real army as the employer of last resort of the young or needy of pre-retirement age. It was a criminal act to expose them to violence. It might have been correct to invoke their aid for the Court in its hour of need. To expose them to violence on the border was shameless and cynical. But there was real hope that our uniformed women and men, in spite of their orders, might be spared the anguish of opposing their poor Mexican sisters and brothers.

The Chief Justice, the Court as a court, might enjoin their use by the Executive branch. Papers for that purpose were being drafted according to the best information she had. Moreover the personnel of the Army were human beings with their own conscience and feeling. They were not so many machines and might well refuse the role of automata.

It sounded to Harry as if Dorothy was, as the phrase went, inciting to mutiny. If so, Planet might be, even he might be, regarded as an accomplice. Dorothy, sincere, with a heart as big as a house, kept the lawyers busy reading their books and distinguishing cases. More to the point she kept him worrying. He was about, maybe, to call her, when Secretary Snow, in person, arrived.

Harry's first reaction was that Marietta did not look her best. She had a new designer dressing her. So far as he could see, the last one was better but Marietta was always changing designers. She was plain but not satisfied to be plain. She was always in pursuit of a miracle that would make her another Helen of Troy or at least another Louisa. She looked more earnest than usual -- a sign of trouble as Harry knew -- and thanks to this last designer, bedraggled. Even Harry could see that she had been weeping.

"Well, Marietta," he said.

She sat down, dabbed at her eyes. "I've come to you as an old friend, Harry. I have resigned." She dabbed at her eyes again.

Harry was astonished. He had never thought that Marietta regarded him or anyone as a friend. And he would never have expected that she would resign. President was better, but Secretary of State was respectable.

"Did you hear me, Harry? I said that I have resigned." Marietta began weeping again.

Harry tried to comfort her, to say something consoling.

"These tears," Marietta said, "are not tears of regret. I never regret anything, Harry. I'm crying because I am angry."

Harry gave her a handkerchief. The best therapy according to experts on human emotions was talk, unrestrained talk.

"Tell me, Marietta. Tell me what happened."

"Thank you for the handkerchief," Marietta said, wiping her eyes. With all his faults, in spite of all the money he had, Harry was not as bad as he wanted people to think, not as hard, not as callous, Harry was considerate. Harry was a nice man.

"Tell me what happened."

Marietta told him her story. She had been at the White House in the afternoon. It was no secret that the Mexican thing had brought on a crisis and that she and Louisa Clymer were on opposite sides.

"She's a hateful woman," Marietta said. "Reckless and stubborn." Actually Louisa was really not like a woman at all. She was really more like a man, some men at least.

"You were at the White House," Harry said.

"Yes. I was at the White House and when I left, Walter had agreed with me that Louisa should not be allowed to do anything that might endanger our good relations with the Eurasian Republics. This is a very delicate balance, Harry. Ambassador Scriabin had been to see me in the morning, to caution me that his government regarded itself as the protector of the Mexican people and would treat any unfriendly act towards them as a serious matter."

"Meaning what, Marietta?"

"He didn't use the words casus belli but that was what I understood him to mean. That was why I went to see Walter. To warn him. You know what casus belli means, Harry?"

Harry nodded. He knew casus belli.

"Ambassador Scriabin told me that feeling is running high, very high, in all of Eurasia, demonstrations, crowds, banners, all concerned about justice for Mexico and the outrage in Mexico City. A very wide, very deep, spontaneous feeling which Scriabin's government cannot ignore."

"I see it all," Harry said.

Marietta looked at him. Harry was being the hard, sceptical Harry Fresser who preferred to be blind to what was clear to everyone else.

"No, you don't see it Harry," she said to him. "You don't really believe the Eurasians are human and you don't understand their system at all. They have a strong government but it has to respond to its people. They are people like us. Don't forget I was there and can judge them. And Cheka's one aim is peace."

"All right," Harry said, "I'm not going to argue."

"I had Walter's word. He was going to keep Louisa under control. So when I got back to the Department I called Ambassador Scriabin and assured him. I gave him my word that we were committed to peace just as they were. That we would do nothing to the detriment of Mexico or its people. I told him he could assure his government that we understood their position and that we respected it." Then tears came again.

With an effort Marietta went on. "I knew nothing until Dorothy called me. She wanted my comment. Troops were being sent to the border. Why had I kept it a secret? I was humiliated, Harry. Not so much for having Dorothy learn that I was ignorant about something important. But worse, much worse, I had misled Mr. Scriabin. I had misled his government. You see what Louisa had done to me, Harry. She had made me a liar." There was more weeping.

Looking at Marietta, Harry was convinced of the truth of something his mother once told him: women were not at their best when they cried. In particular, Harry thought, plain women should not cry in public. In the circumstances, the best he could do was to beg Marietta not to worry about Scriabin. Scriabin would understand.

"And he won't be embarrassed," he said reassuringly. "His people in Moscow will understand what happened. People are always changing their minds. We all change our minds."

Marietta knew about changing your mind. You were going to put on one dress, then you decided to wear something else. That was simple and harmless. But this was high policy and in the midst of a crisis, a world crisis at that. If Walter had changed his mind, Walter was weak.

"Men are weak, Harry," Marietta concluded, "much weaker than women. Not in physical strength, morally weaker. Easily moved." There were ways a woman like Louisa could manage a weak man like Walter. It was disgusting even to think about what Louisa would do to persuade a weak man like Walter to do what she wanted. She would never consider doing what women like Louisa would do.

Harry conceded that Blossom seemed less resolute than some people he knew. As for Marietta's hints about Louisa and what she may have done, he had his own doubts. Louisa was effective enough as a bulldozer with someone like Blossom. There would be no need for her to play the part of a siren. But the sensible thing was to disregard the whole point. He said again that he was not going to argue.

"At this moment," Marietta said, "the world hangs by a thread. This use of force could make the thread snap. The Eurasian Republics might move their own troops. There could be war. The end of everything, Harry, the world, the whole race destroyed."

Harry Fresser had thought about that subject before. His views were peculiar. In a sense the world came to an end when anyone died. Eliot's world ended when Eliot departed. He was getting on himself so his world would end.

What the Mariettas worried about was having a simultaneous ending for everyone's world, young and old, in between. The Mariettas were unhappy at the prospect of there being no more generations in their own likeness, more lives like their own, going on forever and ever. Their hearts broke at the thought that there would be no more human race, no more of this marvelous creature and its marvelous doings.

After a lifetime he thought the ultimate blasphemy was the statement that God had made man in his own image. This self-described, complacent image of God had murderous rages, blew up and burned its own handiwork, cut its own throat, shot itself, stabbed itself, cooked itself: then, having calmed down, it enjoyed the blessings of what it called peace.

It attended concerts, admired whatever treasures survived in its museums, borrowed money to buy things and pleasures that did it no good, looked at beer advertising, advertising of every thing, wished it were rich, wished it were what it thought of as a celebrity, envied the rich, looked down on the poor, looked at itself in mirrors, found its own smell disgusting and fell into its rages again.

But raging or calm this image of God had always one certainty: it owned the creation and without it the creation was meaningless. Such thoughts, Harry realized, were best kept to himself. Disclosed to the Mariettas or anyone else, such ideas would require professional attention. Forty doctors would compete to heal his sick spirit at so much an hour. Lawyers with enterprise would find a suitable judge to certify his incompetence.

It was bad enough that he had agreed with Eliot to set up an Eliot and Harry Fresser foundation to further the art of communication and high national causes. He could see them all now, expensive lawyers and highly paid mandarins gorging themselves on his and Eliot's remains. There was the old joke: you could not take it with you. But it was better to turn everything over later rather than sooner. He conceded that it would be a calamity to have. the whole race destroyed. After all God had spared Noah and family.

Marietta finally came to the point. She was no longer weeping. She had an objective.

"You have power, Harry," she said. "I think you could save us. You could be another Noah. A Noah."

Harry looked troubled. Marietta had been reading his mind. He had thought Noah; she had said Noah. All he could hope was that she had tuned in, so to speak, just at the end of his thinking. He invited her to explain.

"I want to come back to Planet. I want time, lots of time -- to tell people why I resigned. To tell people what they are facing. To make it all clear. Maybe I could do it alone. Maybe, and better, I could get the Chief Justice -- a fine woman, Harry -- to come on the air with me. We could sit and talk, maybe in my house or her house, or in her chambers. Planet would announce it was canceling all its regular broadcasts, for an hour, maybe two hours. Planet was using all its resources to save mankind from the greatest danger that has threatened it since the Flood."

"Just you, or you and the Chief Justice?"

"I might want other people. Perhaps you should bring back Harrison Swing. Maybe the current Science Adviser, Finemind, Salvador

Finemind. One or two others. Witnesses, Harry, people who can make the picture more vivid."

Harry considered. This was outdoing Noah. There was no need for an ark. Marietta and the Chief Justice plus her witnesses would keep off the rain.

"You think that would do it, Marietta?" he asked.

She was sure that it would. The people were teachable, as she had proved over the years. Given a choice and given instruction, they would always make the right choice. History, at least that of the past 20 years, was proof of it. They would listen and they would open their eyes. They would see and speak out. Everything would be saved. It was his choice, only his choice, and, she was practical.

"You won't lose much advertising money," she said by way of conclusion.

"And when do you want to save the world, Marietta?"

Time was, in the lawyers' phrase, of the essence. Two broadcasts might be better than one. She could use a half hour or an hour at the end of the evening to tell why she had resigned, was resigning.

"You mean you haven't resigned?"

"It will be more dramatic if I resign on the air, Harry," Marietta explained. Few high officials, if any, had ever resigned on the air. She would like to do tonight, her announcement, her reasons, then with Dorothy -- she had spoken to Dorothy -- some questions, some answers. They would want Planet to pass the word -- a big thing at the end of the day, something no one should miss. As a matter of fact her public resignation tonight would be a sign to Scriabin and to his government that they should do nothing at once, should wait for developments. She would conclude tonight by telling her audience that there would be another urgent broadcast tomorrow on which their futures depended.

Harry wondered if he were awake or asleep. Was this real or was it some kind of fatuous nightmare?

"Please don't hesitate," Marietta implored. "I came to you as a friend, the only friend who could help. And not just me, Harry. Everyone needs you tonight."

Well, Harry thought, what they all want is excitement. Business was business and it was his business to keep them excited -- up to a point. Excitement and novelty. Secretaries of State did not, as Marietta put it, resign on the air. The public would like it. They could sit up late and talk and drink beer, consume what his advertisers offered for sale. For Marietta's sake he would be Harry Fresser the grand executive, a demon at making decisions, shrewd, clear-eyed, smarter than any competitor in calculating public reactions.

"You had better get going, Marietta," he told her, if you're doing this resignation tonight. Dorothy is ready?"

Marietta had arranged with Dorothy. She had counted on Harry who was her friend.

"I can think about the sequel. But I will have the boys put Harrison on the rocket, in case we want him. You let me know in the morning about your Chief Justice. But I'm not committed. You understand that?"

Marietta, getting up, nodded. But she knew he would do the right thing.

"That's the problem," Harry said, "to figure out the right thing. And," he added, "change the dress, Marietta. Something simpler is better for resigning in public."

20

Late News Breaks in on Marietta's Resignation: Alamo Burning, Texas Seceding

There was something anticlimactic about Secretary Snow's late evening appearance. For an hour or more the national audience was on the alert. Planet had a sensation in store for them. It was something like advertising an ancient newspaper extra but this would be free. Moreover, no one would be obliged to run out in the street to chase after the newsboy. You could sit at home in comfort and the excitement would arrive on its own.

Marietta came on, to use the technical term, together with Dorothy. Dorothy introduced Marietta, saying, of course, that she needed no introduction. Secretary Snow, Dorothy said, had a statement to make, a significant statement, an important announcement, one to concern every American citizen, not to speak of the inhabitants of every island and continent.

Marietta, having followed Harry Fresser's advice and changed to a simpler dress, told the world that she was, even then as they watched, resigning her position as Secretary of State. It was not only a matter of her personal conscience but of her duty to every American woman and man, to every human being, female or male, on the great globe.

The Mexican crisis had brought humankind to a fork in the road. One road was marked war, one was marked peace. She had fought like a tiger and worked like a slave to have us follow the second road. The elements responsible for the outrage in Mexico City and for denying justice to the Republic of Mexico were moving us on the road headed toward war.

The President knew her position. She had gone down on her knees. She had begged and implored. He had turned a deaf ear, turned a blind eye, in short, had ignored her. Her resignation by itself would have no effect. The sinister elements, of which she had spoken, now dominated the President. But she had faith that by resigning and explaining her reasons, by speaking out as she threw herself under the Juggernaut, by crying out a last warning, the people would heed her last desperate message and save themselves even at the last minute of the last hour of the last day.

She had no need to tell them of what was at stake: their children, always their children, their churches, their schools, their houses, their fields, their forests, their rivers, their full, happy lives, every blessing they enjoyed each day -- or thought they enjoyed.

Dorothy, watching and listening, had tears in her eyes. She was moved by the passion and eloquence. Privately she had always thought of Marietta as wanting in feeling, not a communicator of communicators as billed, too restrained, too prim, too much the teacher. She realized, as she watched, that Marietta had depths she had never suspected. Marietta was a woman of feeling, a piano player with fire but perfect control.

At the last, Marietta, having moved from utter despair to absolute hope was shining like a bright light. Even Dorothy envied her radiance but she was contented with having been on stage, even as no more than an extra, to see the performance.

As for Harry Fresser, he was pleased with himself. He had placed his bet, given Marietta her time, in the expectation that Marietta would give the audience something dramatic, something to bring them awake, something to provoke a reaction. As always, or almost always, his judgment was proved to be sound.

He was still in his prime when it came to knowing what would float, what would sink, no sign of failing, no sign of slipping. He had fed the audience something strong, something raw. It had been a genuine deathbed scene, lighted and wired for sound and leaving, he figured, a large part of the audience scared out of its wits. Or perhaps it was a colossal prayer meeting with Marietta as what they used to call the revivalist.

Unfortunately, before he could decide which it was, he was interrupted by a call from Ed Dunkel, the night supervisor. There was a big story from Texas. Should he break in on the Marietta-Dorothy number? Harry heard, Harry decided. The answer was simple: Planet was first, always first, in informing the people.

The ladies had barely begun the questions and answers, the crowning interview of Dorothy's day, when the audience got the apology. Planet was cutting in, breaking in on Miss New and the Secretary. Planet had a man in San Antonio, a man in Austin with late developments in the tremendous Mexican story.

First the San Antonio chapter. Crowds had begun to gather there about nine o'clock Washington time, probably in response to the announcement that large Army units were being sent to the border and elsewhere. The crowds were quiet at first. Then there were signs of resentment as the local police came on the streets.

There was always bad feeling, of course, when police elements tried to intimidate people exercising their right to assemble but the local authorities were still largely Anglo and had disregarded the guidelines laid down by the local Federal Court in its recent decision in Chicano v. the City of San Antonio. A few stones had been thrown by the crowd. The police had used fire hoses. The response of the crowd was to open fire, some members of the crowd being armed.

The police had unwisely returned the fire and naturally the crowd was enraged and attacked. Guns were used. Knives were used. The crowd, having swept the police force from the streets then marched quietly to the Alamo and overpowered the few night guards who offered resistance. The building was burned by an apparently disciplined group calling itself -- to Planet's reporter -- the Sons and Daughters of Santa Anna, a very orderly group with a woman apparently in command.

The whole affair was, according to your Planet reporter, very much like the Boston Tea Party, a sign of determination by women and men, maybe more women than men, to express their aspiration for freedom. The fire from the Alamo had spread because of the high winds that were blowing. The crowd had refused to allow the local Fire Department to function. But the crowd was enjoying the spectacle in a good-natured way.

Your Planet reporter would keep you informed. There would be, he hoped, films of the crowd and the action later. For the present he was not sure which cameramen, cameras and films might have survived. He would report the casualties --police and otherwise -- later. Harry had no time to worry about his insurance coverage for cameramen before a call came in from Austin.

"Harry," the rough voice said, "Othman Frick here." Othman Frick was the Governor, money, much money, old money, starting in land and cattle, increased fifty-fold when Texas was oil, moved on into communications, soft drinks, software, electronic marvels. Frick Communications did business with Planet, considerable business. Now Othman was in the political game. He had wanted the Governor's mansion. He bought it.

Harry wished the Governor a good evening.

"Good evening, my ass," Othman said. I've got a question."

"Yes," Harry said. "Ask the question."

"The question," Othman said, "is where in the Christ do you find the mealy-mouthed bastards who work for you."

"Which one," Harry asked.

"That goddamned reporter who just went off the air, telling us about the Boston Tea Party."

Harry sighed. "I get them" he said, "at the same place you get your mealy-mouthed bastards. You're in the same business. You've got reporters. We all buy the popular model."

Othman Frick grunted. "We'll drop that subject, Harry," he said. "But aren't these fellows bright enough to see that all hell is about to break loose?"

Harry did not think they were bright enough. If these fellows were bright enough they would not be working for him or for Othman.

"Well," Othman said, "at that they aren't any worse than our President Blossom. I tried to get some reaction from him for a week, but he kept dodging or telling me he had to think. What in the hell is wrong with him, Harry? The only man in that crowd is Louisa Clymer. She can make up her mind."

Harry appreciated that for Othman to call Louisa a man was a compliment. He was a man.

"She finally got Blossom to move," Othman went on. "But we're still way back in the woods. And you people back in the East don't give a damn."

Harry objected. There were people back in the East who were troubled.

"You're right," Othman admitted. "The Speaker, Bright Dismukes, Miss Clymer. But the horses are running away and they don't seem to know how to stop them. That crazy Chief Justice. Your ex-broadcaster Secretary of State."

Harry told him that Miss Snow had resigned on the air.

"I'm glad I was too busy to watch her. And I can't talk much more. I'm going on the air, myself, Harry. You're welcome to watch me."

Harry thanked him. "What are you telling us, Othman," he asked.

"I'm going to speak the God's truth. If it has to, Texas will go it alone. We went out once. We can go out again. Nobody is going to give us to the Mexicans."

Harry asked if Texas could really go it alone.

"If we have to," Othman said. "But we may not have to." For the last two or three days he had been talking to Monte del Monte, the Governor of California, the sweet singer of Monterrey loved by everyone before he swung over to politics. Monte del Monte was pretty sure that California would stand shoulder to shoulder with Texas. So would, Othman thought, the rest of what the damned Chief Justice referred to as the Mexican states. The sister states on their borders might stand with them too. Monte had done some talking. He, Othman, had made some approaches.

"Jesus Christ," Othman concluded, "we could end up with everything on the right side of the Mississippi River if push comes to shove."

Harry listened, had questions. But Othman had to go on the air. They would talk maybe later, surely tomorrow. Harry told Othman to do his damned best. Othman assured him he would tell them the God's truth, give it to them with the bark on. It was late but he knew he had a big crowd waiting to hear him.

"You listen too, Harry," he said. "I haven't told you half of what I have to say."

So Harry listened and watched. Othman was as good as his word. He gave it to them with the bark on. Texas had come into the Union as an independent republic. It would go out again if it wanted. Texas would decide its own future and fate.

He had ordered the United States courts to be closed. All the judges and the court personnel, all the U. S. attorneys and staffs had been rounded up and were being sent on to Austin. He would deliver them to Washington in the morning. Their jurisdiction in Texas was over. Units of the armed forces of the United States were welcome in Texas. Texas had not altogether seceded but it would unless it had guarantees from the Washington government that it regarded the Union as sacred. He could say, further, that if Texas had to go it alone, it would go it alone. But he was confident that other states who felt their security threatened by the action and inaction of the Washington government were likely to join with Texas.

As the old saying went, a word to the wise was sufficient. He hoped his hearers were wise, especially the high and the mighty. This is he said by way of conclusion, Othman Frick, talking for Texas, and wishing everybody good night.

If a diamond, as people had said, Othman Frick was a very rough diamond. If Marietta's performance was a masterpeice of its kind, Othman's was in the same class. Harry was pleased. Planet was certainly keeping people informed and awake, inducing insomnia on a mass scale.

Among the victims, naturally, was President Blossom, alone for a change. It had been a long day. The Speaker and Bright Dismukes had come to see him late in the morning. They were concerned about what they called the craziness of the Chief Justice. The system would work if everybody went by the rules and one of the rules was to remember that logic had limits.

The Chief Justice was ignoring the rule and the rest of the Court was tagging along. They, themselves, accepted part of the blame in having confirmed the appointments of such a collection of idiots to the Court and the lesser courts. You could argue, the Speaker had said, over how we had arrived where we were. He thought it was like what doctors spoke of as arthritis, a slow painless process which came to a painful conclusion. The pain by now was intense.

The Chief Justice was out of control. Even the minor judges had caught the contagion from her. Othman Frick had been calling him. Del Monte had called with the same warning: enough was enough. In both the House and the Senate even the liberal Popular members, even the ladies, had come to him and to Bright to say that they were getting too many complaints from back in their states. They were being pushed over the edge, some kind of edge. Somebody had to make the Chief Justice see reason.

"Who?" Blossom had asked. He was no good with high-powered women.

"You," the Speaker had said, "or if you're afraid to go to her alone, Bright and I could go with you."

Blossom thought the Chief Justice was allergic to men, especially men who gave any sign of resisting her.

"A woman, then," the Speaker had said. He had Louisa Clymer in mind.

"That," Blossom had told him, "would be like throwing gasoline on a fire." Neither one liked the other.

The Speaker had one more suggestion, maybe the best one, Marv Mazo. He could tell the Chief Justice that she was tired, overworked was the word, needed a rest, four or five or six months of quiet, then could come back, take on lighter burdens, share the responsibility for running the country. Failing that, Marv could say, tactfully, very tactfully, there was a risk that she might find herself exposed to removal by those who misunderstood her, misconstrued her objectives.

They agreed on Marv Mazo. Blossom sent his callers away. The Speaker would talk to Marv and Blossom was comfortable until

Marietta arrived to tell him what she had learned about what Louisa intended. She, Marietta, had the concession for foreign affairs. Louisa was trespassing. Louisa was about to endanger the peace of the world and Scriabin had warned her.

She had assured him that she and the President saw eye to eye on the need to maintain the confidence of the Eurasian Republics. All she wanted from Walter was the assurance that he would refuse his approval of any move Louisa proposed that would damage that confidence. The more earnest Marietta became, the more Blossom agreed with her. He would, he would, he would let Louisa do nothing that might cause Scriabin or Globus or Cheka to regard Marietta as a woman whose word was unworthy of trust.

Blossom had done his best when Louisa came in. He had told her about Marietta and his commitment. But she had had information the night before from the old man, himself -- she had gone to see him -- that dangerous plans were being made to the South. Schmiedegen was in charge. Medusa Mendes was acting as his number one agent. He had explained something about Schmiedegen's history, about Medusa Mendes' career.

Othman Frick, an old legal and banking client, had called her from Austin because Blossom was ignoring his calls. There was no worse reputation than to be known as a man who did what he was told by the last woman who spoke to him. Blossom knew that but he gave way. Louisa was saving him from himself and, for better or worse, he felt safer with her than anyone else.

All that would have been enough for one day but he had the Chief Justice's call to arms, as he thought of it, to worry about. He respected women. He had been brought up to defer to them. He knew what was owed to them after thousands of years of their being excluded from high-paying jobs. All the same he was President of the United States and, according to protocol, Chief of State. He had a kind of royal position. When he went into a room, everybody stood up. Nobody could go home from a party while he was around on the premises.

But the Chief Justice had done just that a few days ago -- departed before him, not stood up when he entered. Her explanation had been privately given, and passed on to him, that the time had come to recognize the supremacy of the judges. If she had not pushed herself forward, he and Cheka could have talked out the Mexican thing without creating the mess in which he was involved. He would have known how to handle a man who did what this woman had done and was doing. A few words, very firm, a little strong language. Essentially men were more reasonable, more willing to live and let live. That was their weakness, his weakness.

He felt that again when Marietta resigned on the air without giving him warning. She had neither called nor sent word. All she did was resign. But you could always refuse to accept resignations. That had to be his kingly prerogative. He had no sooner settled that in his mind when he regretted not having given Othman Frick a chance to come and see him and talk. However Texas was only half way out of the house and wanted, apparently, to be coaxed back in the door. If the Chief Justice -- damn the woman -- would let him.

He went to bed after sitting in Lincoln's room for ten minutes and invoking his guidance.

Another interested listener was, of course, the Chief Justice. Dorothy had told her that Marietta had a statement to make and that she would approve. Nita was not in the best of her moods. Olga Feemster's account of her meeting with Miss Clymer had, by itself, ruined her day. The disclosure that troops were being sent to the Mexican border had set off an explosion. Blossom had signed the order and that was defiance, worse than Louisa's defiance.

He was acting on a matter that was, again as the lawyers put it, sub judice. The President was intruding on her jurisdiction, her jurisdiction. It was all Marv Mazo could do to get her to leave her chambers without issuing another injunction or holding another press meeting at the end of the day.

"Queenie," Marv said when she was at home, "forget the whole thing for the evening. Read something. You mustn't let the Court's business swallow you up. Listen to some music." Not that

she liked to listen to music. "Have your dinner. Forget about the world for a few hours."

She consented to dinner but not to forget about the great world to Marv's real regret. He had gone to talk to the Speaker and Bright Dismukes at the Speaker's request and undertaken to do what they asked. Their aim, he had been assured, was to release the pressures, wind down the crisis, without harming his friend. They knew his concern, were talking to him out of old friendship. They had relied on his skills in the past in resolving what had seemed hopeless conflicts. He had insights they could not have. He would know what to say but he had to act quickly. What he needed was a few peaceful hours. Unfortunately Nita had given her word to Dorothy: she was morally obliged to watch the Snow broadcast.

Nita watched and listened to Marietta, as a critic, calmly, and commenting. Marv agreed that Marietta was not what you could call a good-looking woman. He agreed, too, that there was a touch of hysteria in the performance, a want, maybe, of dignity. Nita thought Marietta's concern was probably more with her loss of what she called a big job than with anything else. Marv thought she, Queenie, was right. Up to the last he was relieved. Nothing exciting, nothing upsetting.

The story from San Antonio blew up Marv's plans. Judicial action was called for. The police would have to be punished. The local governments, all of them, had outlived their usefulness. The San Antonio judges would have to exercise their authority. And then we transfer you to Austin.

Nita found Othman Frick horrifying, disgusting. Marv tried to explain: Othman Frick thought of himself as a Texan. Othman Frick, if you asked him, would say he loved Texas.

"Texas?" Nita demanded.

"It's his state. Some people still love their states."

"Texas? States?" Nita said. They did not exist any more except as names on a map. A convenience for children in school geography classes. How could you love Ohio? And she came from Ohio. Did he love New Jersey?

Marv admitted that he did not love New Jersey. New Jersey was special. New Jersey could not be called loveable.

"And he's taking Texas out of the Union, threatening to go it alone, as he says. He ought to be in a period costume."

"But," Marv began.

"He's putting his dirty hands on my judges." Nita was Chief Justice again, minus her robes. "What happens to Texas," she pronounced, "is for me to decide." And it was not something minor, not a national issue. The world was involved.

"Good God," Nita said as she measured the implications of Othman Frick's conduct. "How will this look to the Eurasian Republics? What will they think? This could be war, Marv. This could end in -- We all know how it could end. Marv, I've got to call them. I've got to get Cheka at once. Now, before it's too late."

Marv tried to quiet her. It would be difficult to get Cheka. What could she say?

Nita looked at him. Perhaps he did not really understand who she was. She assured him she knew what to say. All her life she had known what to say, first unofficially. As for later, he could read her opinions. And the Court was well managed, superbly managed in fact. She had foreseen a possible need: she had a number to call if she felt it necessary to talk to the Manager or Chairman of the Republics or whatever he was. If he wanted proof, he could watch, he could listen. It would be an experience for him to remember.

She placed her call, waited. A voice came on. Who was calling? Whom was she calling? She was the Chief Justice of the United States. She was calling his Excellency, Cheka. The call was urgent, most urgent. Life or death. The most urgent. Maximum life. Maximum death. She waited again.

21

Cheka Told of Lenino Particles Emerging from Black Hole

Cheka had just begun to talk to a mental patient, Adam Lumens by name, when one of what was referred to as the Inner Secretariat came in. Most apologetically -- Cheka did not like interruptions -- he explained there was a call on one of the second high priority numbers, a woman, speaking English, he thought, an American probably. She seemed to be describing herself as the Chief Justice of the United States. She sounded confused, overwrought. Should he ignore the call? What should he do?

Cheka apologized to Lumens. He would speak to the caller himself. The Americans did have a woman Chief Justice, an arrangement peculiar to the Americans. Conceivably she could have obtained one of the second high priority numbers. From his information she was given to fits of excitement. Yes, he would talk to her. Lumens got up. Cheka motioned to him to stay.

"Cheka here," Cheka said. It was one of the visual lines set so that he could see without being seen. There was a man in the background, looking unhappy. The woman -- he recognized her from photographs -- was indeed the Chief Justice. She was apparently stricken dumb for the moment.

"Cheka here," he said for the second time.

The woman found her voice at last, a surprisingly small and uncertain voice. "Excellency," she said, "I am calling you in despair. I am calling to make an appeal, a human appeal. A desperate human appeal."

"Esteemed lady, I listen." The Americans were a very odd people. "I listen." He waited.

Nita hesitated again. Cheka's voice was calm, a voice of kindly authority. She was being spoken to as though she were a child caught in a small childish crisis. Cheka must know the world was at stake. It was not easy speaking to Cheka.

"Excellency," she found her voice again. "You know about our latest developments?"

"Yes," Cheka said. He kept abreast, as the Americans put it, of the latest developments. The Americans had been getting ready to hang themselves for a good many years. They had tied the noose and the esteemed lady was part of the noose. The noose was in place.

Painfully Nita realized her position. She was a suppliant. She was asking a man for a favor and to make it worse another man, Marv, was a witness. Nevertheless, hers was the grand role, her sacrifice was saving the world.

"Please," she said, "you must not think that I have lost control of my people here. You must not be offended by what you have heard. You must be forgiving and patient."

"Of course," Cheka said. "Why should I not be?"

"You would be justified," Nita told him, "in regarding us as a people who have broken our word, as a people to punish."

"No, no," Cheka said. "How punish?" The question was like a pat on the head.

Nita had seen it all clearly: war, the last ultimate war. That was the punishment due the Americans for what they had done in Mexico City, for resisting the justice owed the Mexican people, for all their many transgressions.

"You will give me your word, you will promise?" Nita said.

"Any reasonable promise." Cheka thought the woman was mad. He could understand why the man in the background looked so unhappy.

"You will promise not to make war on us? You will give me a day, maybe two or three days to see that justice is done to you, to your claims?"

"Even four days," Cheka said. "And now you must excuse me. I have someone waiting to talk with me."

Nita was grateful. She had his word. She had two or three, even four days. The stay of execution was granted. She could act in that time. She thanked, she excused Cheka. In a way she was pleased that Marv had been present. Without question, the story of what had happened had a great theme: a woman responding to crisis, she, at the last hour, turning to Cheka, treating with Cheka power to power. You could sum it up as a woman's courage, a woman's persuasion, personal triumph. Marv would know how to present it.

As for Cheka, he apologized again to his caller.

Lumens demurred. "No," he said, "my time is yours. You have great affairs to attend to."

Cheka shook his head. "Perhaps not so great. That will depend on what you will tell me. Did Brilliant tell you what I had in mind?"

"I did not see the Adviser," Lumens explained. "There was only a message. I was to leave, shall we call it, my refuge, to come here, to answer your questions and then be taken back to my refuge."

"About going back to what you tactfully refer to as your refuge, that we will decide. Now about your work in your pre-refuge days?"

"My work goes on," Lumens said. "They are kind enough to allow me to amuse myself at the refuge. They even provide what I ask for. My refuge, you know, is quite special."

"Then your continuing work. I know a little about it. After all you are one of our medalists. The lenino. The discoverer of the lenino."

Lumens nodded.

"The lenino," he said, "my discovery -- they say now my delusion -- and my ruin."

"You will tell me about the lenino."

Lumens told him about the lenino. He was a theoretical physicist, more exactly, what he would call a cosmogonist, puzzling over the beginning of things, looking, recording, playing elaborate mathematical games. The usual thing, as he said, for men of his kind. The universe, no doubt, existed, expanding, contracting, one age or another.

Time, of course, was a mystery. What was it? How did it start? Would it stop? We talked about billions of years but no one knew what that meant. There was light, which everyone recognized. Some experts thought it was related to time. Light had speed whatever speed was. The speed of light was an absolute in some way and there was general agreement, perhaps if they could grasp the inner nature of light, they would understand everything, maybe time. There were particles, old ones and new ones. Maybe they bred like so many amoeba.

"So," Lumen said, "I found a particle in nature, not in a laboratory. My particle, very remarkable, so remarkable that it got me a medal. Its discovery was a credit to everyone. They honored it by calling it after your namesake. So my lenino."

"I had supposed you had chosen the name," Cheka said.

"No," Lumens told him, "there are committees, always committees. There is a committee for picking out names. But the lenino deserved something notable."

"Why?" Cheka asked.

"Very rare. A natural particle. Not, should I say, manufactured. I observed one, a long wait, then another. My discovery, of course, was confirmed. But the source -- if that is the word – was the thing. It started me on my way to the refuge."

"And the source?"

"A black hole," Lumens said. "Black holes like light and time are commonplace. School girls, school boys, can explain them, give you details. Everything goes in. Nothing comes out. Nothing can come out as a matter of physical law. My leninos emerged from a black hole."

"Did you know from which one?" Cheka asked. Lumens was an odd fellow. Brilliant had underlined that Lumens was a patient in the Hospital for Intellectual Casualties, had been for years, never gave any sign of responding to treatment.

Lumens knew from which one. He watched. He kept track. He, in fact, had volunteered to be a watcher-listener. The refuge was comfortable but he did not really like it. They had denied his petition. Probably they thought his disorder might infect the other listener-watchers. But Cheka wanted to know where the leninos came from. He gave the location.

"My misfortune," Lumens said, "is that I am stupid. There is an orthodox truth which sensible men do not question. It was wrong of me to say that my leninos were emerging from a black hole. It was as bad, maybe worse, when I wrote a paper that proved my leninos had a velocity greater than light. Many times greater. And, then, as a climax I suggested that this lenino was a kind of anti-universe particle."

"An anti-universe particle? And what would that mean?" Cheka asked.

"A destroyer particle. A particle that eats up our universe. There were the missing space colonies, disappearing in silence. No alarms. No warnings. They were there; they were gone. My suggestion was leninos, a party, a company, a shower, touching, pouring into, maybe only passing close by -- and the colony gone. Naturally it is only a guess. To be sure I would have to own a lenino, keep it in a box, examine it closely, weigh it, measure it, make sure of its properties. But, as you see, if I were right the box and my instruments and I, along with them, would disappear too. A man with such an idea was inviting retirement to a refuge."

"Let us go back," Cheka said, "to the black holes. Like the children, I know all about them. But you have other ideas?"

"We only think in terms and use figures that are familiar, if that is the word," Lumen explained. "So I say volcanoes. We both have seen or seen pictures of volcanoes. We know what they are. We know they erupt. A black hole, using a figure of speech, is a kind of volcano. Volcanoes we say are extinct, and yet extinct volcanoes explode. My guess was -- is -- that a black hole is much the same thing. We have never seen a black hole erupt but we have not existed, perhaps, long enough to observe. And if a black hole were to erupt, who can say we would survive to write learned papers about such an event?"

"So you think the lenino may be a sign that such an event is about to occur? The first spewing out?" Cheka was on notice that this was a mental patient lost in a fantasy. But who could be sure?

"Yes," Lumens agreed. "The first spewing out, the first vapor, the earliest rumbling. Even so."

"The speed of the lenino. You spoke about that. Could you measure it?" Cheka asked.

"In part conjecture," Lumens admitted. "We probably have no instruments to make such a measurement but with those that I had I could only say that the lenino went faster than our absolute limit."

"So," Cheka said. "I think I see where you are going. But you must tell me. I am a more ignorant man than you are accustomed to. You must bear that in mind. You are telling me that this black hole of yours may contain a new universe which could come out like a rabbit out of a hat."

Lumen smiled. It was a nice way to put it: a rabbit out of a hat, magic, a marvelous trick.

"Very good," Lumens said. "A very good way to express it."

"And our universe was a rabbit?" Cheka suggested. Lumens nodded. That could have been so.

"You give me the hat -- the black hole. You give me the rabbit -- which is all of us, everything. Where is the magician performing the trick? Was there a magician?"

"As scientists," Lumens told him, "we are honor bound to find no magician."

"Of course," Cheka said. "No one in or outside the hat performing the trick. You know the word God?"

Lumens looked at him. This was Cheka, V. I. Cheka, owner of limitless power, master of men, director of the affairs of all the Eurasian Republics. He had been unnerved when he was told he was being taken to talk to him. He had expected, what had he expected? A different man. That Cheka would want to talk to him was an impossible error. Had he heard the word God? The answer was yes, an occasional reference.

"So have I," Cheka said. "And assuming, unscientifically, the existence of God, would the black holes be a suitable residence?"

Lumens smiled again. Again a nice figure of speech.

"Let us talk in the confidence that neither of us will disclose what is said. It could be very dangerous." Cheka went on. He explained. They believed in all kinds of marvels, in billions of years. They might, if persuaded, believe in an infinite number of universes exploding out of an infinite number of Lumens' black holes.

The only belief no one could hold was in the existence of God. Even the Americans, the most anarchic of people, had been instructed by their highest judges that to use the word God on public property or on premises owned by someone or something receiving public money was a violation of their constitution, their most sacred document. Why? Self esteem. The need to maintain self respect.

God, any god, was a menace, an admission of imperfect authority, of inferior, of limited knowledge. The concept was unsettling, could lead to uncertainty, could undermine confidence. Did Lumens agree?"

Lumens agreed though he had never had the matter presented to him as Cheka presented it.

"Look," Cheka said, "we get now to the reason for our talking together." Brilliant had told him about the noise, the incomprehensible noise that had been reported by the listener-watchers keeping their ridiculous vigil -- for which he was, he admitted, responsible. No one thought it a program that should be continued, no real interest to scientists of any certified standing.

The senior academicians who knew all languages, past and present, maybe future as well, found the noise a jumble. He had had Brilliant describe it as well as he could. He, himself, had listened to recordings. He himself had gone and listened along with the listener-watchers, who were so many failed members of his, Lumens', own brotherhood, drudges, so many drudges. Brilliant's description was, he found, satisfactory. The incomprehensible noise was Many Many Tackle, just as Brilliant had said. Had Lumens any comment to make?

Lumens looked at Cheka for a minute. He had decided that Cheka was a humorous man. Was this some kind of joke? He gave a safe answer. He was not a linguist. Language had not been one of his subjects.

"Then we are both equally handicapped," Cheka told him. "Knowing your handicap I wait for your comment on this incomprehensible sound."

Lumens shrugged his shoulders. "Mene Mene Tekel," It could be chance, accident, nothing but accident, something like stone worn by wind or water until it looked as though it had been shaped by some human intelligence.

"A happy thought," Cheka observed. "And why had the professional linguists not said Mene Mene Tekel," he said. Afraid, all afraid. Mene Mene Tekel was bad news, very bad news. Why should they bring bad news to the Chairman of the Republics. For that matter it was or could be bad news for themselves, private bad news, best ignored, best disregarded. Moreover they might lose professional standing. As students of language they could look at old books but Mene Mene Tekel was an old wives' tale, superstition.

Lumens said nothing.

"I will now read your mind," Cheka went on. "Reading minds is one of my gifts. You are astonished that I am impressed by such nonsense, am serious about an old superstition. Am impressed or may only be impressed. Am I right?"

Lumens nodded. Cheka was right.

Cheka had a question. Would the sound come from a lenino, or a stream of leninos? Were they audible? Could they produce sound?

Could? That Lumens could not say. Had he heard any sound? No but he was not sure about his equipment.

"Finally," Cheka said, "a last revelation. I hear this incomprehensible noise as a voice. You understand the distinction?"

Lumens understood the distinction.

"Now," Cheka said, "before you spread the alarm that I am out of my mind, you will come with me. We will go and visit the listener-watchers. You will hear for yourself. Then you can tell me perhaps where the sound comes from. Also perhaps you can tell me if the Americans could be playing a game. There are still some clever Americans. And if we are about to have a cosmic eruption we will both be interested, scientifically interested. The human mind, Lumens, is a curious, what shall we say? A curious part of the existing creation. And you could tell me too if we could survive a rain of leninos and what might come after the rain?"

22

Cheka Agent Concludes Killing Old Man Key to Success

Zenner and Boregard Dodge had spent the evening together, drinking and assembling the proofs that were needed for the presentation of the Eurasian and Mexican claims. Zenner had provided every thing that Justice Dodge had requested.

There were fingerprints of Bolkonsky, fingerprints of the late Dudorov, photographs of Bolkonsky as a youth, as a young man, recent photographs. There were similar photographs of the deceased. Madame Dudorov would appear with her children and deny the fugitive was their husband and father. Madame Bolkonsky and children would identify the fugitive as their own beloved but wayward father and spouse.

In support of an indemnity, the Eurasian Republics had prepared figures, handsome claims for Troyenko and the hundreds of Embassy personnel who had disappeared in the blast, plus a claim for the mental anguish of each and every citizen of the Republics, all statistically sound. The total would extinguish the outstanding foreign debt of the Union and leave the United States in debt to it by an amount equal to the gross national product of the Americans for the next 23 years.

The Mexican claims, measured in money, were substantial but less. The loss of Mexican lives in the blast could only be fixed by an estimate -- a reasonable estimate, and the same was true of the property damage. Nevertheless, there was a figure, again statistically sound. The charts and graphs were, Dodge agreed, just what he needed.

As for the Treaty claims, there were documents from the Mexican archives to establish the coercion exerted on the Republic of Mexico to sign the Treaty of Guadalupe Hidalgo. Zenner had also supplied the secret correspondence between Nicholas Trist and the authorities in

Washington City bearing on the negotiation. They referred frequently to bribes paid by Trist to Mexican officials for the purpose of insuring their acceptance of the American terms.

"This correspondence," Dodge said, "is remarkable, really remarkable." No one had known it existed. Where had it come from?

"Archives," Zenner said. "The Mexican archives are rich." The Mexicans had access to everything Trist sent or received. They had read and made copies. The chief Mexican archivist could appear and authenticate. He had examined and tested the paper. The age of the copies would be attested to by experts on paper and ink -- if they were needed. Did Justice Dodge think they were needed?

"Yes," Dodge said, "in a normal proceeding." But this was not a normal proceeding. He felt the Court would accept the Trist correspondence along with the documents proving the use of coercion.

"Of course," Zenner agreed. "The Chief Justice, your whole Court is committed to justice. All this will make their task easier." There was a presumption, too, that governments in the past had been corrupt. The documents matched the presumption. Did Justice Dodge think that was so?

"Exactly so," Dodge conceded. Zenner's mind worked like those of his former sisters and brothers. Zenner would have been an ornament to the bench. "And now," Dodge went on, "now that you have given me the proofs that I need, let me tell you that I have spoken to Dudorov."

"Dudorov?" Zenner could not understand.

"You know," Dodge said, "you must know that Mr. Carmody and I are old friends." Naturally Zenner knew of the friendship.

"We have talked about this affair," Dodge went on. "My first suggestion was that he turn over Bolkonsky and the state property without any proceedings. As you can guess, he refused, gave his reasons. Eventually he allowed me to talk to what he referred to as his combination fugitive-guest."

Zenner said nothing except that they knew Justice Dodge and Mr. Carmody had conferred on several occasions.

Dodge nodded. He assumed they would know of the meetings. Zenner assured him they had no objections. It was all proper, quite proper. Able counsel always attempted to resolve disputes, always hoped for what the American lawyers spoke of as settling a case, always informed themselves as fully as possible of their adversaries' position.

"After talking to him a number of times," Dodge said, "and having heard his story and having asked questions I have had to conclude that the man you want as Bolkonsky is our Dudorov, no one but Dudorov."

Zenner poured another drink for himself, another for Dodge. They drank and looked at each other.

"So I continue," Dodge said. "The fingerprints and the photographs, the women, the children. What do you think I make of them?"

Zenner said nothing. He filled their glasses again.

"And the materials from the Mexican archives?"

Zenner said nothing. He emptied his glass.

"I think," Dodge said, "you have answered my questions. Now a third question. Do you know General Dudorov?"

They had met, Zenner told him, met on occasion. Their acquaintance was slight. He, himself, was an outsider, as the Americans put it. Dudorov was an insider. But he knew about Dudorov, that is the usual stories. Dudorov's standing was high, very high. The family distinguished. Dudorov able, well regarded by Cheka.

There were those who thought that Dudorov might be a successor, after Ulianov, maybe in place of Ulianov. These were matters beyond his own competence. For a man in his place it would be imprudent to speculate or even to think about such arrangements. He had no opinions himself. He was only reporting what he had heard, stories and rumors that were current among the journalists with whom he spent much of his time. In the circumstances Dudorov could no longer be living. A Dudorov could never defect -- as the Americans called it. It would be against nature. The Union, the Revolution were sacred.

"So there has to be a Bolkonsky?"

"Exactly," Zenner agreed. "There has to be a Bolkonsky as an explanation for Dudorov." A fit of insanity was also out of the question. All senior officials of the Republics were tested, selected, their reliability and balance were proved.

"Dudorov," Dodge observed, "is sane enough. I can give you my word for it." He had talked to him in Mr. Carmody's presence and he had talked to him alone. Did Zenner know about the state property?

Zenner did not. No one had described it to him. Accordingly it was not his business to ask. He had his position and he was told only what it was necessary for him to know. His position was in fact very good but the nature of the state property was something about which it was best for him to be ignorant. He assumed that it was special, of peculiar importance. Did Justice Dodge know?

Justice Dodge did.

Zenner preferred that Justice Dodge respect his, Zenner's, need to be ignorant. He filled the glasses again. He hoped these proofs presented the Justice with no more than an intellectual problem. No moral problem.

Dodge smiled. "You mean will I have any scruples about making your case, about offering the proof to the court?"

Zenner nodded. That was the question. As he understood it the American lawyers had the highest ethical standards. They were concerned with the truth, always the truth. They were also bound to do everything in their power for the cause of their clients. If the lawyer had doubts about the evidence offered him by the client?

This time Dodge laughed. "It won't make any difference," he said. "Suppose the worst. I tell the Court all the proofs, yours and the Mexican, are fabricated, manufactured to order. The Court does what the Chief Justice says. Apart from the fact that I don't like her and that she doesn't like me, she is committed to saving the peace of the world by giving your Union and the Mexicans whatever they ask for. Knowing her, and the way she goes about things, I assume she has her opinion already written -- with blanks to fill in, references to the facts. So my doubts mean nothing. As we say, she is the trier of facts and she will have the proofs the occasion requires."

Zenner expressed his relief. Justice Dodge, then, had nothing to worry about.

"Nothing to worry about," Dodge said, "is a good way to put it."

"No dilemma. You escape the dilemma."

"I escape the dilemma. Have another drink while I explain how completely I escape the dilemma."

Zenner filled the glasses, admired this Justice Dodge who could drink like a man and had a conscience that he was able to manage. The Americans were always uneasy when left alone with their conscience. But not Justice Dodge.

"Let me explain," Dodge said, "why I have no worries about Dudorov and what may happen to him when the Court decrees that you recover him. Can you guess?"

Zenner was unable to guess.

"The answer is," Dodge went on, "that you won't recover him. My old friend, Mr. Carmody, has no intention of giving him up. Neither him nor the state property we were talking about."

"But, no," Zenner said. He was astounded. It was something he could not believe. "Your respect for the law. Your respect for judges. Your reputation as a people. Your whole reputation."

"We are talking about Mr. Carmody," Dodge told him. "My friend, Michael Carmody. One man, a particular man. Like me he's too old and too well informed to feel respect for the law and the judges. Also he knows that Bolkonsky does not exist. Dudorov came to him and Dudorov stays with him. With the state property."

"But your courts have power," Zenner insisted. "Even a great man like Mr. Carmody is under the law." At least he hoped that was so. The success of his mission depended on the delusion of the Americans that they would be struck by lightning if they disobeyed a court order. The success of his mission. But what if it failed? He had been sent to Washington with instructions. Scriabin, informally, was to be his subordinate. His mission was a tribute to his accomplishments and talents. In his mind he had anticipated his reception when he returned: approval from Cheka, certain prizes that Cheka would give him.

Failure, he had not thought of failure. That would mean a different reception: loss of favor, even disgrace, questions about his ability, questions, even worse, as to his loyalty. If they raised up, they would also strike down. Everyone knew of examples. He would forfeit his comfortable quarters, the deference he had enjoyed, the pay and perquisites to which he was accustomed.

Cheka had the reputation of being more restrained in his punishments than some of the masters before him, but Cheka had told him -- perhaps it was a warning -- that his success was of the greatest importance to the Republic. A disappointed Cheka? Or suppose a Cheka who felt his own position damaged by his, Zenner's failure? It was improper even to imagine what went on in the highest of circles. Nevertheless, as a certified novelist he could imagine.

Justice Dodge had told him that old Carmody, the old man, Cheka's old enemy, stood in his, Zenner's way, was a threat to Cheka, to the Republics. That was all he needed to know.

"Enough of this is enough," Zenner said. "We will listen to your latest news. As a journalist, I am what you call addicted to news."

What they heard and saw was Othman Frick talking for Texas. Three or four years before -- he was not sure which it was -- Zenner had interviewed Othman in connection with a series called American Pictures. A big man who liked to hear his own voice. But smart, as the Americans said, crafty, good at the American game they called making money. When Othman wished every body goodnight, Zenner asked Justice Dodge if this was a serious man.

"You're asking me if Othman is bluffing. I don't know and he doesn't know. Othman is a kind of untrained musician. He's, as we say, playing by ear."

"And his friend, Governor Monte del Monte?" Zenner asked.

Dodge thought the sweet singer of Monterey, if playing, was also playing by ear.

"I am shocked," Zenner said. "Mr. Carmody, the Governors, maybe more governors, all defying your Court. This has never happened before."

"It's been a long time coming," Dodge told him, "maybe too long." He had warned the Chief Justice and her judicial sisters and brothers that they were overplaying their hand, crowding their luck.

What would happen, Zenner wanted to know, if something happened to Othman Frick today or tomorrow or the day after, if he were no longer on the stage. Would the people in Texas behave as they were supposed to, show their respect for the law? What did Justice Dodge think?

Justice Dodge had no way of knowing. And Othman enjoyed good health. He was not likely to disappear by the day after tomorrow.

Zenner had his own thoughts on that subject and there was no reason to share them. He proposed a last drink for the evening, filled the glasses again.

"You asked me to guess," Dodge said after a moment. "I'll ask you to guess. What happens if the Court rules for you and nothing comes of the ruling? What do my clients do?"

"Your clients?"

"You, your people, the Eurasian Republics, what do they do? Suppose you get nothing out of the judgment, no Dudorov, no state property, no Texas, no so-called Mexican states, no indemnity. It won't be the first worthless judgment that went on the books. I've had my share in my time." Dodge knew about uncollectible judgments.

"Do?" Zenner asked. He understood that among the Americans judgments were sacred, always enforced.

"No," Justice Dodge told him. He cited two or three from his own experience, adding an odd American saying, something about getting blood out of turnips. They had come as far as they had because the Chief Justice and half of the people, maybe more than half of the people, the women and God knew who else, were convinced that there would be war if the Republics did not get what they were demanding. Zenner had asked if Othman were bluffing. Were his people bluffing? And if they made war, would they use all of those marvelous weapons? Would they use them on Washington, say, without letting Zenner or the Ambassador or the rest of their crowd know in advance? Would he, Zenner, like everyone else go the way of Troyenko and the other unfortunates who disappeared in Mexico City?

199

Zenner found these unpleasant questions. Justice Dodge was old. How and when death came to him was no longer important. But Zenner had many good years left in his account. Being vaporized, of course, might seem a suitable penalty for his failure and Scriabin's for that matter, to complete their assignments. Dodge's questions were enough to insure that any sensible man would do anything in his power to go the last step, make the last move to obtain his objective.

"Well?" Dodge asked. "What can you tell me? Or don't you know Cheka well enough to have an opinion? I don't really know about your arrangements. Are you an archangel or something more modest, only one of the heavenly choir?"

Zenner explained. He was at best one of what Justice Dodge spoke of as the heavenly choir. No more exalted than that. He had met Cheka. There were occasions on which Cheka had honored him by talking to him in more than a casual way. But an expert on Cheka? He was not an expert on Cheka. Cheka was patient -- his patience was famous. When Cheka said he hated war, he was telling the truth.

Cheka had wonderful weapons but less impulse to use them than some of what Justice Dodge described as archangels. There was Globus and his new son-in-law, Shishak, the ranking single Marshal of the Republics. Could they persuade Cheka to be less forbearing if they were disappointed by the Americans?

"Let us hope," Zenner said, "there will be no disappointment. We will both do our best." He had brought with him -- at Ulianov's suggestion -- three or four reliable men, not equal to the late Speck, but with well-earned reputations and very good training.

23

Armed Mob Besieges Intelligence Center;
Dudorov Guns Down Assassins

"I think," Boregard Dodge said, "that you had better get out of town." It was the morning after his evening with Zenner. He was talking to old Michael Carmody and Dudorov.

The old man objected. Why should he get out of town?

"Because," Dodge said, "I drank too much last night. Drank too much. Talked too much." He told them about the drinking and talking -- about the infallible fingerprints and the rest of the proofs, the Mexican archives, the wives and the children. "And," he concluded, "I told him that, so to speak, the whole exercise was a futility. That you were not going to surrender either the General or what he called the peculiar state property."

"He should have foreseen that," the old man observed.

"I think," Dodge said, "he was shocked. He was sure we were great respecters of law, very devout, very obedient." An idea came to him. "You know he probably regards the Chief Justice and her Court as being for us something like Cheka and his inner circle for him: You bow the head, bend the knee. No questions asked."

"How does that make me leave town?" the old man asked.

"Mike," Dodge said, "one of the beauties of being as old as I am is that I know the human heart, also the inhuman heart. Zenner. But you ask the General. He'll know what conclusion to draw. He told us something about Zenner. He knows about important assignments."

Dudorov nodded. He understood Zenner's needs. No one got prizes for failing. There were times when success was essential, or could be essential even to merely surviving. If Zenner thought Mr. Carmody stood in the way of returning to Cheka with his mission accomplished, he would do what he could to remove him. And if he thought in terms of survival? Either way he had to move quickly. There was no time for intrigue, for indirect means. As for the direct approach, Zenner had people available, competent people whom he had brought with him, Meshbesher and Assad. Osbeg had arrived two or three days later. He had explained their functions when Mr. Carmody had told him they had been added to the Embassy staff.

The old man listened without being persuaded. What did Assad and Meshbesher and Osbeg have to do with him, Michael Carmody?

"Professional killers," Dudorov said. "Killers to order. Taking their orders from Zenner." The last was important. Mr. Carmody and Cheka might have their own understanding: no attacks one on the other. But Zenner was ignorant, to a degree an outsider, and he would be fearful of the consequence of his failure. He would think that with Mr. Carmody out of the way no one would disobey the Court's inevitable order to return Yuri Bolkonsky and the stolen state property.

"The man is a fool," the old man said, "if he thinks everything is that easy." He had told Louisa Clymer that if anything happened to him she was to regard Dudorov as her ward and she had also understood what was involved in the possession of the four cartridges. One had gone to her weapons people, one to his friends; he had kept two for an emergency, giving Louisa instructions where she would find them.

"And what happens if Louisa is in the Chief Justice's jail?" Dodge asked.

"She won't be," the old man said. "Not Louisa Clymer." He had, he conceded, no idea of what was going to happen except that the Chief Justice and her Court were not going to deliver the goods, the so-called Mexican states and everything else, indemnities, Dudorov, cartridges. It was the end of a road.

This time there would be open resistance. Civil war? He thought the Chief Justice would relish it, a civil war to establish her primacy. What would the President do? He would want to do nothing. It would depend on whether he followed Louisa or their Secretary of State and Attorney General. The Congress was in agreement for once. They saw the Court as leviathan and they would -- or try to -- put a hook in its nose. The Speaker and Senator Dismukes looked to Louisa and such reliable troops as she had to hold the country together.

"You know," the old man said finally, "Cheka ought to be satisfied if he gets no more than a civil war out of this Court." He looked at Dudorov. Did the General agree?

"I don't know," Dudorov said after a moment. He knew Cheka, but not as his father had. The Americans, of course, he could not understand. Supposedly they were a rich and powerful people who were always assuring themselves of their pride in their freedom. And the strength of their institutions. Would they let themselves be destroyed by the folly of a few appointed officials? It sounded impossible. But if they allowed it? Well, there would be problems for Cheka.

"Vladimir Ilyich," he explained, "is. a very intelligent man. You Americans are what you call indispensable to him in more ways than one. You have been his supplier, openly, secretly, money and goods. Ideas. The kind of disorder you talk about would be a misfortune. You would have nothing to give him. He would see that. And he may see more being an intelligent man. My father used to say that the Americans by simply existing preserved our own order. That it was our fear and envy of you that kept us in balance, canceled out contending factions and forces. But you will know more about these things than I do."

"Maybe so," Dodge said, "but that doesn't dispose of Zenner and helpers. I think, Mike, that you -- and the General -- ought to get out of their reach. The Court will be sitting tomorrow. The Chief Justice is going to demand custody of the General sometime today. You see the possibilities as well as I do, the Marshal, the Judicial Guard ragtag she has been deputizing since yesterday."

The old man would worry about the Marshal, and the ragtag when they arrived. He had his own people. And he had a detachment of troops, courtesy of Louisa. They had their orders. No one was to enter the gates except the Marshal herself with no more than three or four deputies. He and the General could take care of themselves.

"All right," Dodge said. "I've done what I can. And if anyone asks, officially I've been here to persuade you to turn the General over to me in a last effort to settle at least that part of my case."

"You can count on me to remember that," the old man said, "if anyone asks."

An hour later even the old man might have had second thoughts. Not long after Justice Dodge left, the gate called to report that a large and noisy crowd was arriving in trucks following Marshal Feemster of the Supreme Court in one of the Court limousines. The Marshal was demanding that she and all of her deputies be allowed to enter the Intelligence compound. The gates were closed and would stay closed unless Gate received contrary instructions. Gate felt obliged to tell Mr. Carmody that if anyone undertook to break down the gates he had orders to resist. In the meantime, also in accordance with his instructions, in view of the size of the crowd which apparently numbered in the thousands, he had asked for reinforcements. They would probably arrive by air within a few minutes. Did Mr. Carmody have any comment?

"Is the crowd armed?" the old man wanted to know.

Gate thought they were. Side arms. Some rifles. But he could not be sure about what the crowd had. There were more trucks arriving and he could not be sure what might appear when the whole crowd assembled.

"Are they staying in the trucks or dismounting?"

Some staying, some dismounting, Gate told him. A disorderly crowd. Unpredictable.

The old man was not surprised. Crowds by their nature were undisciplined which was why crowd users used them. Their threat was in their being beyond human prediction. If possible, he told Gate, he would speak to the Marshal herself and see if he could quiet the waters.

While he waited the old man went to his window. He motioned to Dudorov to come with him. From the window he could see the gate a couple of hundred yards away. It was well guarded. There were barricades, guns in position. Dudorov pulled him away. A man with a rifle with telescopic sights was always a danger. Two seconds later the window was shattered.

"They're not playing," the old man said, half to himself, half to Dudorov as Dudorov pushed him out of the room. Overhead they could hear the noise of the helicopters bringing the reinforcements that Gate had called for. From the outside there was a sound of firing, sporadic, then a heavy volley, then quiet. Gate was evidently engaged in an exercise of what was called crowd control. Gate called. Marshal Feemster would, after refusing at first, speak to the Director. But she was indignant. The word, maybe, was outraged.

"Carmody," the old man said.

"This is the Marshal of the Supreme Court of the United States," Olga announced. "With orders to take you and Yuri Bolkonsky into my custody. At once, now. I demand.... "

The old man interrupted her, more exactly tried to. He would tell her that someone had tried to kill him a minute or two ago, had fired at him as he stood by the window in his inner office.

"Don't you break in on me." Olga half shouted. "I demand that you stop this lawless behavior at once. I intend to perform my lawful duties." She went on. The gates were to be opened. She was to come in with her deputies. She would serve her papers or he would take the consequences of being in defiance of the Chief Justice, herself, under whose orders she acted. No, she would not leave her papers with Gate. She would serve them in person.

She would not be intimidated by force or the threat of it. The troops had fired at her deputies -- well, over their heads. Some of her deputies may have fired first but they were in the lawful exercise of their duties as members of the Judicial Guard Force, all lawfully attached to her office as Marshal. They could overpower the troops if necessary. Any troops. She could call up more Judicial Guards and she would.

"Madam," the old man said after a time, "enough is enough. You have a choice. My buildings are not open to everyone. Gate will pass you in -- with an escort -- with two or three deputies. Otherwise you can leave your papers. Or otherwise -- you understand what you will be doing."

It was not an easy decision for Olga. Michael Carmody was evil personified, the source of all wickedness, the implacable enemy of the human sisterhood for which the Chief Justice strove. He was sinister. His buildings were sinister. They were a center of plots and destruction.

He had arranged for the horrible blast in Mexico City. And he was never accountable. No one so far had dared to question his power and the work of his agents who acted and hid in the dark.

Now the Chief Justice, and she as her right hand, were breaking the spell. She would like to see her guards break through the gates, break into the buildings, empty the files, burn all the papers, turn into ashes all the false information, gathered in hatred, gathered illegally, lies about the Eurasian Republics, all aimed to prevent the achievement of eternal peace on the planet. She owed as much to her mother who had devoted her life to peace work, who described herself as a peace worker, always hopeful and always frustrated by Carmody and his schemes.

Moreover the files, as they all knew, were full of lies about everyone who questioned those schemes, hints about their most intimate doings. She could imagine what was in a folder devoted to her, or the Chief Justice. The best ending would be a bonfire, the buildings, their contents, a holocaust devouring -- it might be sinful even to think it but it would be right -- Mr. Carmody and his personnel.

Gate broke in on her. What was her decision? She had been humiliated by the Clymer woman's dismissal with an escort, her papers ignored. Then she was alone. This time she had her own forces, eager and ready. But Gate was heavily armed and the helicopters kept coming. Gate had tanks, machine guns, field pieces. She was an educated woman. She had read history and history encouraged her -- up to a point. There was the Bastille, the Swiss Guard. There was Smolny. Crowds had unforeseeable powers. On the other hand there was the young Napoleon, the cannon, the whiff of grapeshot that undid so much.

If Olga had declined a place on a Court of Appeals as too quiet, less scope than she had in charge of her Court's vast enforcement activities, she had not envisioned herself as Joan of Arc, a judicial Joan of Arc, assaulting what began to look to her like an armored division. Probably the Chief would understand and approve her decision. She would go in with a few guards, deliver her documents and if opportunity offered they might somehow seize Mr. Carmody and his Bolkonsky. Somehow get out. And if no such opening offered, she would speak with dignity for the Court and depart. She told Gate her decision.

Yes, she would meet with the Director but she would take a dozen Guards to insure her own safety. Gate argued, explaining she needed no guards. No one threatened her safety. (Gate began to think the woman was a little unbalanced.) She explained it was a matter of her position, her dignity as the representative of the highest court in the land. Gate called Director who sighed and said to let her have four people come with her. The sooner she was in and out, the better for everyone. So having left instructions to her lieutenants and conferred with her chosen four attendants, Olga and her four were escorted to the old man.

As the old man waited, Dudorov cautioned him. "Please," he said, "only the woman. Only the woman. No one else comes into the room. You are older and wiser but I have had more recent experience with violent men." He took a gun out of his pocket. "This I will keep ready. But only the woman."

The old man turned to one of his deputies. "I don't want the General to worry about me," he said. "We will do what he asks. See that the Marshal comes in alone." The deputy left.

What happened next, happened quickly. In a minute, maybe two or three minutes, there was a sound of voices, low and then louder, a sound of scuffling, then a couple of shots. The Marshal appeared, propelled through the door by three men who pushed the door closed. One ran to the window, took up a chair and broke out the glass. Two of the men moved toward the old man and stopped as Dudorov spoke in Urdu or Uzbek or God knew what language. They looked at him astonished. They knew him, they also knew he was dead. Before they could act he had fired twice, three times, four times, five times. He emptied the clip before they could fire. They had not intended using their guns.

When Gate's escort and the deputy came into the room they found Dudorov standing. The old man sat in his chair, unbelieving. The Marshal of the Court was on the floor in a faint. On the floor were the three men -- two dead, one living, the one by the window.

The old man spoke first. "The General," he said, "was worried about me. The General was right. But what," he turned to Dudorov, "were they doing?"

Dudorov took a half minute, maybe a minute to come back to the real world. He had acted as if in a dream, one of the nightmares by which he was troubled. "That is Meshbesher," he said, "by the window. They made a mistake. Meshbesher's doing. Meshbesher likes disposing of people by throwing them out of windows. And he was senior -- in charge. These other two, Osbeg and Assad were to carry you to the window. So they did not bother with guns. And I was unexpected -- and I was a ghost."

"And what did you say to them?" The old man asked.

"Nothing," Dudorov answered. "Sounds. Sounds that came to me." By that time doctors had arrived. They revived Olga, who got up, looked around her and fainted again. They examined the bodies. Meshbesher was hurt but would live. Unfair, Dudorov thought, his choice of murder had killed Assad and Osbeg and he had survived.

The doctors revived Olga again who this time fell into a fit of shouting and sobbing as they led her away. They removed the bodies and Meshbesher. The deputy called Gate to report and cautioned him to prepare for what he called disturbing reactions. The old man inquired what had happened outside in the corridor.

"The three men," the deputy said, "had pushed their way past Gate's escort, pushing the woman before them. A fourth man opened fire but the escort had not returned the fire for fear of hitting the woman. Had that been a mistake?"

"Thanks to General Dudorov, no," the old man replied. And where was the fourth man. The deputy had better bring the man in.

The fourth man was brought in. Dudorov knew him, spoke to him. The man responded at length. The man was led out.

"And this one?" the old man asked.

"Hovani," Dudorov said, "one of the regular Embassy staff but one of our own. A colonel. Assigned to me once. He said Zenner told him you were to be killed. No waiting. At once. He was to get the three in the woman's entourage -- among her recruits and he was to oversee the performance. He told me the whole thing was too careless. No plans. No real thinking. Too hurried. I think he may have been apologizing to me for the failure. All he knows is that Zenner will blame him for the disaster -- he called it."

"Will he talk?"

Dudorov thought. "Hovani is in my situation," he said. "Hovani will talk."

"And was he surprised to find that you were alive?" The old man said after a moment.

Dudorov shook his head. "He said Zenner drinks more than he used to and had told him one report of his mission involved a great miracle, raising Dudorov from the dead."

The old man sat and said nothing. Then a last question. "General," he asked, "have I thanked you for saving what is left of my life?"

24

Cheka Calls, Thanks Dudorov for Saving Old Man

Within not more than an hour Dorothy New had the whole shocking story of the events in Mr. Carmody's office. Olga had been given something to quiet her nerves. The marvelous thing was that she remembered every detail, every expression, told everything clearly. She talked to Dorothy, having first reported to the Chief Justice. And as she talked Dorothy felt that she too had been at the scene.

Olga had gone to the Intelligence Center with a large number of the newly sworn in Judicial Guards to arrest Mr. Carmody and the murderer Yuri Bolkonsky. The Guard had been carefully selected, mainly thousands of young lawyers and law students who loved the profession. They were intended to protect her from treachery on the part of Mr. Carmody, a dangerous man even in his final senility.

Thanks to the illegal collusion of Louisa Clymer the Center had been turned into a fortress. Olga had been denied access. Then, worse, she was persuaded she could enter with a small group and take custody of the old man and Bolkonsky without interference. What had happened next was an indescribable horror. Tears came to Olga's eyes at the memory.

She had been led down a corridor and pushed through the door of the old man's secret office. As she entered, Bolkonsky, the killer of Dudorov, opened fire and she had escaped only by having the presence of mind to throw herself on the floor. She had been allowed a small escort, four men, old and faithful employees of the Court, old faithful friends, and three of them -- she remembered this clearly -- had followed, her to protect her.

Of these three veterans in the Court's service, one had attempted to escape by breaking a window in a desperate attempt to get out of the room at the risk of his life. He was shot down as were the two others.

Olga had heard the Intelligence Center doctors pronounce two of them dead. One of them was critically injured. She could not tell Dorothy their names until their families were notified.

Olga was dazed, naturally dazed. But she recalled being brutally handled by the Intelligence staff, even the doctors. She remembered their slapping her face, not once but repeatedly. Then she was forcibly returned to the gate through which she had foolishly entered. There she was manhandled again, this time by the troops, and then allowed to return to the safety of her own people. She had thought of some kind of action but she was mindful of firing earlier, indiscriminate firing, by the Clymer woman's armed bullies and they had been reinforced, were being reinforced by the minute. It was her duty to prevent a massacre of her guards. She had left.

The implications were, she said to Dorothy, of the most sinister nature: the attempt on her life, a confidant of the Chief Justice, a high official of the Supreme Court, could only suggest that old rumors of secret executions at the Intelligence Center were founded in fact. She had heard them, had doubted. She no longer doubted.

Since her return and her reporting to the Chief Justice, Olga had learned two things that made the picture more ominous.

One of the men who was killed might have been a ranking member of the Eurasian Security Services who had accompanied her to identify the killer Bolkonsky and had pathetically and ironically been, like poor General Dudorov, one of his victims. Dorothy would have to forgive her if she was confused about some details.

And the other thing -- a fourth man was involved, a senior officer of the Eurasian Embassy staff detained by the Carmody people. The Chief Justice had been told something about it. Reporters had asked, were coming to her for a writ. Their demands to see and talk with the men had been denied by one of the Carmody aides though the whole thing was illegal. Diplomatic immunity, she thought, was involved. Everything that had happened brought the threat of war closer.

Then Olga gave up. She had told Dorothy everything. And she counted on Dorothy to use the truth as only she could.

Dorothy went directly from Olga to Harry. She played the story back -- just as she had heard it. Dorothy had an infallible memory. Harry listened, asked what she wanted. Dorothy wanted Harrison to get to Cheka, at once, Cheka himself. She would brief Harrison. Harrison would play it all back to Cheka; get Cheka's comments and come in on her regular broadcast or an earlier one if they got something in time. This was a special, an extra special event, one more stone in the pyramid and getting close to the top. "You believe all this?" Harry asked.

Dorothy did. "How about the old and faithful retainers turning into Eurasian security types?"

"Only one," Dorothy said. "The other is Embassy."

"The same thing," Harry told her. "Half of the Embassy, the half that has any function is made up of security majors or colonels. And have you checked this out with the old man or anyone in his crowd?"

Dorothy had not and saw no reason to do so. She would get from them nothing but lies. It would have broken his heart if he had any -- to see the condition Olga was in. "When people are really broken they tell the truth, Harry," Olga was broken.

Harry looked at her. "I said not long ago that I was going to break my contract with you, Dorothy. And then I was stupid. This is getting too hot. I'm not smart enough and you're not smart enough to stay in this game. Planet can fill the news time with more analyses of the weather. Or Planet can cut back the news and spend more time on culture -- chamber music is good for people. Or song recitals. You don't call Harrison. He's a fool anyway. And you can take the evening off. The next dozen evenings. Harry Pleasants can do minor accidents. This is too big an accident for Planet to play with."

Dorothy started to argue but for once she thought Harry might have meant what he said. Perhaps she should have gone through the motions of getting something from an Intelligence spokesman. Not that the old man paid much attention to the Fourth Estate of the nation. He was an odd selfish old man who kept what he knew to himself.

But it was already too late for Harrison Swing to play it all back to Cheka. Ulianov had already reported. He had come into Cheka's room, looking unhappy.

"Now what?" Cheka asked him. He thought you could read Ulianov's mind at a glance. His face, as the Americans said, gave him away. No sphinx our Ulianov, he had often said to himself. Nothing inscrutable. It was a weakness -- and troubled him -- in a successor. Ulianov hesitated. "Now what? Sit down and tell me."

"Zenner," Ulianov began. "I have bad news from Zenner. Zenner tells me he has lost four of our people. In Mr. Carmody's office."

"You said in Mr. Carmody's office?"

Ulianov nodded.

"And lost? How lost?"

"Two of them dead, or so Zenner thinks. One badly hurt. He thinks Dudurov did it. An ambush. They walked into a trap."

Cheka looked at him. "What three," he asked.

Ulianov recited the names.

"And the fourth?" Cheka asked.

Ulianov said the fourth was Hovani.

Cheka looked at him again. "What, if I may use the expression, Josef Vissarionovich, what in the name of God were they doing in Mr. Carmody's office?"

Ulianov gave him Zenner's version. They were there to protect a woman named Feemster or Teamster. Zenner was not sure of the name. She was something having to do with the Chief Justice. She had gone there on the Chief Justice's business. Something about papers. It had to do with the American rituals, their courts, their hearings. Zenner thought the woman needed protection.

Cheka had two comments on Zenner. A liar. A fool. "I should never have sent him," he added, "which makes me a fool." He thought about Zenner. The man was too ambitious, too much in a hurry, an outsider who had delusions about being adopted. A man who thought his prizes were the result of his merits. The Nobel Prize, the Tolstoy medal, the critical acclaim from the world critics which meant really the geese in New York.

He, Cheka, had ordered and stage managed the whole process with the idea that a Zenner was needed, a useful figure to produce on certain occasions, a useful ventriloquist's dummy. A decoy like Scriabin but painted another color. Ulianov had suggested Zenner, recommended Zenner as the right instrument for them in the last phase in Washington but Ulianov only made recommendations. He, Cheka, made the decisions.

"A liar?" Ulianov asked after a minute or so.

"Meshbesher. The other two." Cheka said. "I know who they are. Assassins. Gunmen. Stranglers. Cutters of throats. Knives in the back. Meshbesher was the fellow who claimed to be as vicious as Speck." He had felt they were well rid of Speck. A question -- who had sent them to Zenner? Ulianov swallowed. Zenner asked for some men who might take care of unforeseen last minute problems.

Cheka nodded. He understood. The request was routine. They had a stable of Meshbeshers, trained and fed and kept ready to dispose of last minute problems. Their grandfathers, or great grandfathers had been down in the cellar with the Romanov family. An elite crowd, a revered corps, respected, maintained in comfort. He should have wiped them out long ago, let them kill each other off in a tournament, crowned the winner as king of the cannibals and shipped him off to administer villages five hundred miles up the Congo.

"I can guess," he said, "the last minute problem."

Ulianov swallowed again. He understood that Cheka had drawn a line around Mr. Carmody. He had known it for years. He had made a suggestion one day and Cheka had stared at him and told him he did not want to hear such a suggestion again. And he knew Zenner was lying. Protecting the Feemster woman (or was her name Teamster?) was a dodge for getting into Mr. Carmody's presence. Very bold and commendable if it succeeded.

The American scheme was proving more difficult than Zenner had planned on. The Chief Justice was meeting resistance. So Zenner had decided to distinguish himself, take the initiative, demonstrate how resourceful he was. Ulianov told Cheka that even he could guess the last minute problem.

Cheka considered. He could get Zenner back in a matter of hours or he could relieve him from duty and leave him to wait for further instructions, officially ill, a sudden, even a terminal, illness. It would give Zenner something to think about. Scriabin would resume charge of the Embassy, consulting Hovani.

Ulianov took a deep breath. Hovani was not exactly available. Zenner had spoken of four men. The fourth man was Hovani. He had told Cheka.

Cheka nodded. He noted to himself that he was as incompetent as the rest of them, a forgetter. And where was Hovani?

"Zenner thinks Mr. Carmody is holding him," Ulianov explained.

A bad day, Cheka thought, a remarkable day. There had been an attempt on Mr. Carmody's life and in Mr. Carmody's office. A violent violation of rules. A violation of an understanding between them. It involved his honor. It also involved more than honor. Mr. Carmody had the four missing cartridges and if Mr. Carmody thought that he, Cheka, had been responsible for the sending of the killers to call on him he was in a position to strike, strike very hard.

Both honor and prudence required him to show that he had nothing to do with the events of the day, that he regretted, deeply regretted. In an emergency he and Mr. Carmody had understood that they had better talk to each other. This was a time for them to speak. Then he reflected that if Adam Lumens were right there was -- in a sense -- nothing to worry about. The world would come to an end. All the same he would call.

Cheka sent Ulianov off to call the Washington Embassy and tell Zenner that he was ill, a dangerous illness, confined to his room, doctors attending him. Scriabin was to be told that he was in charge again, and was to do nothing. He was to be himself, his old sociable self.

Cheka instructed one of his aides. He would speak to a party in Washington. The call would be made on the highest Special Number 1 line.

The old man was not surprised when he was told there was a call on the reserve line, highest priority. He turned to Dudorov. A friend of yours, he said to him. They were still both recovering from Meshbesher and friends, Dudorov more slowly than the old man. But that was expectable.

The old man had been a spectator. Dudorov had had the leading part in the play. The old man spoke. "Carmody."

"V.I. Cheka," Cheka said.

"Who else?" the old man said.

"Does my calling surprise you?"

"No," the old man said. "I thought that you might get in touch with me today, of all days.

"I won't ask you why," Cheka said. "I know something happened. I have had a roundabout story. I think a series of lies. You will tell me. You were not hurt?"

"No," the old man said. "Thanks to General Dudorov. He will tell you about it. It was all too fast, over before I could grasp it. Here is the General." Dudorov began. They were in Mr. Carmody's room, they had been talking, then the door opened. There was Meshbesher, Assad, Osbeg. Everything happened.

Cheka listened. At the end he thanked Dudorov. "You have done me a great service, Constantin Constantinovich. Mr. Carmody will know how great a service it was. A matter between us. Your father also would have known. I am only sorry that you had to do what you did."

"It was nothing I liked," Dudorov told him. No choice. It had been like a corner, a small piece of a battle scene, kill or be killed. Some men could do these things and feel nothing. He could at one time but no longer. He had had too much of it. He heard Cheka's voice again.

"Mr. Carmody," Cheka was saying, "you will assure me that you understand that I did not order what happened today, knew nothing about it, would have forbidden it. An agent out of control. One I will punish. The one responsible."

"I did not need you to tell me that," the old man said. But, he thought, but for Dudorov, orders or no orders, the agents out of control would have ended his worries. No more concern .about the future of his poor countrymen.

Cheka wanted to know -- if Mr. Carmody had no objection -- if they had talked to Hovani, what Hovani had said. It was important to him to know what had led up to the unfortunate business.

Mr. Carmody had no objection. The General had talked to Hovani, and the General would give him Hovani's account.

"So," Cheka said, when Dudorov had finished. "As I thought. No better, no worse. A last question, if it is permitted. May I ask Constantin Constantinovich about" -- he hesitated, "what happened in Mexico City?"

"That," the old man told him, "is for the General to decide." He looked at the General.

"Vladimir Ilyich," Dudorov said after a moment, "I can only tell you what I have told Mr. Carmody," He repeated his story.

"Then it was Troyenko. In character to the end. Difficult. Always assertive."

"And I had had enough of destruction," Dudorov added.

Cheka looked thoughtful. He was thinking about Adam Lumens, the leninos, the singularity that Lumens described. He picked up Dudorov's words.

"We may have all had enough," Cheka said. "Mr. Carmody," he went on, "we keep a close watch on each other. Do you know about the signs that disturb me, the sounds, what I think of as a voice?"

"We are not responsible for them," the old man said to him. "We thought perhaps that you were, that they were one more bogeyman intended to frighten us."

There was a silence. "That makes it worse," Cheka said when he spoke. There they were, everything tied in a knot, demands knotted with threats, the American Chief Justice thinking she was presiding over the knot, thinking she could untie it with universal thanks and rejoicing if everyone did what she ordered.

The knot was his doing. He had labored and labored to create this climactic confusion through which he was to reach his life's goal. And the end was at hand. He thanked Constantin Constantinovich again. He told Mr. Carmody that he regretted the events of the day. "After so many years, Mr. Carmody," Cheka said finally, "a surprising thing. I am not so sure of the future as when we talked long ago."

The old man observed that he had known for years that neither he, himself, nor anyone else had control over the future.

25

Gazette Dismisses Story of Mob Attack,

Marv Mazo talked to Hovani. The Speaker had made the arrangement after hearing about the wild doings at the Intelligence Center. He had called to be sure that the old man was safe and the old man had said that he was. There had been three men involved and disposed of. He had a fourth man, a Colonel Hovani, a higher ranking security type, a regular at the Embassy. The three men were imports, one purpose types. The General, Dudorov, knew the whole lot, knew Hovani, Hovani knew him. That was enough for the Speaker.

"Mike," he had said, "my father and my grandfather before him used to say once a lawyer, always a lawyer. So in a way I may still be a lawyer. Let me make a lawyer's suggestion." The Chief Justice, as everyone knew, was bound and determined to return one Yuri Bolkonsky to the Eurasians as the killer of one C. C. Dudorov, all as set out in the papers. The Eurasian authorities had forwarded proofs of the identity of the aforementioned Yuri Bolkonsky. But if Dudorov were alive? If there was proof that Dudorov were alive? A live witness, a Colonel from the Eurasian Security Forces would confound the whole case, would even cast doubt on the rest of the package that they had been told of by Dodge.

The old man told the Speaker he heard him. What did he propose? The legal mind was a mystery to him, more mysterious as the years passed.

The Speaker explained that there were times when lawyers -- at least on one side of a case -- preferred the truth to a lie. The truth sometimes even had its advantages and should not be concealed from a court. His suggestion was to have someone talk to Hovani and report Hovani's story in print or directly to the Chief Justice or both. The best person, his recommendation, would be Marv Mazo. His reasons were obvious though Marv had not been effective with Madam before. Still it might be useful even if the only result was the lead story in the Gazette. He would call Marv if Mike had no objections.

"I leave it to you," the old man had said. But in his opinion, he added, the Chief Justice and her sisters and brothers would ignore anything they preferred not to know.

Marv saw Hovani and recognized him at once. He was the Ambassador's chauffeur. Or he had answered the door at the Embassy. Or he had been a kind of major domo at Embassy parties. When the introductions were made by the old man with Dudorov in attendance, Hovani went through his story again. He was a colonel in the Security Services, senior, quite senior; assigned to the Embassy. Scriabin was his more or less opposite number. Then the Chairman had sent Zenner to oversee everything. To make sure that nothing went wrong with the plan.

"Zenner," Marv asked. Was he referring to Zenner, the writer, the prize-winning Zenner? Hovani said there was only one Zenner.

"He called me," Marv said, "as an old friend. To arrange an interview with the Chief Justice."

Hovani said the interview was in accordance with the instructions Zenner had from the Chairman.

Marv found that a little disturbing. Zenner was celebrated, novelist, poet, journalist in the best sense of the word, former President of the World Writers' League. Was it proper to ask if Zenner were involved with the Security Services?

Not a regular officer like himself, Hovani explained. Someone used on special projects as needed. But like himself, subject to orders. He did not know Zenner's rank in the Services. That was probably a matter between him and the Chairman. There were a number of men in that category, musicians, scientists, cultural types, highly regarded, well advertized cultural types.

"Zenner," Hovani went on, "arrived at the Embassy a week ago, maybe ten days ago. Took over, as you Americans say. I had word from the top. I was to take Zenner's orders to insure that the plan was successful."

"The plan?" Marv asked. Just what was the plan? It was the second time Hovani had referred to the plan.

The old man broke in. The plan was always the same. To reduce the United States to something like zero. Remove them as an obstacle. The current version was the Mexican business, to abrogate the Treaty of Guadalupe Hidalgo, break up the Union by a court order. Not order from chaos but chaos from a court order.

"That's one way of looking at it," Marv said. The old man was difficult and he saw him rarely. No real source of news. The same old point of view. No change. Never a change. The perfect example of a one track mind and on the same track for the past 50 years. He looked at Hovani. He had asked Hovani the question.

Hovani nodded. He was not accustomed to contradict what was said by his betters and Mr. Carmody was equal to Ulianov, or Cheka for all that he knew. And if what Mr. Carmody had said was maybe crude, maybe rough, without shadings, refinements, it was one way of describing the plan. He nodded again.

"So you were taking orders from Zenner?"

"Yes," said Hovani. "He brought two men with him. A third came a day or two later. Specials but different from Zenner. Members of the regular service but used for one purpose." It was hard to find the right word. Murder? Liquidate? Kill? Very harsh words. "They were sent to get obstacles out of the way, to simplify matters. Early this morning Zenner told me that there was a difficulty, that Mr. Carmody might make it impossible for us to recover possession of General Dudorov and certain important state property."

"General Dudorov?"

"The General," Hovani said, nodding toward Dudorov. "The General here."

"But," Marv said, "our information is that General Dudorov is no longer alive. But you know the story."

Hovani nodded. Of course he knew the story. Naturally he had accepted it.

"But you say this gentleman is General Dudorov." Was he sure?

Hovani nodded again. Of course he was sure. He had known the General for years, many years. The General had been his superior officer on occasion, the man he reported to. On one occasion he owed his life to the General. On a very difficult mission which he was not free to discuss. The present situation was also not for him to discuss but he knew the General as well as he knew anyone in the Security Services. There was no question about it.

"We can come back to that," Marv said. "You were talking about orders from Mr. Zenner. About Mr. Carmody."

"My orders," Hovani went on, "were to take the three men -- they already had their assignment from Zenner -- to the Intelligence Center, see that they got in and performed their assignment."

"Which was?" Marv asked.

Hovani searched for suitable words.

"That they get Mr. Carmody out of the way," he said after a moment. He explained what had happened -- up to a point. They had joined the crowd. There was the affair at the gate. They had gone inside. He had stayed in the corridor.

At best the undertaking was foolish, no planning, the kind of operation that only an amateur would have ordered, the worst he had seen in all his years in the Services, nothing professional.

So the worst had happened. The specials had found themselves dealing with General Dudorov. Not at all what they had expected. Even trained men, as they were, were no match for the General. He had, as he said, been in the corridor -- to head off the Intelligence people. All he personally knew was that there had been eight shots. In a matter of seconds. Two men dead. Meshbesher surviving. A fiasco of Zenner's creation.

No escape route even if the specials had accomplished their purpose. Stupid. Everything stupid. But, Hovani concluded, they were not to think that he regretted the outcome. He had tried to tell Zenner that Mr. Carmody was out of bounds for the Security Services and been threatened with being reported for questioning orders.

Marv wanted to know if Hovani was willing to testify in court, under oath, to identify Dudorov under oath.

The idea did not appeal to Hovani. There were dangers of a kind that he thought it would be indelicate to speak of to a stranger. He considered. Cheka was no friend to failure. He might be less drastic than some of the Chairmen, or whatever title they chose, who had presided over the Republics before him, but no one could be sure what his reactions would be. There were always replacements for Meshbesher or Assad or Osbeg and he might be their target. His predicament was bad enough as it was.

To contradict the official line, publicly, in a court, would make him a pariah, an outlaw. He could recall two, maybe three, similar cases and he knew what had happened. Since being seized in the corridor he had been slowly realizing his status. It was no better than Dudorov's, probably. Like Dudorov he needed protection, to become and to stay invisible like people in stories he had read or been told as a child. He told Marv that he had reasons, private reasons, for not wanting to make a public appearance.

"You understand those reasons," the old man observed.

Marv both did and did not. He lived in one world. These people lived in another. He had known Scriabin for years, a very agreeable, civilized man, full of news and stimulating ideas. The Eurasians generally were agreeable, civilized people, quite open, as they said not really unlike the Americans. The same aims, the same interests, the same concerns about maintaining a peaceful, comfortable order of things.

He and Scriabin had always talked freely. The atmosphere of the Embassy was pleasant and friendly. Marv knew that there were those who thought the air of friendship and ease a deception, old-fashioned in their distrust of the Republics' aims and objectives. He was aware there were conflicts of interest but that was part of the normal relationship between powers and empires, minor disputes to be worked out and resolved.

Still it was disturbing to have this man, Hovani, a senior officer in the shadowy Security Services describe himself as more or less Scriabin's opposite number, to hear that his Zenner, the world renowned Zenner, was also to a degree Security Services, that his Zenner had sent what Hovani referred to as specials to -- there was no way to avoid the word -- to assassinate old Michael Carmody.

Hovani's complaint was that Zenner was clumsy, that there was no real preparation for the attempt. And then Hovani had referred to a plan, had acquiesced in the old man's way of explaining what the plan was. Also Hovani was sure that it was Dudorov who was sitting there with the old man, Dudorov, not a ghost.

Marv recalled Scriabin's telling him about Dudorov, a man of fine quality, distinguished family, distinguished career, with who knew what future before him, beautiful wife, promising children, strong, original mind, his death a real tragedy, a loss to them all, a deeply felt loss, and a death shocking in its barbarity, killed in cold blood, and, with the killer taking refuge with what Scriabin had called "your Mr. Carmody."

The implication was clear. He, Marv, and all the Americans were guilty of Dudorov's death at the hands of Mr. Carmody's agent. But if Dudorov had never been killed? There was no question of Scriabin's sincerity. You could say almost that Scriabin felt a personal grief which he could not hide, an unusual reaction in a generally worldly, unemotional man.

He was certain that Scriabin had not meant to deceive him. Or could he be sure? Scriabin was a diplomat, the accomplished practiced ambassador. Ambassadors, according to the old jest, were men who were sent to lie abroad for their sovereigns. He could give Scriabin the benefit of the doubt, but the Chairman? Was the Chairman demanding the return of Yuri Bolkonsky in the belief that he had in fact killed Constantin Dudorov or was this part of the game as the old man defined it?

Marv also recalled what the Speaker had told him: that Dudorov was under the old man's protection, having taken sanctuary after the disaster in Mexico City; that Dudorov had brought him four explosive devices, deadly miniatures intended first to destroy the American Embassy in Mexico, then to destroy selected cities, ending in Washington.

Marv had listened and put it all out of his mind. The Speaker's information was tainted, from a source that no one could trust, namely, old Michael Carmody. They knew, all experienced journalists knew the old man lived in a dream world, conspiracy, counter conspiracy, an endless struggle with the forces of Evil, the United States always under threat of destruction, but if Dudorov were alive?

Marv had once been a reporter, running around in pursuit of simple, every day facts such as whose dog had started the dog fight. He was on the highest plane now. He had facts served up to him on a platter, exalted facts, facts concerning only the most important matters that concerned the minds of men who would be noticed and written about in the history books.

If the man who sat next to Mr. Carmody were Dudorov, the least he, Marv, could do as a reporter, low or high level, was to ask the obvious questions. Why was General Dudorov there? And what explanation did he have for the Yuri Bolkonsky business? Marv asked if he could put a few questions to General Dudorov, if Mr. Carmody would allow the General to answer them.

"I have no objection," the old man said. "The General can answer or not as he pleases. But first we will dismiss Colonel Hovani." And Hovani was turned over to a couple of Intelligence helpers who struck Marv as somewhat forbidding.

"Now," Marv said when Hovani had left. He put his first question: why the General was there. He listened. Dudorov had his assignment from Cheka. First the American Embassy in Mexico City, then so on and so on. Did Mr. Mazo know Troyenko? Yes, Mr. Mazo had been acquainted with the Ambassador. It was Troyenko who had spoiled the first operation and he, Dudorov, had been so shaken by what he had seen that he had abandoned the scheme that he was to execute, had come to Mr. Carmody with what was spoken of as the state property. He was a ruined man but he thought he had made the right choice. Did he regret? Only the loss of his family.

And about Yuri Bolkonsky? Cheka was clever, always resourceful. Cheka understood the Americans. They might be uneasy about turning over a Dudorov who could be looked at as a political refugee. They could be counted on to turn over a criminal, a man who had committed a murder, especially the murder of a high or moderately high Eurasian official. That was all there was to it. Was he bitter?

"No," Dudorov said, "probably not. Vladimir Ilyich I have known all my life. He was a friend of my father. What you call a protege, in his early days, of my grandfather. A political man. Not a man who often thinks in terms of small human lives. Dedicated to making the Republics the only power on the face of the Earth. The habit of a lifetime and he is not a young man. Am I bitter? I regret the loss of such friendship as I had with Vladimir Ilyich. An interesting man. Misguided now as I see it. A danger to your people here though they may not see it. You may not see it. Mr. Carmody has told me you are the Mr. Mazo of the Gazette. Most influential. Vladimir Ilyich has told me he approves of the Gazette. Broad-minded he says."

There was silence, no questions, no answers, broken by the old man's saying amen. "Very good, General, " he said, "Mr. Mazo has heard you and, for that matter, Colonel Hovani, and he doesn't know what to make of it. It is not the kind of thing the Gazette likes to touch."

Marv had one final question. Did the Chairman know that General Dudorov was with Mr. Carmody; Mr. Carmody personally?

"Yes," the old man said. "He spoke to him today."

"Spoke to him?"

The old man nodded. "My friend Cheka called not long after the incident -- we can call it that-- to ask after my health. To apologize. Express his regrets. He spoke to the General, thanked him for his intervention."

Marv had been almost persuaded that Dudorov and Hovani were real but this was too much. The old man did live in a dream. The two men he had spoken to could only be a couple of actors, probably Intelligence types playing parts in the fantasy. Cheka calling to express his regrets. That was too much. What Olga Feemster reported rang true. It matched everything that he knew, had known for years.

He had a story, an important story for the Gazette: Michael Carmody was the victim of senile delusions and he had the proof. It was important that the public should know this and he should probably tell the President first.

26

Cheka Still Refuses Open War on US; Uzbeks Poised to Strike

There had been no public mention that the widow Troyenko had consoled herself within a matter of days by marrying Marshal Shishak, the ranking single marshal of the Eurasian Union and commanding officer of its armed forces under the old Double Marshal.

Among the informed, the marriage caused no surprise. Madam Troyenko and Shishak had been more or less paired off for a number of years. Shishak was assumed to be a bachelor. At least there had never been any sign of his having a wife since he had risen to a position of prominence. Madam Troyenko -- she had been Anastasia Globus -- was recognized as the ambitious daughter of a principal hierarch.

Apart from being an ill-tempered man, Troyenko had been a disappointing match, a man who had depended on his connection with Globus for his career and fated never to be a personage in his own right.

When Madam and Shishak first met, each had responded. Ambition had called to ambition and it was assumed there were other factors at work. Madam had style. Shishak looked like a marshal. As hostess for Globus Madam for the most part stayed in Moscow where she and the Marshal were, as the phrase goes, thrown together in the highest official society. The first attraction was followed by friendship and that by more personal feelings.

Immediately after the disaster in Mexico -- Madam had been in Moscow when it occurred -- Shishak asked the Double Marshal's advice: would it be acceptable if he were to marry Madam Troyenko forthwith? The Double Marshal approved, regretting that he was not 30 years younger.

Globus approved, approved very much. With Shishak as his son-in-law, he felt his views on the policy of the Union would be given the respect they deserved. The Double Marshal would still speak for the armed forces of the Republic but he, Globus, would guide Shishak who would in turn guide the old Double Marshal along the right path.

Globus was willing to give Cheka full credit for having accomplished the Merger and the moves that had followed. But Cheka was too patient in his dealings with the Americans, too much the pragmatist. Fabian was the word. The triumph of the Eurasian Republics was certain, so the sooner the better. History had to be helped on its way.

There were times when he wondered if Cheka was wanting in zeal, always reluctant to force the issue with force. With Shishak allied to him by marriage Globus saw himself in a position to act if Cheka's moves did not end the American game, even if there were the least question of how it would end, the least hesitation on the American side. He would invoke the armed forces. One blow from them, only one blow would achieve the triumph foreseen by the Founders.

Even Ulianov was concerned when he heard of the marriage of Madam Troyenko and Shishak. After all, though he was the chosen successor, successions had not always been painless. He spoke of the marriage with Cheka.

"Yes," Cheka said. "It was all very correct. Semyon Semyonovich spoke to me -- for the bridegroom. I gave them my blessing. All very correct." Family alliances at the top of the pyramid were recognized as matters of consequence, sources of power, also sources of misunderstanding as to the motives involved, subject to approval. "An affair of the heart," Cheka concluded.

Ulianov insisted that he was not questioning Vladimir Ilyich's judgment. He never questioned his judgment. But was it only an affair of the heart?

"Let us call it that," Cheka said. "The heart is complex. The very young heart is moved by one thing, the older heart by another, maybe others. The heart, Josef Vissarionovich, grows more complex as it grows older. Madam Troyenko and Shishak are past their first bloom, still blooming but past their first bloom. We will assume the presence of love -- however defined -- and perhaps other reasons."

"But," Ulianov asked, "how does it look?" Troyenko gone for only a matter of days. No sign of mourning. The haste. How would it look?

"They are setting a good example, " Cheka explained. "The possibly irregular now becomes regular. Very discreet. Madam Troyenko -- Madam Shishak -- looks well in black. She will continue her efficient duties as hostess for Globus -- wearing black for a suitable time."

"But," Ulianov objected, "Shishak has a wife, as we know, other wives maybe."

"That," Cheka said, "is something we will hope he has explained to his latest wife. It is her concern. A personal matter. Shishak is a Timurid on his mother's side. Or so he chooses to think. He is H. T. Shishak. Hulagu Timur. Timurids are accustomed to have a number of wives. It is all part of his idea of himself as a marshal. As a Timurid he can do things that we may need but would care not to do for ourselves. The Deccan. Java. A great restorer of order."

Ulianov saw the point. They had had problems -- they still had problems -- after the Merger. They had talked with the Double Marshal at length. Shishak, he said, was reliable. They had turned Shishak loose. He was to use his best judgment. "All the same," Ulianov said, "you look on Shishak as I do, a butcher in uniform, a marshal's uniform now."

"But," Cheka observed, "butchers are useful. In their way an indispensable trade. No butchers, no banquets."

"In their way, yes," Ulianov said. "In their place, yes. But Shishak is one with ambition. So too is the woman."

Cheka reflected. Ambition was said to be what distinguished man from what were called the lower animals. It was, or was said to be, what kept the houses warm in the winter, made the harvest possible year after year, made a great people. "You were ambitious," he said after a moment. "I was ambitious, Josef Vissarionovich."

Ulianov conceded as much. But there was both dark and light ambition. Shishak's ambition was dark. And Globus' daughter's. And Globus'.

"So," Cheka said, "I agree. I agree. You think the pair can cause trouble? I think they would like to. Our ambition was light. Their ambition is dark."

Ulianov set out what he knew. There had been conversations, Madam and Globus, Madam and Shishak, Shishak and Globus, Madam and Shishak and Globus, tentative, soundings, the Americans, what to expect, the Mexicans and their claims, how best to insure that the imperialists were brought to their senses. "Some things recorded," Ulianov said. "Some heard and reported. People I trust. People you trust."

Cheka nodded. They had people they trusted. It was a world in which it was wise to be cautious. From a distance a forest was quiet, no movement. In the woods you could see or hear the comings and goings of hundreds of creatures.

It was the same for the hierarchy over which he presided. To outsiders it was calm, everything, everyone fixed in a perpetual order: but it was different inside. Semyon Semyonovich was the Double Marshal and old enough to be satisfied. The younger ones were anxious or eager, uncertain about who they were, afraid of falling or bent on advancing.

You could regard them as harmless but they had to be watched to be sure that they did not injure themselves or unsettle the order which insured their well-being and maintained the pyramid on which they all lived. Even the greatest pyramids had to be built with regard to stresses and thrusts. Each was a combination of balance and weight, required care in the building, care in the maintenance over the years. Cheka asked what was recorded, what the trusted people had heard.

"They are talking about what happens if the --" Ulianov found it difficult to find the right words. These people were contemplating something that it was improper to contemplate.

"If the apple does not fall from the tree? If my plan fails?" Cheka suggested.

Ulianov nodded. It was better for Cheka to say it.

"And they would like to chop down the tree?"

Ulianov nodded again.

"Well," Cheka said, "they may be right in one thing. The apple may not be as ripe as I thought. President Blossom. We are right about him and the lady Secretary of State and their lady Chief Justice. Maybe right about almost all the Americans. But even a few can cause problems. A few old ones. And their Madam Clymer. Younger but a throwback as the Americans say."

Ulianov was not sure what Cheka was telling him. Was Cheka saying that the Americans might not commit suicide according to schedule? And, if so, what happened next? He was the successor but he was Cheka's chosen successor.

Cheka looked at him. Poor Josef Vissarionovich, anxious, uneasy. "So," he said, "you want to know what happens if the apple stays on the tree? Shishak is the axe. Do I take the axe to the tree: Let us consider. The axe is ambitious. The axe's wife is ambitious. Globus reads the old fairy tales and believes them. They would gain less than they think if the tree were cut down. And if we need an axe, we can find an axe safer than Shishak."

Ulianov agreed. They could find another axe, one with more modest ambitions. Would the Double Marshal agree?

Cheka was pleased. It was to Ulianov's credit to ask such a question. Semyon Semyonovich was wonderfully useful. The Double Marshal and trained at the right time, understanding that marshals did not give orders but took them and without too many questions. Consulted and treated with deference he could go on for years. Offended, he might want to retire or simply melt away like the snow at the end of the winter.

Cheka had considered the choice of a new Double Marshal. None of the single marshals had the respect and authority that the old Double Marshal enjoyed. Shishak maybe came closest. But neither Shishak nor the rest had gone through the school that the old Double Marshal had attended long ago in his youth. The thing to do was to keep the old Double Marshal for as long as possible. He thought for a moment of what Lumens was telling him. How long was possible? An interesting point.

"So much for apples and trees and axes for the present," Cheka said. "We will make up our minds. And what else was recorded or heard?"

Ulianov explained. It was a delicate subject. The time spent with Lumens. The time with the listener-watchers. These they had known about. The implications. The possible inference. These were discussed.

"And they concluded I am out of touch with reality?"

Ulianov said nothing.

"And they had a duty to act?"

Ulianov nodded. "Have, could have a duty."

"Naturally," Cheka said. "Globus is a very serious person. A responsible person. But, Josef Vissarionovich, what is reality?"

It was not, Ulianov explained, something on which he could give an opinion. He had not been trained in philosophy at the Higher Technicum or later at the Higher Military Academy. They had not studied reality. It was not one of the subjects. Other things, yes. Reality in the deeper sense, no. And Cheka's question was, of course, concerned with the deeper sense.

"And the deeper sense?" Cheka asked. Reality however Ulianov chose to define it. Who dealt in reality, Globus or Lumens?

Ulianov ventured an answer. Each dealt in reality. They were separate realities. Globus looked at this world. Lumens -- from what he heard -- looked at the universe. But Globus' world and Lumens' universe had nothing to do with each other. Science was science, and useful if you could, as they said, apply it. But the stars, the beginning and end of the universe, what was there to apply? Perhaps it was a kind of reality but it would mean nothing to Globus or Madam or Shishak. Nothing to interest them. Nothing that could concern what they did.

"You put that well," Cheka said. "A very good answer. But suppose the universe were to end tomorrow or the day after tomorrow, or the day after that?"

"How can I suppose that?" Ulianov asked. No one could contemplate such an event. People used to believe that the world was about to come to an end. That much he had heard about, maybe read about. But the world had gone on. No one had ever talked about the end of the universe. The universe, so he understood, was eternal, whatever that meant.

In spite of himself he began to wonder about Cheka's questions. He knew about Lumens, the medal, the refuge business, the rest of it. It was his business to know. Cheka's interests were broad, at times perhaps a little peculiar. Still Cheka could not be serious about the kind of ideas that Lumens was said to present to anyone who would listen.

"But you know," Cheka said, "that people die every day. For our own people we have some kind of figures. How many? Ten thousand a day. Twenty thousand. Then the wild creatures. How many of them? The trees. How many of them? Each is a partial end of the world or the universe. Expected, unexpected. But quick. The light extinguished. So the entire creation could end. Not piecemeal, as we have observed, but altogether, one ending."

"No," Ulianov said. "It is too much for me. I cannot conceive it."

Well, Cheka thought, there is no need for him to. Lumens could be right or he could be wrong. They had been to the listener-watchers. Lumens had agreed there was a sound, very distinct, and the sound was what Cheka had said. But he was mystified by the sound. His leninos were soundless; or so he had thought. Perhaps there had been fewer, more distant. That could account for the difference.

As for Mene Mene Tekel, the correct view, scientific, detached, would be, accidental, coinciding by accident with the sounds in a story, a book. The source out of our galaxy. Not even a neighboring galaxy, but a black hole, one he had watched, had named Kidinnu Sigma, very far, very far – if distance existed. What had been called, a singularity, naked.

Then Lumens had told him, a day or two earlier, the listener-watchers had been confounded. An observing, reporting device in space, blind and silent for years, presumed to be dead if instruments died, was alive and busy. There was no question about its identity but it was in the wrong place -- so far as place had a meaning. It should have been in our galaxy, after calculating its last position, the time elapsed, the speed at which it could move.

Nevertheless the images being sent seemed to be from one of the most distant galaxies, billions of light years away. They were confounded. It was impossible that they could see the images that they saw. The images ought not to arrive until a year with an impossible date -- billions of years in the future. No doubt Brilliant would tell him about it. It was a matter the listener-watchers had no authority to dispose of. They could report but the significance of their data was for their betters in higher circles to discuss and decide. They were only eyes and ears. Above them were Institutes, a composite mind which would consider and arrive at conclusions on the data received.

Cheka had listened and asked Lumens' opinion. Lumens had seen the images. He knew the theory. He was part of the composite mind. "No," Lumens had told him, "I am in a refuge. A certified casualty. Wild. Disqualified to participate in the work of the Institutes or to have an opinion on problems presented them."

"Right," Cheka had said. "But as a favor to me, a member of none of the Institutes." Lumens thought the sensible view was to assume that the listener-watchers were wrong in their reports; that they had not seen what they claimed; that they were misled as to the point from which the instrument was transmitting its pictures.

Second, you could conclude that the instrument was either deranged or was lying; that its pictures were in some way distorted, inaccurate, false. Otherwise, Lumens explained, this was a disaster, every accepted truth contradicted, the size, the age of the universe thrown into question, the immense advance of science reduced to so much deception, the highest mathematical thinking reduced from truth to some speculation.

"What difference will it make," Cheka had asked, "if this black hole of yours erupts and everything ends -- or everything starts over again?"

In that event, Lumens conceded, you might not regard it as a serious matter, nothing to worry about. At least there would be no one to worry about it. Ulianov could not conceive it. Maybe no one could conceive it, not even Lumens. As for himself, he knew Lumens was counting the days, seemed to think it was a matter of what they called hours, but he could dismiss what Lumens was talking about except for the noise -- the voice -- which was real. The Americans heard it and old Michael Carmody had told him they supposed it was one of his, Cheka's tricks, something to frighten them.

Ulianov got up to leave.

Perhaps I was wrong," Cheka said. "Delay is delay. It can do harm. We had better talk to Semyon Semyonovich. The Americans may not behave as we thought." If Lumens were wrong he had better be what was called practical, attend to the affairs of this world. And if Lumens were right no harm would be done. His great grandparents, it occurred to him, would have resorted to the consolation of prayer if they thought the end of days was at hand.

27

Communications Down; Gazette Reporter "Vaporized"

The western governors had met in Austin and called on the governors of the other states to join with them in forming a new national government if the present government in Washington failed in its duty to preserve the existing union intact. They proposed a convention of the states at which the present government would be declared dissolved, the writing of a new constitution and the creation of a new central government based on it. The response had been good, with only a few of the eastern governors showing some reluctance to join in the plan.

There had evidently been an attempt to destroy the Capitol in Austin where the meeting was held but nothing was clear. Planet had shut down its operations. Othman Frick had closed his. Seeing was believing and without cameras and broadcasts the world no longer seemed real. There were written reports but they lacked conviction, words, only words. To read of explosions and rioting, to read of armed bands and street fighting carried little conviction.

What people wanted was to see, to be spectators, to watch buildings burn and crowds on a rampage. Even the rioters in spite of themselves, felt discouraged at the thought that their rage was not being recorded for the national audience and future generations as well.

The reporters, too, felt less enthusiasm for the proceedings than they had expected. There were attacks and counterattacks, noise and blood, ambulances arrived and departed, bodies lay in the streets but the uplift, the glow, the excitement was wanting. It was true in Austin, in the California cities, in all the principal centers, New York, even Chicago where Castillo's demonstrators had undertaken to strike a blow against those who were withholding their rights.

But if they were discouraged by the absence of cameras, they were discouraged as well by the presence of troops sent by Louisa. The troops were unsympathetic. Some even fired real bullets. Castillo demanded an end to what he called the white terror but he was handicapped by being denied his right to be seen and heard by his usual admiring millions. Even he felt the performance was flat. He used all the usual words, all the usual gestures but he had a sense that the effort was wasted, no scope, no reaching out.

Mark Antony may have been satisfied with a small street crowd in the Forum. Castillo was accustomed to working on a larger, less local scene and Fresser had shut him up in a closet. Castillo knew he had the most sacred constitutional right -- First Amendment right as they called it -- to be heard by the public en masse and yet there was, for the moment, no way to enforce it.

He knew the Chief Justice would grant him an injunction if he went around to apply but for the past ten days her injunctions had been unproductive. She had, so to speak, been firing so many blanks, duds that failed to explode. Castillo saw himself the victim of a sudden disrespect for the law.

Castillo felt this most painfully when he was ruled out of order by the Speaker when he rose to demand that the House make an immediate inquiry into the murders ordered by the Director of Intelligence and committed in his presence in his own office. The Speaker also refused to allow him to address the House on the unlawfulness of Othman Frick's actions and of the use of armed troops to prevent the people from exercising their right to assemble and make their grievances known. His usual allies were silent.

The Treaty state delegations had friends, many friends, and the word was out that they would all support the Speaker and vote to expel any member who favored the breaking up of the United States by court order or otherwise. Their cowardice disgusted Castillo. The Speaker was being arbitrary and lawless.

In the cloak room they were talking again of impeaching the Court, all of the court, possibly all of the judges. There was some talk of supporting Othman Frick's proposed convention of states and the writing of a new Constitution, of starting life over again. The situation was, Castillo decided, dangerous, critically dangerous. They had been accumulating statutes for over 200 years. In the whole mass one or two or three of them ought to be useful. It was a problem for Luanda and his staff and computers. Certainly the Attorney General could come up with an answer and get some kind of court order, assuming anyone would respect it.

The difficulty was, all too clearly, in the sudden epidemic of disrespect for the law. But he went to look for Luanda and was told he had gone to the White House. He followed him to the White House. Perhaps the thing to do was to see Blossom, himself, and demand that he move to protect the rights of the people.

Unfortunately for Castillo when he got near the White House, there was a crowd, armed and unarmed, with posters stating demands, protesting and angry. Louisa's troops were spoiling the game, heavily armed, a few tanks, quiet and giving no sign of responding to exhortations to join their sisters and brothers.

Castillo got out of his cab and began to push and shove his way through the crowd so that he could get to the troops and then on to the White House. After all he was a star of the House, a representative of the people of Illinois, a person entitled to deference and welcome wherever he went.

The problem was to get through the crowd, make himself known to some officer in charge of the troops and, then with an escort, proceed on his mission to Blossom. Progress was slow. In some ways he admired the crowd, surly, contentious, giving a promise of violence. But he wanted it out of his way so he redoubled his pushing. He pushed with authority. There was some muttering, some pushing back. He was almost at his goal when he gave what he hoped was a last shove. The heavy squat figure refused to give way, turned and pushed back. Castillo spoke to him.

"Out of my way," he commanded, pushing again. "I am Castillo. Out of my way." He saw an officer a few yards away watching him. Castillo raised his hand, motioned to him, called to him.

The heavy squat figure looked at Castillo. He was being addressed in English. He did not understand it. It was the language of tyrants. The English speaker, a friend of the officer, was treating him with contempt. Some unknown but friendly person had been passing out hand guns and had given one to the heavy squat figure. The heavy squat figure considered. He could fire it or use the butt as a club. He chose the latter, swung the gun hard, brought it down on Castillo's skull with a smash. Castillo went down. The heavy squat figure kicked at him. Someone else kicked him, a second, a third, a fourth. The officer to whom Castillo had called saw what had happened, moved in with a half dozen men, reached Castillo, tried to get to the heavy squat figure, met with resistance. Hand guns were fired. Troops fired back.

It was a quarter of an hour later that the reporters on the scene learned from each other that Castillo had been a victim of the violence of the Armed Forces of the United States, beaten and kicked to death by them while he tried to quiet the crowd of protesters as it sought to assert its right to assemble and make their case to the President. Taken with the murders at the Intelligence Center, the death of Castillo revealed the brutality of the elements committed to maintaining the United States as they were.

For Blossom the news came as a terrible shock. He had been troubled by the protesters. He had been troubled by the presence of the troops Louisa had insisted on bringing in -- as she said -- to protect him.

His impulse had been to go out to the crowd, make clear his good will, express the sympathy he felt for them. Marietta agreed. It was the right thing to do. It was honest, courageous. All he needed was to speak from the heart. Luanda agreed.

It was Blossom's duty to hear and to speak to the people. Louisa told him to stop acting the fool. The crowd was paid for, so many extras at so much an hour, and some of them armed. He would go out at the risk of his life and for nothing at all.

His kind words would mean nothing. And there were serious things to attend to. The western governors, all the governors were serious. He had to give them an answer. The crazy Chief Justice and her crazy court were supposed to be sitting tomorrow. Would he allow it? Could he in some way postpone it?

If he wanted to calm anyone, it would be better to calm the court than a ragtag of a crowd. And then, beset as he was, there came the ghost of Castillo, done to death, so to speak, in his presence.

The working press was downstairs asking his comment. They had their story. What had he to say?

He was Commander- in-Chief and his agents had murdered Castillo. There was blood, Castillo's blood, on his hands. What was his, the murderer's, comment? The working press had a right to know the murderer's comment, something to go down in the books, something for the historians or maybe a writer of plays. What did Augustus say when he got the word about Cleopatra? There were no reporters to ask.

These were better times and he had a duty to speak to the press which guarded the liberties of the people.

Marietta understood the situation at once. "You had better see the reporters," she said. "You can only tell them the truth. You are grieved, sick at heart. You will punish the guilty. A great public loss for which we all must atone."

Luanda agreed. Marietta was right. And the accent must be on a public loss, personal guilt, certain punishment for the guilty. Furthermore this was the time to withdraw all the troops, all the troops everywhere, maybe disarm them, dispel the threat that they posed to government by the people. He looked hard at Louisa. She was a dangerous woman.

Blossom listened. He turned to Louisa. "I think they're right," he said to her. "Marietta is right. We have sinned and we must pay for our sins. You may not have liked Castillo but he had a good heart. He felt and resented injustice. I had better see the press."

Louisa shook her head slowly. "No," she said. "Don't see them now. Not until we know what happened outside. We can dry our eyes in the meantime. As you said, I had no use for Castillo alive. I like him no better dead. There should be witnesses. Let me talk to our people and get their report. The reporters can wait."

Marietta objected. She knew the profession. They had a story to file. Time was important. It was an impatient profession. Everyone had a deadline. They would leave and how would it look if the President had refused to express his sympathy with all those who would mourn the death of Castillo, especially in the circumstances in which he had died?

Louisa's answer was that there was nothing to worry about. The reporters were there in the White House. They would stay until they had permission to leave. And she would get a report from the senior officer present. A half hour later she had talked to him, talked to the officer to whom Castillo had called, had their accounts of the martyrdom. She stopped in the press room.

Those who were present remembered the session they had with Louisa. They were feeling annoyed. They had, in effect, summoned the President and had been kept waiting. They had a big story. They knew the public was eager to have it.

When they threatened to leave they were told it might be unsafe for them. The crowd or part of the crowd was still outside and still ugly. Anyhow the President had their message. Marv Mazo's number two man was the ranking journalist of the group by virtue of being from the Gazette, and took the view that Blossom was preparing a suitable statement. He thought they could expect the President humble in spirit, contrite, very contrite. What they got was Louisa.

Louisa began by saying that she had heard the story relayed to the President. She wanted to know who had seen Castillo being beaten to death. Nobody had, but they had seen the body. They were sure about the cause of the death. How did they know that the troops were responsible? Marv's number two man had the answer: who else could have done it?

"You were there," Louisa observed. "Maybe you did it. Or maybe it was another one or two or three of you. You say you were part of the crowd."

Marv's number two man thought the joke -- if a joke -- in bad taste. Moreover he did not like being questioned. The press asked the questions. Louisa persisted. She wanted to know the size of the crowd. They thought 2,000, 3,000, maybe 5,000. Someone thought, maybe, 10,000. Louisa's comment was sharp: they did not seem to be sure of their facts, not very accurate. And, also, why were they sure that no one in this crowd of from 2,000 to 10,000 had murdered Castillo?

Marv's number two man had the answer again. He explained, patiently, carefully, that when they saw Castillo there were troops by the body.

"Have any of you ever been police reporters?" Louisa inquired.

Some of them had been. When they got to the scene of the crime had they found police officers there? They conceded that was the usual state of affairs. Then, did they assume the police had committed the crime?

Marv's number two man thought the Castillo situation was different. How different? It was hard to explain. A matter of instinct. Had they asked the officer in charge of the troops what had happened? No. But there was no reason to. They could use their own eyes. What else could they think? And how did they know Castillo had been trying to quiet the crowd? Had anyone seen him? No one had seen him.

Louisa gave up. Who, she asked had started the story that had been passed on to the President? Marv's number two man said he had pieced it together. That was reporting. The Secretary might not be familiar with the techniques of reporting. You picked up the facts, sorted them out. It was like putting a puzzle together. And you had to know human nature. It was like all kinds of writing. Imagination had to be applied to the facts. Reporting was an art in its way.

Enough was enough. Louisa looked at Marv's number two man. "My advice," she told him, "to you and to all of you is to wait to file any story about the death of Mr. Castillo until you know what you are talking about." She suggested they talk to the officer and men who had recovered Castillo's body after seeing him struck down in the crowd.

Marv's number two man declined for the group. He was sorry he had to be blunt. All they could get would be self-serving statements. They could not expect honest confessions. And with all deference to the Secretary, they could not expect her to face the disagreeable truth, that her agents -- and, of course, the President's agents -- were out of control. Or were they out of control in attacking and killing a major political figure who condemned the Secretary's defiance of the Court as it moved to deal with the Mexican crisis?

Marv's number two man would have said more. He resented Louisa. Louisa disgusted him. In one way women disgusted him. He could admire their minds. Their minds were no different from the minds of their fathers or mothers. But apart from their minds, they were disgusting. That was the only word to describe the effect they had on him.

He respected Mr. Mazo sincerely except for his involvement -- was the word -- with the Chief Justice. Feet of clay was the usual phrase. However Mr. Mazo was old, twice his own age, maybe more and in Mr. Mazo's time the style for almost everyone was for men to pair off with women or try to. Style was decisive.

The style of his generation was different and he had no obligation to look at Louisa except as she was, a woman and an overpowering woman at that, repellent, offensive, disgusting. He looked at Louisa. Another Messalina, another Theodora, another Poppaea. Marv's number two man had a sound education and he could see in Louisa all the infamous women he had read about in the books.

They were females who got and loved power, who enjoyed being female and holders of power. Each one a tigress, a man-killing tigress. Like all the well informed members of his profession he knew Louisa's whole history, the success at the bar, the Eternity Trust Company, the political phase, ambitious and reckless, a threat to everything. that was decent.

The time had come for someone to tell her all this to her face. Castillo's death demanded that someone speak out. Everyone else might be, but he was no coward. He was not afraid of her. He opened his mouth, spoke the first words. Then the sound of his voice faded, became a low whine, disappeared. And he disappeared, faded away with his voice, disappeared with his voice. There was an empty space where he had stood.

The survivors, if that was the word, stared at Louisa. They were stunned. Then they were anxious. Anxiety turned into terror.

As reporters they knew everything, knew all that was hidden. The military had a disintegrating device that was super top secret. No one was to be told of its existence but they had all heard about it. It was the latest and most deadly ultimate weapon except that probably the Eurasians, in self defense had something as good. And before their eyes, Secretary Clymer had used it.

Even as they watched she had vaporized one of their colleagues not that they saw any vapor. Whatever she used, the demonstration appalled them, done in cold blood, silent, no warning, with what they could swear was an invisible weapon. They had detected no move by the Secretary but there had to be remote controls that would be brought to light later.

All they could report was that the Secretary had done away with a member of the staff of the New York Gazette who was critical of her. They knew they were in danger. The Secretary might vaporize them. They hesitated. What should they do? What should they say? Then they fled, leaving Louisa astonished at the disappearance of Marv Mazo's number two man.

28

Marshal Shishak Defies Cheka Order, Invades US to Burn, Panic Cities

Schmiedegen had gone north with Aleman Villa to look at the encampment where more millions were assembling on their way to the Border. There were difficulties, delays. And Marshal Shishak had come in by rocket to join them for a couple of hours.

Shishak was angry. The schedule, they were not meeting the schedule. He had sent supplies and advisers, 50,000 advisers to superintend and keep the mass moving but it would not move. They had talked together, the three of them.

Aleman Villa had tried to explain. His were a poor people, a people oppressed. They were eager to take over their promised inheritance but they had been getting bad reports back from the river. The United States troops, they were hostile. His people were cautious but they had tried a number of crossings and had regrettable losses. Some of the wounded had made their way south with discouraging stories.

He could engage his own troops but he was not sure what would follow. They were brave, very brave. Nevertheless, the United States was a great power, demoralized but not as demoralized as expected. Everything would be solved if the Eurasian Republics would act, an ultimatum perhaps. Better still if their soldiers took the lead, attacked, broke the Americans, opened the door for his people to enter. Without such help, his people might lose heart, begin to swarm back. There could be a stampede. Everything would fall into pieces.

He had said all this to Ambassador Schmiedegen. What was the Marshal's opinion? The Ambassador and the Marshal indicated they were not unsympathetic. They would confer by themselves.

"Vermin," said Shishak after Aleman Villa had left. "So many lice."

Schmiedegen thought Shishak's language was strong but soldiers were soldiers.

"So many lice," Shishak repeated. "As bad as what we have in our East and our South. Even worse."

"The world is the world," Schmiedegen said philosophically. "We take the world as we find it."

Shishak shook his head. No philosopher, Shishak. He was offended. These people were useless for the purpose intended and he had had no confidence in them. They were Cheka's idea, the always resourceful Vladimir Ilyich who preferred indirection, one clever move after another, successful up to a point.

Even he had admired the Merger. But with the Merger he had seen no reason for any further delay. There was no need after that to be clever. He was no chess player but he knew checkmate when he saw it and the Merger was the end of the game. His honored father-in-law with his talk of principles and doctrinal purity was a fool but Globus was right in saying to him that Cheka was a waster of time, time that no one could recover.

The armed forces of the Republic were a hammer. One blow would do it. The Americans were nothing but an overripe melon. All that was left was to pick up the pieces. He had said it all to the poor old Double Marshal. Grabkin had repeated it, argued -- he said -- the point to Cheka. And Cheka always said no, that it was better to wait, that it was unwise to push even the Americans into a corner.

Cheka was always using what were called figures of speech. He had told the old Double Marshal that the Americans were, he could assume, an old toothless lion. But old lions had claws. Old lions were dangerous, especially old wounded lions and the hunter might fail to kill with his first blow. When Shishak asked to see Cheka, to make sure that poor old Grabkin had presented the case as he should, Cheka had sent word that it was the Double Marshal and only the Double Marshal with whom he as Chairman, or whatever he was, dealt on matters involving the armed forces of the Republics.

Now this miserable Aleman Villa had offered an opening. Schmiedegen was Security. Whatever he amounted to in the world depended on his standing with Ulianov who was supposed to be the successor and over him, for the present, Vladimir Ilyich. All the same he would try him. What, he asked, did Schmiedegen think?

"Think?" Schmiedegen was trained to be prudent. "Think about what?"

"About the fellow's proposal," Shishak said. "About opening the door for this scum."

Schmiedegen did not approve the choice of words. The Mexicans might be a deplorable lot but vermin, lice, scum? They were clients, maybe some kind of protected species, possibly useful though apparently not to the extent he had hoped.

Assuming soldiers were rough, Shishak was being rough for a soldier, an ambitious soldier at that. He knew about the Globus connection. The Double Marshal was an ancient of days and with the authority that went with his age kept the single marshals in line. They all knew the single marshals were hungry for more occasions to earn themselves new honors, new medals. Shishak clearly was a man with a large appetite. He told Shishak he would report Aleman Villa's proposal to Josef Vissarionovich.

"Recommend? Not recommend?" Shishak asked.

Schmiedegen explained these were matters, issues beyond him. He had no competence to form an opinion. This went to the military capacity of the Republics, the military capacity of the Americans.

"Take my word for it," Shishak told him, "compared with us the Americans have a minus capacity."

Schmiedegen assured Shishak that he respected and accepted the Marshal's judgment. But all he could do was to pass on what Aleman Villa had said and leave action to the proper authority. He would add what the Marshal had said. It would not be right for him to take a position himself.

Shishak was annoyed. The man was either too smart for his own good or too stupid. To pass on the Indian's proposal, request, the beggar's prayer, however you put it, was to invite instructions, the usual instructions, instructions to wait, do nothing, look for developments, reassess the situation as it matured. He had something different in mind.

Shishak had his 50,000 advisers, Uzbeks, so many animals, no brains, no conscience, two-legged man killers only waiting to be let out of their cage. Their grandfathers, so to speak, had cut throats, cut off heads at Nishapur, Baghdad, wrecked cities, smashed canals, turned whole countries into a desert. He could move them north to the river, let them loose. Maybe they would explode with enough force to break through the Americans. Maybe not.

They were animals born to kill or be killed. One way or the other, it made little difference to them. And it made little difference to him how the move would turn out. If the Americans broke and ran -- and they probably would -- all would be well. There would be pandemonium, a general collapse, the United States would no longer exist. He could see very interesting prospects, personal prospects. And if his Uzbeks failed and were chewed up in the process, the Republics would be engaged in and committed to a war that had to be fought sooner or later.

War was a matter of will. The Americans were a degenerate people, so many mongrels. Their older elements might want to resist but they would be washed away by the rest who would want to be left at peace in their sty. The will of the armed forces of the Republic was bound to prevail or, more simply, his personal will. He could see it clearly and he hesitated -- he despised himself for it -- only because of Cheka.

Vladimir Ilyich looked soft, inclined to be reasonable, cultivating a reputation for being humane. All the same Cheka never gave up many inches. For 20 years he had kept everything in his own hands. Those who had pushed him had always regretted it. If he, Shishak, senior Marshal, next to the Double Marshal himself, were to brush aside Cheka's well understood prohibition against an American war he was likely to end in a contest: his will or Cheka's, his life or Cheka's. He could move, though, with caution. He could move his Uzbeks only because of a crisis, an emergency move. Schmiedegen would corroborate, confirm that a crisis existed and the need for action, immediate action.

"Your Indian friend," Shishak said. "It looks to me like he's losing his nerve."

"Let us say Aleman Villa is troubled."

"Demoralized is more like it," Shishak said. "Ready to run, he and his Indians. A bad day for Cheka."

"A bad day for Vladimir Ilyich?" Schmiedegen asked.

Shishak pointed out that the plan, Cheka's plan, required the vermin to mass on the border, push, cross, inundate the old Mexican states or at least make a threatening show. If the vermin stampeded, started to flee, the few Americans who had wanted to resist would gain strength, gather support. The Americans might not give up, break down, surrender.

Schmiedegen conceded that the Marshal was probably right.

"So," Shishak told him, "your mission ends in a failure. More important Cheka's plan fails. A serious business."

Schmiedegen nodded. The Marshal's analysis was correct. He looked thoughtful.

"The failure of your mission," Shishak went on, "is your personal affair. You Security people know your own world. Among us, in the Armed Forces, a failure is serious, even fatal at times. You know what I mean. But for Cheka's plan to break down ...." He left the sentence unfinished.

Schmiedegen thought. His being sent to replace Troyenko had been the reward for long years of service, an opening to a future of higher rank than he had ever expected. For his mission to fail would be a kind of abortion, the end of his glorious future. He could even go home in disgrace, be blamed for what happened. Ulianov would receive him, tell him of Cheka's displeasure, reveal the punishment that Cheka had chosen.

It might be no worse than obscurity, the kind of assignment that was a badge of incompetence. And, as Shishak suggested, there could be something worse, something much worse. Shishak was rough spoken, harsh but perhaps he could be useful. Shishak might have a rough and harsh way to retrieve what was lost or on the way to be lost. Shishak interrupted his thinking.

"We don't have time, you and I, to report and wait to be told what to do," Shishak told him. "This is battle. We act in a battle. Make a decision. Act on the decision. You understand this is battle."

Schmiedegen nodded. He understood.

"All right," Shishak went on. "We have heard Aleman Villa. We are facing a rout. The dam is ready to burst. So I -- with your agreement -- am throwing my force of advisers, my Uzbeks against the Americans, closing the breach; steadying the whole mass that is piled up at the river."

Schmiedegen agreed that in the situation Shishak's move was the only one open. They would both say so. They would stand together when the crisis had passed. But would it be better for Shishak's Uzbeks to be a little disguised, to wear Mexican uniforms, have some Mexicans with them? There would be casualties; unfortunately, casualties. Perhaps some Uzbeks might be taken prisoner. There was the matter of language. It would be better perhaps to conceal so far as they could that Eurasian troops were involved.

"No," Shishak said, "my Uzbeks have pride. Wear Mexican uniforms? Never. As for language my Uzbeks don't speak a language. They grunt. They make sounds but no human language. Anyhow when my Uzbeks hit them, the Americans will know that they are not up against these Mexican dregs."

A half hour later Shishak was pleased. His people were on their way north. They would attack the border positions during the night, a storm blown up in the darkness. His Uzbeks were going off in high spirits, expectant, sure of themselves. He would follow them shortly, had sent word to Moscow that he would stay over till morning. And he had a question: why the encampment? Why were the masses piled up where they were?

Schmiedegen had the answer. He had asked Aleman Villa and Aleman Villa had explained there was a stub of an old extinct volcano nearby, dead, dead for centuries, Axidentl they called it. The Humming Bird God had spoken from the volcano, out of the volcano, to the Chichimec people, promised to guide them south to Anahuac, to a great kingdom where they would have endless victims to sacrifice to him, to lay on his altar and kill, cut open.

The Humming Bird God was a god who liked hearts, human hearts, a particular god but a strong god for the Chichimec and he had kept the promise he made until the Spanish arrived. But the Spanish were only an interlude. The Chichimec would triumph again. Schmidegen had heard about the Sons and Daughters of Moctezuma? They were Chichimec.

He, Aleman Villa, was Chichimec, had a Chichimec name in addition to the name of Aleman Villa. Soon, he thought, they would discard the interlude names and go by the names of their fathers, the true names of their fathers.

Shishak made a face. He found these natives disgusting. They were vermin and, even worse, cannibal vermin. He had heard, perhaps even read, long ago that the Aztecs gave the hearts of their victims to their murderous gods and dined off the rest of the carcass. It was enough to turn a strong stomach. War was killing.

He was proud that his ancestors were great makers of war. They slashed right and left, piled up skulls, sold their captives as slaves, but they were a hearty vigorous lot. No one had ever said that they slaughtered to eat. No cannibals they. They were a people with culture. These Indians were to them what jackals and crows were to lions.

Schmiedegen heard and conceded the Marshal was right. If they were to be graded as human these people, these Indians, were far down the list, somewhere near the bottom. Superstitious as well.

Schmiedegen told the Marshal one thing that held the millions where they had encamped was the rumor that the Humming Bird God was about to speak to them again. They claimed they heard noises, groaning from deep in the earth, saw fires at night rising out of the ground, felt the ground shaking and trembling.

Even Aleman Villa was both eager and frightened. He dressed himself up Europe style, was and called himself President, but even he thought that the Humming Bird God might have a message for him, some word, some guidance.

Shishak felt more disgusted as he listened to Schmiedegen. These were savages, abject and groveling savages. Groanings and messages out of the earth, a god laboring to make himself heard. The Republics had their share, more than their share, of low types but nothing like Aleman Villa and the swarm camping around them.

In spite of himself, he felt some sympathy for the Americans in resisting this pestilence that was about to undo them. But he could see that later, when the United States had fallen apart, he and the lesser marshals could take hold and do what the Spanish had done, reduce this slave population to order, reduce its numbers by half, or three quarters, nine tenths. It would take time but it had to be done. The immediate task was to get the Americans out of the game.

"I am going north," he told Schmiedegen, "for two or three hours. Take a look. Give some orders. Get back to Moscow." He had had second thoughts. It would probably be better to be in Moscow when the message came in that his Uzbeks had done what he expected. He would have a complaint from Cheka, tempered by an admission that he, Shishak, had followed the correct course and thanks for achieving the success of Cheka's own plan.

Suddenly both Shishak and Schmiedegen were conscious that someone was groaning, a vast, mournful sound. Then they both staggered. The floor of the tent heaved and subsided. Then there was a kind of wave motion, a ripple. Then they heard yelling, much yelling, excited, jabbering voices.

"An earthquake, a minor earthquake," Schmiedegen said. Minor earthquakes were a routine occurrence but to judge from the noise you would have thought that these Indians had never experienced such minor disturbance before.

"What a vile people," Shishak said with contempt.

He and Schmiedgen went out. Off in the distance the stub of Axidentl looked unchanged except for a small curl of smoke that seemed to issue out of its side, an occasional curl, appearing, disappearing, appearing.

Aleman Villa came towards them, uneasy. What had they decided? He had understood the military advisers were going, had gone on towards the river. The Marshal was about to follow them? Perhaps the

Marshal would permit him to join him. He would like to be present, to see the victory the Marshal had prepared, with such generosity, such brilliance, such skill. Once the victory was secured, the mass at Axidentl would follow, exploit the opening. For the immediate present the mass was wavering, teetering. The minor shock taken with the rumors had paralyzed it for the moment. But with the Marshal's victory ....

"All right," Shishak told him. He could go north with him. He, himself, was off to Moscow in a couple of hours. Perhaps Ambassador Schmiedegen would go north, a matter of company. Shishak's private opinion was that Schmiedegen had better keep an eye on the Indian.

As they stood together there was another groaning sound, more ripples.

"We had better move," Shishak said as he heard more yelling, more jabbering voices.

29

Dudorov Knows Uzbeks' Achilles Heel, Tells Louisa

Marv found it difficult to make sense out of the accounts of what had happened to his number two man. The survivors -- that was how they had described themselves -- had hurried from the White House to his office. They were all solemn. They each had a big story to write -- really two stories -- the death of Castillo at the hands and feet of the military, the appalling, shocking, truly horrible vaporization of a most promising member of the staff of the New York Gazette.

Vaporized by Louisa. And yet they had agreed that before writing their stories they owed it to the profession to go as a delegation to Marv, bear witness to what they had witnessed, tender condolences and -- to be blunt, ask for advice. How could they protect themselves against disappearing in a sad, lonely whine if they, like Marv's number two man, were exposed to vindictive authority? They all had to deal with the Secretary armed with a disintegrating device. What should they do in the face of this new occupational hazard?

Marv heard, almost disbelieved. He got a second version to confirm the first version. A third reporter confirmed the number one and two versions, from the protest outside the White House, the finding of Castillo's remains, sending a message to President Blossom, the Secretary's arrival and questioning them in the Press Room and the sad denouement.

The one thing that was clear was that their First Amendment rights were in jeopardy. The Secretary had committed not only murder but an unconstitutional murder. What they needed was something like a prior restraint on anyone who had access to the disintegrating device. Marv was an old hand, senior officer present, knew the ins and outs of the professions, knew everyone of any importance. They were the flock; Marv was the shepherd. They were turning to him. Hour of need. All the rest of it.

Marv considered what he had heard. There was a time when he would have rejected it as impossible. The group of mourners -- which was one way to look at them -- were a poor lot judged by the high standards of the Gazette. He would not have hired anyone in the lot. Still they were, or seemed to be, sober, unaffected by any drugs so far as he could observe. Their story might be fantasy but they all agreed on the fantasy. And the story fitted into a pattern.

There were the executions in Mr. Carmody's office. Beginning with them, the brutal death of Castillo was credible. The disappearance, the death of his number two man, however induced, had to be treated as part of the pattern. The element that lived in the past, the haters of change, were in their last desperate days striking back. In a way they could be seen as pathetic in their loyalty to a cause lost long ago.

Nevertheless, they were a danger to all that had been accomplished in the past generation or two and to those who fought for and effected the changes for the general good. Shooting was evil. Beating and stamping to death was worse, more brutal and worse. To disintegrate, to vaporize was in a way the ultimate horror. There could be no funeral, no burial, no traditional rites to honor the dead, nothing to rise at the Last Day, no ashes, no dust to rise from. No one had had such a fate in the past. Men had been blown to bits, atomized, but there had been somewhere fragments, remnants.

Of his number two man there was evidently no trace, only an empty space and there had been no warning, no explosion, no blinding flash, only a voice fading into a whine.

Naturally he had heard the rumors about a secret disintegrating device. He had even asked Louisa about it and been told it was nonsense. She had even laughed, said it would be useful, said she regretted that the rumor was groundless.

So she had lied to him and he had believed her. Queenie knew he found Louisa attractive and had warned him against her. Now he had better warn Queenie. She was to hear the great Mexican cases tomorrow.

She was still set on having Louisa present in court. He owed it to Queenie to put her on guard.

Suppose Louisa came into court with whatever it was that had disintegrated his number two man. Queenie would be exposed to it. With all her faults, he had to protect her.

"What, Mr. Mazo, what should we do?" One of the group brought him back to what they regarded as their immediate, personal problem. "What shall we do?"

Marv gave the only advice that occurred to him. He told them they had better stay away from the Secretary. That was the best thing to do for the present. He hoped he would have something better to suggest to them later. They thanked him. They left. Marv called the Chief Justice. She was busy. He told the law clerk or whoever it was that it was important, imperative, that he speak to her. She would, he was told, spare him a minute -- only a minute.

"Only a minute, Marv," the Chief Justice told him when she came on the line. "I'm in the middle of something important. I have the solution."

"The solution?"

"Yes, Marv," the Chief Justice said, "I don't want to say anything more than that now. You have something to tell me?"

"Yes," Marv said. "You've heard about what happened to Castillo?"

"No," the Chief Justice said.

"Dead," Marv said. "Some people who were here just told me about it, a protest in front of the White House. A crowd. Castillo evidently beaten to death by troops guarding the White House."

"That good man," the Chief Justice said after a moment. "That poor good man. You say the troops did it?"

"There doesn't seem to be any question about it, Queenie. The people who told me about it were there. Reporters."

"I've got to do something about all this," the Chief Justice said. "My solution will take care of this kind of savagery."

"And Queenie," Marv went on, "my real reason for calling is this. It has to do with my number two man."

The Chief Justice tried to visualize Marv's number two man. A young man, a somewhat not one thing or the other young man, but a well connected young man. She asked about Marv's number two man.

"He disappeared, Queenie."

"You mean you can't find him, Marv. Kidnapped? Taken away?"

"It's worse than that, Queenie," Marv said. He described the circumstances. The scene in the Press Room. Louisa. The back and forth. The final sad protesting whine. Then the emptiness, nothing, no trace, no sign that he had ever existed.

"The thing, Queenie," Marv explained, "is that the people who were there are sure that the Secretary did it with some kind of disintegrating device. Some new secret weapon. You can guess how they felt. They thought she might do the same thing to them. They asked me for advice. I told them to stay away from Louisa. Queenie, are you still trying to get her before you tomorrow in Court?"

The answer was yes. Olga was out and determined this time to get her hands on Louisa.

"Let me urge you, Queenie, to leave Louisa alone."

The Chief Justice made it clear that the laws applied to everyone, high and low, applied even to multiple Secretaries. No one was immune from the law. No one could frighten the law.

"1 know that. Everyone knows that. But, Queenie, I don't want you exposed to whatever it was that made my number two man vanish away."

The Chief Justice bristled. No one could make her disappear. No one would dare. They were accustomed to assassination, accustomed to violence. It was part of everyday living. The explosion in Mexico City was shocking but normal.

This was a technological age, an age of ever advancing scientific advance. Knowledge piled up and the higher the pile the greater the potential for everyone to kill everyone else. It was odd but this was the price of progress. And it was man's nature to go on progressing, to struggle upward out of his ignorance and to master the universe.

There were books on the subject. Lives were always at risk. That was why she was determined to protect the Americans from the punishment of a war which they could bring on themselves by resisting the justice due the Mexicans and their protectors. But as Chief Justice, an institution and sacred, no one would dare to strike her. She was head of the priesthood. She told Marv she was not afraid of his friend Louisa, not afraid of his friend.

Marv sighed. "All right, Queenie," he said when she had finished. "We'll talk about it this evening. I only made my suggestion because I want to protect you. And you can tell me later, perhaps, about your solution."

Queenie said she would be home after Olga returned. Then she, Queenie, would leave the Court with a detachment of guards. She told Marv she realized the danger involved in her doing her duty. She would not take any chances.

At the Intelligence Center the Director was troubled by the latest reports from his people in Mexico. He showed them to Dudorov. What did he think? Shishak was the ranking marshal next to the old Double Marshal. Why was he there? Was it usual for the ranking marshal to go off by himself? And these advisers, who had been arriving for the past several days. Who were these advisers? And why all the equipment? Dudorov considered, gave his opinion.

It would not be routine for Shishak to be meeting with Aleman Villa and Schmiedegen. Knowing Cheka's general position it seemed unlikely that Cheka would have approved it. It was hard to conceive the marshal would act on his own, but some earlier messages from Mr. Carmody's friends had indicated that there was something peculiar in Moscow.

Cheka must have approved the marriage of Madam Troyenko and Shishak which meant a kind of marriage between Globus and the armed forces. It was odd that Cheka would have allowed such an alliance. And the story that Cheka seemed to be concerned with data from the listener-watchers, was spending time with Medalist or ex-Medalist Lumens was enough to mystify anyone.

The old man had a comment on that. It could be coincidence but his people kept telling him that for the past several days their satellites were, as they put it, malfunctioning, working, then breaking down, then working again. And there was this noise about which he had spoken to Cheka. It seemed to get louder but they had nothing like the program the Republics maintained and the instruments that went with it, nothing like the listener-watchers. The Americans had given up on a space watch, too costly, taking money that everyone said should be used for big social improvements.

Dudorov went back to Shishak and the advisers. He thought the Director should pass the reports on to his friend, Madam Clymer. She would probably have her own information but the Director would know about that. The old man had his doubts. He reached her at the White House. They would meet at her office. He thought she should hear General Dudorov's views.

On her way from the White House Louisa puzzled over the disappearance of the Gazette's young man. She had never seen anything like it before. A substantial young man, head, body, arms, legs, a voice, a complete normal young man. Then nothing, like a trick at a children's party. Was it illusion? Some parlor magic that the young man had mastered? Evidently the group, his associates, the other reporters thought otherwise, had stared at her, fled. Evidently they thought the magic was hers, that she was some kind of witch. She was still trying to reconstruct the whole business when she arrived in her office to meet Mr. Carmody and Dudorov.

The old man told her he had reports from Mexico -- if anything later came in it would be relayed to him at Louisa's. Marshal Shishak had come over, had met Aleman Villa, at Axidentl, the big camp south of the border. Schmiedegen had been there, had been part of the group. He and Shishak had talked alone after talking to Aleman Villa. The 50,000 advisers had then been sent north to the border. Shishak, Schmiedegen and Aleman Villa then followed. Dudorov would explain the significance.

"The advisers," Dudorov told her, "are special, Uzbeks, Shishak's own, the First Asiatic Strike Force. Shishak used them in the East and the South after the Merger, to bring about order, get some elements under control. A completely reliable corps, perfectly trained, no quarter given, no quarter asked, armed up to the limit. Cheka's orders were to keep them east of the Urals, well east of the Urals. Admirable troops at a distance, at a great distance.

Cheka regards tham as Shishak's praetorian guard and watches them closely -- especially after Shishak proposed to use them as Moscow Garrison. A mistake. Army stays out of Moscow. We use Security Forces there, only Security Forces."

"So what are you telling me?" Louisa asked.

"That Shishak moved them to Mexico beginning last week."

"With Cheka's approval?"

"We don't know," the old man put in. "Maybe yes, maybe no. Anyhow, as Dudorov says, they began arriving last week. The General told me about them when we first got the word."

"So you think they are about to attack?"

"Tonight, " Dudorov said. "That was the warning the Director had from the field. And that would fit with what I know about Shishak and this fighting force moved to the north. Shishak favors surprise. These Uzbeks are trained and armed to attack in the dark."

"You know them? Have seen them?" Louisa asked.

Dudorov nodded. He had been assigned for a time to look at and appraise the armed forces of the Republics, to keep Cheka informed about the commanders and their commands. It was just after the Double Marshal had made Shishak next in command to himself. He had taken a very close look at the First Asiatic Strike Force. The Secretary would understand why. A formidable group, useful but to be handled with care.

When he had made his report, Cheka had said to leave them untouched, not to disband them -- he, Dudorov, had suggested breaking them up -- to keep them surrounded by enough other troops to contain them if they caused trouble. The First Asiatics had been useful before: perhaps they would use them again.

"The truth is," Dudorov said, "I thought at the time that Cheka wanted to avoid an argument with the old Double Marshal about his choice of Shishak. You understand. We too have to keep things in balance. A political matter."

Louisa nodded. Did the General have any advice?

The answer was yes. "You can expect a storm in a matter of hours. The Director will have later reports. You will know where to expect this attack. Put in the best fighting force that you have. The larger the better."

"What," Louisa asked, "what would be their objective? Shishak's objective?"

"Break through your dam at the border. Smash north. Suck the Mexicans after them. Wipe out anything in their way. A hard blow. Maybe a series of blows. Then you collapse out of terror. The Uzbeks are good. Very good about terror."

"Weapons?" asked Louisa.

Dudorov knew how the Uzbeks were armed. Their armament very complete, up to date, nothing omitted. A small number of men but equipped with the means to do maximum damage. He described the usual materiel allotted to the First Asiatic Strike Force. He thought Shishak would have that much, maybe more for this mission.

"Cheka," Dudorov said, "likes your American phrases. I don't know them as well. But he would say something like all Hell will break loose. That is what you must expect. Have you a counter-force for all Hell?"

The old man looked at Louisa. "The General," he said, "has probably put it all very well. You know what to expect. Is there a counter-force?" He did not say it but he thought it would be a miracle if there were.

He knew that the Military Equality Act guaranteed that no resident of the United States could be excluded from any military unit or group on grounds of race, sex, political or religious belief, or handicap, mental or physical. The judges had been strict in enforcing it. The aim was to achieve what was hailed as a democratic army, all the units and parts perfect cross sections, everyone entitled to serve -- if that was the word -- until of an age entitling them to retirement pay, perpetual retirement pay.

Louisa knew what the old man was thinking. She nodded. She had a counter-force, two, maybe three, in violation of the statute and the judicial decisions. Luanda had appealed to Blossom. The Secretary was ignoring the law. As Attorney General he could not and would not defend her in the numerous cases that were being brought by military personnel excluded from the new groups she was forming.

The situation was terrible. The Secretary's conduct reflected on the Administration itself. The Secretary should realize she was an outlaw, that she was subject to heavy personal penalties. Nevertheless she had her counter-force. The United States had their defenses.

"Well, Louisa?" the old man asked.

"You have your counter-force," she said, "and we will hope time to use it."

30

Uzbeks Wiped Out Reloading Rocket Racks

The First Asiatic Strike Force was moving, full speed to the north. The light scout carriers led and covered the flanks and the rear. The heavy carriers moved in the center, with the replacement and ammunition reserve carriers moving closely behind them.

The whole formation was Shishak's latter day version of a Mongol invading force, an army of Genghis with all the modern improvements. The replacement carriers were so many spare horses. The ammunition carriers with their racks of rockets were so many camels with their burdens of arrows. The men in the carriers, heavy and light, were the horsemen, riding and dealing their blows, going through or over or around every obstruction as dictated by tactics but scattering or stunning any force in their way.

The aim was to shock and destroy and to paralyze by the certainty of further destruction. Better than any army of Genghis they could move a hundred miles in an hour. With their special fuel the carriers could move a thousand miles and return. Their arrows were rockets with a range of 50 miles from the carriers. And the rockets were firestorm rockets, designed to generate a heat equal to that of the sun where they struck or double the heat of the sun. They had been tested and proved at Calcutta, Hongkong, Jakarta where there was some resentment over the Merger.

As for their armor, the heavy carriers had nothing to fear from the Americans. As the Strike Force crossed the border there had been a moment of resistance, no more than a moment. Then a small group had been turned east with orders to destroy Tucson and Phoenix before turning west to rendezvous with the main force as it returned from its mission.

Tucson and Phoenix would be a feint, to divert any American force, not that it would be a serious threat. The main force had more important objectives, the principal California cities along the coast and the smaller cities in the Central Valley as it returned. It had found nothing in its way as it struck San Diego with a dozen of the bigger rockets from 40 miles out and left it a pillar of fire by night.

The next target would be the whole Los Angeles cluster. After that, San Francisco. With the main centers burned out, there would be no remaining will to resist but the smaller settlements would take only a rocket apiece in passing and their destruction was scheduled. There was nothing to block them, nothing to fear. A feeble attack from the air had been brushed away ten minutes before.

Then the two lead scouts reported back. There was something ahead. Communications were the only problem so far, an occasional failure but a constant roar, rising and falling, troublesome. The Colonel-General commanding got the range from the lead scouts. Then the flank scouts sent a signal. Something was ahead of them on the flanks.

The Strike Force sent off a salvo, small rockets. A scout carrier to the west reported it had been hit, was out of control, then an explosion. Two other scouts were in trouble. The Colonel-General ordered another salvo, adjusting the range. The scout carriers reported no hits but there was something ahead. The Colonel-General considered sending up flares but decided against it. Instead he ordered another two salvos. Still no results.

His second in command suggested restocking the carriers with heavier rockets. They would stop, come in to the camels, reload their racks, move on against the something ahead. Whatever it was would be no match for them with their rocket racks refilled after the salvos. The Colonel-General heard and agreed. The advance scouts would slow down, circle with caution, keep him informed. Their own camels would come to them and then the whole force would get in motion again. Flank scouts would pull into the main force and take on rockets if needed.

It would be a matter of minutes, an operation for which they were trained, rehearsed and rehearsed, by day and by night.

The big carriers circled around to be loaded. The camel crews did their work, out of their racks, into the carriers. A few small flank carriers moved in towards the center, into the center, closing up to the loaders.

In a way no one would ever know what happened to Shishak's Strike Force. Nothing like it had ever happened to one of Genghis' armies. It was in the dark and it was over in a matter of seconds. A flank carrier fired its rockets into the open port of Heavy Camel Four as its crew began to unload. There was a giant flash that flooded the sky as the whole main formation with all its cargo of rockets exploded. Only the outer circling advance scouts lived through what happened.

Minutes later there was a message, in code to Marshal Shishak, from the commanding officer of the Advance Scouting Carriers of Asiatic Strike Force One: Strike Force destroyed. We are only survivors. We are turning back. Then carefully, the exact latitude and longitude. Then, as a postscript -- cause of destruction unknown to us. Will rendezvous with East group. Then the date and time, 3:37 California. It was 15:37 in Moscow. The message came through, faint, then stronger, then faint. It was decoded, taken to Shishak.

Shishak read it. He had always prided himself on having no temperament, no ups, no downs, no nerves, never depressed. It gave him an advantage, an immense advantage, over those weak enough to be affected by good news or bad. At best he despised them. They were so many women. He read the message again.

For the first time in his life, he felt unsure of himself. When he had been told that Cheka had ordered his Uzbeks to be kept well east of the Urals, he had understood the order and grinned.

Cheka was afraid of his Uzbeks. He, Shishak, had been their inventor. He had created them carefully, picked them himself, planned their armament, designed the whole force with care. It was his personal weapon, to use as he pleased, to use when he wanted. He had tested it in the East and the South, a perfect machine. It was more than a match for any two or three or four of the Republic's armies taken together.

He had moved it to Mexico -- surprised that Cheka made no objection -- to exercise it again. A little blooding was healthy for troups, good for their spirit. He had been sure the Americans presented no dangers. At worst a few losses, a kind of war game. It was true he had thought if the worst came to the worst he would have traded his Strike Force for a full scale full blown American war but it had not been a serious risk. Now he would have to deal with Cheka but stripped of his Uzbeks. He would have to use the old Double Marshal. He would bring Globus on stage. He had to act quickly.

In spite of himself he looked at the message again. What did it mean? Strike Force destroyed. But how? Nothing about any engagement. The Advance Scouting force were the only survivors. But how? How could that happen? There was no point in asking for more information. The poor idiot who sent the report was evidently running for his life and too confused to explain how Strike Force was destroyed and how he survived. He would go into the next room, talk to the old Double Marshal.

Grabkin was sleeping upright in his chair when Shishak came in. He started awake.

"Semyon Semyonovich," Shishak said, very respectfully. "A message." He handed the message to Grabkin.

The Double Marshal lit a pipe that lay on the table in front of him. He put on his glasses, gave himself time to wake before reading the message, read it. "No," he said. "Do you believe it?"

Shishak said that he did. He had no reason to question it. The sender had used the Strike Force emergency code. No one else but Strike Force could have it. They -- the message specialists -- had issued it at the last minute. Only a Strike Force commander in charge of a group could have received it and used it.

"But no explanation."

Shishak agreed. There was no explanation.

"Nothing said about fighting," the Double Marshal observed. "What had they done?"

Shishak told him. Not much had come in. There had been no real opposition. What there was, token, pathetic. A small diversion had gone east into the province of Arizona, had burned out a couple of cities.

Main Force had gone west, had burned out the first target, were going north to the big city, everything in good order, everyone confident of their expected success. Then this last message.

The old Double Marshal shook his head. He felt sympathy with the Commander of Advance Scouting Force, poor devil, to be a survivor and to have to make such a report. A question: did Cheka know of this message. Shishak doubted it and was wrong.

Ulianov had, in fact, received the message. Security had a monitor for any message to Shishak. Ulianov took the message to Cheka at once. Cheka saw it, thought for a moment, looked at Ulianov, commented.

"Grosjean," he said. A very brave man -- if that was the word. He had said he could do it. He did it. But how could he have done it? It had sounded impossible.

Ulianov reminded him that he had seen Grosjean alone.

"So much the better," Cheka said to him. "This is on my conscience, not yours -- if you have a conscience. I have one, maybe two. One from my mother, one from my father. A double inheritance. We can now talk to our Timurid marshal. Not as large as he was. Shrunk by a couple of sizes. Minus his Uzbeks." He motioned to Ulianov to sit down.

"Josef Vissarionovich," Cheka went on, "you were, you are what I believe is spoken of as the successor, my successor, my heir. What do you expect to succeed to? What do you expect to inherit?"

Ulianov was embarrassed. Heirs were supposed not to hint about legacies. It was bad manners to anticipate legacies. Also bad luck. He said so to Cheka.

Cheka laughed. "You inherit prizes. You also get burdens, old problems, old debts. The entire estate. And sometimes the estate is not as large as everyone thought. So I ask your estimate of the estate."

Ulianov said that Vladimir Ilyich's estimate would be better than his. Vladimir Ilyich had more understanding, more insights.

Cheka asked what Josef Vissarionovich thought about the weather today.

Ulianov was puzzled. An odd change of subject but Cheka had his own way of proceeding. He might not be changing the subject. It was a poor day, dismal, surprisingly dark. But there was something about major volcanic activity, in Mexico, elsewhere perhaps. Communications were poor, perhaps related to the major volcanic activity.

"Right," Cheka commented. "And we have reports from some of the big power units -- what they always describe as malfunctions."

Ulianov nodded. He had seen a summary of the power administration reports. A serious matter? Could it be a serious matter?

"Coincidence? Maybe related?"

Ulianov supposed coincidence only. The Electric Power Ministry was on notice. The minister was concerned. Ulianov had talked with him.

Cheka suggested a connection. The weather, the communications, the supposed volcanic activity, the power failures, all fitted together or could fit together. All of it was part of the legacy. "But so much for my estate, your estate, for the present. Another part of the estate is our Timurid Marshal. You will tell him that I want to see him, here. We will give him time, give him an hour. In the meantime you will have Lumens come in. And the message will stay here until the conversation with Shishak."

While he waited for Lumens, Cheka thought about the message to Shishak. Dudorov had inspected Shishak's Uzbeks and had not liked what he saw. His advice was to disband them before they made trouble. He had talked to them, got drunk with their senior commanders. A dangerous crowd. The senior Security officer attached to them had reinforced his reaction, Grosjean, a serious intelligent man.

Dudorov had called him an 18th century heirloom, French Swiss going back to the first Peter or possibly Catherine the Great. More European than Russian, an orderly man. He had told Dudorov that Shishak's senior commanders boasted when they were drunk that their Strike Force would be, probably already was, the real source of power in the Republics.

With it Shishak could make himself whatever he wanted and they would get their rewards. Even he, Grosjean, an outsider, would get his prize. They looked on him as part of the Strike Force. They needed a little more training, their full armament, then they would be ready. Grosjean's account largely matched Dudorov's own impression. They had been a little more cautious with him, had probably not done their usual drinking; but they were confident of themselves, felt contempt for everyone else, everything else.

"Constantine Constantinovich," Cheka had said, "I value your advice and your judgment. You are probably right about disbanding this strike force. But there are considerations that make me hold off for the present unless you see some immediate threat."

Dudorov conceded he saw no immediate threat. Nevertheless, he pointed out that no one knew when or how a fire would start. He thought at least Vladimir Ilyich might talk to Grosjean alone, judge Grosjean for himself. The man had a good record, not given to crying wolf in the past, a reliable officer. He could get Grosjean to Moscow, routine reporting. If Cheka saw him, Grosjean was discreet.

Cheka recalled his conversation with Grosjean, oddly still 18th century Swiss, formal, not a man to accept or approve a collection of Uzbeks. He repeated their boasts. He had heard them too often. Of course men talked wildly when drunk, but in vino veritas.

Also -- and he had not spoken of this to General Dudorov -- he regarded Shishak as evil. Shishak had been in Leningrad a year ago, drunk, on the prowl, had abducted his, Grosjean's niece, his sister's daughter, attacked her, a brutal affair. And the girl had killed herself. It was a personal thing.

He begged Cheka's pardon. It sounded melodramatic, out of an opera. The authorities had done nothing when his sister went to them. He himself had done nothing. He would wait. He had no family, only this sister. He would see that justice was done. Cheka asked how. Cheka listened.

It was, as Grosjean put it, out of an opera, the whole business was out of an opera, Shishak drunk, seeing the girl, stopping, forcing her into the car, attacking her. It was the kind of thing that people said Beria had done in the days of the sainted Stalin.

And the authorities were wary of Shishak. The girl, after all, was nobody. Shishak was Shishak. Nevertheless, the girl had an uncle, prudent, realizing the limitations of his very medium rank, but in a position to exact his revenge -- or try to. He would cut off Shishak's arm and at the same time make it certain that the Uzbek savages would never realize their drunken ambitions when the time came and he thought it would come -- unless Cheka forbade it.

He made it clear. He was not asking Cheka to see that justice was done to his sister and niece. Unless Cheka forbade it, he would do his own justice. Cheka sent him away, saying nothing except that he would think about what Grosjean had told him. Grosjean would get word from Dudorov. A week later he had a formal notice from Dudorov that he had been advanced to the rank of Colonel in the Security Forces. The Uzbeks when they heard about his promotion got especially drunk in his honor.

As Cheka recalled the whole passage he wondered what Shishak would have done if he had known that the girl in Leningrad had been Grosjean's niece. Probably nothing. Shishak had risen too high to concern himself with people so far below him as Grosjean. He, himself, wondered about what was described as human behavior.

He was too old perhaps to understand Shishak's violence or the girl's killing herself. Conceivably he would have come closer to understanding them 20 years or 30 years earlier. He was not sure, not at all sure. He had always been inclined to watch, even himself, with detachment. Passion and patience. For him patience was stronger.

He had just spoken to Ulianov about his having a conscience, a double conscience. Grosjean's niece ought now to be on his conscience since in a sense he was responsible for Shishak's behavior. But only in a sense.

Single human lives were not, as the Americans said, in his line. He dealt with lives wholesale, in bundles and bales. He knew that a man ate so many pounds of food in a year, but not the details, his choice of food day by day, the recipes used in the cooking. There were too many individual lives for him to be involved in them all, or even in any.

The God of his grandparents or their parents before them probably was in the same situation, occupied with the larger issues, the overall planning, obliged to concentrate only on averages, unable to spare time to protect anonymous girls from the transgressions of a creature like Shishak.

That might be the answer to the problem of evil that men used to worry about, a problem resolved if, as they also believed, there was a Day of Judgment when everything came to an end. He looked up as Lumens came in.

"The latest?" he asked. "What is the latest?"

Lumens had much to report. He thought they were getting on to what could be the climax. His leninos were out in full force, a regular stream seemed to be flowing and spreading and spreading. The instruments could no longer count them or measure them. More than a stream, it was turning into an ocean and disturbing everything that it touched. The usual instruments were no longer reliable. The satellites seemed to be out of commission or going out of commission. Communications were being disrupted, space and terrestrial.

The Chairman no doubt would know about the big power plants. The technology gave signs of no longer working but it was based on data that might not be valid where the leninos intruded. Then Lumens had talked to the regular police who were being swamped with calls about people who were suddenly missing. He, Lumens, concluded that he no longer understood what was occurring. He was only watching and guessing.

"So," Cheka said, "you think we are getting near to what you call the climax. And what is the climax?"

"I only guess," Lumens told him. "The lights go out. The big ones, Sun, Moon and stars. Our poor little lights. Maybe everything ends. Tomorrow, today, an hour from now."

Cheka wondered about the next hour when Ulianov called to say that Shishak was waiting. With the Double Marshal and Globus.

31

U. S. Principals Gather, Battles, Vanishings Reported

At about four o'clock in the morning Marv was wakened by a call from the publisher of the Gazette himself. Himself said they were getting garbled reports in New York about what might be Eurasian troops attacking well inside the Mexican border. The communications were bad. Maybe they were being disrupted. They were only working sporadically. There was something -- he thought it had to be false -- about the destruction of Tucson and Phoenix, also San Diego, about their having been set on fire, terrible fires.

The Los Angeles bureau reported a panic. The people there thought they were next on the list; the result of irresponsible rumors. The whole thing had to be false, a fabrication. It had to be false. The Eurasian Republics, the Republic of Mexico were about to get everything that they wanted. Someone was playing a game, a sinister game. Could Marv find out what was going on from his usual high sources? When Marv got the truth and passed it to him, Himself would be in a position to kill off the rumors.

Himself added that even if there were a Eurasian force north of the border he hoped to God the people in Washington would have enough sense not to resist it. Resistance would be insane, the same thing as suicide. If there were resistance, the Eurasians would have no choice but to strike harder. Everyone and his brother would try to get out of New York. There would be a stampede, like the rumored one out of Los Angeles. A hopeless tangle and no one could escape.

Himself was afraid of the Clymer woman and what she might do. She had closed all the securities markets a week ago. He, the Gazette, were locked in. Their investments were probably worthless, certainly would

279

be if there were resistance. Then he had, personally had, properties in San Diego and Phoenix, more in Los Angeles and in Frisco. He felt he was staring poverty in the face.

There was something else, something wild from the bureau in Mexico City, mostly a garble: a giant volcanic eruption somewhere that sounded like Accidental, an earthquake, in fact a whole series of volcanic explosions and earthquakes. Could Marv get the Washington version as well.

The earthquake types whom the Gazette had consulted reported figures that made no sense to them. They were guessing that their seismic devices had all gone out of order at once. And, finally, what would the Court do if all these crazy rumors were true. Would it meet? Would it act? They all relied on the Court to settle the whole Mexican mess, to get things back on the track, to calm everything down. Himself was sure Marv could get the answer to his Court questions.

The connection was bad but he hoped Marv could get around, quickly, get back with the truth. They were holding the presses. Anyhow they could get out an edition with the true story when Marv called it in. The truth would reassure, release all the tensions, dissipate the hysteria that could do all kinds of harm. As for Himself, he was keeping his head. The whole Gazette staff was keeping its head -- except, Himself noted, the people in Los Angeles and Mexico City who seemed to have lost their usual critical judgment and were accepting every rumor they heard and treating it as legitimate news. Himself hung up after getting Marv's promise to go on the hunt and to get the facts to Himself.

Marv's first impulse was to call Queenie and tell her about what he had heard from Himself. Then he decided it would upset her. She was, she had said, preparing herself in spirit for the Court's session. There were finishing touches for the opinions, to be handed down from the bench, that would dispose of the Treaty, the Eurasian claim for indemnity for the blast in Mexico City, the minor issue of Dudorov.

There were also finishing touches for the papers needed to effect her grand solution of all the domestic political problems. They had agreed after dinner to spend the evening apart. He was to join her for breakfast, go on with her to the Court, watch her perform. For the present it was best not to disturb her, certainly not at 4 o'clock in the morning.

He called one important number after another. The connections were poor, voices faded, grew louder, faded, were interrupted by crackling noises but the various aides and assistants all told him their principals were at Defense Operations.

Everybody was there except the President and he was taking no calls, no calls from anyone. He had, Marv was told, retired to the Lincoln Room with instructions that he was to be left undisturbed, unreachable. Marv had the unhappy feeling that he had missed something big. His number one man had probably relied on the now disembodied number two man to do the night duty, ignorant of his having faded away. There was no point in blaming either one of them. The thing to do was to get to Defense. Marv summoned his driver and went on his way.

Defense, to Marv's surprise, was in darkness but there were barricades on all the roads to the main building. No one could enter except that Marv's special pass, plus a call to the Secretary's secretariat made him an exception. At the only open entrance the major general in charge of building security confirmed that the Secretary and all the top people were in Operations, had been all night.

He had no idea of what was involved. All he knew was that a crowd had come over from the White House at about ten o'clock just after he had a signal that Defense was now in Readiness One. Apart from that he had no information. He could give Mr. Mazo an escort to the Operations Room but he could give no guarantee that Mr. Mazo could enter. He was sure something was wrong. How wrong or what? He had no answer so far.

He would appreciate Mr. Mazo's letting him know what everything was about -- if Mr. Mazo found out. He gave Marv the escort. Once at Operations Marv had to wait. Then he was told he could enter. The major general had told him the truth. A crowd had come from the White House. Except for Blossom everybody was there, what Marv's mother would have called la creme de la creme, civilian and uniformed, looking worn down but showing some signs of relief. The one surprise was Dudorov's -- if he were Dudorov -- presence. Marv as Gazette was almost official. Beginning with Marietta he started to put the story together. It had been a big evening.

The gathering at Defense Operations had in fact adjourned there not long before ten o'clock in the evening Washington time after a kind of opening session at the White House. Louisa had returned there, with the old man and Dudorov, to break the news to Blossom that a Eurasian force was definitely headed north to the border and likely to cross. She had a plan of action in mind. She wanted approval. Blossom's response was to summon Marietta and Luanda to an emergency meeting. This was a crisis, the crisis he had meant to avoid.

As the evening went on a large supporting cast, military and civil, began to assemble. There was an attempt to communicate directly with Cheka but something was wrong with the circuits. Blossom had to make a decision. Louisa gave her report and recommendation. Then came the protests. Les, as Attorney General, gave his opinion that with the matter sub judice, with all the issues before the High Court to decide, it would be illegal to oppose the Strike Force.

They all knew, as he pointed out, that Guadalupe Hidalgo would be set aside as a contract entered into as the result of force and coercion. No one could doubt it. It followed, strictly speaking, that the Strike Force would not be, was not in fact, invading any territory of the United States and that the United States, legally speaking, had no right to oppose it. It was, Blossom thought, a very neat argument, very persuasive.

There was, moreover, an even more powerful argument to be made against Louisa's proposal. Marietta presented it. There was the larger issue, the higher morality. Force was evil. And it was evil to meet force with force. The greatest spirits had all agreed on this point. Nonresistance had been proved stronger than force. Gandhi had proved it. It had been proved over and over again in the struggles that had won for every minority in our own country its claim for a preference over every other minority. The practice of non-resistance was certain to be effective.

This so-called Strike Force would be abashed if no one opposed it. Indeed it would be wise to welcome it, to treat its members as brothers. Furthermore, and this was true, incontrovertibly true, the Strike Force could not be destructive, could intend no destruction. The Republic of Mexico was on the verge of receiving its own, taking back what belonged to it. The so-called Strike Force could want only to keep the peace, preserve the properties that belonged to its Mexican allies.

As for any physical threat to the population of the Treaty States, that too was out of the question. Probably a majority were Mexican citizens and their well being would be the primary concern of Eurasian troops coming north. They could only be coming in the role of protectors and guardians. What Secretary Clymer was urging was, in short, illegal, immoral and foolish.

Blossom said he was persuaded by both the Attorney General and the Secretary of State that the best course was to wait. They were probably being alarmed over nothing. He hoped Secretary Clymer agreed.

Louisa did not. There was someone available who had personal knowledge of these protectors and guardians. The President had better hear him before he made a decision. Who? General Dudorov. Marietta objected. Les had legal objections. To begin with, he asked, who was the man? His identity, again, was sub judice. Before he could be Dudorov, they would need the High Court to say so. And as Marietta made clear, if this man were Dudorov and not Dudorov's murderer, he was still an assassin. He was known to be the man guilty of the executions at the Intelligence Center.

The old man interrupted. "I am an old man," he said, looking at Blossom,"much older than anyone here. Older than you. Older than your Secretary of State. Older than your Mr. Luanda. I have been concerned with the Eurasian Republics from the time when you were so many children. Once Cheka talked to me, openly, freely. He told me what he wanted. A very simple objective, the end of the United States as a power. He told me there would be no need for a war. Pressure and terror would do it. That we would fall apart after a time under pressure, shaken by terror. He thought we would end without any will to survive. I thought he was wrong. Now it seems he was right. Perhaps it would be better for you not to hear what General Dudorov has to say. It will be disagreeable."

Marietta broke in. There was, as the Attorney General had pointed out, the identity issue. And, again, the man was a murderer.

The old man looked at her with contempt. He had seen Secretaries of State come and go, all equally foolish. Now this one, an ex-lady news star who had made a career out of being publicly stupid.

"Madam," he said, "I can vouch that this man is General Constantin Dudorov. You and your friend Mr. Luanda have referred to a bloody affair in my office. Let me tell you something that happened after that business. I had a call from Vladimir Cheka. He called to express his concern -- he had his own special reasons -- to tell me what had occurred, the attempt on my life, was without his knowledge, without his authority. He asked to speak to General Dudorov. He thanked him for what he had done. He told me he was grateful to Dudorov.

"I do not need what Mr. Luanda refers to as the High Court to express an opinion as to the identity of the man who saved my life -- the little that may be left of it. Now," he finished, looking at Blossom, "you may ask General Dudorov to tell you about this Eurasian Strike Force -- as he calls it -- if you please. If I were in your place I would think it my duty to get all the information I could. I have regarded that as my duty for 40-odd years. You will do what you do."

Blossom was silent. He had a feeling that he had been spoken to by his father or uncles. Then he spoke. They would see General Dudorov.

Dudorov was brought in, looked around, recognized everyone, though Blossom made, so to speak, the introductions, was waved to a seat by the old man. Blossom had questions. Dudorov answered. Yes, he had some knowledge of what was officially known as Asiatic Strike Force One. The Chairman had ordered him to inspect them. Yes, he knew the Chairman, reported to him directly or through the Vice Chairman.

He had spent enough time with the Strike Force to acquaint himself with its commanders, its men, their weapons, potential. He also knew Marshal Shishak and the strategic concept in creating the group. They were intended to be and they were -- certainly for their size -- the most formidable fighting force of the Republics. Their aim? To destroy and paralyze by destruction.

They had been exercised, tried and tested at Hongkong, Calcutta. Shishak had been satisfied with the results. Were the stories exaggerated? Blossom had been told that they were a libel on the Republics. No. Dudorov had been to both sites -- he had not been to the third site of their operations, Jakarta. Nothing was left at Hongkong, at Calcutta nothing, ashes, if ashes. Total incineration.

Marshal Shishak had ended whatever objections there had been to the Merger. His Strike Force and its firestorms had broken any will to resist -- which was their purpose. No, he had no doubt that they were coming north on a similar mission.

Blossom explained that the Secretary of State thought the best course would be not to resist, that the Strike Force would be best dealt with by what she had called Gandhian tactics. What did Dudorov think? And was it possible that the Strike Force would destroy what was about to be returned to the Republic of Mexico?

Dudorov admitted that he had no knowledge of Marshal Shishak's instructions to the Strike Force commander. But he would assume the worst possibility, new versions of what Strike Force had done in their East and their South. With all deference to the Secretary of State, Gandhi had not been faced by Marshal Shishak or his Strike Force One.

What would he do in the President's place? He would try to protect his people from the firestorm rockets. The California and the Texas cities were large. They were the probable targets. He did not, of course, know what resources the President had. In the President's place he would use what he had, all that he had. He would only say that he had seen the sites of Calcutta and Hongkong. It was a matter of millions of lives, millions of deaths.

Blossom considered. In a moment of folly he had allowed Louisa to make him President of the United States. He should have seen that it would end in something like this. Decisions had always been painful and all he had was one decision after another. This last one was too much for him. Someone else would have to assume it. All he wanted was to be left alone, completely alone.

He had had enough of trying to keep a balance between a couple of women who had no use for each other. It was, he supposed, like having two wives and trying to keep peace in the family. The old man was always reminding him of his great experience. The old man could make the decision. It would be to go with Louisa which made as much sense as anything else. Dudorov, if he were Dudorov, had pretty much shown that there was really no choice.

There was the Protocol of Manila which pledged the United States and the Republics to fight their wars with conventional weapons, at least at the outset. Were these firestorm rockets conventional? The Eurasian Academy of Physics had invented them as an exercise of their talent. They had got Louisa excited. She thought they should have something like them. He had allowed her to go ahead over Marietta's objection.

He was not going to worry about it. He would turn over the mess of the day to the old man and he, himself would go think his own thoughts. He could find out tomorrow what happened. He looked at the old man. Then he got up and walked out. A minute later one of his aides came in to say that the President had retired for the night and asked the Director of Intelligence to make any decision he wanted on the matter that was under discussion. Marietta felt cheated and so did Luanda. Walter had decided against them by deciding not to decide.

It was then that the party with its attendants had adjourned to Defense Operations, ignoring the usual regiment of reporters with the usual questions. As they left they also ignored the usual crowd with the usual signs demanding justice to Mexico and to the Eurasian Republics, all homage to the Supreme Justice, death to the United States of America.

Before going to the White House Louisa had ordered into position the groups which were to oppose Shishak's Uzbeks. By the time she arrived at Operations there was already trouble. She had not believed Dudorov's estimate of the speed at which the Strike Force would move. He had been right. The Strike Force had already crossed the border, shattered and scattered the troops in its path and gone its way.

Again, communications were faulty. The signs, though, were that Strike Force had divided, one part going west, one going east. California or Texas? Louisa asked Dudorov for an opinion. He knew the Strike Force and, more important, he was acquainted with Shishak, could fathom Shishak's intentions. Dudorov reasoned.

In the Mongol tradition one move was a feint. Los Angeles would be the main target -- the largest American city. The main force would go to the west and make the best of the night. Texas was too far to the east and there was no city to destroy that would have the shock effect of the destruction of the whole of Los Angeles, the trunk and the limbs. If the Americans could cover anything, that was what they should cover. But he did not have to tell her the danger of dividing forces against an attack.

As the night passed Operations tracked Strike Force by messages, complete, incomplete, from details reporting its movement, some places attacked, some ignored. Then Tucson was gone. At about the same time there was word about San Diego and Phoenix. Fires, terrible fires, seen at a distance. The information system was only partially working but there was no question of what the Strike Force had done.

An attempt to hold it away from San Diego had been blown away in a storm and then the city was gone. It was almost enough to shake Marietta's faith in the Protocol of Manila, the inherent good will of the Strike Force, the concern of the Republics for the lives and territories of their Mexican ally.

After San Diego, Strike Force moved north. And what could be done? The bulk of what Louisa had thought of as a counter-force was assembling and moving but its striking power and armor were doubtful in the face of the Uzbeks.

The old man's efforts to get through to Cheka were fruitless; the circuits were closed, blocked, failing. Nothing got through. There was a proposal: maybe they could save Los Angeles, declare it an open city. But that would require communicating with Cheka or the Strike Force command. And neither was possible. The only course was to hope against hope, to throw the counter-force in front of the Uzbeks.

Dudorov watched, listened, pondered. Shishak had moved the Strike Force to Mexico but Cheka would have known and he would have allowed it. Cheka knew Shishak had ambitions and that Strike Force was probably indispensable to them.

Cheka had motives for whatever he did. He would not want a triumph for Shishak and another fearsome demonstration of the power of his Uzbeks. He knew Cheka's opinion of the Americans. Cheka would not have looked to them to destroy this modern version of one of Genghis' armies.

Then he remembered Grosjean, the 18th century heirloom whom Cheka had seen, talked with, advanced two grades after he saw him.

Grosjean had probably told Cheka just as he had told him, Dudorov, that Shishak's Strike Force was like Achilles, vulnerable at one spot and that he knew the spot. Grosjean had described it. It had something to do with reloading the carrier racks, destruction and self destruction at once. A queer idea, an odd man. Cheka must have thought Grosjean was serious. Hence the double promotion.

He spoke to the old man, he had a recommendation. They spoke to Louisa: throw the counter-force in front of the Uzbeks, provoke the greatest possible use of their rockets, hope for the best. If there were drones, use the drones. If not use their own manned carriers. The thing was to provoke the Strike Force to use up their rockets, stop to rearm.

When the Strike Force scouting units reported something ahead they were right. There were drones, a few manned carriers, mostly drones. The main counter-force, such as it was, stood further north, the last shield for what lay behind it. The Strike Force commander was a careful, experienced man. This night, this operation would make him a Marshal.

However feeble, there was an American force still in being, probably desperate but committed to use what power it had. Its advance elements were in front of his scouts. He would smother them and prepare for incinerating the rest. Certainly the Americans would make a last try to stop him before he sent his firestorm rockets into Los Angeles and swept further north. He ordered the smothering fire, ordered reloading.

The gigantic explosion and fire that destroyed the Uzbeks was felt and seen two hundred, three hundred miles away. For the first minutes after it was reported to Operations no one knew what it meant. Dudorov thought he understood its significance. There were more reports, confused and unclear. There were more reports.

The advance units of the American force were reporting that the main Strike Force no longer existed, its scouting force carriers had turned and run south. It was impossible to approach the site where the main Strike Force had somehow been destroyed. It was a little after that point when Marv had arrived. Operations was still anxious.

The portion of Strike Force which had burned Phoenix had turned away to the west and had to be dealt with. But the masses at the border had not followed the Strike Force. They had begun to flee south. Something had happened to the camp in the south. There were reports, always garbled and broken, about volcanoes erupting and earthquakes in Mexico, then a confusion, more eruptions, more earthquakes worldwide. Perhaps Shishak's Strike Force had been less than it seemed, no more than a manmade disaster.

32

Court Meets, Finds for Eurasian Republics, Audience Vanishes, Power Fails

The Chief Justice looked out over the Warren Memorial Court Room and felt completely at peace for the first time since she had heard of Michael Carmody's monstrous crime in Mexico City.

Even a few hours earlier she had been disturbed to the point of outrage by Marv's account of the events of the night. Eurasian peacekeepers had been illegally attacked and destroyed on the orders of the Clymer woman in the old Spanish province of California which was and had always been lawfully a part of the Republic of Mexico.

That unlawful attack was one more count in charges that the Clymer woman would face. Moreover the destruction of San Diego and the Arizona cities would be the basis for three additional counts. Marv had been duped by the show at Defense Operations. The destruction of the three cities was plainly the work of the Clymer woman's own weapons, an excuse to justify the attack on the Eurasian peacekeeping force. Nita had suggested it to Marietta who had agreed.

The Clymer woman had insisted on procuring firestorm rockets over her, Marietta's, objections a year or more earlier. Marietta confessed that she, like Marv, had been taken in by the playacting at Defense Operations until Nita had spoken. If there was any doubt, it had been dispelled by one simple fact: there was no trace of the so-called Strike Force that was supposed to have burned out Tucson and Phoenix. At least so far none had been found. And Marietta suspected the Clymer woman was involved in the volcanic -- and earthquake activity and all the other confusion.

Old Mr. Carmody had presented stories to the President and the inner Cabinet about Eurasian schemes to bring about such disturbances but Marietta now understood the whole plan: a cover for the Clymer woman's own plots and designs.

Anyhow they had reached the hour of reckoning. She, the Chief Justice, had a sense of perfect calm and repose as she looked out over her favorite court room, in a sense a memorial to the Chief Justice whose name it bore but even more a monument to Aunt Wanita.

The court room was magnificent in scale and in style, with its 4,000 seats, its boxes, its marble columns 80 feet high, its allegorical murals and tapestries, its 500 seats for the press, its perfect acoustics, its instant translating system into 17 languages, its lighting, the piped-in choral music with which the sessions began and were ended, the great bench that lifted and lowered the Court at the beginning and close of each sitting.

Aunt Wanita had thought out every detail, even handsome colored robes for the Justices and lesser judges to replace the old unbecoming traditional black on special occasions. Aunt Wanita had commissioned choral works to recall the great deeds of the Court, tapestries and murals as well, to mark its progress from what it was to what it had become.

She looked out. The court room was packed. The press section was full. She had summoned all the federal judges to be present. The judges of the appellate courts, impressive in scarlet, sat in the boxes. The lower court judges filled the first rows below her, in their rich royal blue. She looked right and left.

In her purple and gold she looked better than anyone else. She waited while the chorus sang the concluding words of the Bill of Rights Oratorio: Indulge the Transgressor. Always the guilt is collective. It is you who have wronged him. The evil is yours. We protect him and guard him. With the Bill of Rights as his shield.

As she listened she looked overhead. Aunt Wanita had commissioned the most famous artists to do something worthy of her conception of the role of the Justices. The result was grandeur itself! Aunt Wanita a Greek goddess nude (was the word) to the waist, flanked by eight smaller figures in ancient Greek costumes, leaning over from the Heaven in which they were floating and showering justice down to the needy and lowly, who with faces uplifted, held their hands high to receive the justice raining down from above.

As she looked, the music came to an end. She heard Olga rap with her gold headed baton and cry out that the Court -- there was only one Court with a capital C -- was in session. The lights changed from color to color and focused on her, perhaps a little unsteady, then steady, the silver lavender that she felt showed her at her best.

She looked towards the front row of the press where Marv sat and watched. She waited a moment for the usual throat clearing and rustling. It seemed to take longer than usual. Then there was silence, mixed with excitement if there were such a mixture. She took a deep breath and began.

"This," she said slowly, "is the most solemn occasion on which this Court has assembled. The times are troubled. The people full of anxiety."

Here and there voices called out. Amen, sister, they said. It was true. The times were troubled and they were full of anxiety. Early in the morning Harry Fresser had brought Planet back on the air and they had heard broadcasts, jumbled a bit, not up to the usual standard, reporting attacks, the destruction of cities, the destruction of a Eurasian army, volcanic eruptions and earthquakes.

For weeks the tension had grown. Real estate futures had fallen to zero. All the securities markets had been closed after collapsing. But financial ruin was not the worst of their worries. That really concerned only the propertied elements. What was worse was the fear that things had been done in the name of both rich and not rich that had displeased the Eurasian Republics and would move them to show that displeasure by a vast, final attack.

They would all die. Everything would be lost, the ease, entertainments, all the good things of life. Dying, they knew, they could take nothing with them. To strike back would be futile. Nothing that they had and prized would be left. The progress of all the generations before them, all the effort that had come to a perfect, at least almost perfect, climax in them would end in a few minutes, maybe only seconds, of horror.

Those who cried out Amen, sister, spoke from the heart, all of their hearts. Suddenly they were all standing, shouting Amen. They looked to Sister. Sister would save them, nurturing Sister.

The Chief Justice waited, moved by the shouting. In spite of herself there were tears in her eyes. Even Wanita had never enjoyed such a demonstration of love and dependence. She raised her hand to command silence even as Olga beat her baton on the desk and cried out for order.

When there was quiet again Nita went on. She had told Marv she had a solution. Now she made it officially known. The papers had been prepared. She had signed them. The affairs of the United States after something over 200 years had been so mismanaged -- she was assigning no blame until after a full inquiry and then those at fault would answer for what they had done -- that a receivership was in order.

Receiverships were well known at the law. The United States was not bankrupt. All that was needed was a firm hand and wisdom and all would be well. She was naming herself as receiver. The burden was crushing but it was her duty to bear it. The judges of the lower courts would act as her deputies within their jurisdictions. The appellate judges would oversee the local judges in the discharge of their duties.

The assignments and tasks for the whole federal bench were now posted in the office of Marshal Feemster to whom they would report for the present. They could examine the instructions in the marshal's office when the session was over and they would be given three copies of their instructions for guidance.

The receivership, of course, was not limited to the executive branch. The legislative branch had been equally unsatisfactory and the receivership would take over its functions. She did not need to say that in both the House and the Senate the Speaker and the Majority Leader were victims of age. With the receivership she saw a bright day ahead.

The reference to a bright day ahead set off a new demonstration. The day, the day on which they had gathered was dark, very dark, frightening in its darkness. The clocks all proclaimed it was day but except for what the clocks said it was night. Supposedly, the darkness was the result of all the volcanic eruptions, or even the terrible fires that had burned in the Spanish provinces.

But whatever the cause, they rose and cheered the Chief Justice. They wanted, they needed the sun. The Chief Justice would bring back the sun.

When there was quiet once more, Nita continued. They had met as a Court to hear and dispose of certain legal issues that had been presented to them for their judgment. With these issues disposed of, with justice done to the petitioning parties, the United States would make good its claim to be a champion of peace on earth and fellowship among all its peoples. The Court had before it all the papers and proofs bearing on the petitions.

Boregard Dodge rose at that point from his chair at the counsel table where he had been sitting with some odd looking characters.

Nita looked at him. She despised Boregard Dodge, a disagreeable, disruptive old man. It was probably acceptable to have some men sit as judges but not a man of Boregard Dodge's background and views. He had been nothing but a troublemaker when he sat on the Court and it was a happy day when he left.

"If it please the Court," Dodge said, very polite. He knew what the woman was up to and also what she would do. All the same he would leave his mark on the day's record. "I have something to say about the documentary evidence before you."

The Chief Justice assured him that the court needed no comment on the documentary evidence. They were all satisfied with the documentary evidence.

"Precisely," Dodge said, "and I feel it my duty to advise the Court that I have a number of witnesses present."

What would those witnesses say that would interest or be of use to the Court?

"The Court," Dodge told her, "has a number of letters supposedly written and signed by Nicholas Trist. My first witness would demonstrate they are forged, and not very good forgeries. The leading handwriting expert, Dr. Theodore Signs.

"The Court has also before it certain documents from the Mexican archives which my next witness, Dr. Raul Cortez Hidalgo, will testify were prepared under his direction for use in this case. Dr. Raul Cortez Hidalgo was until this past week the Deputy Director of the Archives of the Republic of Mexico.

"My last witness is Professor Pushkin K. Winthrop, Distinguished Professor of the Contemporary Russian Theater at Yale University. Professor Winthrop will tell you that the woman whose testimony was given this Court as the testimony of Madame Dudorov and who appeared in the Moscow proceedings on the matter is in fact Madame Alla Theatrova of the Great Russian Drama Society."

The Chief Justice asked if Mr. Dodge wished to discredit the evidence presented by his own client. Mr. Dodge answered he felt it his obligation as an officer of the Court to protect it from fraud, even fraud on the part of his client. He had submitted the documents in the belief that they were authentic. Having learned the truth it was his duty, etc.

"Mr. Dodge," the Chief Justice asked, "how long have you been engaged in the practice of law?"

The reply was 53 years.

"In 53 years, Mr. Dodge, you must have learned that the main, almost the sole duty of counsel is to devote himself to the cause of his client. I can only say that your conduct is unbecoming a member of the bar of this Court." Mr. Dodge was fouling his nest, in the old phrase and Nita said so in so many words. And did Mr. Dodge have anything more to say to the court?

Mr. Dodge did. And he thanked the Chief Justice for inviting him to speak further. There was first and foremost in any proceeding before any court the question of jurisdiction. He had had second thoughts since he prepared and filed the papers on which the Court was proposing to rule. The Court in his opinion was without jurisdiction on constitutional grounds.

The treaty making provision was complete in itself. There was nothing to indicate that the Founders intended treaties to be reviewed by judges. Perhaps they could interpret. No more than that. We all knew, all understood the principle of the separation of powers. But beyond that another question had been presented by the events of the last 24 hours. His client, he regretted to say this, had invaded the territories of the United States and by its action -- this was his view -- had withdrawn the issues he had presented for consideration by the honorable Court.

Distinctly, he regretted to say this, but could a foreign power proceed in the courts of the United States while engaged in war on the United States de facto, though perhaps not de jure?

The Chief Justice glanced at the Court's official reporters. They were carefully making a record of every impudent word, like the industrious fools that they were.

"Counselor," she said, "I can only admonish you. Your performance this morning can only be construed as in contempt of this Court. The only saving circumstance is your age, the obvious infirmity of your age." He was in a class with the Speaker and that old wreck Bright Dismukes and the almost extinct but still dangerous old man who clung to the Intelligence Group.

Boregard Dodge bowed, smiled. "There is some benefit then in senility."

The benefit was limited the Chief Justice told him. She, the Court, had heard enough, more than enough. He would do well to sit down. Mr. Dodge thanked the Chief Justice for her patience. He had no more to say. He sat down.

Before going on to the cases before them, the Chief Justice said, there was one more matter about which the Court was concerned. It had to do with the Treasury Secretary. The Secretary had been contumelious, that was the only word to describe it, had defied an injunction, actively acted to injure the Court even after warning and notice.

The Secretary had resorted to violence -- through her agents -- towards Marshal Feemster in preventing the Marshal from taking her into custody. For the present the Court would content itself with a fine -- in the amount of 10 million dollars and an additional million dollars a day beginning on the following noon. Failing payment the Secretary would be imprisoned until she purged herself of contempt.

The Court had no choice before it. The Court dealt evenly with high and with low. Even a Secretary of the Treasury was subject to obedience to the Court's orders. A plea that compliance with that order would be in conflict with an act of the Congress was specious. The Court's orders were the law of the land.

There were a few cries of Amen, Sister, but only a few. The audience wanted the main event to begin. That was what they had come for, the grand resolution of the whole Eurasian Mexican crisis. The Chief Justice sensed it, knew it, responded accordingly.

The opinion had been written with care, rich in scholarship, historical, legal. The minor Dudorov matter had been more interesting than she had expected. Zenner had given her the fascinating background of the affair. Dudorov's murderer was one of the Carmody agents. Dudorov had discovered the Carmody plan to destroy the Eurasian Embassy in Mexico City. Accordingly Director Carmody had ordered his death.

What added a special poignance to the story was Zenner's revelation that in the innermost uppermost circles in Moscow it was understood that Dudorov was almost surely Cheka's own son. Knowing that, Nita grasped the importance to Cheka of having the Carmody agent turned over to him for trial -- a fair trial of course -- and punishment for the crime. She was not sentimental by nature but she sympathized with Cheka in his personal tragedy and to a degree marveled at his forbearance in his response to his loss. Another man might not have contented himself by seeking justice in the American courts.

The indemnity for the Eurasian losses as the result of the explosion in Mexico City had been worked out by the economists on the Court's staff. Literally they had worked day and night. They had calculated the indemnities for the death of each member of the Embassy staff and, separately, an indemnity for the affront to the Republics as such.

Their grand total equaled five times the average annual gross national income of the United States for the preceding three calendar years. She was awarding that amount in money and goods to be paid in ten annual installments and she was prepared to increase the award if the Republics thought it too little. As receiver she could arrange and oversee the paying over of any indemnity.

Zenner had also been helpful on the Treaty question itself. He had given her copies of letters from Abraham Lincoln to the American

Minister in St. Petersburg late in 1864 and lately discovered, almost by a miracle, in an old desk in the building where the American Minister had resided 200 or more years earlier.

In those letters Lincoln had stated in so many words that with the Civil War ended he meant to make amends to the Mexicans for the crime of the Mexican War. He had opposed the War at the time but his protests had been ignored. As he had written to the minister in St. Petersburg, he hated war, was a man wholly devoted to peaceful persuasion and had resolved when a member of Congress to abrogate the Treaty of Guadalupe Hidalgo if he should ever have the power to do so.

Her opinion used those letters to underpin her whole argument - - Zenner had given her permission to use them at her discretion -- for setting the Treaty aside. Not that the letters were needed. Equity alone dictated such a result. But the great brooding presence of Abraham Lincoln and the sensation of the letters, now brought to light after so long a time were certain to make her opinion a classic, one that would be read and reread.

She announced that the Court would sign the orders in the following cases, giving their styles, Scriabin, etc., after the opinions were read.

And she began reading, looking up, reading. After a minute or two the lights faded, went off for a second, came on. But the amplifying system went off and stayed off. Instead of the full, strong, powerful voice, to her surprise and annoyance her voice was small, very thin. The press leaned forward to listen. The whole audience leaned forward to listen.

From the back of the court room there were calls: could she speak louder? She took a deep breath, began reading again: read a few lines. Then there was a moaning sound that changed to almost a roar. It sounded like Many Many Tickle or Heckle, repeated over and over again. Nita paused, looked up. The audience was apparently not making the sound. She started to read again. The voice, or whatever it was, was suddenly silent but the court room seemed to fill with some kind of turbulence, like a wind -- except that the great allegorical tapestries gave no sign of movement. Nevertheless, there was a sense of increasing pressure as though the court room were in some kind of storm. Nita read, looked up, was surprised.

It was incredible, a breach of the rules. Apparently people had left while she read. More incredible, a worse breach of the rules, a number of judges had also departed. One or two boxes were almost deserted. The District Judges had thinned away by a half. She looked to her right; she looked to her left. The chairs beside her were empty. She looked at the Press. Marv was there but almost alone. Even as she looked the court room was emptying, no sounds, no figures retreating, only more and more empty seats.

A lesser woman would have lost control of herself. Was she in some terrible dream? The answer was no. She was in the Earl Warren Memorial Court Room. She was Chief Justice. She was handing down opinions in cases of planetary importance, opinions that would be read and discussed by not only legal scholars but by women and men of the highest distinction.

If there was ever an historic occasion, this was an historic occasion. She was making good her promise to Cheka. She was doing justice, big justice. She was saving what the ignorant once described as mankind.

She read on, would have read to the end but the bench, the wonderful bench that lifted the justices out of the cellar into the court room and lowered them back to the cellar as the Court's sessions opened and closed, began to descend, no button pushed, no command given.

Halfway down, level with the floor of the court room Nita, in spite of herself, screamed. The lights had gone out. The wonderful bench was stuck, out of commission, no longer working.

33

Dissension in Kremlin, Cheka Sees End at Hand, Blackness Descends

"So," Cheka said, looking at Shishak, "you have brought company with you. My instruction to Josef Vissarionovich was to tell you that I wished to see you. Only you."

Ulianov said that was how he had delivered the message. Shishak said nothing.

Cheka considered. A sign of weakness by Shishak. Shishak did not want to see him alone. Shishak felt in need of support. It might be better to have the Double Marshal and Globus stay and hear what he had to say.

"All right," Cheka went on, Semyon Semyonovich stay. And you Osip Gabrilovich stay. I will, though, speak to the Marshal as though he were alone. About his Uzbeks. The loss of his Uzbeks."

Shishak said nothing.

"Well," Cheka asked, "what have you to say about the loss of the Strike Force?"

Shishak said nothing.

"You understand that no Eurasian marshal has lost an army for years, many years. But there are precedents, old precedents, for marshals responsible for the loss of an army."

Shishak looked at Grabkin. There was a price for losing an army and he had expected that Cheka would ask for the payment. The old Double Marshal was to make a speech at that point. He had told the old Double Marshal what he was to say and rehearsed him but the old man was silent.

"Well," Cheka said, looking at Shishak, "what have you to say?"

Shishak, as prompter, noted that Marshal Grabkin wanted to comment.

Cheka understood, watched. Shishak had retained counsel.

"Semyon," he asked, "what do you have to say for your client?"

Grabkin smiled, lit his pipe. "A small army," he said, "not really an army. A strike force. Only a strike force."

"But very expensive," Cheka observed. "It cost as much as four or five of your regular armies. New and special equipment. Designed, redesigned. Special weapons. Everything done to the specifications the Marshal presented. And we had a guaranty from the Marshal. An irresistible force. And shall we say an invulnerable force? I understood the Marshal had a very high opinion of the possibilities offered. Shared by its officers. Shared by its men.

No, Semyon, we will have to count it at least as an army. We should probably count it as more, given the Marshal's opinion of what it could do." The old Double Marshal nodded. No fool, Vladimir Ilyich. He, himself, had not thought much of the point that they had lost only a strike force. Cheka was right about what it had cost, money, the time of the experts, the special factories required to produce what Shishak had called for. He might not have given his authorization, and got Cheka's approval if he had known what Asiatic Strike Force One was going to take from the funds that Cheka assigned him.

"And then," Cheka went on, "there was, shall we say, something irregular about the procedures. The Strike Force was sent abroad without clearance from me."

Shishak finally spoke. The Chairman was being unjust. It was true that he had not asked for permission to move the Strike Force. But the Chairman was always getting reports. The Chairman knew everything that was done. The Chairman had made no objection. No countermand had been given Semyon Semyonovich. There had been nothing hidden, nothing concealed. There were problems in Mexico. He had acted to deal with them. Advisers were needed. There had been an appeal from Aleman Villa.

"Which you did not refer to me," Cheka observed. "That was for me to dispose of."

Shishak explained. A matter of need, urgent need. There was no time to waste.

"So," Cheka asked, "you think it a waste of time to bring matters to my attention? How long have you thought so?"

Shishak complained. The Chairman was twisting his words. He understood that the Chairman's judgment was paramount.

"And you felt no need to consult me?" Did he have the Double Marshal's approval?

Shishak explained. The Double Marshal was not present when the message came in. Again the answer was urgent. But he had told the Double Marshal about what he had ordered as soon as he was available.

"And you, Semyon?"

"It was done then," Grabkin said. "Strike Force was already moving. Half of it up in the air, on the way, I cautioned the Marshal that you would not like it."

"That was bad enough by itself," Cheka said. "You are an indulgent father, Semyon Semyonovich. To me the Marshal is a Marshal of the Eurasian Republics. An honored position, but a position with duties. Free to act within limits. The Marshal has exceeded those limits. My orders were clear. No act of war against the Americans. The Marshal sent his Strike Force inside their borders. An open attack. And the Marshal has lost his Strike Force in disregarding my orders."

The Double Marshal heard, blew a smoke ring. Cheka was right in saying he was indulgent. Cheka was also right about his orders. His orders were clear and a marshal of the Republics was bound by those orders. You could say that Shishak was young. The young were ambitious, easily carried away, impetuous. All the same you obeyed Cheka's orders. He had obeyed them, not very willingly once or twice but eventually he had admitted that Vladimir Ilyich had probably seen things that he himself had been blind to.

Shishak looked to Grabkin for a word of support, and getting none, defended himself. The decision was a battlefield judgment. Marshals, of course, had limited power but on the battlefield they could not ask for guidance. All they could do was to act, protect the interests of the Republics, use their full means to defend the honor and dignity of the Republics. That was what he had done. Nothing more.

Ambassador Schmiedegen had been with him. He had consulted Ambassador Schmiedegen and he had agreed that the situation required the use of the Strike Force north of the border. They were concerned only with insuring the success of the Chairman's own plan, to make the Americans realize that resistance to the Chairman was hopeless.

"When his time comes," Cheka said, looking at Shishak, "I will deal with Ambassador Schmiedegen. Let me point out again that you have lost Strike Force One and that this demonstration of our irresistible force proved only that it was resistible. And a question. Could the Marshal explain what had happened, how he had lost such troops with all their equipment?

Shishak found it a disagreeable question. And what was the answer? The Americans were a weak sort of people, used up, debauched by their wealth. Their army was no more than a pretense of an army. Half of it consisted of women, more than half; with a woman in charge, though he was told a formidable woman.

The Americans had, he was told, a few units that might be well armed, thanks to the efforts of the peculiar woman in charge, but only a few, very few. They might have damaged the fringe of the Strike Force, nibbled away at the edge, but they could have caused no serious loss.

The rest of the American forces were trash, to be run over, scattered, blown away by the wind. All the same his Uzbeks were gone. No question about it. One message, nothing more heard. No later report to account for the disaster. He had no other word to describe it. And he, himself, Hulagu Shishak, a Timurid, was the loser.

It was as though someone had cut off his arm, both of his arms. without his Uzbeks, his personal Uzbeks, he was what Cheka said, no more than another marshal of the Republics. He looked at Cheka. Had Cheka led him into a trap? They, the armed forces of the Republics, had their own intelligence service, very good in its way; but ultimately they relied on Security and Security reported to Ulianov who reported to Cheka.

Could Cheka have been reading his mind? And could Cheka have made up an elaborate plan, using Aleman Villa and Schmiedegen, to lead him into exposing his Uzbeks to a secret American battle group of which security had kept him in ignorance. Perhaps he had underestimated Vladimir Ilyich. The Double Marshal and his new wife's father had spoken of Cheka's resourcefulness but he had discounted what they had said. A couple of old men talking about another old man who had got the upper hand over them long ago and whose power they accepted as a matter of habit. He had calculated that Cheka was finished, ready to be pushed out of the way by his Uzbeks.

Again Cheka asked. Did the Marshal have any explanation of how Strike Force One came to its end? Shishak shook his head. He had no explanation. Did the Marshal have at least some suggestion of what could have happened to Strike Force? The Marshal had no suggestion. Shishak might have said that he suspected the Chairman of having outmaneuvered him, stripped him of Strike Force but that would be foolish. There were still other moves.

"I come back," Cheka said, "to the simple fact that the Strike Force is gone, Marshal Shishak, and there is the price to be paid. You will, of course, have a choice." The Marshal could choose between an honorable death by his own hand or being reduced to the rank of a private soldier, with service for life and any promotion forbidden.

"The time has come," Globus broke in, "for me to speak up. "

"First," Cheka said, "the Marshal has a choice to make. Then I will hear what you have to tell me."

Shishak took a deep breath. "No," he said, "I will put off my choice. My wife's father has something to say." It was time. He had talked to Globus, talked to the old Double Marshal, and agreed on the speeches. They were to have taken the lead, attacked at the outset but they had let Cheka lead them away from the demand they were to make. "No," he said again, "my wife's father has something to say."

A clumsy fellow this Shishak, Cheka thought, with his description of Globus as his wife's father. More exactly his latest wife's father. He had a number of wives, with fathers probably living in tents. He looked at Globus, glum, sour Globus, probably the last true believer, the idiot ideologue. "The hour has struck," Globus announced.

"The hour has come. Marshal Shishak's choice is nothing. History has no concern with his choice. But history watches us while we come to a greater decision, a final decision."

Cheka asked what final decision.

"Vladimir Ilyich," Globus said, "the final struggle has come. We must settle once and for all with the Americans, the imperialists, the issue of whether the Revolution is to prevail. They have dared to attack. They have, to our shame, destroyed one of our glorious armies.

"The Revolution requires revenge. The last chains must be broken. History dictates that we make war with every means that we have. Today. This very hour. I have been patient. The Double Marshal and I have waited to see you bring the Americans to their knees by your own methods. But now -- and the Double Marshal agrees, we must wipe them out. Only then will mankind be free and the vision of our teachers fulfilled."

Words, Shishak said to himself. If History had no interest in whether he blew out his brains, History was as much a fool as his revered father-in-law. And mankind would be free. He wondered if the old man had any idea of what would happen to him if mankind were free. As for the teachers and the books the old man liked to quote, he had been made to look into them at Junior Command School and they had put him to sleep. Still his honored father-in-law had his uses. He was calling on Vladimir Ilyich to make his accounting to History.

"So you want the Americans brought to their knees," Cheka said looking at Globus. "We were told about final struggles as schoolboys. That is what you propose Osip Gabrilovich?"

"War," Globus told him. "Ultimate. Final."

"Marshal Shishak was making war yesterday and you see the results," Cheka observed.

"Limited war, with limited weapons," Globus insisted.

"But very good, very effective weapons. Or so I was told when I gave my approval for building them."

"Limited, " Globus repeated.

"And you want to use what?"

"Look," Globus said, "we all know that we have the ultimate arsenal, the birds with their warheads that can fly anywhere on the Earth. Not like the Marshal's carriers with their firestorm rockets and their limited reach. You touch the button. Anyone touches the button and that is the end of it. There will be no imperialist threat. The Revolution will be safe forever and ever."

"And if the Americans should strike back?" Cheka asked.

"They will not, cannot," Globus said. "It will all be over before they can respond. Marshal Shishak has told me the War Planning Study staff is sure of it. You have seen its conclusions. Even I have seen the conclusions. "

"Yesterday Marshal Shishak was confident that his Strike Force would carry out its mission without any real loss," Cheka noted.

"Yesterday," Globus said, "we had a choice. We have none today. Yesterday the Marshal's Strike Force was turned into so many ashes. That will give the Americans confidence. Has given them confidence. They are already attacking."

"Attacking us?" Cheka asked.

"These disturbances," Globus said. "We have all been aware that some force was at work. Now there are stories -- you must have heard them -- earthquakes, volcanoes, great damage in the Asiatic Republics, the day turned to night. This can only be the Americans' doing."

"You believe that?" Cheka asked.

"What else can we believe. Our Institutes thought they could do it themselves. The Americans have got there before us. We must act or they will destroy us and the Revolution for which we are the guardians."

"You know," Cheka said, "that these birds that you speak of are dangerous birds. We destroy and we may end by being destroyed. No guarantee. No quarantine."

An old wives' tale, Globus thought, the same old excuse, made over and over. He was no soldier but he was more of a soldier than Cheka. You struck, took your chances, but struck.

Anyhow they all knew there were shelters for those whose safety the Revolution required, protection for those who were needed. Position One put them on notice. He and the Double Marshal had taken the precaution to give the Position One notice.

Already those who had been chosen were making their way discreetly to the places assigned, some deep in the Earth, some, the more essential, ready to be carried into what they still spoke of as Space. Position.Two would lock all the doors. Position Two would set off the space vehicles. He might as well tell Cheka about the Position One order.

"So you anticipated my decision," Cheka told him. "You are behaving like what I will call your daughter's new husband. And did you approve, Semyon Semyonovich?"

The answer was both yes and no. War was his business. But he was old-fashioned. He understood that the day of single combat was over, hero to hero. Nevertheless, battle was battle, a testing of strength and of nerve. There was something unsuitable about the procedures that the Academy of Sciences presented as war-making. The Position Two business made it all worse. They were to start this new kind of war and leave, ride around and around, come back when it was over. Everything was vague after that. He had been persuaded, though, that there was no other choice.

Shishak's Strike Force had been erased. It was worse than what they had done to the Germans a century ago. Then some survived, to retreat, survived to be driven on home. That was yesterday. Today earthquakes, storms. For several days they had told him, his own people, that there were disruptions, malfunctions, they called them. Globus was probably right.

The Americans were attacking, the people they had told him were objects for only contempt. Very confusing. Cheka had tried to outwit them. Cheka had always been cautious, even after the Americans had presented themselves in Geneva and given every sign of being ready to give up their contest with the Republics, an abject crowd except for a woman whose face he remembered but whose name he forgot. Cheka was right to be wary. A cunning, dissembling lot, the Americans. A people to punish -- if they could be punished.

Cheka listened to the Double Marshal with patience. "If," he said, "if they can be punished. And if they are attacking. Suppose I tell all of you that these earthquakes and volcanic explosions are not the Americans' doing?"

"But what else can they be?" Globus demanded. "What other cause can there be?"

Cheka tried to explain what he had been learning from Lumens. "A cosmic disturbance."

Shishak interrupted. "Bah," Shishak said. "You tell us this all comes out of the sky. I have been up in the sky. Far up in the sky. There is nothing there, emptiness. I have looked. I have seen with my own eyes. Nothing but emptiness. The sky can do nothing to me here on the Earth."

"I go a step further here on the Earth," Cheka said. "Suppose I refuse to put my finger on this wonderful button? Suppose I leave the birds in their nests?"

"Then," Shishak said, "I give you the answer. We have agreed on it. Then you are no longer Chairman."

"And if Josef Vissarionovich refuses?"

"He will have nothing to do with it," Shishak almost shouted. "Osip Gabrilovich will replace you as chairman and he will press what you call the wonderful button."

Cheka looked from Globus to Grabkin. "And this is why you came to see me together?" he asked. "My answer is that the birds stay where they are."

The lights which had been dimming, recovering, dimming, faded out altogether, struggled back. As they came on Shishak stood leaning across Cheka's desk, one hand almost on the button, nearing the button, on the wonderful button.

The moment had come, the inevitable moment for which money had been spent, measured not in billions or trillions but thrillions. The best minds had prepared for it, generations of the best minds, tested, examined, massed in the Institutes. The brightest children had been combed out and schooled and encouraged to use their fullest intellectual powers to ensure that this moment would come, encouraged, honored, indulged, raised high over parents in nameless villages, trained, weeded out, re-weeded, selected so the button would give its command.

The birds were, as Cheka said, in their nests, 100,000 birds ready to fly, from nests in the mountains, nests in the plains, under the sea, placed carefully all over the planet, carefully aimed, targets allotted, the most refined controls in control, watched over, treasured by their loving creators and guardians.

A million lives, maybe two million lives were centered on assuring a perfect response to the button, men and women, women and men, young, middle-aged, growing old, devoted 24 hours each day, seven days in the week, every week in the year, whole lifetimes spent in preparing and caring.

At last the moment had come. Shishak had touched, pressed, with his whole weight, given the order.

When Shishak spoke his voice was hoarse. "Now," he said, "Position Two. We must hurry."

Globus got up. Grabkin, astonished, stayed where he was. Ulianov, who had been silent was silent, his eyes on Cheka.

Cheka sat back, looking at Shishak. Very slowly he took a gun from his desk. "Shishak," he said, "you are a fool as well as a boor and a scoundrel. You have no cause to worry about Position Two. Nothing has happened. The button signals back that its order is given. It has given no order. Nothing has happened."

And it was true. No message had gone out to the nests. The birds were still asleep where they were, undisturbed in their mountains and plains and under the sea. For days now their beautiful, delicate circuits had been exposed to strange ebbs and flows until they were burned out, worn out, no longer able to receive and give orders, victims of Lumens' leninos, victims of something, and all the lives and care and intellectual skill lavished on them for almost a hundred years gone to waste.

Shishak stood considering. Cheka had insulted him, was treating him with contempt. But Cheka could be playing a trick. Who could tell if the button had worked? Maybe Cheka was trying to keep him from the safety that Position Two provided marshals of the Republics. As for the gun that was nothing. He would lunge for it. Cheka was old and probably had no idea of how to move or would be too slow moving. He moved slowly, got himself ready.

Then from nowhere there was a noise, a howl, a terrible feeling of pressure and the lights failed, came on.

Cheka and Ulianov were there. Grabkin was there. Even Osip Grabilovich Globus was there. But where was Shishak? Shishak was gone. The four men looked at each other. Cheka thought he knew what had happened. They had reached the climax that Lumens had spoken of. Then the lights went down, were gone and they were in darkness.

34

Mene   Mene   Tekel . . . Says it All

The survivors, if that is what they were, called it the Blackness. There was uncertainty over how long it lasted. The sun apparently neither rose nor set and all the clocks stopped, every clock, every watch. On one side of the world everyone knew that the Eurasians had brought on the Blackness. On the other, they knew it had been created by the Americans. More or less it was what everyone had expected, a lifelong expectation.

From infancy on, the inhabitants of all the islands and continents, North Pole to South Pole, had known that the brightest and best of them concentrated on producing the means to bring on the Blackness. There had been protests, of course, but protest was foolish and futile.

The Blackness, somewhere in the future, was the price that had to be paid for the high, ever higher, civilization in which they all lived. War was the mirror image of what was called peace, involving the same brilliant inventions and marvels but adapted to a different objective.

So they largely accepted the Blackness, all but those who by virtue of their superior standing had a claim to special protection and shelter. There were arrangements to preserve high to middle officials, experts, those with notable talents, certified medalists, and, among the Americans, people with significant fortunes.

There were also numbers of people who had made their own private arrangements by payments of money or even what were described as sexual favors to insure themselves against the Blackness if it should come. All of these felt the Blackness unfair, grossly unfair.

For several days there had been signs of some possible trouble, the communications systems were faulty, the power systems were faulty. Then there were rumors of the always possible war. Then at last there

313

were rumors of earthquakes, of volcanoes exploding and the Blackness began.

Everywhere, caught where they were, people waited for the arrival of the means of destruction that they knew were to come out of the sky, the weapons in which they had all invested for the past generations. But there was no thunder, no flashes of fire, at the worst no more than a howling, a sense of being out in a storm.

Then there were the vanishings, people fading to nothing. Those who saw the vanishings reasonably thought they were no more than a refinement of the usual weapons, a variation on the standard commonplace means of destruction, quieter, perhaps more humane. Gradually the vanishings arrived at their climax and gradually ebbed.

Those who lived through it feared that the Blackness would continue for months or for years as vast clouds of dust and ash circled high overhead or whatever it was that brought on the Blackness.

Actually on the sixth day the wind rose and on what would have been the following day the sky cleared. There was light and with the light warmth. It was then the survivors, if survivors, came out from their places of refuge, met, talked, compared notes. People talked to each other about having seen family, friends, strangers disappear from their sight. Had it been real or was it some kind of dream?

Certainly people were missing. But they could have got lost in the Blackness, fled, wandered off in the confusion. They could reappear now the Blackness had ended. In the meantime there was much to be done. The whole apparatus on which they had depended and which had failed in the Blackness had to be looked to. The whole network of electrical power and everything that was moved by it, the whole apparatus of civilized life in the cities, the towns, the villages, even the countryside.

The individual generating machines had failed too and all the self movers with their own small electrical systems. The engineers and the technical workers would restore order and life would go on. The process of repair would take time, days, maybe weeks. The Blackness had probably been a prodigious, unparalleled electrical storm, a storm that had burned out every circuit. The engineers would know what to do.

Unfortunately the supply of engineers and assistants was less than expected. They assembled, were assembled, such as they were, made their inspections, were baffled. The diagnosis -- burned out electrical circuits -- was wrong. They looked, examined, found nothing damaged, moved levers, threw switches, pressed buttons, studied the manuals, step by step followed instructions, got no result. Nothing moved; nothing turned over, no humming, no purring.

First one genius here, one genius there recalled something out of the elementary books, rubbed substance on substance. Again nothing happened. No spark, no trace of a spark. The result was impossible. There was no electrical force on the planet. There might, in fact, be none anywhere. The whole universe might not be what it was.

There was no announcement that the engineers had tried and failed. The accustomed means of communication, of course, no longer functioned. The failure was, so to speak, self announced. No lights came on as the days ended. No water moved in response to the pumps. More than anything the want of water brought on the exodus from the cities.

But the cities were useless, actually all but the most backward settlements stranded like so many fish on dry land. Everything that they lived on had to be brought to them. And there was no way to supply them with food or anything that was needed. Moreover there was nothing to do in the cities and towns, or little to do.

By and large most of their working forces had been occupied with the remembering machines which no longer remembered. Even the captains in charge of the clerks and subordinates were helpless. There were no deals they could make.

Even George Sidon was helpless without the means to communicate orders, to buy and to sell. And worse, without the electric machines George Sidon and the other great captains were no better than beggars.

Fortunes here, fortunes there were not even on paper, they were nothing more than electronic impulses and past human reach so far as anyone knew. The splendor of Sidon's office on the 90th floor had faded away for obvious reasons. How could he reach it? There were too many stairs. And the triplex penthouse, as it was called, on the 60th floor of the Babylon Tower was also beyond reach.

George Sidon, all the George Sidons, were reduced to the level of everyone else. Their fortunes had vanished. Their investments were meaningless. Their flair, their talent, their insights were worthless. Their world of money and dealing with money, whatever money might be or have been, had vanished when the Blackness set in.

The cities had constituted much of the wealth of the rich, giant buildings and everything that had served them.

Now the rich were no better off than those who had admired or envied them. Now they were all on the same level. What could they do? Where could they go? And if the power of money was gone, so too was the power that was known as the Government.

Among the Americans there had been arguments as to which power was paramount. Who had depended on whom? Which had come first? Probably they had been symbiotic, had lived on each other. They vanished together. Both controlled their worlds through the same means, reducing people and things to so many numbers stored in the remembering machines.

They ruled, issued orders, levied payments, distributed proceeds, exerted their will minute by minute through the same devices, all fashioned by servants trained and modestly paid to use their minds as scientific observers and technicians of various kinds.

The electric impulse was the leash with which all the managers managed their subjects. It was true among the Americans. It was true in the Eurasian Republics where Government had swallowed everything generations before.

Cheka had sat out the Blackness by the light of candles, not uncomfortably but wondering what the future would be. There had, of course, been disappearances in the various ministries but the head of the Power Ministry was still in being, still making worried reports, offering apologies. Power Ministry would do what it could.

Power's staff was in chaos. He had sent, however, such messengers as he had. He was trying to locate his principal engineers and their main helpers. Some he had found. They were trying in turn to find their assistants. On the seventh day when there was light again the Minister was decidedly hopeful. But at last he was faced with the terrible burden of bringing Cheka bad news, very bad news. The fact was he did not realize the gravity of it.

Cheka heard him. The engineers had tried every trick in the book. They had exhausted themselves. And nothing had happened. Could it be that the trouble was peculiar to Moscow? The main generators were lifeless and the emergency generators as well. His people had tried the small units in the self movers. There was no response from them. But was it peculiar to Moscow?

"No," Cheka said. Lumens had already told him what to expect. Also Lumens had a theory. It was not just the world that had come to an end, but the whole universe with which they were familiar. This was a new universe, an idea they would have to explore. For the present all Cheka could do was to thank the Minister and his staff for making their effort. He could have said something about Lumen's theory but he decided against it.

The Minister had another question: what should he do?

"A very good question," Cheka observed. "You must understand what follows from your report."

The Minister felt himself on the point of fainting. He could plead that he was not to blame for what he had had to report. He had been honest. If anyone was to blame it was his engineers. But if they were incompetent, their fault was his fault. They would be punished and he would share in their fate. He had selected them and had exposed the Republics to their shortcomings. He would have spoken. He opened his mouth. His voice was gone.

Cheka recognized the old symptoms, fear of him and what he embodied, the State which was lord over everything, proposing, disposing and everyone helpless, bound to obedience, whatever the order. Power Minister's name was Yelevsky, Diamat Diamatovich.

"Diamat Diamatovich," Cheka told him, "no one is at fault. Not you. No one else. But if there is no power there will be no Ministry, nothing for you to administer. Certainly not at the present. We will have to consider what we all do. Perhaps ... "

He was about to explain that perhaps they would have to abandon Moscow, forget it, try something smaller, something less ponderous. But that, he could see, would be too much for Yelevsky who had been given the Position One warning, been caught in the Blackness, been exposed to the shock of uncertainty after a lifetime of boundaries and rules. To be told that the Ministry was superfluous was enough of a shock.

To be told that Moscow itself might be discarded could be too much for him. There was no sense in provoking a heart attack or a stroke.

"Perhaps," Cheka went on, "the thing to do is to submit your findings to the Physical Institute. Get their comments, get their opinion." Always assuming, Cheka thought to himself, you can find the Physical Institute or anyone there.

That evening Cheka told Lumens about his conversation with Yelevsky, about Yelevsky's report. Lumens nodded. They were in a new universe. There had been a new creation. They were all of them new, newly created, like his namesake, so many Adams, the women so many Eves.

Cheka shook his head. Lumens was wrong. There was memory. "Did the first Adam have a memory, Lumens?" he asked. "And look out the window. You will see Moscow, a city, no Garden of Eden. The same world, Lumens, the same universe, only changed. For better or worse. That we will find out." He wondered what the Americans made of it.

Groping in the dark Boregard Dodge and Roscommon Brown, a nephew of Louisa, rescued the Chief Justice and eventually restored her to Marv. They were the last to leave the Earl Warren Memorial Court Room and not many people went there thereafter.

Washington, like Moscow and cities in general, was another balloon from which the gas began to escape. The population drained away, slowly, then quickly, into the countryside. The city's function had ended, a world capital which had lost touch with its world.

After the Blackness began no one ever saw Walter Blossom again. No one was sure if he was among the vanished or if he had simply wandered away in the darkness. Later, for years there were those who claimed to have seen him or at least someone who looked like him. But no one was sure. When the light returned after the Blackness there was talk of replacing him, discussion, serious, in what had been known as the highest circles. There would be appointments, resignations, the formalities and Louisa would inherit the White House. Nothing came of it. Louisa objected.

She had talked to her nephew. Roscommon Brown was the scientist in the family. He had told her what -- or something like what -- Lumens had told, was telling, Cheka, and on similar evidence.

Something had happened, the Clerk Maxwell equations no longer applied. There was no electrical impulse. The nervous system of the body politic, of the whole social order, no longer worked.

There was no instantaneous sending and receiving of orders. At best they were back 200 years in the past but without even the benefits of the arrangements of 200 years earlier. For the present they were uncertain about the extent of the vanishings. How many people were left? What would they live on? How would they live? First things, first, was Louisa's conclusion.

The truth was that the incidence of the vanishings varied. It was greater in cities and greater among the youngish, greater still in certain parts of the world. In some places, only half of the population had disappeared but in others the losses were greater, considerably greater. But at the beginning no one was sure.

Moreover -- and this became apparent after the elapse of a year, no children were born. It was not until well into the second year after the Blackness that this was remarked on. In the third and fourth years when there were still no children people began to despair.

There were deaths but no births.

The Blackness had evidently brought on a universal sterility. As the years passed the human species would dwindle to nothing. Everything else was fruitful and multiplied. The human species was the only exception, a cosmic tragedy past understanding.

Then another effect of the Blackness began to appear, human beings seemed to live longer. At least many of those who were old or almost old at the time of the Blackness lived on, were apparently vigorous, in some way renewed and restored. Cheka lived on. Even Michael Carmody, the old man himself, lived on. Louisa, paired off with Dudorov, showed no signs of diminishing force.

But occupations were different. They were concerned with first things, with the need for food, so they gardened, raised food, lived with the animals that their forebears had lived with. Gradually, as the years passed, they and other survivors -- if survivors -- began to restore the order of the older society of ten generations before them.

Roscommon Brown figured in the restoration, as it was called. In the sixth year after the Blackness he and a crew ventured across the Atlantic by sail and discovered that the Eurasian experience had been like that of the Americans, the same Blackness, the same vanishings, the same loss of power. Life was local again. The Union of Eurasian Republics no longer existed and there was no will to revive it. Years later on another voyage, Brown made his way east and at a small settlement west of Moscow met Adam Lumens who led him to Cheka. They talked, the three of them.

What was the Blackness? Lumens explained. It was the Creation, the universe, maybe a Universe had come into being. He knew Cheka's objections. There was the matter of memory. He conceded that he himself had a sense of having existed before the Blackness began. But that was illusion. And there was no reason to think that at this Creation there would be a blank slate. What had come into being was a well furnished universe, complete with languages, records, structures, used or abandoned, the phenomenon they spoke of as memory.

Cheka's comment was simple. "I know who I am," he said, looking at Brown. "I am V. I. Cheka, though I use a different name now. I was Chairman of the Union of the Eurasian Republics and devoted for a lifetime to establishing the supremacy of the Republics over the Americans, scheming, endlessly scheming for their destruction, a game of a kind, an implacable game, hoping to avoid, but preparing, always preparing, for war, using every resource, the best minds, the accumulation of knowledge to reach the ultimate end, control, complete and perfect control over the Earth.

"Then," he went on, "there was the noise. I was told about it. A puzzling sound. I listened.

"My friend here, Adam Lumens was, shall we say, an unfrocked medallist of one of our Institutes, the discoverer of what he called the lenino, an heretical particle. I knew something about him. I thought he might have an explanation for the puzzling noise. I had him brought in to talk to me. He listened. He had an explanation just as I hoped. Leninos. A black hole. Leninos emerging. The end of everything, everything. But we never agreed on the sound, the noise, what I called the voice."

"The voice?" Brown asked.

"Yes," Cheka told him, "I called it the voice, repeating a phrase or so I considered it. The phrase Mene Mene Tekel. It meant something to me. And to you? Has it any meaning to you?"

Brown nodded. It had a meaning for him but only as a detail out of a story. It was strange that this man, V. I. Cheka, seemed to attach any great significance to it. Still, a mind overthrown, the embodiment of earthly power reduced to life in a village, his empire fallen apart in a day, and not a young man, but aging and brittle, no longer resilient, unable to understand what had happened, explaining this cataclysm through which they had lived in terms of an ancient story and the delusion of a mysterious voice.

He had known of Cheka, as they all had, dangerous, tireless, the shrewd, calculating, always analytical mind. Seeing him transformed, Brown felt something like pity.

Cheka watched him, sensed what he thought. "Look," he said, "my friend Lumens talks nonsense. Let me tell you what happened That voice I heard was a warning, not only to me but to everyone. We were weighed. We were found wanting. There were other stories -- the apple that was not to be tasted. The tower of Babel built too high and thrown down. We had built our tower too high. We had eaten too many apples. We looked into mirrors and adored the image we saw there. The whole creation belonged to us as we added power to power. You follow me?"

Roscommon Brown followed him.

"And it was too good to last. Also too bad. A dangerous part of the creation, this species of ours. A tool maker. A maker of toys designed to destroy their makers and everything in their reach. So the warning, what we call the Blackness, the vanishings, the loss of the tricks that we lived by. And we are fewer each day. You think we will disappear in the end?"

"On the evidence, yes." Roscommon Brown, as Louisa said, was the scientist in the family. He went by the evidence, by the facts. People died. No one was born. Communications were poor but no one had heard of a birth, none for years. There were theories of why it was so. It was one of the results of the Blackness. The time would come when there would be a last man or a last woman, and then that life would end, an unhappy certainty.

"Maybe on the evidence, no," Cheka told him. "We will survive. Forty years after the Blackness, more or less 40 years, there will be a birth here, a birth there. This will be like the 40 years in the Wilderness. If we had been wholly wanting, we would have all disappeared in the Blackness. We are able to do less mischief now, even less as the numbers diminish. In another generation it will be safe for us to multiply slowly."

Many years later Brown thought about his meeting and conversation with Cheka. It was about 40 years after the Blackness and in the countryside where he lived there had been more births than deaths. As a man trained in the old disciplines he had puzzled over the nature of the Blackness. The Lumens explanation had never persuaded him though it had its adherents.

He could not believe that the Blackness had been the creation, with a new universe brought into being complete with monuments, records and personal memories of an existence before the Creation.

He was inclined to accept the explanation that the Blackness had marked the recurrence of a cycle that occurred every 13 or 26 or 39 million years, an intrusion toward the solar system of a star, a cousin of the sun, which approached and departed and affected the sun with its system of planets by this intrusion.

Whole species had disappeared in the past as the cycle recurred, not all species, some species. Humankind had survived this latest recurrence.

It was a good explanation, impersonal and remote. But Cheka had been right about what he had spoken of as the 40 years in the Wilderness. Could there have been a voice? And could Cheka have been right in regarding the Blackness as some kind of intervention to save mankind from the consequences of what it considered its triumphs? He put the question to the still vigorous Louisa. She thought for a minute, maybe two minutes.

"It was all too complicated and foolish," she said. "And dangerous. Perhaps Cheka was right."

Printed in the United States
203832BV00003B/202-339/P